A STRANGER AMONG US

❧ Stories of Cross Cultural Collision and Connection ❧

Edited by Stacy Bierlein
Foreword by Aimee Liu

OV BOOKS
an imprint of
Other Voices
magazine

Chicago, Illinois

See specific author credits starting on p. 390.

Library of Congress Cataloging-in-Publication Data

A stranger among us : stories of cross cultural collision and connection /
edited by Stacy Bierlein ; foreword by Aimee Liu.
    p. cm.
  ISBN 0-9767177-3-5
1. Short stories--Translations into English. 2. Short stories, American. 3. Alienation
(Social psychology) in literature. 4. Outsiders in literature. 5. Aliens in literature.
I. Bierlein, Stacy, 1968-

  PN6120.95.A6S77 2007
  808.83'1--dc22

    2007049326

Cover photo: Susan Aurinko

Cover design by Melissa C. Lucar,
Fisheye Graphic Services, Inc., Chicago

Printed in the United States of America

10 9 8 7 6 5 4 3 2 1

Bookstores: OV Books titles are distributed by University of Illinois Press,
phone (800) 621-2736 or www.press.uillinois.edu

www.othervoicesmagazine.org

CONTENTS

Foreword by Aimee Liu — vii

Introduction by Stacy Bierlein — xiii

SPLEEN — 1
Josip Novakovich

MOTHERHOOD AND TERRORISM — 15
Amanda Eyre Ward

SHOES — 27
Etgar Keret
translated from the Hebrew
by Miriam Shlesinger

IN CUBA I WAS A — 31
GERMAN SHEPHERD
Ana Menendez

AFRICA UNCHAINED — 49
Tony D'Souza

TOBA TEK SINGH — 65
Saadat Hasan Manto
translated from the Urdu
by Richard M. Murphy

THE PROFESSOR'S OFFICE — 73
Viet Thanh Nguyen

THE NEIGHBOR — 89
Goli Taraghi
translated from the Farsi
by Karim Emami and Sara Khalili

THIS IS HOW IT IS — 101
Ehren Schimmel

THE ODALISQUE — 115
Laila Lalami

BORDER CROSSINGS — 127
Luis Alfaro

10 SEPTEMBER — 137
Rashad Majid
translated from the Azerbaijani
by Samed Safarov

THE WAY LOVE WORKS — 145
Mary Yukari Waters

THE NAKED CIRCUS — 159
G. K. Wuori

ATTILA THE THERE — 175
Gina Frangello

SLAVE DRIVER — 199
Wanda Coleman

THE WOLF STORY — 207
Irina Reyn

BEFORE TONDE, AFTER TONDE — 221
Petina Gappah

THE VIEW FROM THE MOUNTAIN — 233
Shauna Singh Baldwin

BHAKTHI IN THE WATER — 247
Shubha Venugopal

FRESH OFF THE BOAT — 267
Dika Lam

ASUNCION — 271
Roy Kesey

KEYS TO THE KINGDOM — 279
Diane Lefer

THE WIZARD OF KHAO-I-DANG — 293
Sharon May

ISHWARI'S CHILDREN — 309
Shabnam Nadiya

WHITE NIGHT FIRE — 317
Yelizaveta P. Renfro

WHAT WILL HAPPEN TO — 333
THE SHARMA FAMILY
Samrat Upadhyay

LE MAL D'AFRIQUE — 343
Francesca Marciano

CURRENCY — 357
Carolyn Alessio

IN THIS WAY WE ARE WISE — 371
Nathan Englander

Contributors — 381
Credits — 390
Acknowledgments — 393

Foreword

We are not Them. This belief underscores our culture (whatever our culture may be). It encourages us to look and act, sound and smell and worship in ways that distinguish us. It nudges us to create art that celebrates our distinction. It orders us to teach our children to salute our flag and, in times of perceived threat, to defend our interests by waging war against Them. It also causes us to recoil, perhaps even turn violent, at the suggestion that some of us might conceivably share bloodlines with Them. Yet we reserve a special nervous fascination for those who actively seek Them out—to study, befriend, or, most appalling (and titillating) of all, to court and marry. Those apostates may betray us, but still, we tell ourselves, they deserve our pity, for though they have left us forever, they never truly can become one with Them. What makes Them different, after all, is so vast. They have mothers and fathers, sisters and brothers, husbands and wives and children they love. They share over ninety-five percent of their DNA with chimpanzees! They fight or flee when frightened, laugh or cry when overjoyed. Humiliation enrages Them. They dare to crave respect. Yes, They have nothing, surely nothing in common with Us.

Alas, no matter how much we might resist such thinking, we cannot escape it. Scientists have established that every human on earth descends genetically from a single African father "Adam" 60,000 years ago, yet our common heritage has no more power to unite us than our immediate fathers had to prevent our childhood sibling rivalries. On the contrary, cultural rivalry runs so deep that we imagine anyone who defies it must possess unnatural tolerance, courage—or stupidity.

In fact, the migrants, expatriates, and seekers like those in this book who dare to leave us for them, or them for us, rarely qualify as extraordinary characters. Most are every bit as suspicious, frightened, and cautious as the rest of us. What turn the lives of these characters into riveting stories are the conditions that prompt their transgressions. Circumstances like war and profit, poverty, romance, and deception will cause otherwise ordinary people to circumvent otherwise inviolable borders. The consequences are impossible to predict.

Just about a century ago my grandparents staked their shared claim as cross-cultural mavericks. My grandfather Liu Ch'eng-yu, at age twenty-nine, had come to San Francisco by a circuitous route. The only son of the third concubine of a reformist viceroy in Canton, he was groomed by his father to challenge China's decaying Qing Dynasty. When Ch'eng-yu's youthful plot to blow up a local armory imploded, he barely escaped beheading by fleeing China for Tokyo. There he fell under the sway of fellow exile Dr. Sun Yat-sen.

Dr. Sun touted Western-style freedom, dress, and government. My young grandfather became so enamored with these ideals that he cut off his queue, the pigtail that Chinese men were required to wear as a show of submission to their Manchu rulers. He traded his scholar's robes for waistcoats and a bowler. In 1903 he stood up at a gala New Year's party and called for democracy in China—causing both the Japanese and Manchu officials present to lose big face. Dr. Sun arranged for my grandfather to move on to California.

In San Francisco, Ch'eng-yu would edit the newspaper *Ta T'ung Daily*, urging support from Chinese in America for the revolution back home. There was just one problem: the Chinese Exclusion Act, which had been in effect since 1882—and would not be repealed until 1943—forbade Chinese to enter America. Exceptions were made only for merchants with an established record of doing business in the U.S., or for students enrolled in American schools. All other "Chinamen" would surely "endanger the good order" of U.S. society and so were denied entry.

Sun Yat-sen pulled strings to get my grandfather a student visa. Ch'eng-yu would have to bang the drum for China's freedom by night and attend classes at U.C. Berkeley by day. But to succeed at school, Ch'eng-yu needed tutoring in English. The university directed him to twenty-five year-old Jennie Ella Trescott.

A slender strawberry blonde with luminous blue eyes, Jennie was the only child of pioneers whose heritage stretched back to England. Her mother died of diphtheria in Fort Dodge, Kansas when Jennie was two. Her father failed first at cattle ranching and then at selling snake oil from a traveling medicine wagon. He loved his daughter but could not support her, so she grew up in the care of trail mates, then made her way to San Francisco, where she supported herself by tutoring foreign students.

Years later Jennie would tell her children how her dapper and passionate Chinese pupil impressed her with descriptions of Peking's Forbidden City and the cache of emeralds, rubies, and gold his father and grandfather had amassed during their service as imperial viceroys. The contradiction between Ch'eng-yu's modern dress and politics and his exotic ancestry only made him more intriguing to Jennie. He promised that if she came with him to China, he would make her his "American princess."

This seemed an impossible scenario. My grandfather belonged to a despised minority in California. Marriage between Chinese men and Caucasian women was against state law. It literally took an earthquake to make my grandparents' union possible.

On April 18, 1906, across the Bay Area all social conventions and regulations were suspended. Streets cracked open. Houses split in two. Fire engulfed downtown San Francisco, forcing thousands to take refuge in Golden Gate Park or escape by the boatload to Sausalito or the East Bay. In the havoc of the Great Quake, no one noticed or cared that a single white woman accepted the protection of a Chinese man. Family stories and documents conflict, but what can be pieced together suggests that Jennie landed in a tent city, with Ch'eng-yu standing guard.

The fire leveled Chinatown and with it the offices of *Ta T'ung Daily*. University classes were suspended. The quake left both Jennie and Ch'eng-yu homeless, but it also gave them at least temporary freedom to break the rules.

The nearest town where a Chinese man could marry a white woman in 1906 was Evanston, Wyoming. To get there required a three-day ride on the Union Pacific. They would not be able to ride in the same car or class, yet Jennie couldn't travel alone without courting danger and humiliation. Ch'eng-yu solved that problem by finding six other couples to accompany them. In a surviving photograph taken en route, my grandfather appears by far the most confident of the group's four Chinese grooms.

In Evanston, the Las Vegas of the old west, the turn around time for a certificate of marriage was just twenty-four hours. On May 29, 1906 Leander C. Hills of the Presbyterian Church pronounced the wedding of Jennie Ella Trescott and "Don Luis Chengyu" legal under Wyoming law. At the Federal level, however, this union would cost Jennie her U.S. citizenship—and render her a Chinese national. She was now officially one of them.

My grandparents returned to San Francisco and lived on the outskirts of Chinatown until 1911, when the Manchu rulers finally capitulated and Ch'eng-yu's dream of a new republic in China was realized. My grandparents and their three-year-old daughter sailed to Shanghai, where my grandfather became China's first senator from Hupei Province.

By 1921 Jennie had given birth to three more children, but her life as an American princess in Shanghai fell far short of majesty. My father, the eldest son, was required by the British who then governed most of the city to begin his education in specially designated schools for half-castes, or "Eurasians." The law changed when he entered secondary school, but his treatment at the hands of his "full-blooded" British classmates was no less discriminatory. For the next eighty years until his death my father would favor English muffins and Tiptree marmalade. He acquired by the dozen leather goods bearing the gold stamp of Fortnum & Mason, Harrods, Smythson of Bond Street, or simply LONDON. He did speak Mandarin and Shanghainese, but only in Chinese restaurants. Otherwise his British accent made him sound like David Niven.

Even my father's name embodied his parents' position in Shanghai's cultural crosshairs. "Maurice," after all, looked French—France being Shanghai's other dominant colonial influence in 1912—yet, as spoken by his family and classmates, sounded as British as "Morris." Dad's middle name, Trescott, conjured up his mother's English ancestors. And his original last name, Luis, was a clever torquing of my grandfather's socially inconvenient family name, Liu.

"It costs nothing to change your name." My grandmother maintained this illusion despite all evidence to the contrary. In Wyoming, it had been Jennie who masterminded her husband's transformation from "Liu Ch'eng-yu" into "Don Luis," an identity that could sound English or American but, on paper, might belong to one of the Spaniards who owned much of California in 1906. Even racist landlords in San Francisco wouldn't hesitate to rent to Don Luis. "You're one of us now," I imagine my grandmother advising her husband, "with just the stroke of a pen."

In China, however, she discovered that it costs far less to convert others than to become a convert oneself. As soon as Ch'eng-yu returned to his homeland he reclaimed his ancestral name, along with his traditional scholar's gowns, dialect, and patriarchal attitudes. He hosted male-only poetry sessions and mahjong parties. He left his family for months at a stretch. He paid filial visits to his mother, the concubine, who called his American wife a "camel foot."

Now Jennie belonged to a minority, despised by British and Chinese alike. Neither of them would have her, even if she were willing, which she emphatically was not. She clung to her American style of dress, language, housekeeping—and her made-up name. After two decades in China, when she finally returned with her children to California, the ship's passenger manifest listed her still as Mrs. Cheng Yu Luis.

As soon as she landed she took advantage of recently changed U.S. law to reclaim her American citizenship, effectively declaring her divorce from her Chinese husband and his alien culture. Curiously, though, she never quit insisting that *other* people's identities are fungible.

My father, who returned to China as a correspondent working for the China News Agency in 1941, became the only one of his siblings to adopt his Chinese surname, Liu. He was the only one to see his father again before the Communist takeover closed China's access to the West. And he was the only one to remain a Chinese national after World War II. Despite his British accent, Dad felt a clear allegiance to his birthplace and his father. Yet his mother never gave up her campaign for him to ally exclusively "with us."

During the Red Scare of the 1950s, she won, to a degree, when my father finally decided to apply for U.S. naturalization. But for Jennie, this was not enough. "Dear," she wrote:

> *Why don't you drop the name of Liu ....It costs nothing to change your name, just tell them you want to. If China is in the hands of communists, better drop the name. Your life is here now.*

Political fears aside, my grandmother knew full well that life can never be so neatly compartmentalized. Nor can one ever change name, nation, language, and culture without paying a price. My father understood this. He chose to pass on to his own children the true name of his father – as well as his second hand British goods. He fostered in us a respect for Asia, England, and America that at least attempted to give them equal billing. And through the very inscrutability of his character, my father imprinted in us the cultural collisions and connections that had shaped his and all our lives.

The stories in this rich anthology drive home the same truths that have confounded my family for generations. The American wives in Amanda Eyre Ward's "Motherhood and Terrorism" feel no less stranded in Saudi Arabia today than my grandmother felt in Shanghai. In the modern Tokyo of Mary Yukari Waters' "The Way Love Works," a Japanese-American grand-daughter endures the same split loyalties that wrenched my father and his siblings. And the aging Cuban exiles in Ana Menendez's "In Cuba I Was a German Shepherd," suffer the same sense of loss and estrangement in Miami that my grandfather shed along with his Western coats when he returned to his native China.

We are not Them. Nor are we entirely Us. We are neither. We are both. The shared truths of our collective nature are rarely self-evident, but as all these stories remind us so poignantly and painfully, we ignore them at our peril.

—Aimee Liu, October 2007

Introduction: Finding the Words

I have never known the word for it, the feeling of not wanting to leave a physical place. Indians use the word *rasa*—the mood evoked by aesthetic pleasure and powerful emotional resonance—but this most often describes a work of art, not a village, city, or countryside. I've encountered two Japanese words that relate similar emotions, *yoin* and *yugen*. Yoin refers to the reverberations that continue after a bell has rung. Over time, poets altered the literal definition by writing of bells made from human longing rather than metal. Yugen is the awareness of a place that triggers a feeling too deep for words. A perfect haiku is said to evoke yugen.

Nine years ago I had the incredible privilege to visit the Himalayan kingdom of Bhutan. Like travelers before me, I became enamored with the black mountains, the deep wooded valleys, the vision of white prayer flags bustling in the breeze. My days in Bhutan moved quickly and I didn't want to leave. I cannot remember specific details of leaving, packing my bags, the drive to the airport in Paro, checking in, or selecting a seat.

What I will never forget is that my flight from Paro to Bangkok made an unscheduled stop in Calcutta. The elderly British woman next to me—we hadn't spoken until that moment—clutched my right arm with both hands.

"We're not getting off," she said.

I felt the bones of her fingers. She squeezed until my arm went numb.

"If this is Calcutta," she said, "I can't do it again. Vow to me that you'll stay on board, that they'll have to use extreme force to get us off this plane."

Her eyes watered as she searched hard into mine. I wanted to know more, but couldn't think of how to ask without intruding.

"I promise you," I said, "our day won't end here."

It was a promise I had no business making, yet needed to keep somehow. Twenty minutes later we lifted off again. We had stopped for fuel, a stop made usually in Dhaka, the flight attendant explained, but that day our flight had been rerouted.

The British woman wiped her eyes and thanked me, as if I had maneuvered the plane into the air myself. She took several deep breaths, put her right hand over her heart, and kept her eyes closed until we landed in Thailand.

For weeks I wanted to write a story that answered the questions I had been too polite to ask. What happened in Calcutta? What collision had demanded our brief connection? I never arrived at the right images and words; the story was not mine to tell.

In this book I hoped to collect stories that told me something I could not have imagined. I looked for prose where everything seemed connected, where a story accelerated even as it accumulated greater weight, where in the end the reader had experienced something more expressive than she or he would have anticipated.

One of my favorite questions in Neruda's *The Book of Questions* is, "In what language does rain fall over tormented cities?" Recently I learned an alarming statistic from Words Without Borders: fifty percent of all books in translation worldwide are translated from English, yet only six percent are translated into English. In the United States, we export our language and culture with unrivaled vigor.

In Bhutan, I met students who had watched television only once during their childhood, at a community center the year Bhutan entered an archery team in the Summer Olympics. Still, as young men, they knew American music well and had watched bootleg copies of American movies brought into Bhutan from India. They were eager to ask me if Shania Twain was involved with Brad Pitt when she put his name in her song. (I said no, still they insisted yes.) Visiting Tibet, I cringed with the realization that a Backstreet Boys CD was playing on the sound system in a park across from the Potola Palace. If only the ringing of gongs that accompanies a Bhutanese dance, or the vocal range of Tibetan monks chanting in debate, could be equally disseminated across the oceans.

It may seem absurd, but I resisted the reality that this book could not include the whole world. Several months into preparing it, I started talking in my sleep. *Lebanon*, I said. *Bolivia, Armenia*. I'd wake feeling anxious about cultures and settings that may not be represented. I would remind myself that deeply affecting prose would speak to universal experiences—emotional landscape as much as nationality and physical terrain. I'd relax as I recalled what my friend, the artist Francine Matarazzo, once said of writing fiction, "Maybe you're not creating a map; maybe you're creating a directory of the senses."

To visit a place you have never been and feel completely at home—it is a rare experience, another I find difficult to describe, although it is close to falling in love. In 2002, Bali became the place I wanted never to leave and provided the experience that later would endear me to the title for this book.

On our fourth day in Indonesia, a guide accompanied my husband and me to the Balinese sea temples. We arrived first at Tanah Lot. The temple, while breathtaking, lacked the serene atmosphere I'd imagined. It was well worn by tourists; there was a parking lot.

Our guide told the temple attendant that we were from the United States, lived in Los Angeles, and were recently married. He took some time to explain our itinerary, including a description of our lunch in Nusa Dua. He said that we had admired from his van local gardens and the university; that we planned to move to a hotel near Ubud that evening where we would be greeted, of course, with a small mango cake—a Balinese newlywed tradition.

Despite his best efforts, my husband fidgeted. We weren't yet used to such detailed exchanges of information, to the Balinese custom of speaking about new acquaintances like old friends. We laughed with our guide later that day, how the warmth of the Balinese can be disorienting to visitors. He knew from previous American travelers that Americans rarely speak at length with strangers. He said, "We do not have this word, you see, this *stranger*."

It is true. Native Indonesian languages, like native African languages, have no word for stranger. So it intrigued our guide, that we often associate the word stranger with the word intruder, and not the word guest.

Tanah Lot is one in a chain of six sea temples founded by the sixteenth-century Majapahit priest, Nirartha, built in homage to sea gods, each temple in sight of the next. From Tanah Lot one can see the southern tip of the Bukit peninsula, the brilliantly located temples Ula Watu and Rambit Siwi. Nirartha intended this as a lesson, that the ability to see neighboring villages clearly would create a more harmonious existence.

Two weeks later, Tanah Lot entered my vision again—this time on my television at home in the United States—as a backdrop during news reports on the nightclub bombings in Kuta. My husband and I stood in front of the television shaking our heads, angry, not wanting to believe.

Our friends in Bali responded to tragedy differently from our American peers. The Balinese did not speak of extremists, evil strangers who had targeted their island. True to their culture, they looked inward, explaining that the gods must be angered by the corruptness in their lives to have allowed such a thing to happen there.

Acknowledging this kind of difference in world view is important; it proves essential to our education and humanity. Tanah Lot became my enduring image through changing contexts, a setting I recalled again and again reading the stories included here. I wanted to remember the lesson, the ideal, to see neighboring villages clearly.

If we are lucky, books will provide common ground, spaces to explore what we may not share. Last year OV Books organized a panel called "Writing a Larger World," for the Association of Writers and Writing Programs Annual Conference in Atlanta. Anthology contributors Josip Novakovich, Samrat Upadhyay, and Sharon May were among the panelists. We discussed the essentiality of writing across cultures and reactions to various works set in distant lands. A question came from the audience, "How do you answer to the fact that multiculturalism is trendy right now?"

It's a strange and reductive idea, multiculturalism as a trend, yet the man was correct to point out that our forthcoming book—this book—is hardly the first anthology with a multicultural theme. In the past twenty-five years many very fine books have explored racial, ethnic, religious, and national identities.

For our part, we aimed to collect stories where issues of identity emerged in active dialogues between members of different cultures. The call for submissions stated a belief that culture is at its most vivid—and the idea of identity most relevant—when in relationship with another.

Given this context, culture was open to a wide variety of interpretations by writers of divergent histories and passions. We set out to examine the universal desire to connect, as well as the frustrating difficulties of those connections.

As Aimee Liu points out so beautifully in her foreword, "Circumstances like war and profit, poverty, romance, and deception will cause otherwise ordinary people to circumvent otherwise inviolable borders. The consequences are impossible to predict." Our devoted editorial staff read stories of travelers, expatriates, exiles, immigrants, explorers, runaways, lovers, and protectors. Movement, our contributors seem to agree, is one of the key measures of life.

The exile experience is startlingly rendered by Croatian-American writer Josip Novakovich in "Spleen," where a woman survives her attack in Bosnia to find a new homeland in Cleveland. "I've always wanted to be a homebody," she admits. "So it's all the more miraculous to me that I have become a world traveler, an American." The older and introspective Máximo, in Ana Menendez's "In Cuba I Was a German Sherherd" is significantly less hopeful. He realizes the conversations of fellow exiles that "opened in sun, always narrowed into a dark place."

Several vibrant expatriate stories break the Hemingway mold. In Francesca Marciano's "Le Mal d'Afrique," an Italian woman must learn the rules of the wild to survive her love affairs in Kenya. In "Asunción," by Roy Kesey, an American man living in Paraguay investigates the sloppy and risky union of combat and lust.

Nathan Englander's narrator observes his new home in turmoil, noting "Jerusalemites … have come to abide by their climate. Terror as a second winter, as part of their weather. Something that comes and then is gone." Goli Taraghi's narrator in "The Neighbor" is an Iranian living in France. She realizes her joy when taking the opportunity to speak her own language again. "It's as though I had grown wings … I warble like a song bird and swim into an ocean of words."

Amanda Eyre Ward's provocative "Motherhood and Terrorism" introduces us to a pregnant woman living on an American compound in Saudi Arabia. The brewing dread she feels intensifies when the beheading of a Westerner at a neighboring compound fails to command the cancellation of her baby shower.

The Peace Corps teacher in Ehren Schimmel's "This Is How It Is" and the aid worker in Tony D'Souza's "Africa Unchained," are equal parts educator and explorer, weary when placed in the role of protector. As D'Souza's narrator admits, "While I didn't like to think of myself as a coward, my first impulse upon hearing gunfire was to crawl under something."

I believed this book, by definition, would discuss a post-9/11 world. Yet the haunting story "10 September," by Azerbaijani writer Rashid Majid, was one staff editors recalled often and found impossible to resist. The recently translated "Toba Tek Singh," written in Urdu by Saadat Hasan Manto, a writer who passed away years before most of our contributors were born, feels timeless in its satirical appeal.

The United States is, of course, a nation of immigrants. It amazes me how much public discussion seems to avoid this simple fact. Even those of us whose families have called ourselves American for a long time— through my mother, I am a Mayflower descendent—must feel it; the fact that we did not always belong to this land. Certainly the Native American names of our counties, lakes, schools, and streets should remind us.

The children and grandchildren of recent immigrants have impassioned stories to tell, powerfully represented here by Luis Alfaro's "Border Crossings," Irina Reyn's "The Wolf Story," Mary Yukari Waters' "The Way Love Works," and Dika Lam's "Fresh Off the Boat."

We suggested the now canonical work, "The Third and Final Continent" by Jhumpa Lahiri, to potential contributors as a fine example of our theme. The story covers many years in the life of an Indian man and his wife, émigrés to the United States. We were pleased to consider many émigré stories that recalled Lahiri's discernment, notably Viet Than Nguyen's "The Professor's Office," and Shubha Venugopal's "Bhakthi in the Water."

Sharon May's "The Wizard of Khao-I-Dang" tells the unforgettable story of a Cambodian man who emigrates to Australia then returns to the Khao-I-Dang camp as an interpreter for the Australian Embassy. The camp shelters Cambodians who have escaped to Thailand, determined to get to Australia, England, or the United States. The interpreter puts it plainly for his Australian colleagues. "Even after we have lost everything, we still want something."

The history of international literature, and film, is full of endearing runaways, a tradition that continues in Laila Lalami's "The Odalisque," where a Moroccan student becomes a prostitute in Madrid. G. K. Wuori's "The Naked Circus" describes the strange journey of an internet-order bride. In "The View from the Mountain," Shauna Singh Baldwin's reclusive Costa Rican widower escapes his grief by devoting himself to an American hotelier.

For some, running away fails to become an option. Wanda Coleman's "Slave Driver" awards a feminist revision to the title's deplorable term.

Well traveled lovers have their say on these pages. They get lost in New York, accompanied by a South African priest, in Diane Lefer's "Keys to the Kingdom." In Yelizaveta P. Renfro's "White Night Fire," they walk the streets of St. Petersburg "in a stupor of unspoken ardor and regret." Carolyn Alessio's "Currency" relays the unexpected events of an international adoption. As the American couple becomes acquainted with their Guatemalan son, they wonder "if he will ever warm to their voices…if his easy satisfaction is a byproduct of poverty or a more imaginative culture."

Even the youngest of characters have deep emotional histories to navigate. In Gina Frangello's "Attila the There," an American teenager moves with his mother to Amsterdam, adapting to Dutch culture while contending with his mother's love affair and memories of his girlfriend's rape. "Before Tonde, After Tonde," by Petina Gappah, introduces us to a nine-year-old Zimbabwean girl and the tragic consequences of her family's relocation to London. She fears she will forget too much and reminds herself, "I am not so daft I could forget a whole language, just like that."

Finally, three striking stories by internationally acclaimed writers— "Shoes," by Israeli writer Etgar Keret, "Ishwari's Children," by Bangledeshi writer Shabnam Nadiya, and "What Will Happen to the Sharma Family," by Nepali-American writer Samrat Upadhyay—set within single communities, define culture in the largest sense.

I was online corresponding with anthology contributors when an e-mail update from *The New York Times* flashed onto my computer screen. Grace Paley, the great American writer and activist—a true master of the short story form—had lost her long battle with breast cancer at age eighty-four. I'd been aware of Paley's age and failing health, yet I sat stunned by the news. Born within a year of Italo Calvino, Nadine Gordimer, Jose Saramago, and Wislawa Szymborska—international luminaries who also used literature to bridge cultures—she became a devoted teacher to three generations of student writers.

Paley was the daughter of Ukrainian Jewish Socialists. Her parents were exiled to Siberia as teenagers by Czar Nicholas II, then released when the czar freed prisoners under twenty-one to honor the birth of his son. When they arrived in New York, her father became a doctor, setting up a neighborhood practice in his home in the Bronx. The stories Paley learned during her childhood became a rich tapestry of English, Russian, and Yiddish, the tales of Socialists, Zionists, and anarchists.

She cared deeply about those she met growing up in the Bronx, and later, the mothers she met taking her children to neighborhood parks in Greenwich Village. These women, in Paley's words, "lived in all sorts of peculiar circumstances," and infused Paley's works with Irish, Italian, Latino, and African American voices. She was a great believer in *gotong*, an Indonesian word with no direct English translation, meaning "to carry together the burden of our tasks."

Her awareness of her neighbors only heightened her compassion for people in distant parts of the world. As a peace activist, she visited Vietnam, El Salvador, and Nicaragua. Of El Salvador, she wrote, "I have written remembrances of a country my country will not leave alone because the faces of the people I saw in those short days do not leave me."

I had the honor to take Paley's fiction workshop at the Fine Arts Work Center in Provincetown in 1997. She gave me the best career advice I have ever received. She looked into my eyes, nodded her head, and told me with the economy of words she was famous for, "Cheer up." I believe she meant, writing will always be difficult; creating books will present challenges, but you've vowed to do this, so do yourself a favor, and move forward in good humor.

If interviewers asked Grace Paley how she saw her future, she immediately answered, "Too short!" Like many of the characters in this book, she refused to let hardships deprive her of her spark. I would have liked to tell her that editing an anthology reinforced her lessons: that fiction, at its best, allows us to see the individual rather than the general, to participate more intimately in the lives of others. I like to think that the stories and authors presented here would have pleased her. And I would have been glad to tell her that I have cheered up indeed.

—Stacy Bierlein

Spleen

Josip Novakovich

When I found out that a Bosnian family had moved into our neighborhood, just across from my place, I was thrilled. I had left Bosnia seven years before, and I hardly ever saw anybody from there.

To me now it didn't matter whether the neighbors were Muslims, Croats, or Serbs from Bosnia; the main thing was that they were Bosnian, that they spoke the language I loved and hadn't heard in a while, but when I learned that they were a Croatian family from Bugojno, I was all the more delighted.

Maybe it was the timing—nostalgia. Perhaps I could've already gone home, but I didn't trust it: my hometown was in Republika Srpska. Under the NATO supervision, it's possible to go back, and probably nothing bad would have happened, but I still couldn't see sleeping there at night, without streetlights around; I would imagine masked thugs coming in…and I begin to replay in my mind…. Some people had already fled from my hometown because they'd heard the Serb army was coming, but I didn't believe they would bother me. If they were targeting people ethnically, I thought I was safe, since I was half Serb, half Croat. Then, one night, somebody knocked on the door and shouted, Open up! Police.

I looked through the door and saw two men with masks over their heads.

That's not what you'd expect police to look like. What would police need to talk to me about anyway?

I went to the kitchen, took a sharp, midsized knife, put it in my sleeve and waited while they tore the door down. I hid in a clothes' cabinet. The two thugs went through the house, overturning the tables, smashing the china, and they shouted for me to come out. One walked into the basement, and the other opened the toilet. At that moment, I sneaked out of

1

the closet, walking softly, barefoot. But he saw me and ran after me and knocked me down. The knife slid out of my sleeve and fell on the floor but he must not have heard it because he'd knocked down a pile of plates on the way, and they crashed on the floor. He tore my clothes off. Meanwhile, the man—or should I say, beast—downstairs kept smashing the jars of jam and pickled peppers; suddenly he quieted because probably he'd found the wine bottles.

The thug pinned me to the floor and as I tried to throw him off my body, he whacked my head against the boards. I am pretty strong, and I think I could have thrown him off if he hadn't whacked my head each time I moved. It hurt terribly. I thought migraines were the worst headache you could have, but this was worse, it hurt deeper inside, and I was dizzy, as though my brain had turned around in my skull and was now loose and wobbling.

He slid a little lower and sat on my thighs. You must help me to get it hard, he said.

I don't want to.

You must. Here, take it into your hand.

I did with one hand.

It's awkward like that. Can I sit up? I asked.

Sure, no problem.

I sat up sideways, felt on the floor for the knife, grabbed its handle, and without hesitation stuck the knife into him. I wanted to get him in the middle of his abdomen but I missed and stuck it to the side, the left side. I did not think it went deep.

He shrieked and didn't react when I leaped to the side and ran straight out of doors. And so I ran into the hills, naked, in the cold November night. I nearly froze, turned blue, and didn't know where to hide, except in the Benedictine monastery on top of the hill. I broke into the chapel in the middle of matins, five in the morning now, still dark. The poor men crossed themselves, hid their faces, prayed in Latin, and I heard one word, which I liked, *misericordia*. But one of them said, Brothers, don't be silly. Help her! He took off his brown garment, put it over me, and stood there in his striped shirt and long johns.

The monks gave me hot water and coffee, and when I stopped shivering, I wanted to run away. I told them what had happened and advised them to run away as well. The one who had intervened for me drove me west, to Mostar. As he drove he wanted to hold hands with me. No harm, I thought. And indeed, what harm was it? This fifty-year-old man, holding hands. He did not ask for anything more. I think he just loved some female creature comfort. I did not wait for further developments. I stole a bicycle in Mostar and rode it all the way into Croatia, to Metkovic. That was not hard since the road mostly goes downhill. And in Croatia, I appealed to Caritas, who gave me the papers and let me go abroad, to the States. Now that was more adventure than I had hoped to get.

I've always wanted to be a homebody. I never got the joy of travel, wanderlust. Nearly the only aspect of travel I enjoyed as a kid was the homecoming. I'd rush to the side of the train as it crested the hill before my hometown, and seeing the first glimpse of the church steeples and the minaret, and the old castle, made me happy. So it's all the more miraculous to me that I have become a world traveler, an American.

And my workplace, a bank, is nice. Next to it, there's a restaurant, Dubrovnik. I don't need to go into it, but just knowing it's there comforts me; it's a bit of homeland. And just recently, I did go into it with my fellow bank teller, a Polish woman named Maria. We walked up the stairs into the restaurant and entered a tobacco cloud. The guests in the stinging smoke gave me the impression that a group of angels was noisily resting in the cloud. Since I couldn't make out many details I saw only the silhouettes blowing smoke from their cigarettes, feeding their blue cloud, as if the moment the cloud vanished, they would all fall to earth. I liked to imagine that the gathering was a choir of smoked angels but I knew it was unlikely that any of them were angels; most were recent immigrants from Herzegovina and Croatia, and some had participated in the war.

As I savored soft chicken paprikash, Maria said, You know, a Bosnian family moved into our neighborhood, right next door to you. Have you met them?

No. I had no idea that anybody moved in.

They are having a grill next Saturday. They invited me, and I can bring along anybody I want. Would you like to come along?

Maria wiped her shiny lips and cheeks with a napkin from her lap, and added, They are quite handsome.

Her napkin turned red.

The green backyard of my new neighbors was enveloped in the grill smoke; I enjoyed the smell of coal.

That is one aspect of American culture we from the Balkans quickly adapt to, grilling cutlets and sausages, although we add our variant to it, chevapi, spicy mixed meat. The boom box on the windowsill played folk music, the kind that used to bore and bother me, but now made me feel at home. You know: accordion, bass, and a wailing voice.

The bald host wore a green outfit as though he were in a hospital, and when I asked him whether he was a doctor, he said, I work at Mercy Hospital as an X-ray technician.

That's a good job, isn't it? How many hours a week counts as full time? Twenty-four.

So you have lots of free time. Nice.

It could be nicer. I studied to be a doctor in Sarajevo, did very well, but wasn't very wise: I participated in a protest against Tito, had to go to prison, and couldn't go back to the university afterward. I had no choice but to emigrate.

Have you met my nephew yet? He pointed out a man who was facing away from us. The man turned around, balding like his uncle, with a wide bony face and teeth unusually white for someone from our parts—they were also wide-spaced and maybe that's what saved them.

He looked familiar, but the more I looked at him, the more I was sure that I was wrong. That is just it—many people from my native region can give me that feeling of familiarity even without my ever having met them. In my hometown, they'd all be strangers to me, but the familiar kind of stranger, and that is what I imagined I was responding to.

He came over to me and asked where I was from and what I did, the kind of questions you would not expect from someone from our native region, but from an American.

When I told him I worked for a bank, he grew wildly enthusiastic. I need to buy a house, he said. Can you get me a mortgage? What's the best rate you can offer?

That depends on your credit rating.

Credit rating, phew. How would I have any? But I have a refugee status, and a Lutheran church backing me. And I just got a job, as an electrician.

You must be smart then. A dumb electrician would be dangerous.

You are right about that. But maybe I am a dumb and brave electrician.

Have you ever got a good shock?

Of course, who hasn't? Even you have an electrical shock story.

True.

Bank, he said. Isn't it boring to work there?

Not in the least. There are many Croats and Slovenes there but not Bosnians.

So it must be boring!

It's always interesting with our people—they are still to my mind our people. One day a man paid for his entire new house in cash. He opened a brown suitcase—it was full of ten dollar bills. Nothing but ten dollar bills.

Why don't you write a check? I asked him.

Can't trust checks, he said.

And why only ten dollar bills?

Can't trust no hundret dollar bills, he said. Too many Italians here. They are all Mafioso, and that's what they do, they print fake bills. Ten dollar is the best.

He was an old Croatian car dealer. The motto of his dealership was Honest Cars for Honest Cash. You wouldn't imagine that someone completely stuck in the cash economy could become rich, but that man did, bringing half a million dollars just like that. I wonder how he dared walk the streets, alone, with all the cash.

Dragan laughed. Our people are such hopeless hicks! All of us are peasants.

He kept standing closer and closer, and I moved a little away from him, and so we kept moving around the yard. I was keenly aware of it, and he apparently wasn't, or didn't mind. Perhaps I had adopted the American subconscious concept of personal space, which is about an arm's length, so nobody can touch you or hit you without your getting a chance to duck; it's also convenient because at that distance anybody's bad breath would dissolve in the air and you wouldn't have to suffer it and likewise, you wouldn't have to worry that if you had morning breath, you'd make people uncomfortable breathing in your free-floating bacteria. I like this Anglo-Saxon personal space, but naturally a fresh arrival from Bosnia wouldn't understand the space and would find it cold and standoffish.

But after a while it occurred to me that he was not so much after a house and mortgage as after me.

In the meanwhile, his uncle was retelling Bosnian jokes to Anna, who rewarded him with her booming laughter.

We ate chevapi then. I looked forward to the taste, but the meat was overgrilled. Our hosts were too eager to talk and so they forgot the meat. Actually, since we didn't used to have refrigerators in the Balkans, we customarily overgrilled meat, to make sure to kill all the bacteria. Only here did I for the first time see people eating bloody meat, calling it rare and medium rare. With us, there was only one way: well-done. At any rate, while I loved the smell of grilled meat, I couldn't eat the charcoal crusts to get to the meat. Instead, I drank the red wine Dragan offered—and it was spectacular, Grgich, deep red and purple, tasting of plums for some reason. Now both he and I relaxed, and he told me his repertoire of Bosnian jokes. Strangely, though I found many of them funny, I couldn't remember any.

Anyway, I agreed to get together with this man, Dragan—for no serious reason, other than that I loved speaking Bosnian. I guess that's a serious enough reason. We met in our neighborhood beer hall. That's one thing about Cleveland—it has many ethnic neighborhoods, and this was the German contribution.

You know, he said, my uncle is a funny cat. At night, he sometimes dresses like a doctor and pretends to be one, and visits patients in the clinic, even offering them new diagnoses and advising them to undergo surgery; he loves to advise heart patients to get transplants. He was caught impersonating a doctor and fired, but then, there was such a shortage of nurses and medical technicians that they let him come back. He suffers on the job because he imagines he knows much more than his superiors. He is so absorbed in his status struggle that he neglects other aspects of his life. He lent his life savings to a friend of his from Bosnia, forty thousand dollars, without a security note, just on the honorable word. The friend disappeared, and that was that for life savings. What an idiot my uncle is!

How can you speak so badly of him? He takes care of you.

I am not speaking badly of him. Everybody knows what he's done. It's funny.

Mostly sad. He lost so much money. And he pretends to be what he's not. Does that run in the family?

What do you mean? Crazy generosity? Well....

No, pretending.

I don't pretend anything.

I did not say you did. I simply wonder whether what he's doing is a family trait.

Is that how you talk for fun?

Yes, I continue a theme, a thread. So he's your uncle.

And so? What are you getting at? (He sat up from his chair.)

My God, I thought you had a sense of humor.

Yes, I had it.

OK, mellow out. Have a beer.

Good idea. Two Guinnesses please, he asked the waitress, and turned his head. The waitress wore a short skirt and black stockings that went only a few inches above her knees, so there was a stretch of thigh between the hem of the skirt and the stocking.

Good body, I said.

Guinness has lots of body.

She has a good body.

You noticed?

I noticed you noticing.

Oh, here we go again. You are catching me or something?

No.

I noticed her style. I don't know whether she has a good body, but the style's—

Sexy?

I forgot how difficult our women can be. Now I feel right at home.

Same goes for me and our men. I do feel at home. That's the point, I wanted to feel like I was home.

And that's why you agreed to come out with me?

Yes.

It doesn't matter what I am like, the main thing is I'm from over there?

It matters what people are like.

The beer was foamy and cool, and left a creamy edge on his lips, which he never wiped off right away, but talked like that, with the foam on his upper lip.

The second round of ale got to my head. The American bars are dark.

We kissed in that darkness under the spell of dark ale, or under the excuse of it. He tasted of unfiltered cigarettes, and I liked that, it reminded me of home. Yes, I had kissed a few Americans, and nonsmoking immigrants, who before the kiss, regularly chewed mints, so their mouths were cool, slightly antiseptic. Well, the three, four times I had kissed they went to the bathroom to floss their teeth, no doubt, and to brush them, so you'd get a refurbished mouth. But this was a European kiss, old style, with a nicotine bite to it, and an undertone of hot peppers—he must have had feferonki somewhere. The kiss was hotly reminiscent of the old continent, so I closed my eyes and floated into the smoky spaces with Turkish coffee poured from dzezva, coppery vessels, and heavy dregs on the bottom, from which old peasant women read fortunes. Upon drinking a cup, you'd have a few coffee grains left in your mouth, to chew on, to chase around your mouth with your tongue, and that is how the kiss now felt, like a grainy chase. A gritty and biting kiss. I stretched my neck and he kissed it, his five o'clock whiskers scratching me like a rasping paper, raw, but I liked that sensation of hurt.

We went to my home and continued our erotic pursuits so impatiently that we had not fully undressed. I still had my skirt on, and he had his shirt and tie, though everything else was off. I pulled him to me by his red tie, and the tightening grip of his collar, plus the labor of lust, made his face all red, and blue veins popped on his forehead and kept changing their courses, like overflowing tributaries of a river, seeking the most urgent way to the sea.

I wondered why this man trusted me and let me pull the tie. I felt a sudden impulse to strangle him, inexplicable but tempting. Instead, I let go of the tie, and loosened it. He panted with his mouth open, baring his teeth, and again he kissed my neck, and bit it, perhaps playfully, but still that shot a wave of fright through my blood. I bit his ear. We kept biting each other, as though we were two wolves, steadying each other in the playful grip of teeth. Our lust affected our bones, and came from our bones, and flesh was in the way. The bones of our love made us both sharp, not dreamy and sleepy as I used to be in lovemaking, not floating in the delicacy of sensations, but aggressively alert. It was as though we wanted to destroy each other—and that did result in a sensation, the kind you have when your life is in question, jumping off a cliff into a deep azure bay, skiing downhill and hitting a bump which suspends you in the air.

There was an extraordinary undercurrent of hatred in our sex, and it shocked me. I was shuddering, at first I thought in the premonition of an orgasm, but no, from the cold fright. He let go of my neck, and his tie tickled my stomach and breasts as he rocked back and forth. I was nearly strangling him again, holding on to his tie, like a friar to the church bell, while he was smashing his pubic bone into mine in the rhythm of a church bell, and I did indeed hear the ringing in my ears. If the bones were to break, I wasn't sure it would be mine that would give first. Love and lust aren't synonyms, as everybody knows, and hate and lust aren't antonyms, as I found out. Love is usually safe—someone there who can help you, who can spread his arms to keep you from falling—and in that sense, it's antithetical to that sensation of total collapse and abandon that the most intense orgasms are made of. Hatred, however, helps along that delicious sensation of destruction and self-destruction. That is what I realized as I was coming in this sea, not of joy, but of terror. I would not have thought like that if we had not been making love and hate in our sex, and if hate had not prevailed.

I slid my hands under his shirt and touched his stomach. His stomach twitched like a horse's flank when bitten by a horsefly. His skin was smooth and soft. That surprised me because his neck's hairs stuck out above the collar of his shirt. When my hands roamed farther, he gripped them and put them back. That tickles, he said.

So? Tickling is good. You can tickle me, if you like.

I touched him again, and he twitched and lost his erection. That was just as well; we had survived several hours of passion, and both of us sighed perhaps with relief, perhaps with the contemplation of the unsettling nature of our collision.

Even after he was gone, I sat in amazement at what had transpired and the animosity which hung in the air mustily as a war of different body vapors, his sweat and my sweat, his garlicky, mine olivey, his sugary, mine salty.

After he was gone, I wondered why he had kept his shirt on, and that is how I went to sleep. I woke up, certain I had had an enlightening dream, like that biochemist who had a vision of a snake eating its own tail, which was the solution for the circular structure of benzene or whatever it was and is forever, of course. Now, in my dream, Dragan appeared in a black T-shirt. I asked him, Why don't you take it off?

I can't.

I will make love to you only if you take it off.

I'd rather not.

So I undressed and teased him, and when he took off his T-shirt, I saw a brown scar on his left side, under the ribs, in the spleen area. The scar paled, then blushed, and became angry red. Drops of blood slid out of it and went down his flank. Give me back my shirt, he said, right away! I had thrown it behind the bed. I don't know where it is, I said.

Find it! he said. Blood now gushed.

By the time I took mercy on him—though I thought I had no reason to do it—and wanted to hand him his shirt, he fell on the floor, in an oily red puddle. Blood kept coming out of him, and furniture floated, and my bed turned into a sinking boat. I shrieked and woke up with the echo of it, from the attic and the basement, the whole house was empty with the aftermath of my shriek.

I went to the bathroom. The floor was dry. I brushed my teeth. My gums weren't bleeding. I looked into my eyes. They weren't bloodshot.

I had believed in my dreams, but I also doubted them—I had had all sorts of dreams, in some I had lost all my teeth and when I woke up they were still fast in my jaws.

We were supposed to meet again the following evening after my work. I dreaded it. I would not answer the door. I would turn all the lights off and pretend I was not there.

When eight o'clock approached, I grew terrified that the man would not come, that he would know I had figured him out.

Suddenly three police cars screeched to the house, their lights flashing. Ha, I thought, they must have the evidence. Once they got him out in handcuffs, I would run out and tell them what I had to add. I put my Nikes on and tightened them, remembering that Nike comes from Greek for Victoria, female winner. Soon the cops escorted the familiar bald silhouette, which wore green. It was the poor pretend-doctor. The nephew showed up on the doorstep and smoked a cigarette. Of course, it was possible that he yawned because he'd had too much sex. Still, why wouldn't he at least talk to the cops, why wouldn't he be upset? Maybe he liked it this way, maybe he'd even turned his uncle in, to have more space to himself. Now he wouldn't need to buy a house. But what did I know of what had happened there? I went back to the kitchen and prepared some cappuccino, letting it hiss and spit like an angry cat, although it would be hard to imagine a cat being that angry with milk.

Soon the doorbell rang. I let Dragan in. This time he was not formal; he wore a black T-shirt, just like in my dream. He brought in red carnations and a bottle of Eagle Peak merlot. I turned on the music, Mahler's Fifth. Some of the funeral chords in Mahler's music give me chills, so this was masochistic of me, in all the redness and blackness to have these jarring notes in minor keys.

You like that music? he asked.

Love it.

Why not play some real folk music?

Later. This is good for a slow start.

We have been anything but slow and we are way past a start.

I've never heard a man complaining about getting to bed too quickly.

I'm not complaining. But then, maybe I could if you let others sleep with you so quickly. How many were there before me?

Oh, nobody else has been so special to me. (My voice sounded more cynical than I wanted. Yes, indeed, nobody was so special, I had to admit to myself. And I went on talking.) Poor uncle of yours. Why did they take him?

How do you know?

I am the good kind of neighbor, I look out the window.

God spare us from watchful neighbors. Seriously though, my uncle is totally insane. He went around the kidney ward, injecting morphine into the patients. He kept repeating, There's too much pain in the world, too much pain.

He's right about that. That's kind of charming.

It would be if the drugs weren't an additional stress on the kidneys. If he'd done it in the orthopedic ward, maybe nobody would have complained, but what he did was dangerous, criminal. I am ashamed of him.

But he meant well, and probably the patients were in pain, and felt better afterward. Maybe he knows better about it all than we and the cops do. I think it's touching.

He chuckled. That gave me the creeps. Or maybe a particularly well-placed dissonance in Mahler gave me a chill, and if it didn't, it catalyzed it. As though he understood precisely what went on in my spine, he repeated, You sure you like that music?

He smiled, sitting in a slouchy posture. He didn't look dangerous, but almost amiable, low-key, not like an alpha dog but a beta, sitting at a fireplace with his tail curled.

Above his T-shirt and inside it, he massaged his pectoral muscle, slowly, sensually. It seemed strange to me that a man would caress himself like that—it was surprising and slightly erotic.

Out of nervousness, I drank half the bottle, and soon we were kissing on my queen-size bed. I grew excited, partly because this had a forbidden quality to it: I had forbidden it to myself, and now I was transgressing. I had of course planned to get to bed, to check out his scar, but I had not wanted to be aroused, and here, I was.

Under the pillow I had a kitchen knife, just in case. I know, that sounds like some praying mantis kind of thing, and if so, maybe the man should have his last wish, without knowing it was his last, to make love. I didn't mind the idea; in a way, I almost wanted him to become aggressive and dangerous so I could do it. Not that I wanted to do it, but the temptation flashed in my mind.

As we made out, I slid my hand under his T-shirt, to his navel.

He pushed my hand away and said, I'm ticklish.

Yes, I know you said that, but you don't mind being touched elsewhere.

Only my feet and my stomach are ticklish.

I touched his neck and slid my hands downward, but the T-shirt was too tight, from my angle, to go farther.

What are you trying to do? He asked. You like collarbones?

Collarbones are my weakness. Why won't you take off your shirt?

Out of vanity. I don't want you to see how my stomach sags, how my chest hairs are getting gray, and how deep my innie is.

Now that you have told me all that, what's there to hide? I know what to expect, it can get only better. Let's fully undress. Isn't it funny, we haven't been naked yet. We have screwed each other's daylights, and haven't seen each other naked.

All right, but turn off the light then.

I thought about that. I wanted the light to examine him. But I could examine him anyway, I would let my fingers to it. I turned off the overhead light.

Good, that will be romantic, I said. I'll light the candles then.

I took out half a dozen candles and lit them.

He pulled off the T-shirt, his red underwear, and his soccer-style socks, which went almost to his knees. For his age, he was in good shape; his stomach didn't sag. He had lied. I had candlelight coming from all the corners of the room, and bathroom light came through a crack and spread wider and wider across the floor onto the wall, but that was not enough to see his scar. So as he lay down, I put my hand on his flank. He shrank, and his stomach twitched.

Just let go, I said.

All right, I guess you know a technique.

I felt all around, touched his ribs, below them, and I could not believe my fingers. There was no scar. What? Could my dreams have been wrong? It was horrible to think that I had found that man and that he was under my fingertips, but suddenly it was more horrible to think that this was not the man, and the other one was at large, who knew where, if he was not dead. How would I find him? Why should I want to find him? Why didn't I feel relief? I could've been overjoyed to be with a man who made love so vigorously—I could have a boyfriend, maybe even a new family, that wouldn't have been outlandish at my age, midthirties.

I was in such a state of shock that right away I quit the foreplay. I can't do it, I said.

Why not?

Dark thoughts have crossed my mind and they won't go away.

What are your dark thoughts?

And I told him, in detail, the attempted rape, and how I fled, except I didn't tell him about the knife and the wound. I said I knocked down the guy with a candelabra.

That is admirable, that you had so much courage to do that, he said. But why would you think of that right now?

Why admirable? What choice did I have?

Do you know what happened to the guy?

No, and I don't think I want to know. Do you?

Why would I? What a question!

I have no idea.

Did you think that even before?

I did not answer. I decided not to worry about anything. (I could worry; yes, I was tempted. It flashed in my mind that if this was not the first man, this could be the second man, the one who went to the basement to drink wine. But then, how did I know that one drank wine? Simply because he grew quiet? Well, this one certainly liked wine. But then, what's so unusual about that? Oh, no, I decided, I shouldn't keep having paranoid thoughts. They had to stop somewhere. I was wrong once, I could keep being wrong.) We drank more Eagle Peak; he'd brought two bottles, it turned out, and kept one in his laptop briefcase.

Let's shower together, I said. Maybe we'll make love, maybe not, but let's shower.

He obeyed and followed me. I soaped up our bodies, and so in foam, in hot water, we washed, our hair dripping, our eyes stinging from soap, gasping from exhaustion and lack of air in the steamy cubicle, in the trapped cloud of our own making. He tried to grip me, and I clasped him, but we kept slipping out of each other's hold; the evasive slipperiness of our bodies made me lose the sense of balance so much that I enjoyed the illusion of exquisitely falling through the clouds.

Motherhood And Terrorism

Amanda Eyre Ward

Lola thought her baby shower would be cancelled due to the beheading, but she was wrong. Karen McDaniels called early Friday morning to make sure Lola knew how to get to her house on Liberty Avenue.

"Oh," said Lola, "is the shower still on?"

"Well, why wouldn't it be?" said Karen, an argumentative edge to her voice.

"The attacks in al-Khobar," said Lola. "And…and the head." She swallowed. "I guess I thought…"

"Did you know him?" said Karen.

"What? No."

"Phew!" Karen breathed a sigh of relief. "Honey," she said, her voice slipping back into its buttery Texas twang, "it's all quiet now up there. You can't let these Muslim assholes run your life."

"Right," said Lola.

"And I'm making nachos," added Karen.

"Okay," said Lola, hanging up the phone.

Lola's husband, Emmett, looked up from the *Arab News*. "Who was that?" he asked.

"Karen," said Lola. "Of Karen and Andy McDaniels."

"Great!" said Emmett, flashing a wide smile before looking back at the paper. His wispy curls were thinning a little. Lola remembered standing next to him at the altar three years before, looking at his black hair and thinking she owned every handful of it. Now she understood: she would lose it all eventually, and be left with a big, bald head.

"What's in the news?" said Lola.

"Oh," said Emmett, "same old."

Lola knew that the shooting spree on the Oasis Compound was not same old. Twenty-two people had been killed, and the terrorists had promised to rid the Arabian Peninsula of infidels. Infidels like Lola. She had been dreaming of gunmen for weeks. In her dreams, a man with a scratchy beard held her head against his chest. He smelled like lemons.

From the moment she'd stepped off the plane from Texas—her back sore from the nineteen-hour flight, her eyes blinded by desert sun—she had felt a brewing dread. It was cool on the tarmac, and she found out later that the whole zone was air-conditioned.

"They air-condition the *outside*?" she'd said to Emmett.

"They've got more money than you can imagine," said Emmett. "They can do whatever they damn well please."

Day by day, fear had grown in Lola. At the welcoming cocktail parties, the compound softball games, Lola had approached the wives, asking them, *Don't you feel afraid?* and, *Do you ever wonder if we should go home?* She found quickly that these were not the sorts of questions you asked in Haven Compound.

"You sweet little thing," Karen McDaniels had said, putting a hand to Lola's cheek. "You need some hobbies and a little baby or two. And a drink. Somebody get this sweet girl a drink!"

Lola learned to talk about motherhood instead of terrorism.

"You're my wonderful Lola, that's who you are," explained Emmett in bed one night, when Lola had drunk duty-free wine until she couldn't keep from talking. Emmett scratched her back and said, "Maybe take some tennis lessons."

"But I've never felt so *lost*," said Lola.

"Oh sweetie," said Emmett, "yes you have."

Now, he drained his coffee cup. "Off to the races," he said, glancing at his beeper. The damn beeper woke them up some nights, paging Emmett to discuss some drilling mishap. When it went off, Emmett ran to the office as if he were a doctor, though what he worked on was not hearts but oil wells.

"What races?" said Lola.

"I don't know," said Emmett, looking embarrassed. "Just something to say."

"My mom wrote again," said Lola. "She says we're not safe here. She thinks I should come home."

Emmett put his thumb and forefinger to his eyes and pressed, a gesture that made him look old. "We're safe," he said. "I don't know how many times I have to say it. But if you want to go home, then just go."

"I have the baby shower today," said Lola.

"That will be fun," said Emmett, "won't it?"

"Sure," said Lola.

"Take care of Junior," he said, bending to kiss Lola's giant belly. The baby kicked Emmett hard.

She stood in front of her bedroom mirror for some time. The master suite had thick carpeting and carved mahogany furniture. It was a bedroom fit for a sultan, with gold braiding and tassels around everything, even the Kleenex-box holder. When Lola lay on her bed, she tried to understand how she had ended up an oil wife underneath a garish chandelier.

"I don't know about this party," she said to Corazon, the maid scrubbing her Jacuzzi tub. Corazon did not answer. Lola pulled on a black dress her mother had sent from Old Navy Maternity. It smelled of America: crisp, synthetic, clean.

"Are you afraid to be here?" Lola said. "On an American compound?"

Corazon stood up, her hand on her back, and pursed her lips. "What can I say?" she said. "You are a target, and I am in the way of the target."

The baby kicked again. "Fabulous," said Lola.

Lola's mother had e-mailed four times more, begging her to come home from the godforsaken desert with the baby. "They say we are protected," Lola typed back. "The attacks are in the north, and the compounds are filled with guards. I will let you know what I decide. Anyway, I am off to a baby shower!!! (Can't wait for the loot.) LOVE, Lolabee."

Lola clicked SEND, then held her head in her hands.

"Miss," said Mayala, the cook, tapping Lola on the shoulder. "Miss, your lunch is ready." Lola nodded and wiped her eyes. She turned to face

Mayala, a thin woman with her hair pulled severely back from her face. "I made you the frozen pizza," she said, not hiding her disgust. "The Tombstone pizza," she added.

"Thanks," said Lola.

As she chewed the slices, Lola looked around her gleaming kitchen. Just a year before, she had lived in a shabby apartment in Austin. Lola and Emmett had made pasta on a hot plate, drank beer from water glasses on the porch. Then Emmett finished his dissertation and took the job with British Petroleum.

"I don't want to be a professor in some crummy little town," he'd said. "In Saudi, I'll be working with the best scientists in the world, and the fact is we all use gas. Like it or not. Even professors use gas, Lolly. And BP will send us all over the world." His hands moved like birds as he described the years that lay before them. "We'll never worry about money again. You'll have maids—a cook, even!"

Lola was a bad cook, she'd never pretended to be otherwise. And it was true: she'd been bored by her job at the radio station. But now she missed flirting with Crazy Bob, the morning-show host. She missed the drive down Lamar in her Toyota Tercel, a hot cup of coffee between her thighs.

As Lola ate, she saw that Mayala, usually a frenzy of activity, was standing still in the kitchen. Mayala had seven children at home, but spent her days in Haven, cooking for Lola and Emmett. Often, Emmett worked late, and Lola sat alone at the long table with platters of food. She could hear her Filipino staff giggling and speaking rapid Tagalog in the kitchen, but she did not dare to join them.

"Is something wrong?" Lola asked Mayala.

"No ma'am," said Mayala, but she did not meet Lola's eyes.

In two days she would be gone, leaving behind a note saying, "I am sorry. I am scared. Cook pizza for ten minutes at 350 degrees."

After lunch, Lola went for a walk. Haven was surrounded by high walls, so she could walk outside without a head covering or long pants. The pool was filled with kids, and two blond teenage girls lay on either side of a boom box playing Aerosmith. As Lola walked by, one of them lifted an arm and pressed her fingers to her skin, checking her tan. Standing by the pool were two armed Saudi men dressed in guard uniforms, their sunglasses hiding their eyes.

Suzi and Fran waved as Lola passed the tennis courts. As doubles partners, they won every tournament. Suzi's husband, Carl, was Haven's best golfer. Emmett had encouraged Lola to join the Golf Circle, get out, make buddies, but Lola was uncoordinated and became dizzy in the heat. She preferred to read inside her cool bedroom and had joined the Book Ladies only to shut Emmett up. The first book choice had been *Ten Stupid Things Women Do to Mess Up Their Lives*, by Dr. Laura Schlessinger. Lola was not allowed to drive outside of the compound, so Emmett arranged for a chauffer to take her into the city.

As soon as the limousine passed through the guard station, the landscape changed. Abruptly, green lawns and large houses were replaced by desert. The limousine, clean and black as they left the compound, became covered with a thin layer of sand as they moved toward the teeming city. They drove through narrow streets, and Lola saw groups of women in dark robes led by men who walked a few strides ahead of them. Some of the women held hands, and Lola felt a pang of jealousy. She had never had a sister, or a close female friend for that matter. She had always been the girl in the corner of the bar, staring at her napkin.

They passed fast-food restaurants—McDonald's, Kentucky Fried Chicken—and Lola saw the separate entrances for women and men. The limousine stopped at a traffic light, and Lola saw three boys playing with a dog. The dog rolled over, exposing its stomach, and one of the boys shrieked and knelt down, pressing his face to the dog's neck. There were flies everywhere, flies that had somehow been exterminated from Haven.

Lola had walked around the bookstore for an hour, hiding under her *abaya*. From the eye opening, she watched the other women touching each other, pressing fingers to the thick cloth. Lola could not bring herself to buy the Book Ladies pick, and bought Stephen King's *Carrie* instead.

The baby shower was at four. Corazon made Lola sit down, then rubbed blush into Lola's cheeks. At the radio station, Crazy Bob used to sing to her whenever he passed her cubicle: *Her name was Lola. She was a show-girl!* Life was simpler then, before Lola knew she should be ashamed of her bare legs, her car, and her country. She couldn't help it: Lola started to cry.

"I don't understand you, madame," said Corazon.

"My mom wants me to come home with the baby," said Lola. "I don't know what to do."

"How about this nice headband?" said Corazon, taking the plastic band from her own head.

"No, no," said Lola, but Corazon did not listen, sweeping Lola's hair back, jamming the band in place.

"Maybe everyone should stay home," said Corazon. "Maybe everyone should stay at their own home and never leave." Lola looked at Corazon, whose home was the Philippines. "Wear the nice headband," Corazon said, staring coldly at Lola and hissing through gritted teeth.

The worst day had been when Emmett admitted he was glad she was pregnant.

"But how could this have happened?" said Lola. She held the e.p.t. stick in her hand.

"This is perfect, don't you see?" said Emmett. "You're going to be so happy! The other women are happy, right?"

Lola could have flown home, of course. She could have had an abortion. But each day went by and she found herself still in Haven, watching her body change. *A mother*, she said to herself. It could have been laziness and it could have been a decision. Maybe it was both. Maybe a mother was what she was meant to be.

Lola knocked on the McDaniels' door, and Karen pulled it open forcefully. "Lola's here!" she screamed. Lola swallowed and followed Karen down her long front hallway. In the living room, twenty or so suntanned women sat on leather couches.

"Hooray!" said Beth Landings, holding her drink high.

"Do you want a gin and tonic?" asked Karen. Lola shook her head.

"Oh, come on," said Beth, "It's my bathtub special." Lola shrugged, and Beth ladled her an icy glass, saying, "It's not easy to make gin, you know."

"Yes," said Karen, "we do know."

"Carl once lit a cigarette while he was making booze. He almost blew up the house," said Suzi, who had changed from her tennis whites into a dress printed with fuchsia crabs. Suzi was one of the few women who was not from Texas, and she had decided to pretend Saudi was Nantucket.

"How are you feeling, honeybun?" said Karen, leading Lola to a La-Z-Boy. "Sit back now, make yourself at home."

"I'm tired," said Lola, "but otherwise I'm fine."

"Well, just relax," said Karen. Lola watched the hubbub, sipping her drink and eating whatever hors d'oeuvres Karen's maids brought by: deviled eggs, shrimp, nachos. She listened to the women talk about the stupidity of having to wear an *abaya* outside the compound. "For the Arabs," said Suzi, "your hair is like your boobs."

"At the mall yesterday, I saw someone with a few curls sticking out," noted Karen.

"That's like wearing a skimpy bikini," said Beth, seriously.

"That's like wearing a thong!" said Suzi.

"You went to the mall?" said Lola. As soon as she said it, she wished she had not.

"Sorry?" Karen looked at Lola, narrowing her eyes.

"I mean, isn't it dangerous? Should we be leaving the compound?"

Karen sighed. "Lola," she said, "you can either think about the nutters all day long or you can go about your business."

"That's true," said Suzi. She crossed one long leg over the other.

"Has it been this bad before?" said Lola. There was a silence.

Beth Landings ladled herself another cup of gin. "No," she said simply. "I've been here for ten years, and this is the worst. To be completely honest, I'm scared to death."

"We might go to Bahrain," admitted an older woman with very pink lipstick. "I'm sick of this…fiasco," she said. "The Arabs don't want us here. The tide has turned."

"The terrorists just keep shooting people," said Beth matter-of-factly. "They just stormed the fucking compound and shot people in the head."

No one spoke, and Lola felt her baby begin to move slowly, rolling back and forth in its warm home. It pushed against her side, tentatively, and then with force. It was trying to get out, but did not know how.

Karen McDaniels rose and clapped her hands. "Time for the games!" she cried, her face brilliant and brave.

The first game was the string game. Karen made Lola stand up, and each woman cut a length of string that estimated Lola's girth. Nervous hilarity ensued: every single person thought Lola was a good six inches bigger than she was.

The I-Spy game was a silver tray filled with baby items. Karen let them look at the tray for a few minutes, and then she covered it with a sheet. Lola chewed her pencil eraser, trying to remember what was on the tray as the kitchen timer ticked. *Diaper*, wrote Lola. *Rattle, Teddy Bear, Bottle.* In truth, she didn't even know what half the items were. (She would find out later, for example, that the rubber bulb was a nasal aspirator, not a rattle.) This made her nervous, and she resolved to read the books Karen had lent her: *What to Expect When You're Expecting* and *The Girlfriend's Guide to Pregnancy.* Beth won the I-Spy game, remembering seventeen items, including the rectal thermometer.

As Lola opened each present, the women made comments. "A godsend," for example, when she opened the Diaper Genie, or "My Alice couldn't get enough of that damn toy," when she opened the Lazy-Bee Singing Mobile.

Lola looked up from opening her presents, and saw a guard through the window. He was looking straight at Lola, his hand on his gun. What if he was a terrorist? *Look at that pregnant American!* she imagined the man thinking. *Who does she think she is? She's as greedy as the rest of them with her fancy-ass presents. What does she believe in, I'd like to know?* When he saw her looking, the guard nodded and moved on.

Twice during the party, Lola caught herself running her hand along her neck, pressing at the tendons and the bones.

Karen drove her home and helped her unload the packages. Soon, Lola's living room was filled with bright toys. Corazon brought out a tray of lemonade and cookies, and Karen sank into one of Lola's sofas.

"Well, I hope you had fun," said Karen.

"I did," said Lola. "I really did."

"You know," said Karen, "a million years ago, I was in advertising."

"Sorry?" said Lola.

Karen patted her permanent. "You think I'm some dumb housewife," said Karen. "Don't look so shocked, miss. I know."

"I don't..." said Lola.

"You think you're smarter than everybody else," said Karen. "You think you know what's going on out there." She flung her hand, indicating the world outside the compound. "I'm here to tell you, sweetie, at some point you have to decide. And let me promise you, what's going on in there," she pointed at Lola's stomach, "is a hell of a lot more interesting. You mark my words."

"You know," said Lola, "I'm feeling a little tired..."

"Let me finish my piece," said Karen. She leaned toward Lola. "You think you can waltz around here," she said. "You think you don't need all this..." she gestured to the living room, the sunken fireplace, the surround-sound stereo. "Well, darlin', you can't go home again."

"Actually," said Lola, "I think I might be going home. My mom doesn't want me to have the baby here."

Karen snorted, then took a breath and said, "In Texas, you're just some pregnant girl. Here, though, you're a queen. And that baby," she jabbed again, "will have it all. You think about that before you jump on Lufthansa." Lola was silent.

"Thanks for the lemonade, little chick," said Karen McDaniels.

When Emmett got home from work that night, Lola met him at the door. "Hey," she said, "let's go out to dinner."

"Out to dinner?" said Emmett. "What are you talking about?" He opened the side door of his car, took his briefcase out.

"I'm sick of this big fucking house," said Lola.

Emmett sighed. He had grown pudgy from eating too much and sitting at his workstation. Even with the leather shoes and the BMW, though, Lola could still see in Emmett the shy student who had once told her the story of a mountain range as they hiked, explaining with wonder its evolution over millions of years.

"Okay okay," he said, after a moment. "How about the Japanese place?"

"No," said Lola. "Out."

"The Mexican place?"

"You know what I mean, Emmett."

"Out of the compound," said Emmett wearily.

"Right."

"Look, Lolly," said Emmett, coming toward her. "It's nothing great out there. You've been out. You have to wear the—"

"The *abaya*. I know."

He set his face in a mask of calm. "Okay," he said. "All right," he said. "Fine."

Emmett changed into clean clothes and Lola put on the long-sleeved black robe and headscarf. As they drove the BMW down the busy streets, Lola watched the men drinking tea outside the dim cafés, the boys selling cigarettes. "We could have taken the bus," she said. Emmett sighed.

"They hate us here, don't they?" said Lola.

"Of course they don't," said Emmett. Then he added, "Well, some of them do. A few crazy ones."

"More than a few," said Lola.

"You know," said Emmett, "I work with people who are very happy we're here. What I do is important to a lot of people."

Lola turned back to her husband. The anger in her faded when she saw that he was biting back tears. "Emmett…" she said.

"Can't you be proud of me?" he said, staring at the unpaved road where a cow was trying to cross the street. "Can't you just try?"

The restaurant Emmett chose was a steak house lit up like a Christmas tree. When Lola noted this, Emmett told her to keep her voice down. They were seated at a table set elaborately for six. Next to them, a large Saudi family had already been served their dinner. The women scooped food underneath their headscarves gracefully. Lola watched them as she squeezed into a chair, but they took no notice of her.

"Skooch over here," said Emmett. "You're three seats away. And wearing that damn hood."

Lola moved closer, and Emmett put his hand on the fabric covering her knee. "Should we drink from all the glasses?" he said. "Should we eat off all the plates?"

He was trying to be charming, and Lola smiled tightly. Not that Emmett could see. For all he knew, she was baring her teeth.

They ordered filet mignon and Cokes. They talked about baby names, crib styles, how a well-done steak felt like the tip of your nose when pressed. Finally, Lola put down her knife and fork. "Em," she said, "we need to talk."

"Yeah," said Emmett. "I know. Just tell me. Are you leaving?" His eyes were large and blue, with bursts of white around the irises. He blinked in the dim light of the restaurant. There was something in his forehead, in the lines around his mouth: he was just as scared as she was. "And also," he said, "will you come back?"

"I have to go to the bathroom," said Lola.

In the ladies' room, two Saudi women stood at the mirror. They had taken off their headscarves, and above their dark bodies, their faces were bright and topped with elaborate hairdos. Precious stones glittered in their ears and around their necks. One applied very pink lipstick to her lips.

There was a couch in the corner, and Lola sat down. She felt calm underneath the robe, with no skin exposed. She could walk out of the restaurant and into the street, joining the groups of people out for an evening stroll. She could take a cab to the airport and fly home, or to Tahiti. Nobody would notice her: she was just a blank expanse of cloth in the shape of a woman.

Lola thought about going home. She could live with her mother, in Sugar Land. Her mother lived in the same small house that Lola had grown up in, but now it was surrounded by Houston's nasty sprawl. Lola thought about her baby, and her mother's cracked linoleum floor. Lola saw herself: a sweaty, pregnant girl on her mother's front porch, kicking at a rusty metal chair.

Without warning, the lights in the bathroom went out. Lola heard her own, shallow breath. The women at the mirror fell silent. As Lola's eyes adjusted to the darkness, she saw them putting their headscarves back on. They walked past Lola quickly, and she smelled perfume.

She was alone. At prayer time, they cut the electricity, she knew it. But she imagined a man in the doorway of the bathroom. She imagined cold metal against her temple, a blade to her throat. The man would take pictures of her, afterward. He would post a video on the Internet.

The baby moved, and Lola put her hand to her stomach. She felt the baby throb against her skin, a second heartbeat. It kicked and kicked, blissfully unaware. It occurred to Lola that she could tell the baby the Jacuzzi tub was an indoor pool. The baby would think that Corazon loved it whole-heartedly, and not just because she was being paid. And when they were forced to evacuate (which they surely would be, sooner or later) the baby would know only that they were together—a family—and safe. Though she felt far from home or a hope of home, she cradled the baby and whispered, *I've got you*. When it was born, Lola would lie on her expensive sheets and hold the baby to her breast. To the baby, Lola would smell like a mother, and the ridiculous chandelier would look like stars.

Shoes

Etgar Keret

Translated from the Hebrew by Miriam Shlesinger

On Holocaust Commemoration Day, our teacher, Sarah, took us on the number fifty-seven bus to the Vohlin Memorial Museum, and I felt really important. All the kids in my class had families that came from Iraq, except me and my cousin and one other kid, Druckman, and I was the only one whose grandfather died in the Holocaust. The Vohlin Memorial Museum was a really fancy building, all covered in expensive-looking black marble. It had a lot of sad pictures in black and white and lists of people and countries and victims. We paired up and walked along the wall, from one picture to the next, and the teacher said not to touch, but I did. I touched one of them, a cardboard photograph of a pale and skinny man who was crying and holding a sandwich. The tears running down his cheeks were like the stripes on an asphalt street, and Orit Salem, the girl I was paired up with, said she'd tell the teacher on me. I said that as far as I was concerned, she could tell everyone, even the principal, I didn't care. That was my grandfather, and I could touch whatever I wanted.

After the pictures, they took us into a big hall and showed us a movie about little kids being loaded onto a truck. They all choked on gas in the end. After that this skinny old guy came up on the stage and told us how the Nazis were scum and murderers and how he got back at them and even strangled a soldier to death with his bare hands.

Djerbi, who was sitting next to me, said the old man was lying, and from the looks of him, there wasn't a soldier in the world he could beat up. But I looked into the old man's eyes and I believed him. There was so much anger in them that all the attacks of all the hot-shot punks in the world seemed like small change by comparison.

In the end, after he was finished telling us about what he'd done in the Holocaust, the old man said that everything we'd heard was important, not just for the past but for what was happening now too. Because the Germans were still living, and they still had a country. The old man said he'd never forgive them and he hoped we wouldn't either, and that we should never ever go visit their country, God forbid. Because when he and his parents had arrived in Germany fifty years ago everything looked really nice and it ended in hell. People have a short memory sometimes, he said, especially for bad things. They prefer to forget. But don't you forget. Every time you see a German, remember what I told you. And every time you see anything that was made in Germany, even if it's a TV, because most of the companies that make TVs, or anything else, are in Germany, always remember that the picture tube and other parts underneath the pretty wrapping were made out of the bones and skin and flesh of dead Jews.

On our way out, Djerbi said again that if that old man had strangled so much as a cucumber, he'd eat his T-shirt. And I thought it was lucky our fridge was made in Israel, 'cause who needs trouble.

Two weeks later, my parents came back from abroad and brought me a pair of sports shoes. My older brother had told my mother that's what I wanted, and she bought the best ones. Mom smiled when she handed them to me. She was sure I didn't know what was in the bag. But I could tell right away by the adidas logo. I took the shoe box out of the bag and said thank you. The box was rectangular, like a coffin. And inside it lay two white shoes with three blue stripes on them, and on the side it said ADIDAS ROM. I didn't have to open the box to know that. "Let's try them on," Mom said, pulling the paper out. "To see if they fit." She was smiling the whole time; she didn't realize what was happening.

"They're from Germany, you know," I told her and squeezed her hand hard.

"Of course I know," Mom smiled. "Adidas is the best make in the world."

"Grandpa was from Germany too," I tried hinting.

"Grandpa was from Poland," Mom corrected me. She grew sad for a moment, but it passed right away, and she put one of the shoes on my foot and started lacing it up. I didn't say anything. I knew by then it was no use. Mom was clueless. She had never been to the Vohlin Memorial

Museum. Nobody had ever explained it to her. And for her, shoes were just shoes and Germany was really Poland. So I let her put them on my feet and I didn't say anything. There was no point telling her. It would just make her sadder.

After I said thank you one more time and gave her a kiss on the cheek, I said I was going out to play. "Watch it, eh?" Dad kidded from his arm-chair in the living room. "Don't you go wearing down the soles in a single afternoon." I took another look at the pale leather shoes on my feet and thought back about all the things the old man who'd strangled a soldier said we should remember. I touched the adidas stripes again and remembered my grandpa in the cardboard photograph. "Are the shoes comfort-able?" Mom asked. "Of course they're comfortable," my brother answered instead of me. "Those shoes aren't just some cheap local brand, they're the very same shoe that Kroif used to wear." I tiptoed slowly toward the door, trying to put as little weight on the shoes as possible. I kept walking that way toward the petting zoo. Outside, the kids from Borochov Elementary were forming three groups: Holland, Argentina, and Brazil. The Holland group was one player short so they agreed to let me join, even though they usually never took anyone who didn't go to Borochov.

When the game started, I still remembered to be careful not to kick with the tip, so I wouldn't hurt Grandpa, but as it continued, I forgot, just like the old man at the Vohlin Memorial Museum said people do, and I even scored the tiebreaker with a volley kick. After the game was over I remembered and looked down at the shoes. They were so comfortable all of a sudden, and springier too—much more than they'd seemed when they were still in the box. "What a volley that was, eh?" I reminded Grandpa on our way home. "The goalie didn't know what hit him." Grandpa didn't say a thing, but from the lilt in my step I could tell he was happy too.

In Cuba I Was A German Shepherd

Ana Menendez

The park where the four men gathered was small. Before the city put it on the tourist maps, it was just a fenced rectangle of space that people missed on the way to their office jobs. The men came each morning to sit under the shifting shade of a banyan tree, and sometimes the way the wind moved through the leaves reminded them of home.

One man carried a box of plastic dominoes. His name was Máximo, and because he was a small man, his grandiose name had inspired much amusement all his life. He liked to say that over the years he'd learned a thing or two about the "physics of laughter," and his friends took that to mean good humor could make a big man out of anyone. Now Máximo waited for the others to sit before turning the dominoes out on the table. Judging the men to be in good spirits, he cleared his throat and began to tell the joke he had prepared for the day.

"So Bill Clinton dies in office and they freeze his body."

Antonio leaned back in his chair and let out a sigh. "Here we go."

Máximo caught a roll of the eyes and almost grew annoyed. But he smiled. "It gets better." He scraped the dominoes in two wide circles across the table, then continued. "Okay, so they freeze his body and when we get the technology to unfreeze him, he wakes up in the year 2105."

"Two thousand one hundred and five, eh?"

"Very good," Máximo said. "Anyway, he's curious about what's happened to the world all this time, so he goes up to a Jewish fellow and he asks, 'So, how are things in the Middle East?' The guy replies, 'Oh wonderful, wonderful, everything is like heaven. Everybody gets along now.' This makes Clinton smile, right?"

The men stopped their shuffling, dragged their pieces across the table, and waited for Máximo to finish.

"Next he goes up to an Irishman and he asks, 'So how are things over there in Northern Ireland now?' The guy says, 'Northern? It's one Ireland now and we all live in peace.' Clinton is extremely pleased at this point, right? So he does that biting thing with his lip."

Máximo stopped to demonstrate, and Raúl and Carlos slapped their hands on the domino table and laughed. Máximo paused. Even Antonio had to smile. Máximo loved this moment when the men were warming to the joke and he still kept the punch line close to himself like a secret.

"So, okay," Máximo continued, "Clinton goes up to a Cuban fellow and says, 'Compadre, how are things in Cuba these days?' The guy looks at Clinton and he says to the president, 'Let me tell you, my friend, I can feel it in my bones: any day now Castro's gonna fall.'"

Máximo tucked his head into his neck and smiled. Carlos slapped him on the back and laughed. "That's a good one, sure is," he said. "I like that one."

"Funny," Antonio said, nodding as he set up his pieces.

"Yes, funny," Raúl said. After chuckling for another moment, he added, "But old."

"What do you mean *old*?" Antonio said, then he turned to Carlos. "What are you looking at?"

Carlos stopped laughing.

"It's not old," Máximo said. "I just made it up."

"I'm telling you, professor, it's an old one," Raúl said. "I heard it with Reagan."

Máximo looked at Raúl but didn't say anything. He pulled the double nine from his row and laid it in the middle of the table, but the thud he intended was lost in the horns and curses of morning traffic on Eighth Street.

Raúl and Máximo had lived on the same El Vedado street in Havana for fifteen years before the revolution. Raúl had been a government accountant and Máximo a professor at the university, two blocks from his home on L Street. They weren't close friends, but friendly still, in that way of people who come from the same place and think they already know the important things about one another.

Máximo was one of the first to leave L Street, boarding a plane for Miami on the eve of January 1, 1960, exactly one year after Batista had done the same. For reasons he told himself he could no longer remember, he said good-bye to no one. He was forty-two years old then, already balding, with a wife and two young daughters whose names he tended to confuse. He left behind the row house of long shiny windows, the piano, the mahogany furniture, and the pension he thought he'd return to in two years' time. Three, if things were as serious as they said.

In Miami, Máximo tried driving a taxi, but the streets were still a web of foreign names and winding curves that could one day lead to glitter and another to the hollow end of a pistol. His Spanish and his Havana University credentials meant nothing here. And he was too old to cut sugarcane with the younger men who began arriving in the spring of 1961. But the men gave Máximo an idea, and after teary nights of promises, he convinced his wife—she of stately homes and multiple cooks—to make lunch to sell to those sugar men who waited, squatting on their heels in the dark, for the bus to Belle Glade every morning. They worked side by side, Máximo and Rosa. And at the end of every day, their hands stained orange from the lard and the cheap meat, their knuckles red and tender where the hot water and the knife blade had worked their business, Máximo and Rosa would sit down to whatever remained of the day's cooking, and they would chew slowly, the day unraveling, their hunger ebbing with the light.

They worked together for seven years like that, and when the Cubans began disappearing from the bus line, Máximo and Rosa moved their lunch packs indoors and opened their little restaurant right on Eighth Street. There, a generation of former professors served black beans and rice to the nostalgic. When Raúl showed up in Miami in the summer of 1971 looking for work, Máximo added one more waiter's spot for his old acquaintance from L Street. Each night, after the customers had gone, Máximo and Rosa and Raúl and Havana's old lawyers and bankers and dreamers would sit around the biggest table and eat and talk, and sometimes, late in the night after several glasses of wine, someone would start the stories that began with "In Cuba I remember...." They were stories of old lovers, beautiful and round-hipped. Of skies that stretched on clear and blue to the Cuban hills. Of green landscapes that clung to the red clay of Güines, roots dug in like fingernails in a good-bye. In Cuba, the stories always began, life was good and pure. But something always happened to them in the end. Something withering, malignant. Máximo never understood it. The stories that opened in the sun always narrowed into a dark place. And after those nights, his head throbbing, Máximo would turn and turn in his sleep and wake unable to remember his dreams.

Even now, ten years after selling the place, Máximo couldn't walk by it in the early morning when it was still clean and empty. He'd tried it once. He'd stood and stared into the restaurant and had become lost and dizzy in his own reflection in the glass, in the neat row of chairs, the tombstone lunch board behind them.

"Okay. A bunch of rafters are on the beach getting ready to sail off to Miami."

"Where are they?"

"Who cares? Wherever. Cuba's got a thousand miles of coastline. Use your imagination."

"Let the professor tell his thing, for god's sake."

"Thank you." Máximo cleared his throat and shuffled the dominoes. "So anyway, a bunch of rafters are gathered there on the sand. And they're all crying and hugging their wives, and all the rafts are bobbing on the water, and suddenly someone in the group yells, 'Hey! Look who goes there!' And it's Fidel in swimming trunks, carrying a raft on his back."

Carlos interrupted to let out a yelping laugh. "I like that, I like it, sure do."

"You like it, eh?" said Antonio. "Why don't you let the Cuban finish it."

Máximo slid the pieces to himself in twos and continued. "So one of the guys on the sand says to Fidel, 'Compatriota, what are you doing here? What's with the raft?' And Fidel sits on his raft and pushes off the shore and says, 'I'm sick of this place, too. I'm going to Miami.' So the other guys look at each other and say, 'Coño, compadre, if you're leaving, then there's no reason for us to go. Here, take my raft too, get the fuck out of here.'"

Raúl let a shaking laugh rise from his belly and saluted Máximo with a domino piece.

"A good one, my friend."

Carlos laughed long and loud. Antonio laughed, too, but he was careful to not laugh too hard, and he gave his friend a sharp look over the racket he was causing. He and Carlos were Dominican, not Cuban, and they ate their same foods and played their same games, but Antonio knew they still didn't understand all the layers of hurt in the Cubans' jokes.

It had been Raúl's idea to go down to Domino Park that first time. Máximo protested. He had seen the rows of tourists pressed up against the fence, gawking at the colorful old guys playing dominoes.

"I'm not going to be the sad spectacle in someone's vacation slide show," he'd said.

But Raúl was already dressed up in a pale blue guayabera, saying how it was a beautiful day and to smell the air.

"Let them take pictures," Raúl said. "What the hell. Make us immortal."

"Immortal," Máximo said with a sneer. And then to himself, *The gods' punishment.*

It was the year after Rosa died, and Máximo didn't want to tell how he'd begun to see her at the kitchen table as she'd been at twenty-five, one thick strand of dark hair stuck to her morning face. He saw her at thirty, bending down to wipe chocolate off the cheeks of their two small daughters. And his eyes moved from Rosa to his small daughters. He had something he needed to tell them. He saw them grown up, at the funeral, crying together. He watched Rosa rise and do the sign of the cross. He knew he was caught inside a nightmare, but he couldn't stop. He would emerge slowly, creaking out of the shower, and there she'd be: Rosa, like before, her breasts round and pink from the hot water, calling back through the years. Some mornings he would awake and smell peanuts roasting and hear the faint call of the *manicero* pleading for someone to relieve his burden of white paper cones. Or it would be thundering, the long hard thunder of Miami that was so much like the thunder of home that each rumble shattered the morning of his other life. He would awake, caught fast in the damp sheets, and feel himself falling backward.

He took the number eight bus to Eighth Street and Fifteenth Avenue. At Domino Park, he sat with Raúl and they played alone that first day, Máximo noticing his own speckled hands, the spots of light through the banyan leaves, a round red beetle that crawled slowly across the table, then hopped the next breeze and floated away.

Antonio and Carlos were not Cuban, but they knew when to dump their heavy pieces and when to hold back the eights for the final shocking stroke. Waiting for a table, Raúl and Máximo would linger beside them and watch them lay their traps, a succession of threes that broke their opponents, an incredible run of fives. Even the unthinkable: passing when they had the piece to play.

Other twosomes refused to play with the Dominicans, said that Carlos guy gave them the creeps with his giggling and monosyllables. Besides, went the charge, any team that won so often must be cheating—especially a team one-half imbecile. But really it was that no one plays to lose. You begin to lose again and again and it reminds you of other things in your life; the despair of it all begins to bleed through, and that is not what games are for. Who wants to live their whole life alongside the lucky? But Máximo and Raúl liked these blessed Dominicans, appreciated the well-oiled moves of two old pros. And if the two Dominicans, afraid to be alone again, let them win now and then, who would know? Who could ever admit to such a thing?

For many months they didn't know much about each other, these four men. Even the smallest boy knew not to talk when the pieces were in play. But soon came Máximo's jokes during the shuffling, something new and bright coming into his eyes like daydreams as he spoke. Carlos's full loud laughter, like that of children. And the four men learned to linger long enough between sets to color an old memory while the white pieces scraped along the table.

One day as they sat at their table, closest to the sidewalk, a pretty girl walked by. She swung her long brown hair around and looked in at the men with her green eyes.

"What the hell is she looking at?" said Antonio, who always sat with his back to the wall, looking out at the street. But the others saw how he stared back, too.

Carlos let out a giggle and immediately put a hand to his mouth.

"In Santo Domingo, a man once looked at—" but Carlos didn't get to finish.

"Shut up, you old idiot," said Antonio, putting his hands on the table like he was about to get up and leave.

"Please," Máximo said.

The girl stared another moment, then turned and left.

Raúl rose slowly, flattening down his oiled hair with his right hand.

"Ay, mi niña."

"Sit down, hombre," Antonio said. "You're an old fool, just like this one."

"You're the fool," Raúl called back. "A woman like that…"

He watched the girl cross the street. When she was out of sight, he grabbed the back of the chair behind him and eased his body down, his eyes still on the street. The other three men looked at one another.

"I knew a woman like that once," Raúl said, after a long moment.

"That's right, he did," Antonio said, "in his moist boy dreams—what was it? A century ago?"

"No me jodas," Raúl said. "You are a vulgar man. I had a life all three of you would have paid millions for. Women."

Máximo watched him, then lowered his face, shuffled the dominoes.

"I had women," Raúl said.

"We all had women," Carlos said, and he looked like he was about to laugh again, but instead just sat there, smiling like he was remembering one of Máximo's jokes.

"There was one I remember. More beautiful than the rising moon," Raúl said.

"Oh Jesus," Antonio said. "You people."

Máximo looked up, watching Raúl.

"Ay, a woman like that," Raúl said and shook his head. "The women of Cuba were radiant, magnificent, wouldn't you say, professor?"

Máximo looked away.

"I don't know," Antonio said. "I think that Americana there looked better than anything you remember."

And that brought a long laugh from Carlos.

Máximo sat all night at the pine table in his new efficiency, thinking about the green-eyed girl and wondering why he was thinking about her. The table and a narrow bed had come with the apartment, which he'd moved into after selling the house in Shenandoah. The table had come with two chairs, sturdy and polished—not in the least institutional—but he had put one of the chairs by the bed. The landlady, a woman in her forties, had helped Máximo haul up three potted palms. Later, he bought a green pot of marigolds that he saw in the supermarket and brought its butter leaves back to life under the window's eastern light. Máximo often sat at the table through the night, sometimes reading Martí, sometimes listening to the rain on the tin hull of the air conditioner.

When you are older, he'd read somewhere, you don't need as much sleep. And wasn't that funny, because his days felt more like sleep than ever. Dinner kept him occupied for hours, remembering the story of each dish. Sometimes, at the table, he greeted old friends and awakened with a start when they reached out to touch him. When dawn rose and slunk into the room sideways through the blinds, Máximo walked as in a dream across the thin patterns of light on the terrazzo.

The chair, why did he keep the other chair? Even the marigolds reminded him. An image returned again and again. Was it the green-eyed girl?

And then he remembered that Rosa wore carnations in her hair and hated her name. And that it saddened him, because he liked to roll it off his tongue like a slow train to the country.

"Rosa," he said, taking her hand the night they met at the La Concha while an old *danzón* played.

"Clavel," she said, tossing her head back in a crackling laugh. "Call me Clavel." She pulled her hand away and laughed again. "Don't you notice the flower in a girl's hair?"

He led her around the dance floor lined with chaperones, and when they turned he whispered that he wanted to follow her laughter to the moon.

She laughed again, the notes round and heavy as summer raindrops, and Máximo felt his fingers go cold where they touched hers. The *danzón* played, and they turned and turned, and the faces of the chaperones, and the moist warm air—and Máximo with his cold fingers worried that she had laughed at him. He was twenty-four and could not imagine a more sorrowful thing in all the world.

Sometimes, years later, he would catch a vision of Rosa in the face of his eldest daughter. She would turn toward a window or do something with her eyes. And then she would smile and tilt her head back, and her laughter connected him again to that night, made him believe for a moment that life was a string you could gather up in your hands all at once.

He sat at the table and tried to remember the last time he saw Marisa. In California now. An important lawyer. A year? Two? Anabel, gone to New York. Two years? They called more often than most children, Máximo knew. They called often and he was lucky that way.

"Fidel decides he needs to get in touch with young people."

"Ay ay ay."

"So his handlers arrange for him to go to a school in Havana. He gets all dressed up in his olive uniform, you know, puts conditioner on his beard and brushes it one hundred times, all that."

Raúl breathed out, letting each breath come out like a puff of laughter. "Where do you get these things?"

"No interrupting the artist anymore, okay?" Máximo continued. "So after he's beautiful enough, he goes to the school. He sits in on a few classes, walks around the halls. Finally, it's time for Fidel to leave and he realizes he hasn't talked to anyone. He rushes over to the assembly that is seeing him off with shouts of 'Comandante!' and he pulls a little boy out of a row. 'Tell me,' Fidel says, 'what is your name?' 'Pepito,' the little boy answers. 'Pepito, what a nice name,' Fidel says. 'And tell me, Pepito, what do you think of the Revolution?' 'Comandante,' Pepito says, 'the Revolution is the reason we are all here.' 'Ah, very good Pepito. And tell me, what is your favorite subject?' Pepito answers, 'Comandante, my favorite subject is mathematics.' Fidel pats the little boy on the head. 'And tell me, Pepito, what would you like to be when you grow up?' Pepito smiles and says, 'Comandante, I would like to be a tourist.'"

Máximo looked around the table, a shadow of a smile on his thin white lips as he waited for the laughter.

"Ay," Raúl said. "That's so funny it breaks my heart."

Máximo grew to like dominoes, the way each piece became part of the next. After the last piece was laid down and they were tallying up the score, Máximo liked to look over the table like an art critic. He liked the way the row of black dots snaked around the table with such free-flowing abandon; it was almost as if, thrilled to be let out of the box, the pieces choreographed a fresh dance of gratitude every day. He liked the straightforward contrast of black on white. The clean, fresh scrape of the pieces across the table before each new round. The audacity of the double nines. The plain smooth face of the blank, like a newborn unetched by the world to come.

"Professor," Raúl began, "let's speed up the shuffling a bit, sí?"

"I was thinking," Máximo said.

"Well, that shouldn't take long," Antonio said.

"Who invented dominoes, anyway?" Máximo said.

"I'd say it was probably the Chinese," Antonio said.

"No jodas," Raúl said. "Who else could have invented this game of skill and intelligence but a Cuban."

"Coño," said Antonio without a smile. "Here we go again."

"Ah, bueno," Raúl said with a smile, stuck between joking and condescending. "You don't have to believe it if it hurts."

Carlos let out a long laugh.

"You people are unbelievable," said Antonio. But there was something hard and tired behind the way he smiled.

It was the first day of December, but summer still hung about in the brightest patches of sunlight. The four men sat under the shade of the banyan tree. It wasn't cold, not even in the shade, but three of the men wore cardigans. If asked, they would say they were expecting a chilly north wind and doesn't anybody listen to the weather forecasts anymore. Only Antonio, his round body enough to keep him warm, clung to the short sleeves of summer.

Kids from the local Catholic high school had volunteered to decorate the park for Christmas, and they dashed about with tinsel in their hair, bumping one another and laughing loudly. Lucinda, the woman who issued the dominoes and kept back the gambling, asked them to quiet down, pointing at the men. A wind stirred the top branches of the banyan tree and moved on without touching the ground. One leaf fell to the table.

Antonio waited for Máximo to fetch Lucinda's box of plastic pieces. Antonio held his brown paper bag to his chest and looked at the Cubans, his customary sourness replaced for a moment by what in a man like him could pass for levity. Máximo sat down and began to dump the plastic pieces on the table as he'd always done. But this time, Antonio held out his hand.

"One moment," he said, and shook his brown paper bag.

"Qué pasa, chico?" Máximo said.

Antonio reached into the paper bag as the men watched. He let the paper fall away. In his hand he held an oblong black leather box.

"Coñooo," Raúl said.

He set the box on the table, like a magician drawing out his trick. He looked around to the men and finally opened the box with a flourish to reveal a neat row of big heavy pieces, gone yellow and smooth like old teeth. They bent in closer to look. Antonio tilted the box gently and the pieces fell out in one long line, their black dots facing up now like tight dark pupils in the sunlight.

"Ivory," Antonio said, "and ebony. They're antique. You're not allowed to make them anymore."

"Beautiful," Carlos said, and clasped his hands.

"My daughter found them for me in New Orleans," Antonio continued, ignoring Carlos.

He looked around the table and lingered on Máximo, who had lowered the box of plastic dominoes to the ground. "She said she's been searching for them for two years. Couldn't wait two more weeks to give them to me," he said.

"Coñooo," Raúl said again.

A moment passed.

"Well," Antonio said, "what do you think, Máximo?"

Máximo looked at him. Then he bent across the table to touch one of the pieces. He gave a jerk with his head and listened for the traffic. "Very nice," he said.

"Very nice?" Antonio said. "Very nice?" He laughed in his thin way. "My daughter walked all over New Orleans to find these and the Cuban thinks they're 'very nice'?" He paused, watching Máximo. "Did you know my daughter is coming to visit me for Christmas? She's coming for Christmas, Máximo, maybe you can tell her her gift was very nice, but not as nice as some you remember, eh?"

Máximo looked up. His eyes settled on Carlos, who looked at Antonio and then looked away.

"Calm down, hombre," Carlos said, opening his arms wide, a nervous giggle beginning in his throat. "What's gotten into you?"

Antonio waved his hand.

A diesel truck rattled down Eighth Street, headed for downtown.

"My daughter is a district attorney in Los Angeles," Máximo said, after the noise of the truck died. "December is one of the busiest months."

He felt a heat behind his eyes he had not felt in many years.

"Hold one in your hand," Antonio said. "Feel how heavy that is."

When the children were small, Máximo and Rosa used to spend Nochebuena with his cousins in Cárdenas. It was a five-hour drive from Havana in the cars of those days. They would rise early on the twenty-third and arrive by mid-afternoon so Máximo could help the men kill the pig for the feast the following night. Máximo and the other men held the squealing, squirming animal down, its wiry brown coat cutting into their gloveless hands. But god, they were intelligent creatures. No sooner did it spot the knife than the animal would bolt out of their arms, screaming like Armageddon. It had become the subtext to the Nochebuena tradition, this chasing of the terrified pig through the yard, dodging orange trees and the rotting fruit underneath. The children were never allowed to watch, Rosa made sure. They sat indoors with the women and stirred the black beans. With loud laughter, they shut out the shouts of the men and the hysterical pleadings of the animal as it was dragged back to its slaughter.

"Juanito the little dog gets off the boat from Cuba and decides to take a stroll down Brickell Avenue."

"Let me make sure I understand the joke. Juanito is a dog. Bowwow."

"That's pretty good."

"Yes, Juanito is a dog, goddamnit."

Raúl looked up, startled.

Máximo shuffled the pieces hard and swallowed. He swung his arms across the table in wide, violent arcs. One of the pieces flew off the table.

"Hey, hey, watch it with that, what's wrong with you?"

Máximo stopped. He felt his heart beating.

"I'm sorry," he said. He bent over the edge of the table to see where the piece had landed. "Wait a minute."

He held the table with one hand and tried to stretch to pick up the piece.

"What are you doing?"

"Just wait a minute." When he couldn't reach, he stood up, pulled the piece toward him with his foot, sat back down, and reached for it again, this time grasping it between his fingers and his palm. He put it facedown on the table with the others and shuffled, slowly, his mind barely registering the traffic.

"Where was I? Juanito the little dog, right, bowwow." Máximo took a deep breath. "He's just off the boat from Cuba and is strolling down Brickell Avenue. He's looking up at all the tall and shiny buildings. 'Coñooo,' he says, dazzled by all the mirrors. 'There's nothing like this in Cuba.'"

"Hey, hey, professor. We had tall buildings."

"Jesus Christ!" Máximo said. He pressed his thumb and forefinger into the corners of his eyes. "This is after Castro, then. Let me just get it out for Christ's sake."

He stopped shuffling. Raúl looked away.

"Ready now? Juanito the little dog is looking up at all the tall buildings, and he's so happy to finally be in America because all his cousins have been telling him what a great country it is, right? You know, they were sending back photos of their new cars and girlfriends."

"A joke about dogs who drive cars, I've heard it all."

"Hey, they're Cuban superdogs."

"All right, they're sending back photos of their new owners or the biggest bones any dog has ever seen. Anything you like. Use your imaginations." Máximo stopped shuffling. "Where was I?"

"You were at the part where Juanito buys a Rolls Royce."

The men laughed.

"Okay, Antonio, why don't you three fools continue the joke." Máximo got up from the table. "You've made me forget the rest of it."

"Aw, come on, chico, sit down. Don't be so sensitive."

"Come on, professor, you were at the part where Juanito is so glad to be in America."

"Forget it. I can't remember the rest now." Máximo rubbed his temple, grabbed the back of the chair and sat down slowly, facing the street. "Just leave me alone, I can't remember it." He pulled at the pieces two by two. "I'm sorry. Look, let's just play."

The men set up their double rows of dominoes, like miniature barricades before them.

"These pieces are a work of art," Antonio said, and laid down a double eight.

The banyan tree was strung with white lights that were lit all day. Colored lights twined around the metal poles of the fence, which was topped with a long looping piece of gold tinsel garland.

The Christmas tourists began arriving just before lunch as Máximo and Raúl stepped off the number eight bus. Carlos and Antonio were already at the table, watched by two groups of families. Mom and Dad with kids. They were big, even the kids were big and pink. The mother whispered to the kids and they smiled and waved. Raúl waved back at the mother.

"Nice legs, yes?" he whispered to Máximo.

Before Máximo looked away, he saw the mother take out one of those little black pocket cameras. He saw the flash out of the corner of his eye. He sat down and looked around the table; the other men stared at their pieces.

The game started badly. It happened sometimes, the distribution of the pieces went all wrong and out of desperation one of the men made mistakes, and soon it was all they could do to knock all the pieces over and start fresh. Raúl set down a double three and signaled to Máximo it was all he had. Carlos passed. Máximo surveyed his last five pieces. His thoughts scattered to the family outside. He looked up to find the tallest boy with his face pressed between the iron slats, staring at him.

"You pass?" Antonio said.

Máximo looked at him, then at the table. He put down a three and a five. He looked again, the boy was gone. The family had moved on.

The tour groups arrived later that afternoon. First the white buses with the happy blue letters: WELCOME TO LITTLE HAVANA. Next, the fat women in white shorts, their knees lost in an abstraction of flesh. Máximo tried to concentrate on the game. The worst part was how the other men acted out for them. Dominoes is supposed to be a quiet game. And now there they were shouting at each other and gesturing. A few of the men had even brought cigars, and they dangled now, unlit, from their mouths.

"You see, Raúl," Máximo said. "You see how we're a spectacle?" He felt like an animal and wanted to growl and cast about behind the metal fence.

Raúl shrugged. "Doesn't bother me."

"A goddamn spectacle. A collection of old bones," Máximo said.

The other men looked up at Máximo.

"Hey speak for yourself, cabrón," Antonio said.

Raúl shrugged again.

Máximo rubbed his left elbow and began to shuffle. It was hot, and the sun was setting in his eyes, backlighting the car exhaust like a veil before him. He rubbed his temple, feeling the skin move over the bone. He pressed the inside corners of his eyes, then drew his hand back to his left elbow.

"Hey, you okay there?" Antonio said.

An open trolley pulled up and parked at the curb. A young man, perhaps in his thirties, stood in the front, holding a microphone. He wore a guayabera. Máximo looked away.

"This here is Domino Park," came the amplified voice in English, then in Spanish. "No one under fifty-five allowed, folks. But we can sure watch them play."

Máximo heard shutters click, then convinced himself he couldn't have heard, not from where he was.

"Most of these men are Cuban and they're keeping alive the tradition of their homeland," the amplified voice continued, echoing against the back wall of the park. "You see, in Cuba it was very common to retire to a game of dominoes after a good meal. It was a way to bond and build community. You folks here are seeing a slice of the past. A simpler time of good friendships and unhurried days."

Maybe it was the sun. The men later noted that he seemed odd: The tics. Rubbing his bones.

First Máximo muttered to himself. He rubbed his temple again. When the feedback on the microphone pierced through Domino Park, he could no longer sit where he was, accept things as they were. It was a moment that had long been missing from his life. He stood and made a fist at the trolley.

"Mierda!" he shouted. "Mierda! That's the biggest bullshit I've ever heard."

He made a lunge at the fence. Carlos jumped up and held him back. Raúl led him back to his seat.

The man of the amplified voice cleared his throat. The people on the trolley looked at him and back at Máximo. Perhaps they thought this was part of the show.

"Well," the man chuckled. "There you have it, folks."

Lucinda ran over, but the other men waved her off. She began to protest about rules and propriety. The park had a reputation to uphold.

It was Antonio who spoke. "Leave the man alone," he said.

Máximo looked at him. His head was pounding. Antonio met his gaze briefly then looked to Lucinda. "Some men don't like to be stared at is all," he said. "It won't happen again."

She shifted her weight but remained where she was, watching.

"What are you waiting for?" Antonio said, turning now to Máximo, who had lowered his head onto the white backs of the dominoes. "Shuffle."

That night Máximo was too tired to sit at the pine table. He didn't even prepare dinner. He slept, and in his dreams he was a blue and yellow fish swimming in warm waters, gliding through the coral—the only fish in the sea and he was happy. But the light changed and the sea darkened suddenly and he was rising through it, afraid of breaking the surface, afraid of the pinhole sun on the other side, afraid of drowning in the blue vault of sky.

"Let me finish the story of Juanito the little dog."

No one said anything.

"Is that okay? I'm okay. I just remembered it. Can I finish it?"

The men nodded, but still did not speak.

"He is just off the boat from Cuba. He is walking down Brickell Avenue. And he is trying to steady himself, see, because he still has his sea legs and all the buildings are so tall they are making him dizzy. He doesn't know what to expect. He's maybe a little afraid. And he's thinking about a pretty little dog he once knew and he's wondering where she is now and he wishes he were back home."

He paused to take a breath. Raúl cleared his throat. The men looked at one another, then at Máximo. But his eyes were on the blur of dominoes before him. He felt a stillness around him, a shadow move past the fence, but he didn't look up.

"He's not a depressed kind of dog, though. Don't get me wrong. He's very feisty. And when he sees an elegant white poodle striding toward him, he forgets all his worries and exclaims, 'O Madre de Dios, si cocinas como caminas…'"

The men let out a small laugh. Máximo continued.

"'Si cocinas como caminas…' Juanito says, but the white poodle interrupts and says, 'I beg your pardon? This is America, speak English.' So Juanito pauses for a moment to consider and says in his broken English, 'Mamita, you are one hot doggie, yes? I would like to take you to movies and fancy dinners.'"

"One hot doggie, yes?" Carlos repeated, then laughed. "You're killing me."

The other men smiled, warming to the story again.

"So Juanito says, 'I would like to marry you, my love, and have gorgeous puppies with you and live in a castle.' Well, all this time the white poodle has her snout in the air. She looks at Juanito and says, 'Do you have any idea who you're talking to? I am a refined breed of considerable class and you are nothing but a short, insignificant mutt.' Juanito is stunned for a moment, but he rallies for the final shot. He's a proud dog, you see, and he's afraid of his pain. 'Pardon me, your highness,' Juanito the mangy dog says. 'Here in America, I may be a short, insignificant mutt, but in Cuba I was a German shepherd.'"

Máximo turned so the men would not see his tears. The afternoon traffic crawled westward. One horn blasted, then another. He remembered holding his daughters days after their birth, thinking how fragile and vulnerable lay his bond to the future. For weeks he carried them on pillows, like jeweled china. Then, the blank spaces in his life lay before him. Now he stood with the gulf at his back, their ribbony youth aflutter in the past. And what had he salvaged from the years? Already, he was forgetting Rosa's face, the precise shade of her eyes.

Carlos cleared his throat and moved his hand as if to touch him, then held back. He cleared his throat again.

"He was a good dog," Carlos said, pursing his lips.

Antonio began to laugh, then fell silent with the rest. Máximo started shuffling, then stopped. The shadow of the banyan tree worked a kaleidoscope over the dominoes. When the wind eased, Máximo tilted his head to listen. He heard something stir behind him, someone leaning heavily on the fence. He could almost feel their breath. His heart quickened.

"Tell them to go away," Máximo said. "Tell them, no pictures."

Africa Unchained

Tony D'Souza

At 9:00 AM, the doorbell rang. I couldn't see who it was because of the high wall surrounding the house, but after a moment's debate whether I shouldn't just ignore it, I picked up the crowbar we'd been keeping handy and started across the courtyard to the security door. I'd talked with the girls about getting a gun on the black market, but we hadn't gone that far yet. "Jack's a man. He'll protect us," Samantha had winked and said, and I'd shaken my head and told them, "Then consider yourselves dead already." Because while I didn't like to think of myself as a coward, my first impulse on hearing gunfire was to hit the floor and crawl under something. At the door, I raised the crowbar like a baseball bat. I'd never swung a weapon at anyone, didn't know if I could now, but I held it like that anyway. "C'est qui?" I shouted, trying to sound larger and more menacing than I really was.

"Adama, reste tranquille," a woman's voice called to me. "C'est Méité Fanta, ta voisine."

I quickly turned the lock and pushed open the door onto Ama Méité, a weathered old woman with a steel tub on her head, the heads of the fish in it peeking down at us like children eavesdropping on adults. She also had a stick poking out of the corner of her mouth, an extra-large toothpick. Ama Méité was grandmother to the rabble of naked children who played dust-raising ragball on our street in Séguéla, hollering all day like they owned the place, which they did, and who had brought us water, bucket by paid-for bucket, from their well during the last coup when the water and electricity had been cut in the city. Méité's face did not change when she saw the crowbar in my hand. She went on chewing her stick, the local version of a toothbrush, as though it were a carrot, or a tasty piece of licorice.

But I knew from experience that it wasn't tasty at all, that it was infused with a bitter oil as succulent as varnish. People were like that here.

We quickly went through the morning salutations in Worodougou, a cultural requirement you couldn't ignore in the biggest of rushes—even if, say, you felt like the world was ending.

"Manisogoma," I said, lowering my eyes in respect. Good morning, respected mother.

"Say va! Ah see la," Ama Méité said like shouting, which was how it was done. Thank you, respected sir. Did the night pass well?

"Em'ba, Ama," I said. Thank you, respected mother, yes.

"Allah bis sonya!" God bless your morning.

"Amina, ma." Amen, mother.

"Allah kenna ahdi." God grant you beautiful health.

"Amina, ma," I said, touching my hand to my forehead as if bowing in thanks and deference to her benedictions.

"Allah ee balo," she said. God grant you a wonderful youth.

"Amina, ma."

"Allah bato luma." God nourish your home and family.

"Amina, ma."

"Allah bo numa." God bless all that you do.

"Amina, ma," I said louder than before, indicating in their way that I'd received all the benedictions I could bear. "Iniché, iniché. Allah ee braghee." Amen, mother. Thank you, thank you. God bless you in thanks for your benedictions over me.

"Amina, va!" Amen, sir.

"Allah den balo, ma." God bless and protect your children, mother.

"Amina, va!"

"Allah kenna ahdi." God grant you beautiful health.

"Amina, va!"

"Allah sosay djanna." God grant you long life.

"Amina, va!"

"Allah bis sonya." God bless your morning.

"Amina, va! Iniché. Adama Diomandé." Amen and thank you, respected Adama Diomandé.

Then we were done with that and Ama Méité said to me, "Bon," flatly in French because we could now get on with our lives. I could already feel the sweat starting to stand out on my forehead, and the fish in the tub on Méité's head seemed to me to be wilting in the sun now, hanging over the rim like the melting watches in the Dalí painting. She rolled her eyes from the weight of the load and planted her hands on her hips, which were wrapped in a wildly colored bolt of cloth depicting cellular phones. The cloth was a *pagne* celebrating the arrival of Nokia to our stretch of West Africa two weeks ago, and many women in Séguéla were wearing them, were tying their infants snugly onto their backs with them. Coups and guinea worm and female circumcision and HIV and mass graves in Abidjan full of the Muslim north's political youth and the women had turned traditional dances all night around bonfires to celebrate the arrival of the cell phone. This was what West Africa was about: priorities.

"So you already know about the coup," Ama Méité chewed on her bitter stick and said.

"Know about the coup?" I said. "All I know is that I got up this morning and turned on the radio and there wasn't any radio."

"Oui," she said, "so you know about the coup. But what are you going to do with that stick? When the bandits come, they will have guns. Therefore, you should buy a gun. A rich man like you, Adama, with so many wives—"

"They're not my wives!" I started, like a thousand times before. "They're my colleagues. I work with them. Nothing else."

"If they're not your wives, oh, then why won't you marry my daughter Nochia, oh?" she sang in French to embarrass me. "She knows how to cook and likes to work in the fields. If you know how to do anything, she'll give you many healthy children, maybe even twins. And even if you don't know how to do those things, she will teach you. Like that you will be rich in America and make your mother proud. Then you will bring us health and happiness and, of course, many gifts, oh, when you come and visit. Anyway," she said, spitting wads of mulled wood on the ground between us like hay, "you should buy a gun. My son knows a man who can sell you a strong gun washed with good magic."

"We are a humanitarian organization, Ama," I said lamely. "We don't believe in guns."

And she said, "In all the films from America, all is guns. So don't tell me! What I've come to say is this: Don't open the door today, Adama

Diomandé. There are many looters and bandits. They will come and rob you. Everybody knows whites live in this house. And who knows what riches you have in there, anyway? So do not open the door. Now I have to go to market and sell these fish. They don't care if there's a coup or not. All they care is that they want to stink soon."

"Thank you, Ama," I said as she turned to walk back to her compound, where the children were kicking a soccer ball that was really half of a coconut shell, were playing hopscotch in the dirt and clapping and singing like it was the best day ever, like always. She waved her hand back at me and said, "You whites are bizarre, oh! Going to chase away bandits with a stick, Allah!"

I could not remember if this was the third coup or the fourth in the two months since I'd arrived up north, and anyway, talk of coups was a very complex thing because you had bloody coups and bloodless coups and attempted coups and aborted coups and averted coups and rumored coups and the coups that happen that nobody knows about except you go to the post office one day to mail a letter to your retired mother in Florida to say everything's getting all blown out of proportion in the Western media and there's a new general—president smiling at you from the stamp like somebody who's gotten away with something big, and also there were the couvre-feux, which is pronounced somewhat like "coup" but means you can't go out at night or you'll be shot, which should not be confused with coups de grâce, which is how chickens were killed for dinner. All of this is to say that every three weeks the country was erupting into general mayhem from the capital to Korhogo, producing very little change except for a mounting body count and the ulcers growing in my stomach. Oh yes, there was also the matter of a few towns in the far north like Kong and Tengréla that had declared themselves independent states and were being deprived of all services by Abidjan in an apparent attempt to siege them into submission.

There was also the small matter of the new guns that the traditional hunters and witch doctors were showing off in the villages—shiny AKs that they said came from Mecca—and other small matters such as the Christian military kicking in people's doors like storm troopers and beating old women, and the list could go on for a very long time, but after I locked the door behind Ama Méité, I went inside to call the Potable Water International office in Abidjan—my organization—for an update and found that the line had been cut, which wasn't reassuring. Then I sat on the couch and fiddled with the shortwave's antenna.

Just as I was able, with many strange maneuvers of my arms like a semaphore, to draw in the BBC, where the female announcer was calmly saying in her lovely British voice, "…rebel forces in the Ivory Coast…," all the power was cut and I was suddenly very alone in a dark and quiet house in what the U.S. embassy security officer had referred to just weeks before as "the most unstable city in the country." I switched the short-wave over to its batteries. Of course nothing happened. I turned the radio over. The cover to the battery compartment was missing, and so were the batteries. One of the girls knew where they were no doubt, as one of them was out in the bush right now, humming softly as she dug a new latrine, working to the music playing from her battery-powered Walkman.

To make a long story shorter, I had to go out. For one, I was hungry; and for two, I wanted to know what was going on. I got on the bicycle we kept at the house and pedaled out into the city, chased by the vast throng of my neighbors' kids hurrying barefooted and bare-bodied over the piled trash and foamy sewage rivulets of our street, shouting after me, "Everybody! Everybody! Regardez! Regardez! It's the whiteman! Toubabou! Toubabou! Le blanc! Coutoubou! Crazy!"

The best thing about the coups was the opportunity the lawlessness afforded an otherwise subdued people to have some real fun. I turned onto one of the three paved roads in town and started down to the city center, scattering sheep and goats and chickens and beat-up and mangy dogs and children and women carrying huge loads of firewood on their heads as I went. A long chorus of "Regardez le blanc! Coutoubou! Crazy!"—shouted by even the adults for a change—kept me company, and then I came onto a large gathering of young men watching a house burn down. They seemed very excited and happy to see me, so much so that they decided to block my way, their chests glistening with the sweat brought out by the heat of the fire. A leader stepped out from the crowd, set apart from the others, typically, by his massive size, and also by the rainbow-colored clown wig he wore like some kind of insignia of rank—who knows where he got it. I wondered then what this minor general would say to me.

"Whiteman!" he decided to say.

"Oui, je suis blanc. Ya rien je peux faire. Papa blanc, mama blanche. Donc, je suis blanc."

"C'est ça! C'est ça! C'est toujours comme ça! You are white and I am black. There is nothing we can do," he said with enthusiasm, and we shook hands to seal the agreement.

"The fire is pretty, is it not?" he asked me, and I had to agree because after all it was: a two-story pillar of flame rising up from the gutted shell of a one-story house. It lifted its roaring face into the cloudless and suddenly beautiful sky.

"Whose house was that?" I asked him as we appraised this work.

"A swine-fucking policeman's," the young man told me.

"And who lit it?"

"We did," he said, and thumped his chest.

"Yes, it's very beautiful," I said.

The young man turned to me. He glowered under the wig, a completely different person now: the person who had lit the fire. He said, "You are French."

"No, I'm American," I assured him, glad for a change to actually be one.

"Not French?"

"No."

"Certain?" he said, and cocked his head.

"Yes. Very certain."

"Well...," he said, and looked me up and down as if unsure about what to do. "Well, that's really great," he said, and smiled broadly. As easily as that, we were friends again. In English, he said, "Are you fine?"

"Yes, I'm fine."

"Eh? You say what?" he said, tapping his ear and making a hard-of-hearing face. "Speak more slowly."

I said very slowly, "I...said...I...am...fine."

"Yes, okay. Mama fine? Daddy fine?"

"Yes...ev-ry-bo-dy...is...fine."

"Yes, okay. Sister fine, brother fine?"

"Yes…every-body. Every-body…is…fine."

"I speaking English."

"You…speaking…good…English."

Then he puffed up his thick chest and looked around the mob to make sure they had seen and heard his linguistic display, and why not? None of them could do it. Then he was back in French again. "You know Michael Jordan?"

"Yes," I said.

"You know Jean-Claude Van Damme?"

"Yes. Him, too."

"Me, I want to go to America," he pronounced. "You will take me when you go?"

"Yes."

Then he said, "Your bicycle is very pretty. Here in Africa, we don't have bicycles such as this. I admire your bicycle very much. Give me your bicycle. A gift."

"Unfortunately," I said at the prospect of having to travel at the same speed as everyone else on a day like this, "I have to go and see my friend. The older brother of my great, great friend, in fact. I have to pay him many respects. Also, his mother, who is very old. Also, their quarter's imam. The house is very far away, so I need the bicycle. Please forgive me for being so rude. Tomorrow, I will see you and I will definitely give you the bicycle."

"Tomorrow, hey? So, whiteman, you know our ways, is it? Well," the young man the size of a bull and wearing a clown wig and surrounded by a crowd of other young men standing before a house they had destroyed said to me with a smile, "no problem then. Tomorrow we'll meet and you will give me the bicycle. A gift."

"Tomorrow," I assured him. "Don't worry. I won't forget!" I pushed past him, and the crowd of them parted and let me go.

"Hey, whiteman!"

"Yeah?"

"Have a good time!"

At first, I pedaled away at a regular speed because we were friends and everything was normal, wasn't it? Then, away from them, I pedaled as fast as I could. Down by the big intersection where the meat vendors in their shacks lined the roadside among their hanging sheep carcasses and pools of blood, a troop carrier full of grim soldiers holding rifles upright between their knees came barreling along, and I tumbled out of the way and into a gang of goats. Not bothering to brush myself off, I kicked the goats away, hopped back on the bike, and rocketed down the opposite alley-way. When the soldiers met that mob, I guessed it would probably turn out bad. I thought it best to leave them all to it.

First I went to the bank, the reason I had come in to Séguéla from my village in the bush. The heavy metal doors were shuttered and the long iron bar with the padlock as big as my chest was drawn down across them as though the bank would never open again. It wasn't really a very big building. Now it looked like the most secure shoe box in the world.

A very old man in rags was lying on the steps with his eyes open. He looked like a scrap of trash, like someone had tossed him there. First I thought he was dead, but then he turned his head, hacked, and spit—something I understood he'd been doing for a while because of the running gob of spit dripping down the steps beside him like raw egg whites.

When he noticed me looking, his bearded face brightened as though something funny had just happened. He said loudly in excitement, "Hey! A whiteman!"

"Allah noya kay," I said to him. God soothe your illness. And he said back to me, "Amina, Toubabou-ché." Thank you, whiteman. I knew from the filthy rags he wore that he was wildly insane. Though the insane were mostly left to fend for themselves in this part of the world, they were also treated with courtesy. If you ever bothered to ask them a question, some-times you'd even get a useful answer. "Papa," I said, "what's going on with the bank?"

"The bank? This bank? This bank behind me? Ha ha! It's closed!"

"When is it going to open again?"

"Open again? Ha! Don't ask me crazy questions," he said, and laughed. "You whites. You walk on the moon before you walk on the ground."

"Hasn't anyone come by and said anything about the bank opening?"

"Everyone came by and asked about the bank opening. Look at the bank, whiteman. Ha ha! It's closed!"

"I need money," I said, mostly to myself, and the old man said, "Money! You need money! Ha ha! Why don't you go find money on the moon! Don't you know what time it is? It is time for the bank to be open and the bank is closed. So you tell me what time it is now! Les blancs! Don't you make the time, too? Ah, les blancs! Bank and time! Money and the moon! Oh, whiteman! Hahahahaha…"

Next, I decided to go see an acquaintance, Diomandé Kané, at his compound. He had recently gone from being my preferred Séguéla ciga- rette vendor to a Muslim insurgent. I'd had beers with him at the Club des Amis Christian bar on my odd weekends in the city, but in the past week I'd heard he'd bought a boubou and started praying. So it was serious with him, and I knew he'd have news. His narrow compound was set in the vast camp of impoverished Dioula, south of the main market square, beyond the towering and yellow-painted Grand Mosque of Séguéla, its minarets capped in brown onion domes, its latticed windows intricate and mysterious and dominating everything.

As I rode toward the market—a sprawling shantytown of corrugated tin shacks in whose passageways one instantly became lost like in a North African souk—a mixed mass of women and children came spilling out from it like a school of baitfish chased by sharks. They were darting and chang- ing course together suddenly just like fish, coughing and shouting, "Lacrymogène!" which meant *tear gas,* and nobody stopped to call me *white- man,* so I knew they weren't exaggerating. The crowd swept me down the hill past the mosque to Timité Quarter, the poorest section of town, until I pulled myself out of it at a compound I knew there, and where I'd taken refuge before, when I'd newly arrived in Séguéla, just as I'd been waiting for a logging truck to take me into the bush to my village posting for the very first time.

Back then, a throng of young men had come running down the road, stopping only to pick up and hurl stones at another crowd of young men who were chasing them, who were stopping in turn to snatch up the bounc- ing stones and throw them back again. I'd been carried away by the crowd of onlookers who'd gathered themselves up to run away from that, carried down to hardscrabble Timité as though in a wave. In my fright, I'd found shelter in the first compound after the omelet kiosk with the big mango tree rising up beside it like a giant in a coat of green feathers by banging on the gate as hard as I could and yelling, "M'aidez! M'aidez!" and passed an afternoon in silence, stared at by four assembled generations of a Fulani family freshly arrived from Mali to try their luck in relatively prosperous Ivory Coast as many from the neighboring countries did. They'd never seen a whiteman up close before, and the smallest children pulled my toes to see if I was real, while the women simply stared. Now I was at their gate and banging on it again.

"C'est qui?" someone shouted, trying to sound larger and more menacing than he really was.

"Sidibé, reste tranquille. C'est Adama, ton blanc."

The gate was pulled back to reveal the old patriarch of the family in his flowing blue boubou and wide-brimmed hat with the circular Peul designs tooled into the leather. His face was thin and bright beneath the hat, his beard stringy and white.

He said in stumbling French as he tugged me in quickly by my shirt, "Oh, Adama. How nice of you to come and pay us a visit again! Please come and sit with us like before. Tell us all of your news."

I passed some hours in Sidibé's dirt-floor parlor listening to the ticking of his wall clock—a round-faced Seiko, his only real possession—after we'd run out of things to say. One of his grandsons made periodic forays into the city to assess the situation, and came back again and again so breathless and worried that the old man folded his hands on his lap and said, "Oh, Adama, it has been so long, isn't it? Let us drink another tea."

The one time I left the parlor to cross the courtyard to squat over the flyblown latrine hole seething with fat maggots, I saw the smoke from the fires rising up into the sky in columns from the different quarters of the city like trailings, vultures circling lazily around them, high up, as if there were all the time in the world for what they had to do. Then there was gunfire, automatic and small-arms, staccato, right here, far away, patterned layers of jarring sound, just like the Fourth of July in Chicago, where I was from. It was the smoke from the fires that did it, the way it curled into the sky like the black smoke of sacrifices of people invoking the ancestors for help.

It filled me with a stunned dumbness, a weight, a dread that spread through my body like exhaustion. Was this really happening? I mean to say, I did not know how to feel. Fear, exhilaration, nerves, adrenaline: these were all the same species of creature, and ever since I'd arrived in Ivory Coast, life had been this way. Did they really want this fight, this North-South, Muslim-Christian, colonization's hangover civil war, or did they not? Did I? I don't believe anyone could truthfully tell then. Yes, of course people would die, but didn't everyone think, Not I! Not I! And didn't everything taste sweeter since the violence? That cold, cold Coca-Cola, the last Marlboro of the day, sex with your girl, the joy of breathing because the day had ended and you were still alive! Everything had become heightened, everything myopic and refined. How much fun to be had by all!

And of course I couldn't help but pick a side. Forty years of abuse and neglect by the Christians since they'd inherited power from the French at independence, forty years of watching roads and electricity and schools and development traverse the south, while here in the Muslim north it was all hunger and harmattan, military harassment, the men gone to labor in the cocoa fields, coming home once a year with AIDS, no money, no medicine, no schoolbooks for the kids, and even the northerners' nationality stripped away because of the new interpretation of the Constitution. There were good guys and bad guys and I could see them, and over all of this stood the basilica in Yamoussoukro, the largest church in the world— air-conditioned seats, miles of stained glass and Italian marble for a congregation of three hundred on good days, none on most—to spell out the way things were as clearly as its gold dome and crucifix standing up against the horizon. How many hospitals could have been built with that money? How many deep-bore water pumps? And Boigny, the first president, had himself placed at the feet of Jesus Christ in the glass, unleashing this mess! Where was the mosque to stand beside that church? What about this half of the country?

Lastly, there was reality. I was a whiteman. No matter how well I spoke Worodougou or gnushi French or Dioula, or that I obeyed my village's customs and let them take my old name, Jack Diaz, from me and baptize me with a new name, Diomandé Adama; no matter that I lived with them as they did and was ready some days to take up arms with my friends, to stand with them as though their families and grievances were my own, this was a place I did not belong and, more than that, a place where they would not let me belong.

We were the last foreign-aid group still in the field. The last round of rioting had seen even the missionaries driven out. It was only three weeks ago that that Dutch woman, Laurie's friend, was sitting in the living room where we'd gathered for safety, gabbing, fingering the wooden cross on a rope around her neck, laughing nervously, saying, "Well, now that those funny Japanese people have packed up and left, you know, it looks like it's you water people and us Bible people."

Then it was only us because the churches were burned all over the north and they went in a mob to the Dutch woman's house in Séguéla where she lived behind where they welded bicycle frames beyond the military post, thought she wasn't home, and proceeded to loot everything. It was only while they were dousing the walls with kerosene that someone—maybe my friend with his rainbow wig—noticed the bed that they had forgotten to take in the back room, and lifted up the mattress, and there she was like a dusty treasure found in the back of a closet, an old dress your grandmother wore seventy years ago to the prom: a middle-aged Dutch woman who had come to Africa to bring Jesus to Muslims, her skirt damp from her own urine, crying with her hands hiding her face like she wanted to be a child again, and did she curse them as black devils finally is what I want to know.

But the crying and her age and the piss struck a chord in someone, because they helped her up, helped her to gather herself together—to brush her hair from her eyes, to wipe the tears away—helped her find her keys, helped her pick them up when she dropped them from her trembling hands as certainly she did, helped her stagger out of that house on their shoulders, shook her out of her dream of childhood in Amsterdam—the clouds reflected in the canals, the yellow hay fields of the countryside of Gouda—ducked her head down with their hands so she wouldn't bang it as she got into her car, let her drive away. Then they torched her house anyway.

On the road south, she was joined by a convoy of whites with their Bibles piled around them in their Land Rovers like sandbags, their churches and missions burned, for some of them their life's work burned, and nothing left to do now but sift the remains from the ashes of their memories and turn the other cheek. In Sidibé's house then we could hear the singing of the muezzin, a long and mournful wail, like an air-raid siren in the shock and length of it. Sidibé winked at me and tapped the side of his long nose.

"If God says that it is all right to go out now, Adama," he said, smiling, "then certainly it must be all right."

And I did go out into the city again, and I did see many other things to make me feel very quiet inside myself in the memory of them, but here now in the telling of this story, I've lost my direction. What I'd like to tell about now is a monkey.

Across from our house in Séguéla, where I would go on to spend the night under the bed with gunfire and the shouts of angry men around me in the city like the madness in a crazy man's head, there lived a monkey on a chain. This was in the courtyard of our neighbor Méité Fanta, the same woman from the morning, the grandmother of many, many happy children, a kind enough woman who sold us water once on a hot day when we didn't have any. Anyway, they kept a young monkey on a chain attached to a pole in the courtyard and the monkey was really a baboon, but if you were to ask anyone what sort of animal it was, they would simply say, "A monkey."

This monkey's name was Rita—I asked—and I grew fond of her. The children spent many long hours teasing her with leafy tree branches, with bananas she could not reach, and there was also a famous game in that neighborhood called Touch the Monkey, in which each child brave enough would venture forth when they felt Rita was not looking, cross into her sandy area—the radius of her chain, the chain being as long as two or three paces, enough space for a monkey in a poor compound in West Africa, if that can be accepted as a unit of measure—touch her like slapping, scream, and flee, and often I was pleased to see her leap onto a child's back and sink her short-yet-sharp incisors into a neck. I harbored untold sympathy for that tormented creature who somehow managed to keep her spirits up. I got it into my head that she could recognize me, that she could pick me out of the crowd as the one person who did not want to amuse myself at her expense, and she would break into a funny little half-step dance on seeing me, banging her fists against the sand and then leaping and turning as she howled. Of course, this was because I brought her bananas and papayas and other things monkeys like to eat every time I came to town.

"Oh, thank you, Adama Diomandé," Méité Fanta came to me and said one day with the sun beating down on our necks, the gritty harmattan wind caking our pores with dust, chapping our lips and the insides of our nostrils. "Thank you for feeding the monkey. When she is grown and fat we will call you and you must come and share the meat of her with us."

There is little sentiment to be wasted in a place where hunger is a real thing, where meat is scarce and a small and personable baboon like Rita would help the children grow. Still, I chased the children away from her when I could, bribed them with cheap candies to leave her alone, trying to make her short life more endurable, chained as she was around the hips to an immovable pole in a dusty courtyard where chickens scratched for ticks. I honestly believe that she came to recognize me, that she would say to herself on seeing me, That is the good one among them.

Then one day when I was caught in Séguéla while Séguéla burned around me, I opened my door in the late afternoon to a small gang of bandits. They showed me knives, and then they hid them in their sleeves again. I could not get past them or close the door on them and still I did not let them in. In my hand was a crowbar, which in the end I was not able to swing. "You will give us money," the leader of the trio said, and I tried to see his face behind his mirrored sunglasses but could only see my own reflection. It startled me, how white I seemed, and then, how odd. What was this white person doing in this place? I opened my wallet and gave them the money that I had. It was a few U.S. dollars in their currency, perhaps ten, not much by any standards, not much by theirs.

"This isn't enough," he said, holding the money on the flat of his hand as if offering it back, giving me a second chance. "This is nothing. You must give us more money."

"Please," I said. "The bank is closed today. This is all I have. Please." Some long moments passed. I do not know how many. In the silence I heard myself say to them from a faraway place, "Please. Please."

They went away. I cannot remember what direction they took as they left, or what they looked like as they walked away. I could not now pick them out of a crowd. I cannot know how much time passed as I hung there in my doorway, but then, as if waking from a deep, deep sleep, I was in the world again. And what a raucous world it was! In the distance, gunfire; and here, the explosion of goats and dogs and chickens and sheep and dust and feathers and the many and bare-bodied grandchildren of my neighbor screaming as they were chased through the street by Rita—a baboon mistaken for a monkey—her chain broken and free, pursuing wildly now these children who for so long had tortured her. For an instant, I felt a wave of pleasure course through me like love at the sight of the mayhem of her freedom, and for that one instant I can say this: I was happy, I was happy to my core.

Then the monkey spotted me, and my happiness turned to white-knuckled fear as barreling toward my doorway was an openmouthed creature with fangs, shrieking, and I don't know what she planned on doing—on seeking asylum behind my legs, or on sinking her teeth into them—for suddenly I was face-to-face with what I wanted to know but couldn't: Africa, Africa unchained, and there was no other recourse at that moment but to guard hearth and home, and slam shut the door.

Toba Tek Singh

Saadat Hasan Manto

Translated from the Urdu by Richard M. Murphy

Two or three years after Partition, the governments of Pakistan and India decided to exchange lunatics in the same way that they had exchanged civilian prisoners. In other words, Muslim lunatics in Indian madhouses would be sent to Pakistan, while Hindu and Sikh lunatics in Pakistani madhouses would be handed over to India.

I can't say whether this decision made sense or not. In any event, a date for the lunatic exchange was fixed after high level conferences on both sides of the border. All the details were carefully worked out. On the Indian side, Muslim lunatics with relatives in India would be allowed to stay. The remainder would be sent to the frontier. Here in Pakistan nearly all the Hindus and Sikhs were gone, so the question of retaining non-Muslim lunatics did not arise. All the Hindu and Sikh lunatics would be sent to the frontier in police custody.

I don't know what happened over there. When news of the lunatic exchange reached the madhouse here in Lahore, however, it became an absorbing topic of discussion among the inmates. There was one Muslim lunatic who read the landowner's newspaper, *Zamindar*, every day for twelve years. One of his friends asked him, "Maulvi Sahib! What is Pakistan?" After careful thought he replied, "It's a place in India where they make razors."

Hearing this, his friend was content.

One Sikh lunatic asked another Sikh, "Sardar ji, why are they sending us to India? We don't even speak the language."

"I understand the Indian language," the other replied, smiling. "Indians are devilish people who strut around haughtily," he added.

While bathing, a Muslim lunatic shouted "Long live Pakistan!" with such vigor that he slipped on the floor and knocked himself out.

There were also some lunatics who weren't really crazy. Most of these inmates were murderers whose families had bribed the madhouse officials to have them committed in order to save them from the hangman's noose. These inmates understood something of why India had been divided, and they had heard of Pakistan. But they weren't all that well informed. The newspapers didn't tell them a great deal, and the illiterate guards who looked after them weren't much help either. All they knew was that there was a man named Mohammed Ali Jinnah, whom people called the Qaid-e-Azem. He had made a separate country for the Muslims, called Pakistan. They had no idea where it was, or what its boundaries might be. This is why all the lunatics who hadn't entirely lost their senses were perplexed as to whether they were in Pakistan or India. If they were in India, then where was Pakistan? If they were in Pakistan, then how was it that the place where they lived had until recently been known as India?

One lunatic got so involved in this India/Pakistan question that he became even crazier. One day he climbed a tree and sat on one of its branches for two hours, lecturing without pause on the complex issues of Partition. When the guards told him to come down, he climbed higher. When they tried to frighten him with threats, he replied, "I will live neither in India nor in Pakistan. I'll live in this tree right here!" With much difficulty, they eventually coaxed him down. When he reached the ground he wept and embraced his Hindu and Sikh friends, distraught at the idea that they would leave him and go to India.

One man held an MS degree and had been a radio engineer. He kept apart from the other inmates, and spent all his time walking silently up and down a particular footpath in the garden. After hearing about the exchange, however, he turned in his clothes and ran naked all over the grounds.

There was one fat Muslim lunatic from Chiniot who had been an enthusiastic Muslim League activist. He used to wash fifteen or sixteen times a day, but abandoned the habit overnight. His name was Mohammed Ali. One day he announced that he was the Qaid-e-Azem, Mohammed Ali Jinnah. Hearing this, a Sikh lunatic declared himself to be Master Tara Singh. Blood would have flowed, except that both were reclassified as dangerous lunatics and confined to separate quarters.

There was also a young Hindu lawyer from Lahore who had gone mad over an unhappy love affair. He was distressed to hear that Amritsar was now in India, because his beloved was a Hindu girl from that city. Although she had rejected him, he had not forgotten her after losing his mind. For this reason he cursed the Muslim leaders who had split India into two parts, so that his beloved remained Indian while he became Pakistani.

When news of the exchange reached the madhouse, several lunatics tried to comfort the lawyer by telling him that he would be sent to India, where his beloved lived. But he didn't want to leave Lahore, fearing that his practice would not thrive in Amritsar.

In the European Ward there were two Anglo-Indian lunatics. They were very worried to hear that the English had left after granting independence to India. In hushed tones, they spent hours discussing how this would affect their situation in the madhouse. Would the European Ward remain, or would it disappear? Would they be served English breakfasts? What, would they be forced to eat poisonous bloody Indian chapatis instead of bread?

One Sikh had been an inmate for fifteen years. He spoke a strange language of his own, constantly repeating this nonsensical phrase: "Upri gur gur di annex di be-dhiyan di mung di daal of di lalteen." *The lack of contemplation and lentils of the annex of the above raw sugar of the lantern.* He never slept. According to the guards, he hadn't slept a wink in fifteen years. Occasionally, however, he would rest by propping himself against a wall.

His feet and ankles had become swollen from standing all the time, but in spite of these physical problems he refused to lie down and rest. He would listen with great concentration whenever there was discussion of India, Pakistan, and the forthcoming lunatic exchange. Asked for his opinion, he would reply with great seriousness, "Upri gur gur di annex di be-dhiyana di mung di daal of di Pakistan gornament."

Later he replaced "of di Pakistan gornament" with "of di Toba Tek Singh gornament." He also started asking the other inmates where Toba Tek Singh was, and to which country it belonged. But nobody knew whether it was in Pakistan or India. When they argued the question they only became more confused. After all, Sialkot had once been in India, but was apparently now in Pakistan. Who knew whether Lahore, which was now in Pakistan, might not go over to India tomorrow? Or whether all of India might become Pakistan? And was there any guarantee that both Pakistan and India would not one day vanish altogether?

This Sikh lunatic's hair was unkempt and thin. Because he washed so rarely, his hair and beard had matted together, giving him a frightening appearance. But he was a harmless fellow. In fifteen years, he had never fought with anyone.

The attendants knew only that he owned land in Toba Tek Singh district. Having been a prosperous landlord, he suddenly lost his mind. So his relatives bound him with heavy chains and sent him off to the madhouse.

His family used to visit him once a month. After making sure that he was in good health, they would go away again. These family visits continued for many years, but they stopped when the India/Pakistan troubles began.

This lunatic's name was Bashan Singh, but everyone called him Toba Tek Singh. Although he had very little sense of time, he seemed to know when his relatives were coming to visit. He would tell the officer in charge that his visit was impending. On the day itself he would wash his body thoroughly and comb and oil his hair. Then he would put on his best clothes and go to meet his relatives.

If they asked him any question he would either remain silent or say, "Upri gur gur di annex di be-dhiyana di mung di daal of di lalteen."

Bashan Singh had a fifteen-year-old daughter who grew by a finger's height every month. He didn't recognize her when she came to visit him. As a small child, she used to cry whenever she saw her father. She continued to cry now that she was older.

When the Partition problems began, Bashan Singh started asking the other lunatics about Toba Tek Singh. Since he never got a satisfactory answer, his concern deepened day by day.

Then his relatives stopped visiting him. Formerly he could predict their arrival, but now it was as though the voice inside him had been silenced. He very much wanted to see those people, who spoke to him sympathetically and brought gifts of flowers, sweets, and clothing. Surely they could tell him whether Toba Tek Singh was in Pakistan or India. After all, he was under the impression that they came from Toba Tek Singh, where his land was.

There was another lunatic in that madhouse who thought he was God. One day, Bashan Singh asked him whether Toba Tek Singh was in Pakistan or India. Guffawing, he replied, "Neither, because I haven't yet decided where to put it!"

Bashan Singh begged this "God" to resolve the status of Toba Tek Singh and thus end his perplexity. But "God" was far too busy to deal with this matter because of all the other orders that he had to give. One day Bashan Singh lost his temper and shouted, "Upri gur gur di annex di be-dhiyana di mung di daal of wahay Guru ji wa Khalsa and wahay Guru ji ki fatah. Jo bolay so nahal sat akal!"

By this he might have meant: You are the god of the Muslims. If you were a Sikh god then you would certainly help me.

A few days before the day of the exchange, one of Bashan Singh's Muslim friends came to visit from Toba Tek Singh. This man had never visited the madhouse before. Seeing him, Bashan Singh turned abruptly and started walking away. But the guard stopped him.

"He's come to visit you. It's your friend Fazluddin," the guard said.

Glancing at Fazluddin, Bashan Singh muttered a bit. Fazluddin advanced and took him by the elbow. "I've been planning to visit you for ages, but I haven't had the time until now," he said. "All your relatives have gone safely to India. I helped them as much as I could. Your daughter, Rup Kur…"

Bashan Singh seemed to remember something. "Daughter Rup Kur," he said.

Fazluddin hesitated, and then replied, "Yes, she's…she's also fine. She left with them."

Bashan Singh said nothing. Fazluddin continued, "They asked me to make sure you were all right. Now I hear that you're going to India. Give my salaams to brother Balbir Singh and brother Wadhada Singh. And to sister Imrat Kur also….Tell brother Balbir Singh that I'm doing fine. One of the two brown cows that he left has calved. The other one calved also, but it died after six days. And…and say that if there's anything else I can do for them, I'm always ready. And I've brought you some sweets."

Bashan Singh handed the package over to the guard. "Where is Toba Tek Singh?" he asked.

Fazluddin was taken aback. "Toba Tek Singh? Where is it? It's where it's always been," he replied.

"In Pakistan or in India?" Bashan Singh persisted.

Fazluddin became flustered. "It's in India. No no, Pakistan."

Bashan Singh walked away, muttering, "Upar di gur gur di annex di dhiyana di mung di daal of di Pakistan and Hindustan of di dar fatay mun!"

Finally all the preparations for the exchange were complete. The lists of all the lunatics to be transferred were finalized, and the date for the exchange itself was fixed.

The weather was very cold. The Hindu and Sikh lunatics from the Lahore madhouse were loaded into trucks under police supervision. At the Wahga border post, the Pakistani and Indian officials met each other and completed the necessary formalities. Then the exchange began. It continued all through the night.

It was not easy to unload the lunatics and send them across the border. Some of them didn't even want to leave the trucks. Those who did get out were hard to control because they started wandering all over the place. When the guards tried to clothe those lunatics who were naked, they immediately ripped the garments off their bodies. Some cursed, some sang, and others fought. They were crying and talking, but nothing could be understood. The madwomen were creating an uproar of their own. And it was cold enough to make your teeth chatter.

Most of the lunatics were opposed to the exchange. They didn't understand why they should be uprooted and sent to some unknown place. Some, only half-mad, started shouting "Long live Pakistan!" Two or three brawls erupted between Sikh and Muslim lunatics who became enraged when they heard the slogans.

When Bashan Singh's turn came to be entered in the register, he spoke to the official in charge. "Where is Toba Tek Singh?" he asked. "Is it in Pakistan or India?"

The official laughed. "It's in Pakistan," he replied.

Hearing this, Bashan Singh leapt back and ran to where his remaining companions stood waiting. The Pakistani guards caught him and tried to bring him back to the crossing point, but he refused to go.

"Toba Tek Singh is here!" he cried. Then he started raving at top volume, "Upar di gur gur di annex di be-dhiyana mang di daal of di Toba Tek Singh and Pakistan!"

The officials tried to convince him that Toba Tek Singh was now in India. If by some chance it wasn't they would send it there directly, they said. But he wouldn't listen.

Because he was harmless, the guards let him stand right where he was while they got on with their work. He was quiet all night, but just before sunrise he screamed. Officials came running from all sides. After fifteen years on his feet, he was lying facedown on the ground. India was on one side, behind a barbed wire fence. Pakistan was on the other side, behind another fence. Toba Tek Singh lay in the middle, on a piece of land that had no name.

The Professor's Office

Viet Thanh Nguyen

The first time the professor called Mrs. Khanh by the wrong name was at a wedding banquet, a crowded affair of the kind they attended often, usually out of obligation. As the bride and groom approached their table, Mrs. Khanh noticed the professor reading his palms, where he'd jotted down his toast and the names of the newlyweds, whom they had never met. Leaning close to be heard over the chatter of four hundred guests and the din of the band, she found her husband redolent of well-worn paperbacks and threadbare carpet. It was a comforting mustiness, one that she associated with secondhand bookstores.

"Don't worry," she said. "You've done this a thousand times."

"Have I?" The professor rubbed his hands on his pants. "I can't seem to recall." His fair skin was thin as paper and lined with blue veins. From the precise part of his silver hair to the gleam on his brown oxfords, he appeared to be the same man who'd taught so many students he could no longer count them. During the two minutes the newlyweds visited their table, he didn't miss a beat, calling the couple by their correct names and bestowing the good wishes expected of him as the eldest among the ten guests. But while the groom tugged at the collar of his Nehru jacket and the bride plucked at the skirt of her Empire-waist gown, Mrs. Khanh could only think of the night of the diagnosis, when the professor had frightened her by weeping for the first time in their four decades together. Only after the young couple left could she relax, sighing as deeply as she could in the strict confines of her velvet ao dai.

"The girl's mother tells me they're honeymooning for the first week in Paris." She spooned a lobster claw onto the professor's plate. "The second week they'll be on the French Riviera."

"Is that so?" Cracked lobster in tamarind sauce was Professor Khanh's favorite, but tonight he stared with doubt at the claw pointing toward him. "What did the French call Vung Tau?"

"Cap St. Jacques."

"We had a very good time there. Didn't we?"

"That's when you finally started talking to me."

"Who wouldn't be shy," the professor murmured. Forty years ago, when she was nineteen and he was thirty-three, they had honeymooned at a beach-side hotel on the cape. It was on their balcony, under a full, bright moon, listening to the French singing and shouting on their side of the beach, that the professor had suddenly started talking. "Imagine!" he said, voice filled with wonder as he began speaking about how the volume of the Pacific equaled the moon's. When he was finished, he went on to talk about the strange fish of deep sea canyons and then the inexplicability of rogue waves. If after a while she lost track of what he said, it hardly mattered, for by then the sound of his voice had seduced her, as reassuring in its measured tones as the first time she'd heard it, eavesdropping from her family's kitchen as he explained to her father his dissertation on the Kurishio Current's thermodynamics.

Now the professor's memories were gradually stealing away from him, and along with them the long sentences he once favored. When the band swung into "I'd Love You To Want Me," he loosened the fat Windsor knot of his tie and said, "Remember this song?"

"What about it?"

"We listened to it all the time. Before the children were born."

The song hadn't been released yet during her first pregnancy, but nevertheless, Mrs. Khanh said, "That's right."

"Let's dance." The professor leaned closer, draping one arm over the back of her chair. A fingerprint smudged one lens of his glasses. "You always insisted we dance when you heard this song, Yen."

"Oh?" Mrs. Khanh took a slow sip from her glass of water, hiding her surprise at being called someone else's name. "When did we ever dance?"

The professor didn't answer, for the swelling chorus of the song had brought him to his feet. As he stepped toward the parquet dance floor, Mrs. Khanh seized the tail of his gray pinstripe jacket. "Stop it!" she said, pulling hard. "Sit down!"

Giving her a wounded look, the professor obeyed. Mrs. Khanh was aware of the other guests at their table staring at them. She held herself very still, unable to account for any woman named Yen. Perhaps Yen was an old acquaintance (whom the professor never saw fit to mention); perhaps she was the maternal grandmother Mrs. Khanh had never met (and whose name she couldn't now recall); or perhaps Yen was a grade school teacher (with whom he'd once been infatuated). Mrs. Khanh had begun preparing for many things, but she hadn't gotten herself ready for unknown people emerging from the professor's mind.

"The song's almost over," the professor said.

"We'll dance when we get home. I promise."

Despite his condition, or perhaps because of it, the professor still insisted on driving them back. Mrs. Khanh was tense as she watched him handling the car, but he drove in his usual slow and cautious manner. He was quiet until he took a left at Golden West instead of a right, his wrong turn taking them by the community college from where he'd retired last spring. After coming to America, he'd been unable to find work in oceanography and had settled for teaching Vietnamese. For the last twenty years, he'd lectured under fluorescent lighting to bored students. When Mrs. Khanh wondered if one of those students might be Yen, she felt a prick of pain that she mistook at first for heartburn. Only upon second thought did she recognize it as jealousy.

The professor suddenly braked to a stop. Mrs. Khanh braced herself with one hand against the dashboard and waited to be called by that name again, but the professor made no mention of Yen. He swung the car into a U-turn instead, and as they headed toward home, he asked in a tone of great reproach, "Why didn't you tell me we were going in the wrong direction?" Watching all the traffic lights on the street ahead of them turn green as if on cue, Mrs. Khanh realized that his was a question for which she had no good answer.

The next morning, Mrs. Khanh was standing at the stove preparing brunch for their eldest son's visit when the professor came into the kitchen, freshly bathed and shaved. He took a seat at the kitchen counter, unfolded the newspaper, and began reading to her from the headlines.

Only after he'd finished did she put a lid on the pot of bun bo Hue and begin telling him about last night's events. He'd asked her to remind him of those moments when he no longer acted like himself, and she had gotten as far as his lunge for the dance floor when the sag of his shoulders stopped her.

"It's all right," she said, alarmed. "It's not your fault."

"But can you see me on the dance floor at my age?" The professor rolled up the newspaper and rapped it against the counter for emphasis. "And in my condition?"

Taking out a small blue notebook from his shirt pocket, the professor retreated to the patio, where he was writing down his errors when Vinh arrived. Fresh from his graveyard shift at the county hospital, their son wore a nurse's green scrubs, which, shapeless as they were, did little to hide his physique. If only he visited his parents as much as he did the gym, Mrs. Khanh thought. The edge of her hand could have fit into the deep cleft of her son's chest, and her thighs weren't quite as thick as his biceps. Under one arm, he was carrying a bulky package wrapped in brown paper, which he propped against the trellis behind his father.

The professor slipped the notebook into his pocket and pointed his pen at the package. "What's the surprise?" he asked. While Mrs. Khanh brought out bowls of the soup she had worked on all morning, Vinh stripped off the wrapping to reveal a painting in a gilded frame. "It cost me a hundred dollars on Dong Khoi," he said. He had gone to Saigon on vacation last month. "The galleries there can knock off anything, but it was easier to frame it here."

When the professor leaned forward to squint at the painting, the steam from his soup clouded his glasses. "There was a time when that street was called Tu Do," he remarked wistfully. "And before that, Rue Catinat."

"I hoped you'd remember," Vinh said, sitting down next to his mother at the patio table. Mrs. Khanh could tell that the subject of the painting was a woman, but one whose left eye was green and whose right eye was red, which was nowhere near as odd as the way the artist had flattened her arms and torso, leaving her to look less like a real person and more like a child's paper doll, cut out and pasted to a three-dimensional chair. "There's a new study that shows how Picasso's paintings can stimulate people like Ba," Vinh went on.

"Is that so?" The professor wiped the fog off his glasses with his napkin. Behind him was the scene to which Mrs. Khanh was now accustomed: an entrance ramp rising over their backyard and merging onto the freeway that Vinh would take home to Los Angeles, an hour north of their Westminster neighborhood. Her boys used to pass their afternoons spotting the makes and models of the passing cars, as if they were ornithologists distinguishing between juncos and sparrows. But that was a very long time ago, she thought, and Vinh was now a messenger dispatched by the rest of their six children.

"We think you should retire from the library, Ma," he said, scattering a handful of bean sprouts onto his soup. "We can send home enough money every month to cover all the bills. You can have a housekeeper to help you out. And a gardener, too."

Mrs. Khanh had never needed help with the garden, which was entirely of her own design. A horseshoe of green lawn divided a perimeter of persimmon trees from the center of the garden, where pale green cilantro, arrow-leafed basil, and Thai chilies grew abundantly in the beds she'd made for them. She plucked a sprig of mint from her bowl and rubbed it between her fingers until she smelled its tang. When she was certain that she could speak without betraying her irritation, she said, "I like to garden."

"Mexican gardeners come cheap, Ma. Besides, you'll want all the help you can get. You've got to be ready for the worst."

"We've seen much worse than you," the professor snapped. "We're ready for anything."

"And I'm not old enough for retirement," Mrs. Khanh added.

"Be reasonable." Vinh sounded nothing like the boy who, upon reaching his teenage years, had turned into someone his parents no longer knew, sneaking out of the house at night to be with his girlfriend, an American who painted her nails black and dyed her hair purple. The professor remedied the situation by nailing the windows shut, a problem Vinh solved by eloping soon after his graduation from Bolsa Grande High. "I'm in love," Vinh had screamed to his mother over the phone from Las Vegas. "But you wouldn't know anything about that, would you?" Sometimes Mrs. Khanh regretted ever telling him that her father had arranged her marriage.

"You don't need the money from that job," Vinh said. "But Ba needs you at home."

Mrs. Khanh pushed away her bowl of soup, barely touched. She wouldn't take advice from someone whose marriage hadn't lasted more than three years. "It's not about the money, Kevin."

Vinh sighed, for his mother only used his American name when she was upset with him. "Maybe you should help Ba," he said, pointing to the front of his father's polo shirt, marred by a splash of red broth.

"Look at this," the professor said, brushing at the stain with his fingers. "It's only because you've upset me." Vinh sighed once more, but Mrs. Khanh refused to look at him as she dabbed a napkin in her glass of water. She wondered if he remembered their escape from Vung Tau on a rickety fishing trawler, overloaded with his five siblings and sixty strangers, three years after the war's end. After the fourth day at sea, he and the rest of the children, bleached by the sun, were crying for water, even though there was none to offer but the sea's. Nevertheless, she had washed their faces and combed their hair every morning, using salt water and spit. She was teaching them that decorum mattered even now, and that their mother's fear wasn't so strong that it could prevent her from loving them.

"Don't worry," she said. "The stain will come out." As she leaned forward to scrub the professor's shirt, Mrs. Khanh had a clear view of the painting. She knew she was supposed to admire it, but she had never liked Picasso's work. This painting, with the woman's eyes looking forth from one side of her face, did nothing to change her mind. The sight of those eyes made Mrs. Khanh so uneasy that later that day, after Vinh went home, she moved the painting to the professor's library, where she left it facing a wall.

It wasn't long after their son's visit that the professor stopped attending Sunday mass. Mrs. Khanh stayed home as well, and gradually they began seeing less and less of their friends. The only times she left the house were to go shopping or to the Garden Grove Library, where her fellow librarians knew nothing of the professor's illness. She enjoyed her part-time job, ordering and sorting the sizeable collection of Vietnamese books and movies purchased for the residents of nearby Little Saigon, who, if they came to the library with a question, were directed to her perch behind the circulation desk. Answering those questions, Mrs. Khanh always felt the gratification that made her job worthwhile, the pleasure of being needed for only a brief amount of time.

When her shift ended at noon and she gathered her things to go home, she always did so with a sense of dread that shamed her. She made up for her shame by bidding good-bye to the other librarians with extra cheer, and by preparing the house for emergencies with great energy, as if she could forestall the inevitable through hard work. She marked a path from bed to bathroom with fluorescent yellow tape, so the professor wouldn't get lost at night, and, on the wall across from the toilet, she taped a sign at eye level that said FLUSH. She composed a series of lists which, posted strategically around the house, reminded the professor in what order to put on his clothes, what to put in his pockets before he left home, and what times of the day he should eat. But it was the professor who hired a handyman to install iron bars on the windows. "You wouldn't want me sneaking out at night," the professor said with resignation, leaning his forehead against the bars. "And neither would I."

For Mrs. Khanh, the more urgent problem was the professor coming home as a stranger. Whereas her husband was never one to be romantic, this stranger returned from one of the afternoon walks he insisted on taking by himself with a red rose in a plastic tube. He'd never before bought flowers of any sort, preferring to surprise her with more enduring presents, like the books he gave her every now and again, on topics like how to make friends and influence people, or income tax preparation. She never read past the title pages, satisfied at seeing her name penned in his elegant hand beneath those of the authors. But if the professor had spent his life practicing writing, he'd never given a thought to presenting roses, and when he bowed while offering her the flower, he appeared to be suffering from a stomach cramp.

"Who's this for?" she asked.

"Is there anyone else here?" The professor shook the rose for emphasis, and one of its petals, browning at the edges, fell off. "It's for you."

"It's very pretty." She took the rose reluctantly. "Where did you get it?"

"Mr. Esteban. He tried selling me oranges also, but I said we had our own."

"And who am I?" she demanded. "What's my name?"

He squinted at her. "Yen, of course."

"Of course." Biting her lip, she fought the urge to snap the head off the rose. She displayed the flower in a vase on the dining table for the professor's sake, but by the time she brought out dinner an hour later, he had forgotten he bought it. As he nibbled on blackened tiger shrimp, grilled on skewers, and tofu shimmering in black bean sauce, he talked animatedly instead about the postcard they'd received that afternoon from their eldest daughter, working for American Express in Munich. Mrs. Khanh examined the picture of the Marienplatz before turning over the postcard to read aloud the note, which remarked on the curious absence of pigeons.

"Little things stay with you when you travel," observed the professor, sniffing at the third course, a soup of bitter melon. Their children had never acquired the taste for it, but it reminded the professor and Mrs. Khanh of their own childhoods.

"Such as?"

"The price of cigarettes," the professor said. "When I returned to Saigon after finishing my studies, I couldn't buy my daily Gauloise any longer. The imported price was too much."

She leaned the postcard against the vase, where it would serve as a memento of the plans they'd once made for traveling to all of the world's great cities after their retirement. The only form of transport Mrs. Khanh had ruled out was the ocean cruise, for open expanses of water prompted fears of drowning, a phobia so strong that she no longer took baths, and even when showering kept her back to the spray.

"Now why did you buy that?" the professor asked.

"The postcard?"

"No, the rose."

"I didn't buy it." Mrs. Khanh chose her words carefully, not wanting to disturb the professor too much, and yet wanting him to know what he had done. "You did."

"Me?" The professor was astonished. "Are you certain?"

"I am absolutely certain," she said, surprised to hear the tone of satisfaction in her voice.

The professor didn't notice. He only sighed and took out the blue notebook from the pocket of his shirt. "Let's hope that won't happen again," he muttered.

"I don't suppose it will." Mrs. Khanh stood to gather the dishes. She hoped her face didn't show her anger, convinced as she was that the professor had intended the rose for this other woman. She was carrying four plates, the tureen, and both their glasses when, at the kitchen's threshold, the wobbling weight of her load became too much. The sound of silverware clattering on the tiled floor and the smash of porcelain breaking made the professor cry out from the dining room. "What's that?" he shouted.

Mrs. Khanh stared at the remains of the tureen at her feet. Three uneaten green coins of bitter melon, stuffed with pork, lay sodden on the floor among the shards. "It's nothing," she said. "I'll take care of it."

After he'd fallen asleep later that evening, she sat down at the desk in his library, where the painting was still propped facing the wall. The bookshelves lining the library had several hundred volumes in Vietnamese, French, and English. His ambition was to own more books than he could ever possibly read, a desire fueled by having left behind all his books when they had fled Vietnam. Dozens of paperbacks cluttered his desk, and she had to shove them aside to find the notebooks where he'd been tracking his mistakes over the past months. He had poured salt into his coffee and sprinkled sugar into his soup; when a telemarketer had called, he'd agreed to five-year subscriptions for *Guns & Ammo* and *Playboy*; and one day he'd tucked his wallet in the freezer, giving new meaning to cold, hard cash, or so he'd joked with her when she discovered it. But there was no mention of Yen, and after a moment's hesitation, underneath his most recent entry, Mrs. Khanh composed the following: "Today I called my wife by the name of Yen," she wrote. She imitated the flourishes of the professor's penmanship with great care, pretending that what she was doing was for the professor's own good. "This mistake must not be repeated."

The following morning, the professor held forth his coffee cup and said, "Please pass me the sugar, Yen." The next day, as she trimmed his hair in the bathroom, he asked, "What's on television tonight, Yen?" As he called her by the other woman's name again and again over the following weeks, the question of who this woman was consumed her days. Perhaps Yen was a childhood crush, or a fellow student of his graduate school years in Marseilles, or even a second wife in Saigon; someone he'd visited on the way home from the university during those long early evening hours when he told her he was sitting in his office on campus, correcting student exams. She recorded every incident of mistaken identity in his notebooks, but the next morning he would read her forgings without reaction, and not long after would call her Yen once more, until she thought she might burst into tears if she heard that name again.

The woman was most likely a fantasy found by the professor's wandering mind, or so she told herself after catching him naked from the waist down, kneeling over the bathtub and scrubbing furiously at his pants and underwear under a jet of hot water. Glaring over his shoulder, the professor had screamed, "Get out!" She jumped back, slamming the bathroom door in her haste. Never before had the professor lost such control of himself, or yelled at her—not even in those first days after coming to Southern California, when they'd eaten from food stamps, gotten housing assistance from Section Eight, and worn secondhand clothes donated by the parishioners of St. Alban's. That was true love, she thought: not giving roses but going to work every day and never once complaining about teaching Vietnamese to so-called heritage learners—immigrant and refugee students who already knew the language but merely wanted an easy grade.

Not even during the most frightening time of her life, when they were lost on the great azure plain of the sea, rolling unbroken to the horizon, did the professor raise his voice. By the fifth evening, the only sounds besides the waves slapping at the hull were children whimpering and adults praying to God, Buddha, and their ancestors. The professor didn't pray. Instead, he had stood at the ship's bow as if he were at his lectern, the children huddled together at his knees for protection against the evening wind, and told them lies. "You can't see it even in daylight," he'd said, "but the current we're traveling on is going straight to the Philippines, the way it's done since the dawn of time." He repeated his story so often even she allowed herself to believe it, until the afternoon of the seventh day, when they saw, in the distance, the rocky landing strip of a foreign coast. Nesting upon it were the huts of a fishing village, seemingly composed of twigs and grass, brooded over by a fringe of palm trees. At the sight of land, she had thrown herself into the professor's arms, knocking his glasses askew, and sobbed openly for the first time in front of her startled children. She was so seized by the ecstasy of knowing that they would all live that she had blurted out "I love you." It was something she had never said in public and hardly ever in private, and the professor, embarrassed by their children's giggles, had only smiled and adjusted his glasses. His embarrassment only deepened once they reached land, which the locals informed them was the north shore of eastern Malaysia.

For some reason, the professor never spoke of this time at sea, although he referred to so many other things they had done in the past together, including events of which she had no recollection. The more she listened to him, the more she feared her own memory was faltering. Perhaps they really had eaten ice cream flavored with durian on the veranda of a tea plantation in the central highlands, reclining on rattan chairs and swatting at mosquitoes. And was it possible they'd fed bamboo shoots to the tame deer in the Saigon zoo? Or together had beaten off a pickpocket, a scabby refugee from the bombed-out countryside who'd snuck up on them in the Ben Thanh market?

As the days of spring lengthened into summer, she answered the phone less and less, eventually turning off the ringer so the professor wouldn't answer calls either. She was afraid that if someone asked for her, he would say, "Who?" Even more worrying was the prospect of him speaking of Yen to their friends or children. When her daughter phoned from Munich, she said, "Your father's not doing so well," but left the details vague. She was more forthcoming with Vinh, knowing that whatever she told him he would e-mail to the other children. Whenever he left a message, she could hear the hiss of grease in a pan, or the chatter of a news channel, or the beeping of horns. He only called her on his cell phone as he did something else. She admitted that as much as she loved her son, she liked him very little, a confession that made her unhappy with herself until the day she called him back and he asked, "Have you decided? Are you going to quit?"

"Don't make me tell you one more time." She wrapped the telephone cord tightly around her index finger. "I'm never going to quit."

After she hung up the phone, she returned to the task of changing the sheets the professor had wet the previous evening. Her head was aching from lack of sleep, her back was sore from the chores, and her neck was tight with worry. When bedtime came, she was unable to sleep, listening to the professor talk about how the gusts of the Mistral blew him from wall to wall of the winding narrow streets of Le Panier, where he'd lived in a basement apartment during his Marseilles years, or the hypnotic sound made by the scratch of a hundred pens on paper as students took their exams. As he talked, she studied the dim light in their bedroom, cast off from the streetlamps outside, and remembered how the moon over the South China Sea was so bright that even at midnight she could see the fearful expressions on her children's faces. She was counting the cars passing by outside, listening for the sounds of their engines and hoping for sleep, when the professor touched her hand in the dark. "If you close your eyes," he said gently, "you might hear the ocean."

Mrs. Khanh closed her eyes.

September came and went. October passed and the Santa Ana winds came, rushing from the mountains to the east with the force of freeway traffic, breaking the stalks of the Egyptian papyruses she'd planted in ceramic pots next to the trellis. She no longer allowed the professor to walk by himself in the afternoons, but instead followed him discreetly by ten or twenty feet, clutching her hat against the winds. In the afternoons, if the Santa Ana had taken a breather, they read together on the patio. Over the past few months, the professor had taken to reading out loud, and slowly. Each day he seemed to read even more loudly, and more slowly, until the afternoon in November when he stopped in mid-sentence for so long that the silence shook Mrs. Khanh from the grip of Quynh Dao's latest romance.

"What's the matter?" she asked, closing her book.

"I've been trying to read this sentence for five minutes," the professor said, staring at the page. When he looked up, she saw tears in his eyes. "I'm losing my mind, aren't I?"

From then on she read to him whenever she was free, from books on academic topics she had no interest in whatsoever. She stopped whenever he began reciting a memory—the anxiety he felt on meeting her father for the first time, while she waited in the kitchen to be introduced; the day of their wedding, when he nearly fainted from the heat and the tightness of his cravat; or the time they returned to Saigon three years ago and visited their old house on Phan Than Gian, which they could not find at first because the street had been renamed Dien Bien Phu. Saigon had also changed names after it changed hands, but they couldn't bring themselves to call it Ho Chi Minh City. Neither could the taxi driver who ferried them from their hotel to the house, even though he was too young to remember a time when the city was officially Saigon.

They parked two houses down from theirs and stayed in the taxi to avoid the revolutionary cadres from the north who had moved in after the

Communist takeover. The professor and she were nearly overwhelmed by sadness and rage, fuming as they wondered who these strangers were who had taken such poor care of their house. The solitary alley lamp illuminated tears of rust streaking the walls, washed down from the iron grille of the terrace by the monsoon rain. As the taxi's wipers squeaked against the windshield, a late-night masseur biked by in the empty alley, announcing his calling with the shake of a glass bottle filled with pebbles.

"You told me it was the loneliest sound in the world," said the professor.

Before he started talking, she'd been reading to him from a biography of de Gaulle, her finger still on the last word she'd read. She didn't like to think about their lost home, and she didn't remember having said any such thing. "The wipers or the glass bottle?" she asked.

"The bottle."

"It seemed so at the time," she lied. "I hadn't heard that sound in years."

"We heard it often. In Da Lat." The professor took off his glasses and wiped them with his handkerchief. He had gone once to a resort in the mountains of Da Lat for a conference while she stayed in Saigon, pregnant. "You always wanted to eat your ice cream outside in the evenings," the professor continued. "But it's hard to eat ice cream in the tropics, Yen. One has no time to savor it. Unless one is indoors, with air-conditioning."

"Dairy products give you indigestion."

"If one eats ice cream in a bowl, it rapidly becomes soup. If one eats it in a cone, it melts all over one's hand." When he turned to her and smiled, she saw gumdrops of mucus in the corners of his eyes. "You loved those brown sugar cones, Yen. You insisted that I hold yours for you so your hand wouldn't get sticky."

A breeze rattled the bougainvillea. The first hint, perhaps, of the Santa Ana returning. The sound of her own voice shocked her as well as the professor, who stared at her with his mouth agape when she said, "That's not my name. I am not that woman, whoever she is. If she even exists."

"Oh?" The professor slowly closed his mouth and put his glasses back on. "Your name isn't Yen?"

"No," she said.

"What is it?"

She had been worried about her husband calling her by the wrong name, not the right one. They rarely used each other's proper names, preferring endearments like Anh, for him, or Em, for her, and when they spoke to each other in front of the children, they called themselves Ba and Ma. Usually she heard her first name spoken only by friends, relatives, or bureaucrats, or when she introduced herself to someone new, as she was, in a sense, doing now.

"My name is Sa," she said. "I am your wife."

"Right." The professor licked his lips and took out his notebook.

That evening, after they had gone to bed and she heard him breathing evenly, she switched on her lamp and reached across his body for the notebook, propped on the alarm clock. His writing had faded into such a scribble that she was forced to read what he wrote twice, following the jags and peaks of his letters down a dog-eared page until she reached the bottom, where she deciphered the following: *Matters worsening. Today she insisted I call her by another name. Must keep closer eye on her*—here she licked her finger and used it to turn the page—*for she may not know who she is anymore.* She closed the book abruptly, with a slap of the pages, but the professor, curled up on his side, remained still. A scent of sweat and sour milk emanated from underneath the sheets. If it wasn't for his quiet breathing and the heat of his body, he might have been dead, and for a moment as fleeting as déjà vu, she wished he really were.

In the end there was really no choice. On her last day at work, her fellow librarians threw her a surprise farewell party, complete with cake and a wrapped gift box that held a set of travel guides for the vacations they knew she'd always wanted to take. She fondled the guides for a while, riffling through their pages, and when she almost wept, her fellow librarians thought she was being sentimental. Driving home with the box of guides on the back seat, next to a package of adult diapers she'd picked up from Sav-on that morning, she fought to control the sense that ever so slowly the book of her life was being closed.

When she opened the door to their house and called out his name, she heard only bubbling from the fish tank. After not finding him in any of the bedrooms or bathrooms, she left the diapers and box of books in his library. An open copy of *Sports Illustrated* was on his recliner in the living room, a half-eaten jar of applesauce sat on the kitchen counter, and in the backyard, the chenille throw he wore around his lap in cool weather lay on the ground. Floating in his teacup was a curled petal from the bougainvillea, shuttling back and forth.

Panic almost made her call the police. But they wouldn't do anything so soon; they'd tell her to call back when he was missing for a day or two. As for Vinh, she ruled him out, not wanting to hear him say, "I told you so." Regret swept over her then, a wave of feeling born from her guilt over being so selfish. Her librarian's instinct for problem-solving and orderly research kept her standing under the weight of that regret, and she returned to her car determined to find the professor. She drove around her block first, before expanding in ever-widening circles, the windows rolled down on both sides. The neighborhood park, where she and the professor often strolled, was abandoned except for squirrels chasing each other through the branches of an oak tree. The sidewalks were empty of pedestrians or joggers. There was no one except for a withered man in a plaid shirt standing on a corner, selling roses from plastic buckets and oranges from crates, his eyes shaded by a grimy baseball cap. When she called him Mr. Esteban, his eyes widened; when she asked him if he'd seen the professor, he smiled apologetically and said, "No hablo inglés. Lo siento."

Doubling back on her tracks, she drove each street and lane and cul-de-sac a second time. Leaning out the window, she called his name—first in a low voice, shy about making a scene, and then in a shout. "Anh Khanh!" she cried. "Anh Khanh!" A few window curtains twitched, and a couple of passing cars slowed down, their drivers glancing at her curiously. But he didn't spring forth from behind someone's hedges, or emerge from a stranger's door.

Only after it was dark did she return. The moment she walked through the front door, she smelled the gas. A kettle was on the stove, but the burner hadn't been lit. Her pulse quickened from a walk to a sprint. After shutting off the gas, she saw that the glass doors leading to the patio, which she'd closed before her departure, were slightly ajar. There was a heavy, long flashlight in one of the kitchen drawers, and the heft of the aluminum barrel in her hand was comforting as she slowly approached the glass doors. But when she shone the light over the patio and onto the garden, she saw only her persimmon trees and the red glint of the chilies.

She was in the hallway when she saw the light spilling out of the open door to the professor's library. When she peeked around the door frame, she saw both him and the painting, their backs to the door. At his feet was her box of books, and he stood facing the bookshelf that was reserved for her. Here she kept her magazines and the books he'd given to her over the years. The professor knelt, picked a book from the box, and stood up to shelve it. He repeated the motion, one book at a time. *Hidden Tahiti and French Polynesia.* Frommer's *Hawaii. National Geographic Traveler,* Caribbean edition. With each book, he mumbled something she couldn't hear, as if he might be trying to read the titles on the spines. *Essential Greek Islands. Jerusalem and the Holy Land. World Cultures: Japan. A Romantic's Guide to Italy.* He touched the covers of each book with great care, tenderly, and she knew, not for the first time, that it wasn't she who was the love of his life.

The professor shelved the last book and turned around. The expression on his face when he saw her was the one he'd worn forty years ago at their first meeting, when she'd entered the living room of her father's house and seen him pale with anxiety, eyes blinking in anticipation. "Who are you?" he cried, raising his hand as if to ward off a blow. Her heart was beating quickly and her breathing was heavy. When she swallowed, her mouth was dry, but she could feel a sheen of dampness on her palms. It struck her then that these were the same sensations she'd felt that first time, seeing him in a white linen suit wrinkled by high humidity, straw fedora pinned between hand and thigh.

"It's just me," she said. "It's Yen."

"Oh," the professor said, lowering his hand. He sat down heavily in his armchair, and she saw that his oxfords were encrusted with mud. As she crossed the carpet to the bookshelf, he followed her with a hooded gaze, his look one of exhaustion. She was taking down *Les pétites rues de Paris* when he closed his eyes and leaned back in his armchair. Sitting beside him on the carpet and opening the book, she wondered what, if anything, she knew about love. Not much, perhaps, but enough to know that what she would do for him now, she would do again tomorrow, and the next day, and the day after that. She read out loud, from the beginning; she read slowly, taking her time; she read as if every letter counted to a man who was vanishing word by word, page by page.

The Neighbor

Goli Taraghi

Translated from the Farsi by Karim Emami and Sara Khalili

All of us—myself, my children, and the friends who now and then drop by to see us—are scared stiff of our neighbor on the floor below. Our life as expatriates in Paris is full of hidden anxieties and emotions. There is, first of all, a feeling of guilt for having come as strangers from across the border to encroach upon the rights of the native inhabitants. Underneath this guilty feeling lurks a silent, seething rage that must be suppressed, and a nagging sense of humiliation waiting for revenge. And finally there is that millennia-old pride that makes us, the descendants of Cyrus the Great, look down upon modern civilization with a skeptical sneer, convinced that even defeated and miserable and downtrodden, we remain (God knows why) superior to the rest of the world; and that anyhow, if we have lost the glory and splendor that were once ours, you are to blame, you deluded Western exploiters.

Though this may be a false accusation, one thing is certainly true: my present miseries are entirely due to the lady downstairs, who constantly haunts our disrupted and chaotic existence like an evil spirit. We dare not talk or laugh or walk, and having but recently arrived and not yet learned the ins and outs of life in Europe—having, moreover, left a spacious house with a garden full of flowers and trees, as well as our family and friends, to find ourselves in this different world—we move around in circles wondering how to live here without being in each other's way or disturbing the neighbors. The children have gone completely wild. One is five and the other is four. They are overexcited and confused and express their anxiety by letting out earsplitting shrieks and kicking and banging their fists at everything in sight. My son hits my daughter, I hit my son, and the neighbor bangs at our door. Sometimes she knocks at her ceiling with a broomstick, sometimes she shouts at us out of her window, and sometimes she yells and screams on the telephone, raising such a hullabaloo that I can hear her voice not only through the receiver, but also from the end of the corridor; in short her frequent angry outbursts seem to reach me from all four cardinal points and, like the trumpet announcing the Last Judgment, they make me shudder inside and blow my plain, unsophisticated logic to the four winds.

When I open the door to her, my timid glance that remains glued to the floor, my unsteady voice that stammers a few words, my hand that has frozen in mid-air, my foot that is ready to beat a retreat, and my whole body that is rooted to the spot, helpless and terror-stricken, all express utter submission and acknowledgement of my guilt. I promise my neighbor that these inhuman noises will never be heard again, that the children, though they have not yet had their dinner (who cares?), will immediately be put to bed, even if that means beating the daylights out of them, and that I myself will keep my feet off the floor and fly to the end of the hall like a weightless mosquito and stay under the mattress or, if necessary, under the bed for three days and three nights in deathlike silence, and do my best to obey the laws of the land and bow to the principles established by the inhabitants of this city.

Madame Downstairs doesn't believe a word of it. She bristles again, raises her voice again, stares into my eyes again, makes her nostrils quiver again, and punctuates her oh! so long sentences with huffs and puffs and poohs and pahs, giving me to understand, with all these utterances that pour down on me like a violent rainstorm and strike me like a thunderbolt, that the situation couldn't be worse and that the war continues. Our tiny, modest apartment, which even the donkey man of Mahmoudieh would have considered too cramped a living space, is wildly expensive because it is situated in the heart of Paris and has a corridor and some built-in closets. We live on the fifth floor of a building facing a church, and the fact that the churchyard has a few trees with three or four sparrows flitting about, and that there are some fat pigeons living under the eaves, is a constant delight, reminding the children and myself of Tehran and our garden of Shemiran. Another advantage of this mouse hole of ours is that the living room is graced with two square meters of balcony, a welcome space for receiving guests or resting or taking the air. We managed to adorn this blessing of a balcony with as many pots of geraniums and petunias as it can possibly hold, and in the evenings, weather permitting, we spend some carefree moments among the little greenery and the scent-less flowers, eating those overripe cucumbers and tasteless peaches grown in an alien land. And if friends happen to arrive, we bid them join us in this tiny space to share this happy hour with us and forget their home-sickness. The lady downstairs, or as the children call her, the Bogeywoman, does not approve of our use of the balcony and manifests her disapproval at short intervals. "Quiet!" she screams, and this command sounds so final and categorical that it breaks our vocal cords and freezes the smiles on our faces. We abandon our garden parties. I quickly shut the window and tell myself that one should be patient, one mustn't talk back. We foreign-ers, especially I myself with a passport issued by the Islamic Republic and a temporary residence permit, have no right to protest. In this city people just don't sit on balconies, they don't talk nonsense and laugh aloud, they don't waste their precious time on idle gossip. If they want to see a friend, no doubt to discuss politics and philosophy and world literature, they ask him to a café and rapidly settle the matter over a cup of strong coffee. These words are convincing enough for myself, but they hardly have any effect on the children. Cuddled on the laps of grandmothers and aunts and accustomed to an inexhaustible store of love and affection, they con-sider their exile in this cold, joyless, and unfeeling climate as an incom-prehensible injustice. The doorbell and the telephone are a source of joy to them, and they even prefer the visits of the Bogeywoman to the silence and solitude of our new dwelling.

The French do not open their doors very willingly. They first look through the peephole to make sure who it is. They then ask whom the visitor wants to see and for what purpose. When they feel quite safe, they undo the chain on the door, and then unlock the first and the second locks, which gives them time to have another look and ask another question, upon which they decide to half-open the door. If it is simply an unannounced visitor, they send him packing there and then. If the caller has something important to communicate, they let him have his say at the door and settle the matter without asking him in. The door to our apartment has none of these special locks or chains, nor does it have a peephole. We open it imme-diately, without asking any questions, and are overjoyed to have unexpected visitors. The children ask everybody in, even the Bogeywoman, and I quickly put the kettle on and welcome the caller with a smile. I don't like to talk to people in the corridor, I prefer to sit down with them and discuss even complaints and misunderstandings in a leisurely fashion over a cup of tea. The lady downstairs has no time for that, however. She comes up, she knocks at the door, she yells at us, and leaves. It is the same with the concierge. She comes, she knocks at the door, she brings me the mail, and leaves. The same again with the man who reads the electricity counter. He comes, he knocks, he notes, and he leaves. Greeting people and enquiring after their health are things that are not done. Our next-door neighbor is a middle-aged woman. She is not bad-tempered. She does not complain about us. She does not knock at our door. But she might as well not be there, it's as though we don't exist for her nor she for us. Sometimes I meet her on the landing and we take the lift together. Neither of us speaks. If I greet her, she greets me back. If I don't, she doesn't say a word. She goes out early in the morning and comes back in the evening, exhausted. Her solitude worries me, and I shudder at the idea that someone living in her own city can be so lonely. The lady downstairs is alive. She is mad, we fight, and that in itself is a kind of relationship. Not a moment goes by without our being aware of her existence, and nothing we do or say is free of her awareness.

I have entered the children in the local kindergarten and am glad that they keep them there all day, from 8:00 AM to 5:00 PM. My main reason for being glad is that this will please the Bogeywoman, and I even wish they could keep the school open until late at night, and on Sundays as well. Taking the children to school is not easy. They don't like to go, and they are horrified of the teachers, who, of course, don't speak their language. It is dark in the morning and it often rains. We have no car and have to walk three blocks down the avenue. Both of them cry. When we reach the second block, my son starts having his usual stomachache. The pain makes him writhe and clutch at my legs, insisting that we should go back. I feel sorry for him, but the thought of going home conjures up the face of our neighbor and suppresses my maternal instincts. My daughter is sleepy and dazed and doesn't wake up until we reach the school. She sits down on the steps in front of every single building on our way and starts yawning. If I would leave her, she would fall asleep right there. I can only make her go on by giving her sweets and chocolates. The moment she sits down, I tempt her with the colored wrappings. She jumps up and runs a few yards for these goodies, but having eaten them, she sits down again and dozes. I have to grab her by the neck and drag her all the way to the kindergarten. The rain is also a big nuisance. I can't decide which child to shelter under the umbrella. I know they will start sneezing and coughing and running a temperature in the evening, and these sounds will reach the sensitive ears of our neighbor through the chinks in the windows. Were it not for the war, I would have gone back home. Were it not for the fear of bombs and missiles, nothing would have kept me here for a single day. But in fact, the battlefield is right here, and the real enemy is lying in ambush on the floor below. If we had stayed at home, chances are that we could have escaped the bombs and missiles, while here we spend every moment confronting an invisible machine gun specially aimed at us. Saddam Hussein was across the border, while the Bogeywoman is only one floor below us. Like prisoners of war, we are holding our hands on our heads and surrendering without putting up a resistance. The reason for our defeat and the gist of our shortcomings is not speaking and understanding the language. No weapon is sharper than words, and our mouths remain shut, while the enemy's victory lies in her command of words.

A new idea has occurred to our neighbor. She has sent us a long, official letter resembling a legal reprimand and issuing a number of regulations. First of all, we are immediately to cover the wooden floors in our rooms with thick wall-to-wall carpets to deaden the noise of our footsteps. We are not to wear any shoes (especially with high heels) or any slippers with wooden soles or heels. We are not to sit on the balcony. We are not to talk in the bathroom and kitchen, because the ventilators conduct the noise. We are not to take a bath or flush the toilet early in the morning or after nine o'clock in the evening. We are not to slam the doors of the closets or make any loud noises such as laughing, sneezing, or coughing. The last regulation is underlined in red and prescribes that we are to stay at home as little as possible, and that we should try to spend most of our time outside.

We have no choice but to obey. We promptly cover the floors with thick fitted carpets lined with sponge-rubber. We walk barefoot and whisper in each other's ears. When friends drop in to see us, they take off their shoes at the door. Our fear has infected them, too. We have agreed to be careful and silent and to suppress our impulses. We have gradually forgotten that we, too, are human and that each person is free within his own four walls. Automatically and without arguing, we are obeying all the orders and bowing to the tyranny of the Bogeywoman. We are not used to standing up for our own rights, and we don't even know what rights we have in this world. Nor did we know them in the past, because everything was given to us free, and we never had to fight for our ancestral rights. The Bogeywoman is aware of her supremacy over us and makes us feel it more and more. Of all the commands she has issued, the hardest to obey is the last one, "You are to spend most of your time outside." Where are we to go? Most of my friends are artists and writers. They are unmarried and have no children. They are not rich; they live in small apartments and can't receive guests. Each of them lives in a small studio full of books and papers or paints and easels; they have no room for children. Even those who have families have their hands full with their own children and cannot cope with any additional ones. The only solution is to resort to the parks. Opposite our building, there is a measly park which is frequented by the old women of the neighborhood and by Arab charwomen. Late in the evening it turns into a meeting-place for tramps, who sit there and divide up their money. I loathe this park and find it most depressing. The only thing the children can do there is play in the sandbox and go up and down a shabby slide. The Luxembourg Garden is pretty, but it is too far and therefore too risky, considering the unsettled weather in Paris. Before we get there, it usually starts raining, and as we are not used to umbrellas and hats, we are exposed and defenseless and have to stand under a shelter for hours on end and then go home, wet and frustrated. As luck will have it, it always rains on Sundays, so we are condemned to stay at home. We used to resort to our little balcony, but the neighbor's objection has deprived us of this last recourse.

The best hour of the day is when the children are asleep and the lights on the floor below are out and a few letters have arrived from friends and relatives scattered all over the world. I don't read the letters immediately. I keep them to read in bed at night over a cup of hot coffee and a good cigarette. The first letter is from Leily, who lives in Tehran and is happy and content. Her children go to school and have lots of friends with whom they play in the garden or walk about in the neighborhood streets without worrying about war and bombs. She herself is working and does not too much mind wearing the Islamic veil. She goes to a party every evening or hosts dozens of guests herself. The second letter is from Dariush A. It is so sad and bitter that it makes me weep. He is unemployed and penniless. His son has escaped. His friends have disappeared, and his prospects for the future are so dismal that they frighten me. The third letter is from Mr. K. It is a succinct and concise report of all the bad news: his nephew was executed and his mother twice has tried to kill herself. Prices are soaring and soon everybody will starve. The foreign workers raid people's houses every night and cut off the heads of women and children and people of all ages. The Russians and Americans are hand in glove and the partition of Iran is an absolute certainty. The sons of Mashdi-Akbar the gardener have joined the Revolutionary Committee and are planning to confiscate all his property. The last letter is from my mother. There are many pages of it and it reads like a Persian film script. It is full of ups and downs, full of contradictions. The people she mentions are extremely happy, and at the same time desperately unhappy. There is no end of parties and outings and fun and games. People get together and eat and drink and praise the Islamic Republic. Then all of a sudden she sings a different tune. The lines that follow speak of shortages. There is no electric current, there is no water. You can't find any meat. There is a cholera epidemic. There are no doctors, there is no medicine. There is no security. There are no policemen, no traffic wardens. Inflation is skyrocketing and food is short. There are two meters of snow on the ground. There is no fuel. It is freezing cold, and worst of all, she is lonely and misses the children. And toward the end of the letter she abuses Europe and Paris and says that at home she has everything she needs and can live a good life without having to be at the mercy of foreigners, and all those who left the country were ill advised. Then she writes again about parties and meals and having fun and suddenly announces that she has decided to sell her house and all her belongings and buy herself a little hole abroad so that she can at least spend what is left of her life in peace.

It is late and I can't sleep. My daughter has come down with chicken pox and has a high temperature. I am worried and don't know whom to turn to for help. I want to write but my brain isn't functioning. I pick up

a book and try to read. I read one page and realize that I haven't registered a single word of it. It has been raining steadily for two days. I wish
someone would come and visit me. Tehran is sunny in spite of the cold,
and Leily mentioned that she goes for long hikes every Friday morning.
They all take off for the mountains and have breakfast at a roadside inn.
Dariush A. laughs about such things and says that even the mountains are
in mourning and the sky pours black snow over people's heads. The children are asleep. They are both feverish. I am anxious. I tell myself I'll go
back home. At home I at least have aunts and uncles and my mother to
whom I can turn for help. There would be no one living above or below
me. I wouldn't be afraid of the neighbors and could scream in my own
house. I would be able to jump around, laugh, cry, dance. Yes, I'll go back
tomorrow. Dariush A. is the only person who encourages me to stay. My
dear, he says, who tells you you're free in your own house? You're not even
allowed to breathe against the regulations, let alone talk or think or dress
or eat. Even going to the toilet has its rules and regulations. Mating, making
love, even dying is not free, and all the minute details and moments of
your existence have been prescribed in advance. So what shall I do? Stay
or go back?

There's a knock at the door. I listen. I am startled. Who can it be?
The doorbell does not function. Someone is banging at the door. My heart
is beating. I'm sure there's bad news. Something must have happened to
my mother. They must have arrested my brother. It must be the police,
or a friend in trouble. The book drops from my hand. My foot gets entan-
gled in the wire of my bedside lamp. I hurriedly put on a dress over my
nightgown. Who can it be? I'm coming. I say it in Persian and French.
Coming. I open the door. Whom do I see? It's the lady downstairs. This
is most unexpected, since she is usually asleep at this hour of the night,
and besides, she hasn't got any reason to come up. I am stunned and feel
I am going pale. My heart beats faster and I am upset about my awkward
movements and my halting speech. As soon as the Bogeywoman hears me
stammer and sees me in this nervous state, she bristles. Raising her voice,
she asks, "What's going on? What are you doing?"

"Who?"

She asks where all this noise is coming from.

"What noise?" I reply.

I am so used to thinking that she is right that I imagine the children must have got up and are romping about. I take a few hurried steps toward their room. I stop and listen. Absolute silence. She is talking nonsense and had no reason to come here. This time I'm in my rights. It's quite obvious. It doesn't require knowledge of French or of Western culture. It's plain human logic. There is no noise in the apartment and the Downstairs Lady is wrong. This time I won't submit to her aggressive behavior, because I am right. And this "being right" is a great asset that makes me strong and bold. I raise my head. I find my voice. I ask, "What noise?"

Madame's mumbling makes me more daring. A long-stifled rage that had been gnawing at my vitals suddenly erupts and inflames my whole being like a fever. I get worked up, I sweat and yell. The neighbor is taken aback by my outburst. This increases my vehemence. I hear my intestines rumbling. I advance a step. Now I look the Bogeywoman straight in the eye and see her for the first time as she really is. I had a different image of her. I had always thought she was old and ugly, and it wouldn't have surprised me if she had horns and a beard and hooves. In my mind's eye she sometimes resembled Dracula and had long, protruding front teeth. But there is nothing of that. She is about my age and has more or less the same figure that I have. Her short brown hair is greasy and straight. She is dressed without the studied elegance of most French women and wears no makeup. Two deep lines on either side of her mouth make her look bitter. She is tired and nervous. She is pregnant. She looks like all those other sad women who go to work early in the morning and come home in the evening, exhausted and depressed, to collapse in front of their TV sets. I explain to her in my broken French that the children are asleep and that I myself was in bed, and then it suddenly occurs to me that I might as well talk to her in my own language or in English, which I speak fluently. The French are in awe of the English language and resist learning it with a kind of childish pride and reactionary stubbornness, but this aversion is merely for show, and deep down they have a particular admiration for the United States and the Americans.

I have regained the power of speech. It's as though I had grown wings. No one can stand in my way any longer. I warble like a songbird and swim in an ocean of words. My thoughts and my speech are in perfect harmony. No longer do I have to chop up my sentences to make them short and simple. I feel like an orator intoxicated by the impact of his own voice. With this language, which I have at my command, I can heap insult upon injury, and that's exactly what I do. I don't know if the Bogeywoman understands the meaning of my words, but that's unimportant. The tone of my voice, the look in my eyes and the fierceness of my gestures tell her that she must clear off, and if she's ever seen here again, she'll be torn to pieces, wretched, impudent, revolting creature that she is! I yell at her. I gesticulate with my hands and even raise a foot, threatening to kick her out. The more I work myself up, the smaller the Bogeywoman becomes. She looks like a lamb on the way to be slaughtered, while I grow taller and taller. I have the impression that my front teeth are beginning to protrude like Dracula's, that I'm growing horns and a beard, that I've turned into a dragon, and I'm madly enjoying it all. I'm quite ready to devour the poor Bogeywoman. Ha ha! I leap about. Ha ha ha! I charge. Madame lets out a little shriek and rushes to the lift. I can't stop myself. I go on yelling heaven knows what. Drunk with my show of strength, I feel like going upstairs, knocking on all the doors and accusing everybody, telling them they have no right to talk or walk, and clawing at their faces.

The moment the lift door opens, the Downstairs Lady rushes in and disappears, breathing heavily. She literally disappears. We won't see her the next day or any following day of the month, or any day of many subsequent months. Had she melted, or had the ground swallowed her up? A long time later, when I happened to run into her at the entrance of the building, we both looked away and quickly ran off in opposite directions. All I remember noticing was her big belly and her tired eyes. She must have been at the very end of her pregnancy.

The prolonged absence of the Bogeywoman gradually lends our life a more normal aspect. We walk about with our shoes on, we walk fearlessly whenever we want to, and when the sun is shining, we even sit on the balcony and laugh without any anxiety. The children are much calmer, now that the shadow of Dracula no longer looms before them. We go out when we wish, but no longer feel compelled to stay out. At the beginning of the summer, just before daybreak, I suddenly wake up hearing the monotonous wails of a baby. As I listen carefully, I realize that they come from the floor below, and I chuckle.

Years pass. The war with Iraq is still going on and we are still waiting for the departure of the mullahs. The children have grown older and no longer complain about going to school. They can walk there and back on their own. They are less nervous and have quite forgotten their fear of the Downstairs Lady.

Autumn has now started, and it is one of those gloomy Sundays. The sky is covered and a penetrating cold wind is blowing. The children are at home and we are expecting guests this evening. I am on my way to a grocery run by an Arab who keeps his shop open even on holidays. I go past the park where the tramps usually hang out. I suddenly discover the Bogeywoman on a bench, looking at a point in the distance. She is cold and is sitting there with hunched shoulders and with her collar up. She has a half-open book on her lap. A half-lit cigarette rests between her fingers, and her hair is greasy and unkempt as usual. Her right leg is stretched out with its ankle bent, and her shoe has slipped off. Her child is playing in the sandbox. She looks so sad and forlorn that I feel sorry for her. I wonder why she is sitting in this miserable park when it's so cold and windy, and then I suddenly remember her letter. No doubt a neighbor has complained and ordered her to keep her baby outside. I see that another Bogeywoman has bared her teeth to her and this depresses me. In this peaceful building facing a park and a church, ten lambs in wolves' clothing are lying in ambush for one another and blaming each other for their misfortunes. Tired, frustrated wolves with petty desires and trivial aspirations, hoping for better days!

I ask myself, "Could it be otherwise? Could it?" A few raindrops fall on my face. I walk faster. The Downstairs Lady is still sitting there, helpless and dazed. Under the trees lies a drunken beggar, unconscious or perhaps dead. No one looks at him. I hurry on. I am thinking that my guests will arrive any minute, and in my haste to get the shopping done I forget the question I asked myself.

This Is How It Is

Ehren Schimmel

The rat must have lived in the basement, with the warm pipes of the water and sewer lines, before they began overhauling the system. The men stomping around and the sounds of metal against metal probably scared him into the walls where somehow he crawled to my seventh floor. The new system will allow all of us in block nine to control our heat individually with a *centrala termica*—capitalist-style. We will pay for what we use. It is a logical improvement, but they are doing it in January and currently there is no heat at all.

Since the rat entered my apartment several weeks ago, my home has taken on the odd feeling of a detainment center. I have locked him in the kitchen and because he is nocturnal, I live—and certainly he does as well—with a series of awkward and tiresome interruptions.

Every morning at five-thirty he claws on the kitchen door and I cannot fall back to sleep. So I wrap myself in a heavy coat and scarf and walk around town in the hours before work, stopping to buy a cigarette at the nonstop around the corner. I have become accustomed to smoking. It is a pleasant thing to do when walking in the winter, and I walk through the snow-covered park and the deserted streets with stray dogs and wait for the day to begin.

I have done, I think, all the things anyone might do to eliminate the rat, or *şobolan*, from my home. I sealed the hole under the bathroom sink, where I believe he entered, but unbeknownst to me, he was in the apartment at the time. This is how he became shut in.

I have set traps—snap traps, live traps, glue traps, even a primitive homemade one with a bucket and a string—and as an infestation website instructed me, I placed them "against the wall, in high traffic areas."

I have used several varieties of poison. There have also been times when I displayed an uncharacteristic temper and resorted to simple aggression (a period when I was considerably more energetic), and I have swung my baseball bat against the cupboards, splintering doors, denting walls, and chasing the little creature into every pocket or shelf. All attempts have either been ignored or negotiated by what I now consider a sophisticated little thing, and we are currently locked in a sort of stalemate, a predictable pattern of behaviors that is disruptive and allows each of us only a minimal level of function.

The extraordinary thing about the rat is not only that he has survived these attempts on his life, but that he seems to have built up a resistance. The last two traps were ignored, last week's poisoned spoonful of Nutella was devoured, and still he is scratching and pitter-pattering around.

One weekend, I brought in a cat loaned to me by one of my tenth graders, but that experiment also failed. I entered the kitchen one morning and the door banged against the rigor of a dead animal. The cat had eaten some poison, a handful I had forgotten was behind the fridge.

"I am so sorry, Simona," I told the student, a girl with long dark hair and a maturity that makes her appear out of place with her classmates. "I feel terrible. What can I do for you?"

"It is okay, teacher," she said simply, "she was old," then shrugged and muttered "*Asta e*," a familiar phrase, which translated loosely means "this is how it is" as in, my cat is dead and this is how it is, or I have a rat in my home and this is how it is. The Romanians use these words like a reflex, an over-developed penchant to tolerate adversity—to handle things with grace and humor, to be flexible.

The Peace Corps emphasizes flexibility, and in the first eighteen months in Romania I have come to expect unfamiliar problems and obstacles and manage them with surprising grace. I go to six different locations to pay for my gas, cable, water, electric, rent, and heat (I still pay for heat), and I no longer complain when the postman opens my mail or the water is shut off.

I am trying to be flexible with my current problem. I have seen rats in subway stations and landfills and so I have viewed them as I suppose most people do, as unattractive, harmless, tangential things. The website calls them "commensal parasites" because the host is not affected. Of course I find this funny, even tragically false. But in some ways I have managed to adapt. When I want to eat, I go to Restaurant Chicago, a pizza place down the street. Sometimes I walk to a *patiserie* and get a potato pie and a Coke. I have purchased a traditional Romanian hat, a *căciulă*, perfect for my winter walkabouts. I also take my garbage out daily and to better live in coordination with the rat, I go to bed early. I speak to anyone willing to listen about rats and infestation because it is often on my mind, and I have learned all the appropriate vocabulary:

Rat – *şobolan*
Poison – *otravă*
Whiskers – *mustăţi*
Tail – *coadă*
Trap – *capcană*
Hole – *gaură*
Cement – *cement*
Droppings – *excremente de animale*

Through my experience and research I have also developed a begrudging respect for rats, particularly because they are very adaptable creatures. They live in virtually every country and their skeletal structure is flexible, malleable like pipe cleaners. "If a rat can fit its skull through a hole, it can fit its body," the website says.

Although I have found ways to manage, my days now lapse into a lackadaisical fog. I become sleepy and teeter out in the afternoons, playing review games with the children. They have grown tired of me. I can see it in their disinterested eyes. No longer the exotic, creative American, I am just another burdensome teacher. The only one who seems, not to have lost a bit of her interest is Simona, who has not only maintained her enthusiasm but has already developed all the physical attributes and sophisticated mannerisms of a mature woman. She sits in front and diligently takes notes, asks pertinent questions, and does not hide an obvious disdain for her classmates, who behave in all the typically infuriating ways in which teenagers behave. Simona also employs a practiced flirtation, using the rat to continue an ongoing dialogue with me after class.

"Still with the little animal?" she asks me, books pressed against her chest.

"Unfortunately, yes." I maintain a professional air, but do not want to discourage her entirely. I confess that I like the attention.

"I am so sorry you have this problem, teacher," she says softly. "Not all us Romanians have rats in the home."

"I know."

"You will be liberated from the rat, I am sure," she says sympathetically, then touches my arm and turns away. As I watch her walk out, I am aware of a sensation that has become exaggerated in recent weeks. The feeling is not a perverse affection but something like nostalgia, even love—a warm, sad pining for youth and beauty that gives me hope.

After all, the adults have been skeptical, even suspicious of me and seem bothered by my errors of speech, so I have naturally embraced the naive happiness of the children. God bless them, my students. They are mischievous and self-centered like teenagers everywhere but they charm me, especially when they are sitting in class wrapped in winter coats and hats. When we talk of Romania there is a self-effacing humor mixed with stubborn pride, and they are amused that I moved from America to Romania—as if I lost some terrible lottery.

"We all try to leave and you come here!"

I tell them that they should appreciate what they have, that Romania is actually quite nice. And for the most part I believe this. There are romantic, European traits that make Romania a charming place. Cafés and small cars and fresh bread and people taking their time. The towns are pedestrian friendly. The concrete blocks such as the one I live in are ugly and cumbersome, but I view them—as it is my privilege to do—as kitschy, functional monuments to communism, rectangular silhouettes pasted against the sunsets of Transylvania.

It is a beautiful city in some areas. Especially in the winter it can sparkle at times like a medieval fable. The architecture of the old center predates communism by hundreds of years and so it resembles a Western European village, rows of stone shops and hotels with colorful facades. There is the sense that one gets in a small, out of the way town that something magical might occur, that some spectacular revelation may be discovered and draw the eyes of the world.

But my enthusiasm to absorb Romanian life, like a temporary romantic infatuation, has passed. It may be my current mood or an inevitable evolution, but despite the fondness I have developed for my students, I am interested now in only immediate, practical concerns: Kill the rat. Eat warm, healthy meals, and, of course, sleep well without fear of infection or disease. Find a nice young lady and regain a youthful, energetic lifestyle of love, sport, and drinking that others seem to expect of someone in my place.

Instead, because my living area has become so unkempt and somber, I avoid going home after school. I walk along the high banks of the Someş in the afternoon, a river that passes behind my block and lingers into Hungary. There is a stone walkway on the dike and a rusted, rickety train bridge that crosses over the river, and the train moves so gently that people hardly step off the rails to let it pass.

I head home when I feel the cold air beneath my *căciulă*, and I see the gypsies light fires that at nightfall shine like lampposts in a row along the river.

When I open the door to my apartment there is only a mild increase in temperature. It is generally no colder than in New England, but in Romania the cold infects life like a pervasive itch. Collars are tightened, arms are rubbed, toes are curled. The buildings have heat but, like mine, it will be under maintenance or there will be a temporary outage or there will be imperfections and the cold will seep in through the cracks and the thin panes of glass.

I hear the rat scurry away from the kitchen door to the cupboards and the maze of passageways. Each cupboard is lifted a few inches from the floor and he can scurry between each one, behind the refrigerator, the radiator, or the pantry.

In recent days, I have considered a terrible option; something that earlier, I quickly dismissed. My kitchen has two doors. The first is solid wood and leads to my living space, the other has a large pane of glass and a swivel hook latch and leads to my balcony. The balcony is a small space with a foggy, obscured glass divider that stops about ten centimeters short of the floor and separates my area from the other side, a space that is a mirror image of mine, occupied by an older couple, the Niţus. Their area is clean and arranged beautifully, the product of decades of investment and care. I smell fresh meals at the same hour every day: boiled chicken, garlic, steamed carrots, pickled cabbage, *slănină* spiced with paprika.

In warm weather, when windows are open, there is activity on the balcony and I can hear them, sharing their concerns as easily as they share their daily chores.

Sometimes on warm days I pop my head over the railing and they seem pleased at my arrival. We are in good spirits because of the pleasant, still air and we talk with great ease and candor, as if we are close family. It feels as though our little balcony is some small contribution to peace in the world, a tender and fragile thing, and always I hate to end our talks and go inside at nightfall.

I have rejected the possibility of opening that second door, and not only because of my affection for my neighbors. I can imagine their future looks of disgust, seeing me as slovenly or, if they discover my intent, a selfish, deceitful bastard. Or perhaps—and this is the most horrible thought—they will attribute these characteristics to all of my people.

So I keep the door locked. There are other methods, I am sure, and I do my best to manage, though I am losing my will. He is very resilient. There are streaks of dried rat blood on the kitchen door where he scrapes and bites every morning and little red paw prints across the green tile. Wood shavings are scattered about with droppings and a liquid that I imagine is urine or diarrhea but certainly not vomit. "Rats do not have the esophageal strength to vomit," the website says.

"I see you, you little şobolan bastard," I tell him. He is peeking out from behind the pantry. He likes to keep an eye on things, in case I am concocting any more plans.

I am quite sure he is a Norway rat, *Rattus norvegicus*, despite the fact that he is obviously something of a climber. He is so large and has brown-ish fur, and Norway rats are common and notoriously destructive. I will approximate that he is one and a half feet long from the tip of his nose to the end of his naked little *coadă*. His body is shaped a bit like an elon-gated pear, and at the widest point, his hindquarters, I estimate that he is about twelve centimeters. He has small black eyes, and his underside is a dirty, lemony color. It is a he, I understand: male rats have abnormally large testicles. There is a mark on his side, a pale discoloration of fur about the size of a nickel that distinguishes him. I have taken to referring to him sometimes as "Rasheed," for the professional basketball player who shares the same characteristic. *Rasheedus norvegicus*.

At five-thirty in the morning Rasheed is again gnawing on the door, and I am forced awake. I drag myself out of bed and walk to the kitchen in a ritual that has become as routine as brushing my teeth. I push the door open. He used to bolt across the room and toss himself headlong into a crevice, his ass and tail then disappearing as if sucked up by an unseen vacuum. Now he simply stops gnawing and finds the widest entryway on the far side of the room and waddles arrogantly across the floor, his tail sliding through the path of dried blood and *excremente de animale*.

Outside through the windows in my living room I can see that it is snowing heavily, but most students walk to school. Nothing will be cancelled.

I slip on a sweater and coat and my *căciulă* and walk the seven flights down the concrete steps, feeling for the rail in the darkness. At the entryway there is a familiar stray dog, one who appears like the victim of a cruel genetic experiment: mottled fur, asymmetric ears, an imposing terrier-like head attached to the malnourished body of a dachshund or beagle. Despite myself, I often snicker at his appearance. I can't help but imagine the awkward act that created him. He lifts his paw up, showing an open wound. Perhaps the winter is getting to him. One eye is crusted over with infection and there is a slice in his right ear. I drop him a pizza crust, as is my custom, and he wolfs it down and follows me for a few tentative steps before retreating back beneath the overhang.

The snow is piled high in fluffy sheets. There is a satisfying crunch to my steps as I mark a path to the kiosk at the corner. I buy one cigarette, a small coffee, and a potato pie before I make my way to the park.

I choose a bench beside the statue of Vasile Lucaciu, as it feels as though I have company. He is adorned with a regal, cape-like robe and stares off to the West over Hotel Dacia. He did something positive for the Transylvanians in the nineteenth century. The snow has formed on the crown of his head and his shoulders, and wind-blown snow has stuck to the pedestal, blocking out his name and the dates of his life.

At six forty-five I go to school and at the start of my first class it is still dark outside. We huddle in the classroom. Grammar or history seems somehow inappropriate, so we ease into the day with a discussion about sledding and ice skating and how long it takes to walk to school. The rest of the day proceeds predictably. I do a lesson on adverbs for the younger ones and for the older kids there is a quiz on the civil rights movement. I kick Sergiu out of class for being disruptive.

Kids are throwing snowballs in the schoolyard between hours, and the stone hallways are wet and grimy. In the teacher's room, or *sala profesoarala*, there is a birthday to celebrate. We all do a shot of *țuica* with vanilla cake, and we march out of the room red-faced and ready to finish the day. The last hours erode with the excitement of snow and the coming weekend. Kids cannot keep their mouths shut.

After the final bell I go to the *sala*, where the teachers seem as anxious as the students. The closet is stripped clean, coat hangers rocking back and forth. They wish each other a happy weekend. In a few minutes the place is empty, ashtrays full, cigarette smoke settling against the high ceiling. I am at my usual place in the corner, and, all alone, the room appears cavernous with three large oak tables and windows with massive, yellowed curtains. On one end is a Romanian flag and on the other end is a portrait of the great poet, Mihai Eminescu.

In the hall I can hear the sound of giddy students, of laughter and shouting. I sift through papers and recalculate a few grades, gaze through the windows and consider my weekend. The snow has almost stopped. A few big, heavy flakes twist down like feathers, and I have nothing to do. I feel neglected, like that misshapen little dog.

There is a creak of the floorboards near the entrance. Generally, students rarely enter the *sala profesoarala*, and if they do, they are accompanied by a teacher or walk in blushing shyly, as if interrupting something of great importance. But here is Simona, with a bright row of white teeth, walking in with a purse around her shoulder as if she were my date.

"Still working, teacher?" she asks.

"Just finishing up some things is all," I say, and then Simona is sitting next to me, legs crossed in tight jeans. She is waiting to have English lessons with Mrs. Nagy, she explains, and then she looks at me. Big hazel eyes. Her tendency is to look unflinchingly into my eyes for long periods, and it gives her an aura of confidence.

There is a stillness now, which we both seem to comfortably accept, the halls now silent, the world pausing as if in a conspiracy to sequester us. Only the faint buzz of an old Macintosh computer can be heard in the corner of the room. She has a scent, a perfume, something like vanilla, or is it coconut? Shadows are gone from the room. It is darker now, outside, heavy black clouds overhead, and somehow I feel dizzy; perhaps, I think, it would be best to turn the light on. My legs are heavy, though, and that dizziness, where does it come from? I could sleep here, perhaps. The table-cloths could be used for blankets. There are bathrooms, even a coffee machine. What do I tell the janitor? What do I tell him, poor Gheorghe, the janitor, when he sees an American—an American no less!—sleeping beneath the tables in the *sala profesoarala? Sala cu un profesor. Sala mare, si inauntru este un profesor. Profesor American. Profesor American, adormit.*

"What are you drawing?" Simona asks, and I pick my head up. She turns the paper with her thin fingers.

"Oh, teacher!" she says, staring at the crude pictures I have doodled on the back of one student's homework:

She touches my arm again. There is a synaptic response, a flurry of activity inside me. The touch is warm, like a fond memory. She is wearing hoop earrings that graze her cheeks, and though I have become used to less personal space, Simona seems very close. She has untainted, fresh, inoffensive breath, like the breath of a puppy.

"Maybe you should move blocks," she tells me.

"I know," I say. "There is pneumonic plague. Weil's syndrome. Lassa fever. Hantavirus. Lyssavirus. Lymphocytic choriomeningitis. Trichinosis. Salmonellosis."

"Oh, teacher."

"Bubonic plague, of course."

"Teacher?"

Perhaps I have a fever. I feel her jeans, and the knee beneath her jeans brushing against my thigh. I see it first, and then somehow, after, I feel it, her hand. It is in my hand, curled into my moist palm. She is proud of her youth, of her physical perfection, and so she is not timid but expectant. She wants a kiss. Just a brief one, a few seconds to give evidence of our bond. Of course we should kiss, she seems to say. We like each other, and I am very beautiful, and you should kiss me now. It is appropriate that you do so. Our differences are only impositions, superficial creations really, preventing true kinship. They limit our possibilities, don't they? As lovers and as people? We should kiss now, because this is how I feel, and how you feel, and this is right.

And for a brief moment, I feel the same. I see all the foolish obstacles in the world and watch them drift away, harmlessly, like the seeds of a dandelion. Then there is only Simona and she is looking at me, such comforting beauty.

"I have to go home," I say. I gather together my papers and books. "I think I'm a little under the weather," I say, because I know she won't recognize this phrase and she may assume it is something credible. I tap her hand, walk slowly to the door. She is confused, but she does not slouch or pout, or do anything that could be construed as childish, or that would jeopardize a later encounter. She only says, "Teacher," and then, *"da-i drumul."* Yes, yes. I know this phrase. I saw it on a sign, or in the paper, or perhaps I heard it on the radio. *Let it go.*

Outside the air is cold with a mild breeze, and it invigorates me a bit. I follow my general routine, a casual walkabout with a few stops at parks and kiosks and then to a café to get a *țuica* and some pear juice, then pick up a pizza to go. At nightfall I return to my apartment. The elevator is under repair so I walk the seven floors to the top.

As I flip on the light, I can hear him scurry away. I bang on the kitchen door just to be sure and then lay down on the sofa and watch the weather report while I eat. I spend so much time outside, I am attentive to any shift in the weather. The metallic shutters are rattling outside my window, as if the storm is being pushed off to the east, or perhaps another one is arriving, sweeping down from the Ukraine.

"In 1727, *Rattus norvegicus* was observed crossing the Volga river from Russia," the website says. "They later invaded America on the same ships that brought British troops during the revolution." If only Mr. Revere knew of the destructiveness of the little rodent, I think. *"Rattus norvegicus!"* *"Rattus norvegicus* is coming!" I consider this as I move toward the kitchen and slip through the door. He is hiding. I step carefully through the mess. I swear he has organized the wood shavings, feces, and other garbage into piles and pathways that best accommodate his habits. When I reach the other side, I flip the latch and swing the door open, letting in a surge of cold air. I prop it open with a coffee mug and tiptoe back and close the other door behind me.

I lay in bed with an unfamiliar tension. The wind is swirling through my kitchen, rattling doors and cabinets. Perhaps I fall asleep for a few hours, or maybe I don't sleep at all, but I am first aware of the time at three thirty in the morning. Now I only wait. Three thirty becomes four thirty and four thirty becomes five thirty and then six thirty, and because I know the Nițus wake up at seven, I am wide awake on my back with a wool hat, the blankets pulled to my chin. At 7:04 I hear the screams from Doamna Nițu on the balcony:

"*Şobolan! Şobolan! Aaaah! Tudor, hai aici! Este un şobolan pe balcon! Acolo...aaah ah ah!*"

I wait a few moments and then pass through and look over the railing to the Nițu's side. "*Şobolan!*" she screams again. I contort my face into a look of confusion and disgust as Domnul Nițu closes the door to his kitchen, then cranes his neck around the wall to tell me to do the same, but stops short, noticing that I am already prepared, a frying pan in my hand.

The rat moves from one side to the other, sniffing and scurrying for a route of escape. Looking over the rail, I see Doamna Nițu hand her husband a broom. We stand on our respective sides, ready to chase and strike the rat for as long as it takes.

For several minutes, the rat bounces from end to end, running into each balcony door, the back wall, and then, on the side that overlooks the town, he crashes into the aluminum railing that extends to the floor. He tries to use the divider as a shield, but it is too narrow. There is no place for him to hide. On a few occasions I swing the pan. Twice he manages to dart under the divider and the third time, at the last moment, I fear the violence and awful sound of impact, so I slow the velocity of the pan and it only clips his back, stunning him for a moment before he runs across to the other side.

The rat does not seem eager to return to my side of the wall and the wide circumference of the frying pan; he scurries about on the Nițu's side. A blurry, distorted image of Domnul Nițu is visible through the glass as he waves the broom in a pathetic, uncoordinated fashion. His wife is frantically hollering instructions.

The rat is then pushed by a wide sweep of Domnul Niţu's broom under the divider. He has no chance, tumbling like a snowball close to my feet. I catch him before he gathers himself and strike him on the head. The rat takes a few unbalanced steps, his limbs failing him like a drunk. *"Inca una!"* Domnul Niţu shouts, peering around the wall. *"Inca una!"*

I strike him again, in a halfhearted fashion, on the back. He falls and lays on his side, and I can make out a meager rise and fall of his ribs, the mark of discoloration near his tail. From up close he is a bit smaller than I thought, and there are clear signs of malnourishment, his ribs and skull forming sharp lines against his dark fur. His little black eyes are staring up at me. *"Numai inca una,"* Domnul Niţu says, now a faint whisper. Only one more.

I bring the pan down, just heavy enough to kill him, and that is the end of it. Doamna Niţu looks over and makes a face, muttering a Hungarian curse.

I look down at the rat, now still and lifeless, his eyes opaque and empty, and I think how remarkable it will be to return to my old self. It is an intoxicating, transformative feeling, as if I have removed a hideous goiter from my face.

My neighbor hands me a plastic bag around the wall. Then, Doamna Niţu appears and passes over a fistful of toilet paper.

With the paper, I pick up the rat by the tail and lower it into the bag, then tie the bag tightly with a knot. I give a sheepish look to Domnul Niţu and he chuckles. He tells me, "Be sure he does not have friends," and I tell him I am quite sure he does not—not in my apartment.

I walk the seven floors to the lobby and step out into the snow with the bag in my hand. The sun is not yet up, but the sky has lightened to a steel blue, and in the east thin streaks of orange sit on the horizon beyond the river. The streets are covered with snow, untouched, like fresh paint.

The dumpster is a short walk behind an adjacent building, and I bring the bag over and lift up the heavy, steel lid, the metallic thud echoing off the walls of the blocks. A few gypsy children rush over, three of them. They reach up with long, dirt-filled fingernails, snot crusted on their faces, and they beg in sequence, like a sales pitch.

"You don't want this, trust me," I tell them. The littlest one pulls on my pant legs and my coat, saying please, mister let us have it. I can smell them, a scent as powerful as the one from the garbage bin. "Fine," I say and toss it on the ground, a layer of crusted snow and ice. I walk away and turn to watch them tear into the bag. One of them holds the rat up by the tail and they laugh. He tosses it in the air and it lands with a thump. The little one kicks it and then the other one, snow flying up in the air and then they are all kicking it down the street like a soccer ball until they disappear around a corner.

There is no use going back to bed. I am wide awake, filled with thoughts, and I amble around the streets in my usual fashion. In the park, some of the benches have been wiped clean from the wind, and I take a seat and watch my breath curl into the air. It is a clear, cold morning. The town is still, dampened by the snow, and the day feels empty. I have nothing planned. It thrills me, this great emptiness. In that strange manner in which the mind can change so quickly, all my ambitions, the standards by which I measured myself, and all my pedantic concerns are returning to me. It is curious why they ever left. Only hours ago, the world could drift away like the icy snow, and I might have run off with a young girl, to begin a simple life of love-sharing. Now my kitchen is waiting for me, a broken, devastated place, with splinters of wood and pools of dried blood. There is a lot to do. It will take a long time to clean and put everything in order— like starting over.

Oh, dear rat. Oh dear, dear *şobolan*!

The Odalisque

Laila Lalami

The teenager was Faten's favorite client. He wasn't what you would call a regular, like her Friday-night or first-of-the-month men, those who came to her the way they might stop by a bakery and buy an extra pastry to go with their coffee because they'd just gotten paid. In the five months that she'd known him, there hadn't been a regular pattern to his visits, but whenever she saw his car coming up Calle Lucia, she'd arch her back, cock her hip, and smile. He always got out of the car, too, which is more than you could say for the others, the men who talked to her while they bent over their steering wheels, as if spending more than a minute deciding who they were going to fuck was too much of an imposition on their time. He was different.

His name was Martín. At first she'd assumed it was just a fake name, but someone had called his mobile phone once, right after he'd paid her, and she'd heard a hoarse voice at the other end of the line yelling the name. It sounded like a cop—someone with authority, someone used to giving orders. Later on, she asked him who it was and he said it was his father, calling from Barcelona to ask why he was out so late, as if he were still a child. Martín explained that he was the youngest of his father's children from two marriages. He shook his head and put his phone away, grumbling that *el viejo* was losing it.

She did not know Martín's last name. What she did know was that he had recently moved to Madrid to attend Universidad Complutense. He never talked about what he studied, and she didn't ask, for she feared it would bring back memories of her own college life back in Morocco, and she didn't want to think of that time in her life, when the world still seemed full of promise and possibility.

In a way, Faten liked never knowing when he'd stop by. It gave her something to look forward to, and if he showed up, it was like a gift, something she could unwrap and hold up to admire. The later it got, the better the surprise. And there was, too, the possibility that if he came up to see her late in the night he could be her last one, so it didn't matter how long she stayed with him. That kept her going on bad nights, when it rained or when the girls bickered. The Spanish girls often fought with the Moroccans or Romanians or Ukrainians, but it was a useless battle. Every week there was a new immigrant girl on the block.

Martín reminded her of a neighbor she'd had a crush on when she was little. At that time, she had been sent to live in Agadir with her aunt, because her mother couldn't afford to keep her in Rabat, what with her father having left them and the child support the court had ordered him to pay never having materialized. Faten had stayed in the seaside town until she turned fourteen and her breasts grew into a D cup. The single man next door had started coming around on the silliest of excuses, asking to borrow a cup of sugar or a glass of oil. That was when Faten's aunt decided it was time for her to go back to the capital.

Faten had moved in with her mother in the slum in Douar Lhajja, the kind of place where couscous pots were used as satellite dishes. She'd stayed there for six years—and in that short time she had managed to graduate high school, go to college, find God, and join the Islamic Student Organization. She'd had the misfortune of making a derogatory comment about King Hassan within earshot of a snitch but had, rather miraculously, escaped arrest thanks to a friendly tip. So when her imam suggested she leave the country, she had not argued with him. She had done as she was told. Except her imam wasn't there when the Spanish coast guard caught her and the other illegal immigrants, nor was he around when she had to fend for herself in Spain. Now no one could decide for her whether or not she should see Martín.

Tonight had been good. She'd made good money and Martín was her last client. She climbed into his car and pulled down the passenger-side mirror, dabbing her face dry with a Kleenex and reapplying her lipstick. She glanced at him. His light brown hair was falling out prematurely, and his thin lips grew thinner whenever he was emotional. He wore a pair of dark slacks and a loose button-down shirt, where gold arabesque letters danced on a sea of deep red. She asked what he wanted to do.

"Just talk," he said. "Can we?"

"*Como que no*," she said.

He started the car and drove slowly off Calle Lucia, toward Huertas. Faten let her head rest against her seat and stretched her legs, her feet painful from standing too long in high heels. It had been just as hard to get used to the heels as to the short skirts. Before this, back at home, it was always flats or sneakers, an ankle-length skirt, and a secondhand sweater.

"So, where are you from?" he asked.

"Rabat."

"I thought you were from Casablanca."

"I can be from Casablanca if you want." She laughed, wanting him to know it was just a line, not something she'd actually tell *him* with seriousness. She wanted him to know that she thought he was different.

He turned up a side street and stopped the car. She was quiet, watching the lights from the bars up the street, trying to figure out where they were with respect to Lavapiés, where she lived. She spent a lot of time on the street, yet she didn't know Madrid well at all. Since she'd arrived here, she hadn't seen much—only the streets, her apartment, the hospital, and the stores.

Martín spoke softly. "How long have you been in Madrid?"

"Three years, just about."

"I bet you have a lot of regulars."

"A few. Not a lot."

"They don't know what they're missing."

"And what would that be?"

He circled the knob of her knee with his thumb. "So much," he said. "I like the smell of your skin—salty like black olives." He coiled a strand of her hair around his finger, let it spring out, ran his fingers along her cheekbones, cupped her right breast. "And your breasts—ripe like mangoes."

"You're making me sound like a dish," she said.

"I guess you could say I'm a connoisseur."

She looked into his eyes, and for the first time, she wondered if what she had assumed was a flicker of innocence was something else—a twinkle of playfulness, even mischief. "There's something I've been meaning to ask," she said. "About your father. Is he a cop?"

"He's a pig."

"Why do you call him that?"

"Because he's a fascist," he said. He leaned back against the headrest as he spoke, telling her about his father, a retired army lieutenant who had served under Franco as a young man. It was a bit of a tradition in the family, Martín's grandfather having served under Franco as well. Hearing the Generalissimo's name stirred in Faten the memory of her maternal grandfather, a proud Rifi who'd lost his eyesight during the rebellion in the north. It was mustard gas, he'd told his children, and he'd spent the rest of his life begging for a gun to put an end to it all. It was cancer that took him away, though, two years before Faten was born.

Martín said his father hated the immigrants. He shook his head. "But I'm not like him," he said. "I like you."

"You do," she said, in her I've-heard-it-all-before voice.

Martín didn't seem to mind the sarcasm. "I want to help you," he said, stroking her arm. He said he could help her get her immigration papers, that he knew of loopholes in the law, that she could be legal, that she wouldn't need to be on the streets, that she could get a real job, start a new life.

Faten had never expected anyone to make extravagant promises like these, and so she wasn't sure whether she should laugh or say thank you. For a moment she allowed herself to imagine what a normal life would be like here, never having to see the men, being able to sleep at night, being able to look around her without worrying about the police at every turn. She began to wonder about the price of all this—after all, she had long ago learned that nothing was free. He laughed when he noticed her fixed gaze. "But first, tell me about yourself. Where did you live in Rabat?"

She shrugged. "An apartment."

"With your parents?" he asked.

"My mother."

"Any brothers or sisters?"

"No."

"That's unusual, isn't it?" he asked. "I mean, being an only child, in your country."

"I guess."

"And did you wear those embroidered dresses? What are they called? Caftans?"

"Not really."

He seemed disappointed and, looking down at the steering wheel, he bit his fingernails, tearing strands of cuticles with his teeth.

"What's with all the questions?" she asked. "Are you doing a term paper about me?" she joked.

He threw his head back and laughed. "Of course not," he said, slipping his hand down her thigh. She burrowed through her purse, looking for condoms, and discovered she was out. When she told him this, he said he had extras in the glove box. She opened it, and there, between CDs, maps, and gas-station receipts, was a copy of the Qur'an.

"What's this?" Faten said, sitting straight up, holding the book in her hand.

"Don't touch that," he said, putting it back.

"Why? Is it yours?"

"Yes, it's mine."

She blinked. The brusque tone was not something she was used to from him. "Why do you have it in your glove box?" she asked.

"I'm just reading up," he said. He reached out and caressed her hair. "Can we get on with it?"

She shook her head and passed him the condom. In her experience with men, she'd long concluded that even when they said they only wanted to talk, they always wound up wanting some action, too. Maybe Martín was no different after all.

When it was over, she adjusted her miniskirt and buttoned her corduroy jacket. Martín's questions and his offer of help had caught her unprepared; his wanting to have sex had disappointed her. She felt the same sadness that she had as a child, when she'd discovered that the silkworm she'd raised in a shoe box and lovingly fed mulberry leaves had died, despite all her care. She'd cried all day, wondering what she could have done differently to keep the worm alive, until her aunt came home and told her that that was what happened sometimes with silkworms—they died no matter how carefully you took care of them.

He started the engine. "I'll drop you off if you want."

She opened the door and got out. "I'll just take a taxi."

Faten climbed the stairs to her apartment just as the garbage trucks were making their rounds. She heard one of the men hollering at another in Moroccan Arabic, telling him, as he emptied a bin, that the family at 565 had just had a baby. Cleaning out people's trash, the men got to know everything about everyone's lives. Sometimes Faten felt that way about herself, as though she had been entrusted with people's secrets, and her job was to dispose of them.

Faten found her roommate, Betoul, in the kitchen eating breakfast. Betoul worked as a nanny for a Spanish couple in Gran Vía, and she had to take an early bus in order to get there before 6:30, when the lady of the house required her help. Sometimes Betoul couldn't resist talking about her bosses, how the wife was given to depression, how the husband liked to read his newspaper in the bathroom, leaving urine stains on the floor. But Faten didn't like to hear about the husband at all. She heard enough from the men in her job.

Betoul was from Marrakesh, where she had two younger sisters in university, one brother who worked as a photographer, and another who was still in high school. She was one of those immigrants with the installment plan—she sent regular checks in the mail to help her brothers and sisters. In addition, she lived like a pauper for eleven months of the year and then, in August, she flew home and spent whatever was left in her bank account. Of course, her yearly trips only made people back home think that she made a lot of money, and so she always came back with long lists of requests in her hand and new worry lines etched on her forehead.

In Morocco Betoul would never have lived with Faten, but here things were different. Here, Betoul couldn't put on any airs the way she would have at home. She had moved in with Faten because the rent was cheaper than anything else she could find, allowing her to save even more money to send home.

Faten dropped her bag and keys on the counter. "Good morning."

"Morning," Betoul said. "You left the door unlocked last night."

"I did? I'm sorry."

"You should be more careful. Someone could have gotten in here."

"I'm sorry," she said. "I've been distracted lately."

Betoul nodded and finished her slice of buttered bread. She drank the rest of her coffee standing. Then she put a few grains of *heb rshad* in a hermetically sealed plastic bag, which she stuffed in her purse.

"What's that for?" asked Faten.

"For Ana," Betoul said. Ana was the toddler, the youngest of the three children whom Betoul watched while their parents worked. "She's had a bit of a cold, and so I thought of making her some milk with *heb rshad*."

"Why do you bother?" Faten asked.

Betoul zipped her purse closed.

"I'm sure Ana's mother wouldn't want you giving that to her anyway," Faten said.

"What would you know of what she wants?"

"She'll probably laugh at you and throw it out."

"You're the one people laugh at—the way you sell your body."

Faten felt her anger take over her fatigue. She had been wary of taking Betoul as a roommate. She'd heard a rumor that, back home, when Betoul had found out that her husband, a truck driver, had been cheating on her with a seamstress from Meknes, she'd put a sleeping pill in his soup and then drawn Xs on his cheeks with henna while he slept, leaving him marked for days. Faten had finally agreed to room with her because she wanted someone with a day job, someone whom she wouldn't see much.

"I'm not forcing you to stay here," she said. "You can move if you want."

Betoul left, slamming the door behind her.

Ordinarily, after Faten came home she took a shower, slept until two, and then took a sandwich to the park and watched old couples feeding the pigeons or young ones kissing on the benches. If the weather was too cold, she watched television or went shopping. But today her routine was already off. She couldn't sleep. She stared at the ceiling for a while and then turned to look at her nightstand, where a pocket-sized edition of the Qur'an lay, a thin film of dust over it. She remembered her college days, when she'd decided to wear the hijab and preached to every woman she met that she should do the same. How foolish she had been.

She thought about her best friend, Noura, back in Rabat, and wondered what had happened to her, whether she'd kept the hijab or whether, like Faten, she'd taken it off. Noura was probably still wearing it. She was rich; she had the luxury of having faith. But then, Faten thought, Noura also had the luxury of having no faith; she'd probably found the hijab too constraining and ended up taking it off to show off her designer clothes. That was the thing with money. It gave you choices.

She tried to chase Noura out of her mind. That friendship had cost her too much. She knew that Noura's father, who'd taken a dim view of their friendship, had pulled some strings to have her kicked out of the university. If it hadn't been for him, maybe Faten would have graduated, maybe she wouldn't have been so careless in that moment of anger, maybe she wouldn't have said what she did about the king, maybe she would have finished school, found a job, maybe, maybe, maybe.

She got out of bed and went to the bathroom to get a Valium. The main thing to survive this life was to not think too much. She poured herself a glass of water in the kitchen. Her eye fell on Betoul's calendar, taped to the side of the refrigerator. The Eid holiday was coming up and Betoul had circled the date, probably so she could remember to send a check to her family. It made Faten nostalgic for celebrations, even though she knew there was not much to be nostalgic about. After she had moved back in with her mother in Rabat, Eid amounted to an extra serving at dinner. There were never any new clothes to wear, or a barbecued lamb to eat, or shiny coins to feel in her pocket. Still, she had a certain fondness for those special times because at least her mother didn't work on Eid and they could spend the day together. She pushed the memories out of her mind and shuffled over to the living room.

She lay on the sofa, waiting for the Valium to kick in. There was a program on TV about dromedaries, and she watched, eyes half-closed, as the Spanish voice-over described the mammal's common habitat, his resistance to harsh living conditions, his nomadic patterns, and his many uses: as a beast of burden, for his meat and milk, and even for his dung, which could be burned for fuel. Soon Faten's eyelids grew heavy and she fell asleep.

When Martín showed up again a week later, she didn't feel the same sense of glee that she'd had in the months she'd known him. He came out of the car to ask her to join him, and she hesitated. "What's wrong?" he asked.

She shrugged, her eyes scouring the other cars, but he wouldn't leave. "What do you want?" she asked.

"What do you think?" He laughed. She wasn't sure whether it was with her or at her. He held out his hand and she took it and followed him to the car. Again he drove out to Huertas. A song by Cheb Khaled was on the CD player, and as she listened to the lyrics she wondered whether Martín knew what they meant.

After a few minutes, Martín asked her where she grew up, as he had done the last time, as though he were checking that her answer hadn't changed. This time, she had no illusions about what he wanted. She looked out of the window. "Casablanca," she said.

She thought about her first john, her first week in Spain. The captain of the boat that had brought her here hadn't bothered to land in Tarifa; he'd started turning back as soon as they were within swimming distance of the coast. She'd managed to swim to the beach, where the Spanish Guardia Civil was waiting for them. Later, in the holding cell, she saw how one of the guards had been staring at her. She didn't need to speak Spanish to understand that he'd wanted to make her a deal. She remembered what her imam had said back at the underground mosque in Rabat— that extreme times sometimes demanded extreme measures.

The guard had taken her to one of the private exam rooms, away from everyone else. He lifted her skirt and thrust into her with savage abandon. He was still wearing the surgical gloves he'd had on to examine the group of migrants who'd landed that day. And, all the while, he kept calling her Fatma. And he said other words, words she didn't understand, but that she'd grown used to now. Over the years that followed, she'd had time to hear all the fantasies—those that, had she finished her degree, she might have referred to disdainfully as odalisque dreams. Now they were just part of a repertoire she'd learned by heart and had to put up with if she wanted to make a living.

"Where did you grow up?" Martín asked.

"In a Moorish house."

"With your parents?"

"I didn't see much of my father. I spent all my days in the harem."

"With your siblings?"

"With my six sisters. They initiated me into the art of pleasing men."

Martín chuckled. She could tell he was pleased with the game.

"Why do you come to me?" Faten asked. "There are a lot of girls out there. Like Isabel, and—"

"Women in this country," he said, shaking his head. "They don't know how to treat a man. Not the way you Arab girls do."

Faten felt anger well up in her. She wanted to slap him.

"I've been reading up," he said. "About the duties of the woman to the man, and all that. It's a fascinating subject."

She watched his clear, open face become excited as he told her that he knew things about her and her people. That was the trouble with him. For all his studying, all his declarations of understanding, he was no different than his father. He didn't know anything.

She stared at Martín in silence, trying to visualize herself the way he saw her, the way he wanted her to be—that was the price she would have to pay every time if she wanted to see him. When he started talking about how he wanted to help her get her immigration papers in order, how he cared about her, she raised up her palm to stop him. "I don't need your help," she said.

He gave her a look that made her feel he didn't believe her, then continued talking, as though her acquiescence wasn't required when it came to the matter of helping her, because he knew what was better for her.

"Time's up," she said.

He got his wallet out, without interrupting himself in his plans for her.

"From now on, all the chitchat is extra," she added.

He stopped talking, eyebrows raised in surprise, then handed her a few more bills, which she pocketed.

"I think you should find yourself someone else next time," she said. She opened the car door and got out.

Faten hadn't seen Betoul for ten days. Her schedule had miraculously adjusted after their sharp exchange, to the point that Faten always seemed to come home only a few minutes after Betoul left. Faten would walk in to find the toaster still warm, the dishes still dripping on the rack. By the weekend, Faten decided to do something. She was going to cook a meal for Eid and so, rather than sleep, she spent the better part of her day at work in the kitchen. At home with her mother, meals had been simple: fava beans and olive oil, *rghaif* and tea, bread and olives, couscous on Fridays, whatever her mother could afford to buy. Now that Faten could buy anything she wanted, she didn't know how to make the dishes she'd craved as a teenager. The lamb came out too salty and the vegetables a little burned, but she hoped that Betoul wouldn't mind. She rounded off the meal with pastilla from the Moroccan bakery at the corner, set the table, and waited.

When Betoul finally came home, she stood for a moment with her hand still on the door knob and exhaled loudly.

"How was your day?" Faten asked.

"I'm exhausted."

"Is Ana still sick?"

"No, she's better," Betoul said. "But her mother spent all day in bed, crying. She didn't go to work. She said she's too fat and her husband doesn't want her anymore. So after I took the children to school and put Ana down for her nap, I made her lunch and then let out the waist on a couple of her pants, so they'd fit better."

"Well, you should rest now. I made dinner," Faten said.

"Aren't you working tonight?"

"Not tonight," Faten said. "It's Eid."

Betoul looked as though she wanted to sleep rather than eat, but she said thanks, went to wash up, then sat at the table. Faten served her a generous portion of the lamb. Betoul had a taste. "A bit salty, dear," she said. Faten smiled, feeling grateful for the truth.

Border Crossings

Luis Alfaro

CROSSING THE SPIRIT

My Grandmother from Mexico hates where we live.

She refuses to come visit. We beg and we beg, but she's *muy* set in her place.

It's not our house she dislikes. Not even our *barrio* that she's upset about. Not the fact that we live between buildings in downtown L.A.

My Grandmother from Mexico hates the whole country! She hasn't set foot in the USA since *Ama* and *Apa* got married.

So, what do we do?

We meet in a magical place my brother and I call TJ. Tijuana.

We don't like to tell people, especially other kids on our block, because then they'll call us TJs. But in reality we love Tijuana like one can love Knights of Columbus parades.

Tijuana is one of those places that you have to let yourself get sucked up by. It's one of those places that you can't visit with too many expectations.

To the adults in my family, Tijuana means poverty, midnight outhouse trips, and unpaved roads. But to the kids of Tijuana Summers with My Grandmother from Mexico it's one big *rancho* playground where we ride in buses with no doors. The people on those buses carry little pigs and roosters on their laps. And they're alive. Yes, the animals are alive!

In Tijuana Summers with My Grandmother from Mexico, you can sit or run up aisles in Mexican movie theaters with scratchy soundtracks. You can walk down the *avenida* and catch a glimpse of a woman's *chi-chis* in a magazine. On any corner you can buy pickled pork skins, *cueritos*, cut up and served real *especial*—in a funneled-up newspaper. And my favorite Tijuana adventure: *colonias*, the colonies, that are like secret little villages nestled deep in a valley by a hillside.

My Grandmother from Mexico lives in a colonia where the goats go anywhere they want. Cool, huh?

My Ama thinks that My Grandmother from Mexico is *muy loca*. She claims that My Grandmother from Mexico marches through the streets of Tijuana with the ragtag musicians in the *banda de guerras*, holding a shotgun and pledging her allegiance to the State *y la causa*.

My Apa says his mother is a saint, a *santita*, who only wishes to keep the tradition, *la tradición*, of what it means to be a true *Mexicana* in her heart. My Apa says My Grandmother from Mexico is just like *el* Abraham Lincoln.

My Grandmother from Mexico has a gun. One of those big ones like on *Bonanza*. She has never relied on the kindness of men to help her get by in the world. My Grandmother from Mexico has always lived alone.

But, My Grandmother from Mexico has a "friend."

My Grandmother from Mexico is best friends with The Virgen. That's right, *La Virgen de Guadalupe*. She's got a big old altar to her and everything. The only real friend she's ever had is The Virgen. My Apa says it's okay if she's a religious fanatic. The two old ladies can keep each other company.

The other grandmother, My Grandmother from America, she's just okay. She lives in in a dusty town, Delano, and there's not really much up there but grapes. And you know, in kids' terms, that holds your interest for about *un minuto*.

So, when My Ama and My Apa announced they were going to a Catholic couples retreat to work on their "reconciliation," whatever that means, my brother and I were given permission to experience a TJ vacation.

We told the kids on our block that we were going to Florida, 'cause, *you know....*

When we arrive at My Grandmother from Mexico's house, everything is nice and dusty, just the way we like it. My Grandmother from Mexico doesn't like to talk to us too much, or try to hug us, or kiss us. And God knows, we like her distance a lot. Most of the time she spends it talking to The Virgen and knitting things for her or making little *cositas* for her altar.

That summer in Tijuana turned out to be the worst when My Ama and My Apa told My Grandmother from Mexico that we were ready and available to continue our altar boy duties in another country. That we would welcome the opportunity to celebrate the mystery of Christ anyplace that he might be found.

Well, let me just say in my own defense, that it never occurred to me that Jesus Christ might be found in Tijuana. But Our Lord was a big fixture in TJ. He should have opened a nightclub or played in the jai alai. He was that big!

Each colonia in Tijuana celebrates the mystery of Christ in its own unique way. The Sunday we were offered up as the sacrificial altar boys, there was to be a procession to the church and we had to be at the little parish, *Santa* something or other, an hour early to prepare everything for the march.

As we stood outside the church with the priest (I was *incense* and my brother was *holy water),* we noticed a group of about a hundred people gathered in a big circle. Something was going on in the center of that crowd but we couldn't tell what it was.

Slowly the mob moved and as they got closer and closer you could see women with veils on their heads crying. All of the men had taken off their hats as a sign of respect.

As they approached us, the crowd began to part, as if a big Red Sea. As the figure emerged, my brother uttered an "Oh man..."

A woman had crawled on her knees from the center of the colonia all the way to the parish. That's far in knee-walking. With shredded rags she had tied a pillow to each knee to make the journey of penance a less painful one. But the makeshift absorbers were not enough in the unpaved village and as her skin hit pavement, she left a trail of blood behind.

She moved slowly from knee to knee toward us.

I could see the pain and the guilt on my brother's face. He could see the embarrassment in mine. Because, of course, the bloody martyr with the bloody knees of Mexico was a husbandless, nationalistic Mexican who owned a gun and sewed cositas at an altar for The Virgen. A Grandmother from Mexico.

She wasn't My Grandmother from Mexico after that. As far as we were concerned, she never would be again.

Grandmothers from Somewhere Else bake cookies, go to Vegas on weekend turnarounds, and watch *novelas* quietly. They don't crawl through their barrios like freaks, right?

That night, my brother and I lied through our teeth about food poisoning and called our parents back home.

When My Apa came to pick us up, I faked a kiss on My Grandmother from Mexico's cheek. My brother was worse. He shook Grandma's hand and ran to the car shouting, "Good to see you Granny!"

Later, in the car, as we drove past the brightly lit Del Mar racetrack, I tried to sleep, but all I could do was obsess about the bloody knees of Mexico.

In my heart, I know I wanted to go back to the Tijuana I loved. Bumper-car buses, little boxes of Chiclets, armless street-vendors and shops with dead pig heads.

But it was never going to be that again.

From then on it was Summers with My Grandmother from America and picking grapes with the Pentecostals.

CROSSING WHO I AM

This year, my Cousin Weenie, who only eats once a day, is hosting our family reunion in Fresno.

Everyone's happy because she always kills and cooks a pig at the family reunions, and that's something that's really big with us.

My Ama thinks a family reunion is a bad idea because so many relatives died this year and we've already seen everybody at Muriaga's Mortuary. Besides, everybody is just going to be depressed.

My Uncle Abel, the one-legged alcoholic Vietnamer, says he already ordered the kegs of beer and what we should really be celebrating is "those" who are still alive. Which means he's gone off the wagon again and midway through the reunion he'll either fall asleep in the driveway or make somebody cry.

My Ama resigns herself to preparing a tub of potato salad that all the relatives think tastes "restaurant-style."

We hop into the station wagon and head for the Greyhound bus station downtown. All of us wear our Sunday best and I've got my favorite clip-on tie purchased at Sears. Clip-on ties make every kid look important and faithful to God.

We take the Greyhound bus to Fresno because My Apa doesn't want to use up the engine on our brand-new station wagon, which, he says, is only designed "for the city."

At the family reunion I count more than 120 Alfaros.

After the required Big Circle Prayer (totally embarrassing) and the Three-Legged Races with Drunken Uncles, I always go to the backyard and to the garden with my aunt's fish pond. She put it right next to the pig pen because, she says, it makes the pigs more "relaxed and happy." They are more tender as ham because they didn't have a lot of stress in their lives due to their peaceful surroundings.

I love going to see the koi fish in the pond because it is the cleanest place in Fresno and because my aunt designed it all *Chino*-style. I don't know, maybe Auntie's right. Beneath the red pagoda, the pigs look really relaxed and happy.

But the best thing about the garden is that this is where Uncle Constantin, or "Constance," as My Ama calls him, sits and smokes long skinny cigarettes with a holder.

He always hangs out in the garden by himself smoking his Virginia Slims. He is always dressed in white, with a scarf around his neck and rings dripping off his fingers.

Uncle Constantin is the star of our family reunions.

Everybody talks about him as he makes his way through the crowds of family, kissing aunties on their cheeks and shaking uncles' hands. He pretends not to hear them gossip and giggle as he makes his way through the crowd.

Although Uncle Constantin looks like a movie star, I have heard my *tías*, Romie and Cuca, whisper over *cafesito* in the kitchen—about all the times that "Constance" has been in prison.

Uncle Constantin smells all brand-new with the scent of *Tres Flores* brilliantine holding back his salt-and-pepper hair and the Grey Flannel smoothly escaping through the back of his neck. You can only see his dark side when he rolls up the sleeves on his white shirt and you notice the markings. Dark blue, like the color of the ocean at night, the designs snake up the inside of his arm and on the joints of his fingers.

Tattoo names in deep Cholo writing. Aztec symbols pricked by home-made needles. The dot dot dot of prison life covers him like a map on the skin.

When I ask about the markings, he takes a long Ida Lupino drag on his cigarette. He looks skyward and the smoke escapes through his nose and heads to God in heaven.

I want to be that pose. I don't know why, but I can feel it inside of me.

The crease on his pants, the scarf loose on the neck, the markings on the hand, the deep dark mysterious world of *knowing*.

When he looks down at me sitting there on the grass, cross-legged in my clip-on and Sunday suit, he doesn't say anything; he just smiles. And he gives me a look. Not just any look. The look of *knowing*.

"You and I understand each other, don't we?" he says. *Nos entendemos muy bien.*

He says it like he looked deep behind my esophagus and found the tiny heart beating under the shell of me.

We look at each other for the longest time until I get ashamed of whatever it is that is making my heart beat so fast. It's not a love feeling at all, but more like when you're at the zoo and you stare at the animals for such a long time that you end up seeing a reflection of yourself in one of them.

His smile turns to a reassuring gaze.

I smile back and hold it this time. It feels good. I can see the mirror of myself. And I don't know why, but I feel like someone finally looked inside of me and found me. Me, struggling through the gang infested poverty loneliness hate sadness poor Mexican violent crowded dirty drunk corner bullshit drive by horror show, that is my neighborhood downtown.

Someone saw the little garden inside of me.

On the bus ride home, I sit in silence in the last row of the Greyhound. I feel calm as my brother, who is sitting next to me, lowers his head leaning deeper into my shoulder with every breath of deep sleep.

My Ama looks over at us, but her eyes lock into mine. She always looks at me with a worried gaze. She never knows what to make of me. Always wondering and worrying about me, My Ama.

"*¿Que te pasa?*" she says.

But today on the bus, I look back at her and I smile like I smile at

Uncle Constantin. And this time I hold it for her, like a gift. I can tell it freaks her out as she turns to whisper with My Apa.

I watch as we pass the THANKS FOR VISITING BAKERSFIELD sign and I think to myself,

I know who I am....

I know who I am.

CROSSING BOYHOOD

The Three Mexican Musketeers.

That's what we were. Small time change in the big slot machine of a city.

Uno por todo y todo por Uno!

My brother was the head Musketeer and I worshipped him like little kids worshipped Muhammad Ali. I loved him because he always opened the back door of the bus so that I could sneak on.

The third Musketeer was our neighbor, Gabriel Ochoa, the darkest Mexican on our block. So dark they called him *El Negrito*. We befriended Gabriel after his dog, Brandy, died. We felt sorry and and helped dig out a grave in his backyard. Stole plywood from the project's construction site and made a big cross like we had seen at our parish. After that, Gabriel was our friend, even though he ate non-Mexican food like waffles and crepes.

But we had things in common. He was "fatherless" due to a long-ago divorce, and we were fatherless due to a lost-cause dad who spent his days at the *Club Jalisco*.

One summer, we searched the neighborhood for soda bottles. Turned them in for the five-cent deposit so we could pay for bus fare and kids' admission to the movies. We stood in the front of the Tower Theater at Seventh and Broadway looking for somebody who would pretend to be our parent and buy us tickets for an R-rated kung fu movie.

All of a sudden, Gabriel started to cry.

Not just cry, but sob, like he saw the devil, saw a ghost.

"I saw my dad."

That's what he said, just like that. Said he saw his dad drive by in front of the Tower Theater and wave at him.

And I just didn't get it. I told him that if I had seen my dad driving by, I would run up and get in the car and make him buy me a Tommy Burger.

But Gabriel's dad had been gone so long that he made us stand in front of the Tower Theater waiting for his dad for about an hour.

We missed the first showing of *The Chinese Connection*. I prayed we wouldn't be late for *Enter the Dragon*. The thing about Chinese kung fu movies is that if you miss the first five minutes, you miss the whole reason why they spend the rest of the movie fighting.

But I couldn't rush Gabriel, who was waiting for another chance to see his long-lost *Papa*.

Right when it seemed like we were just about to die because the previews were on, that old green station wagon pulled up in front of the theater again. Gabriel's dad smiled all nice like maybe he had only been gone a few minutes. Like maybe a few years ago he just went out to buy milk for the kids and now he was back.

Gabriel didn't even say good-bye. Didn't even give us his movie entrance money or nothing. He hopped in the car and took off like he'd waited all his life in front of the Tower Theater for his dad to just drive by and pick him up.

And that was the last that we saw of Gabriel.

We went in and watched all of *Enter the Dragon* and did not have a clue as to why Bruce Lee was angry.

Later that night, Gabriel's mom came over and started asking where Gabriel was. My Ama brought her into our room and she looked terrified, wearing her tamale apron and her hair up in curlers. When my brother told her that he went with his dad, she fell down on our floor sobbing and screaming. She went crazy right in front of us. My Ama tried to pick her up off the floor as she screamed, "He stole my son, he stole my son. *Me lo robó, me lo robó...*"

I told My Ama to call the police—but no one did. In our neighborhood no one ever calls the police. Sometimes you call the ambulance or the morgue, but never the police. There are too many *illegales* in our barrio, My Apa included, to have the police snooping around looking for wetbacks.

At that very moment, Gabriel and his dad were probably way past the border and deep into the night on a Mexican highway.

And that was the night that the voice went out of Gabriel's mom. She never spoke again.

For the next six months, the remaining two Musketeers, my brother and I, hung out in front of the Tower Theater. Wondering, and maybe hoping, that a green station wagon was cruising down Broadway looking for us.

10 September

Rashad Majid

Translated from the Azerbaijani by Samed Safarov

Leaving the hospital, Rza went toward his car. It was a Zhiguli 06 he'd acquired by entering his name in a queue during the Soviet period. He took the "TAXI" board from between the front seats and fixed it on the roof of the car. He had come to the hospital to see the surgeon. His middle daughter needed an operation, and every doctor he had talked to told him that it would cost no less than $300. An old friend had recommended this military surgeon saying, "He is a professional, but he is not a greedy man."

Their talk was not so bad, indeed. They agreed on a $100 fee, plus $50 for the doctor's assistants. Rza had $100 already. When the first doctors described to him the importance of the operation, he cut down on everything, even the children's food, and saved dollar by dollar. Now he just needed to find fifty dollars more.

He reached the Narimanov underground station and thought maybe he should hurry on to share the news with his wife, that the operation seemed within reach. But there were no other taxis in sight at the car park. If he stopped there would be a fare.

The car park had been his best place for years now. The plant at the end of the street—the place he had worked for seventeen years, receiving awards for his service—had gradually reduced its production then shut down. His neighbor, Islam, had worked at the Azerbaijan Trade Center Base. A rich man then, he had helped his neighbors, sold goods for them without profit. When the base closed, he had to make his living driving a taxi. When the plant closed, Rza took Islam's advice and did the same. At first, he was a bit shy. Sometimes his fares were friends or people he knew, and he did not like to take money from them. As time passed, he got used to it. He found new comrades and workmates

in the car park. There were former workers from the district committee, engineers and doctors among them.

A tap on the windshield brought Rza back from deep thought, and he
saw two Americans, a short, stout man and a medium-sized, thin woman,
both holding full grocery bags. Rza reached back and opened the rear door.

"Please, please," the woman said. She gave an address in the direction of the city, and he turned toward Moskow Avenue. In the rearview
mirror, he saw the man take a baklava out of the grocery bag. They are
always eating, he thought. Americans barely chewed the pastry, but swallowed each piece nearly whole.

He drove into the city, stopped in front of a high building, a new construction, on the woman's order. She gave him a ten thousand manat bill,
the customary fare, thanked him, and hurried away. The man was still eating
and got out with difficulty, dragging the bags. Rza watched them walk toward
the entrance, then drove toward home.

Two months after his marriage, Rza's father had given him the money
he collected from selling his cows and sheep, so he could buy the small
shack where his family still lived. There were two rooms, a little kitchen,
and a yard that could hold his car. Later he'd built the toilet in the entrance
of his yard. Reaching the gate he honked the horn, and his wife came
outside and opened it.

He told her about the military surgeon, feeling glad again, and after dinner
went into the back room to sleep. A window faced his neighbor's yard, and
often the rattle of dishes, the babble of water, and children's noises kept
him awake. But it was silent now. Maybe his wife told them he needed
rest. They were aware of her talent from God and wanted to please her.

His wife had worked as a kindergarten teacher during the Soviet
period. Then there were mainly books about Lenin in the schools, but
when the state was about to collapse, somebody brought religious books
from Iran, with large Cyrillic print, and presented them to the kindergarten. This was around the time the plant shut down. When the kindergarten also closed, his wife brought the books into their home. It seemed
strange to him to see her reading them for hours at a time. She sometimes spoke about the Qur'an and the Prophet Muhammad's life. Often

her comments—those about hellish fire waiting for non-believers—had frightened him.

Rza remembered the party card that his wife kept in her dowry trunk—and his own, too. When Russian troops entered Baku and killed unarmed people, he blamed Gorbachev, not the party. When Yeltsin stopped the party's activity with a decree, he refused to throw away his card. He believed in the return of communism. Surely, such a huge state could not collapse so easily, he thought. In time, life would be as it had been before.

But things did not change and, little by little, the number of religious books increased. His wife began covering her head when she went out. Sometimes women from the neighborhood came to the house to pray; then unfamiliar women came too. One day his wife told him that, in a dream, a saintly man in a white turban gave her something in a gleaming gold basin to drink and, waking up in the morning, she knew extraordinary things.

Unemployment and poverty had caused these changes in his wife, he believed. Still, he was angry with her. He demanded she stop interfering with the lives of their neighbors and inviting strange women to their home.

Then Islam invited him to a teahouse. Totally changed from the fun-loving person he had been, Islam had given up drinking and spent time at the mosque. He wore the short beard favored by religious men. When Rza described his wife's dream, Islam said that God granted such gifts only to righteous, honest people.

"Let her help her neighbors," he said. "It will be pleasing to God."

He gave Rza advice as well. "Give up drinking, my friend, throw away your party card. Remove anything bad from your house."

He suggested Rza go on a hadj pilgrimage to cleanse his soul.

Rza did not go on the pilgrimage, but in time believed in his wife's extraordinary ability. In a dream, she had seen their middle daughter sick and, in two weeks' time, the girl wasn't eating, was getting thin. The first doctor said one of her kidneys must be removed. Two more told him the same thing. He recognized power in his wife then, and felt a bit afraid.

When he woke from his nap it was nearly five. He washed his hands and face and returned to the kitchen for *News at Five* on Space TV. The program began with a report on the return of the Garabagh Armenians to Baku for an international conference the next day, 11 September. Rza watched bitterly, remembering the Garabagh Liberation Organization's protest, their refusal to meet with opposition parties. The West should not interfere with our problems, he thought. They do not know us. He turned away from the television to drink the tea his wife had prepared for him, and noticed a yellow handbag on the table.

"What is this?" he asked.

"Our girls found it in your car."

"Did they open it?"

"I closed it and put it there."

Rza opened the handbag and put its contents on the table. A comb, a credit card, a few thousand- and ten thousand-manat bills, and seventeen hundred-dollar bills.

His wife watched him; his daughters stood by the door. He looked at his middle daughter and smiled. "It belongs to the American couple I picked up earlier," he told them. "I must return it."

His daughters stepped inside. His wife picked up the tea and said, "It has gone cold. Let me change it."

He drank the hot tea, then left the house with the handbag. In his heart, he believed that the couple would be so glad to see him that they would give him one of the hundred-dollar bills. He would have the money for his daughter's operation to present to the doctor tomorrow.

On his way to their apartment, he stopped at the car park by the underground. The taxi drivers made a habit of leaving their doors open while they talked in the shade of the nearby trees, so that the inside of their cars would not get hot as they waited for clients. Akif and the man they called "Doctor" stood up as soon as they saw him.

Akif spoke first. "Two Americans came looking for you and left their visiting card. They had a translator, too. He said they got into a red Zhiguli and left a woman's handbag there, that the driver was black-mustached and short. Is there anything in the handbag?"

Rza was about to answer when Doctor interrupted him.

"They would not have come without good reason. An American will not trouble himself for every trifle. I'm guessing there is a thousand dollars in that handbag. They should give you at least a hundred when you take it back," he smiled. "You must give a little banquet for this reason."

"I am on my way to give it back to them."

Akif held out the visiting card. "I remember the address," Rza said, but took it anyway. The card was in English, of course. He read the name "Jim" easily, but could not read the surname. There was a map on the back of the card, with an arrow indicating floor eleven of their building.

"Do not forget the banquet!" Doctor said.

"Be sure I will give you the banquet, if they give me a hundred dollars!" Rza said.

He got into his car and drove toward Baksoviet, to the building where the Americans lived. It was surrounded with an iron fence, so he approached the guardhouse on foot. He showed the visiting card to the tall security man dressed in black and explained why he was there. The man looked at the card, went into the guardhouse, and talked to someone on the phone. "Enter the lift and go to the eleventh floor," he said when he came out. "They are waiting for you."

Rza squeezed the handbag as he went upstairs. One of the two doors in the corridor was half-open, sound coming from inside. He pushed the door open a bit farther. The stout man was there, holding a small dog in his arms, smoothing its curly fur. "Please wait," he said.

He disappeared and returned with the woman. Rza held out the handbag to her. She took it quickly, opened it, checked everything. She counted the dollars and said, "Right." She replaced the money in her purse and held out her hand to him. "Thank you," she said. "I am grateful."

He let go of the woman's thin, wrinkled hand, and she closed the door. He stood dazed for a long time before turning away. He pushed the elevator button. Waiting, he imagined his wife's face, the face of his middle daughter when he told them the news. He thought of the banquet he had promised his friends waiting underneath a tree. He should have denied finding the handbag, he thought. Who could have proven that it had been left in his car? He felt sick at the thought of it—and foolish for having so many times argued against his friends, who believed Americans came to Azerbaijan only for their own benefit, only interested in oil.

His friends were still there, under the tree.

They stood, glad to see him.

Akif asked, "How was it? Did they give anything?"

"Yes," he lied. "They gave me one hundred dollars."

"Ah, now we are going to celebrate?" Doctor said.

"Let me put away the car first."

"You want to drink I see," said Akif, smiling.

Rza did not answer.

He drove home and left the car at the gate, unwilling to take the trouble to drive it into the yard. When he entered the house, his wife asked, "How was it?"

"They gave me nothing," he said, and turned away from her.

He took off his shoes and entered the bedroom. He opened the built-in cupboard, and from the top drawer counted out ten thousand-manat bills and put them into his pocket. As he put his shoes back on, his wife asked, "Are you going somewhere?"

"I must give a little banquet to the friends," he said.

It was written on his wife's face that she was angry, but Rza walked out the door and got into Akif's car.

They went to their usual café, ordered kebab, waited for Doctor. Vagif was his real name, Rza remembered. A graduate of the Medical University, a children's doctor, who found no profit in it. For a time, he imported foreign goods, but went bankrupt like Islam. Akif had earned a degree in history at the University and worked at the Historical Institute. When the Soviet Union collapsed he was about to defend his thesis. History forgotten, he'd been driving his taxi for fifteen years.

Akif and Doctor drank the first three toasts to Rza, his family, and his middle daughter. The bottle was nearly empty when Rza raised his glass. "I want to drink to our nation," he said. "Anybody would have rewarded me with one hundred dollars. I returned seventeen hundred to them. But the Americans did not give even ten thousand manat. They looked at me as if I were indebted to them. A Russian would give, a German would give." Rza stopped, scratched his head. "An Armenian would give, as well. But the Americans…"

Doctor and Akif looked at each other in astonishment, then at the fatty tail and lule kebab getting cold. Rza went on. "Don't reproach me! I gave this banquet because I never break a promise. I will find money for my daughter's operation. I used to say, you have never known an American so you cannot know what they are like. Why do you speak against them?

"Today I learned it is not so simple. They collapsed the Soviet Union—such a good state—and made us slaves to their benefits. Now they come to take away our oil, and do this as they look down on us. They won't even help to get back Garabagh."

Rza raised his hand. "Malay, bring one more bottle of vodka."

Akif fidgeted in his place. Doctor started to say something.

"No," Rza said. "Let's just drink today."

It was after midnight when they left the café. Akif stopped at the gate. Rza continued his words against America until Akif managed to talk him out of the car.

"What if I put your car into the yard for you?" he asked.

Rza refused. He searched for the key in his pocket so that he could do it himself. His wife came to the door. She said nothing, though he knew she had intended to remind him about the stealing in their neighborhood.

"Let it remain there," he said.

He went inside, threw himself onto the bed.

"Don't take it to heart. Everything will be all right," said his wife.

At first Rza only pretended to sleep.

In the morning, he felt a dull pain in his head. His wife was sitting opposite him on the bed. "I had a terrible dream," she said, shaking, "of huge buildings on fire."

"Have you checked the car?" Rza asked.

"The car is okay."

"What about the girls?"

"They are fine. But something terrible is coming. I beg you…"

"I will give up the drinking," he said.

"I am very afraid…" she continued.

Rza looked into her eyes. He realized he wanted to know more about her fears, to share them, to see the fire in his wife's dreams. "We will get up and go to the mosque," he said.

He noticed her hands still trembling.

The Way Love Works

Mary Yukari Waters

I was thirteen when my mother and I flew back to Japan on what, unbeknownst to us, would be our final visit together. I was eager, after a five-year absence and eleven hours of flying, to see our family. But upon emerging from airport customs into a wall of searching eyes, it took some moments to spot them. They were standing shoulder-to-shoulder, pressed up against the rails: Grandma, Aunt Miho, Uncle Koku, my cousins, Grandpa Ichiro with his special-occasion beret. A fraction of a second later, I felt Mother's carry-on bag swipe my arm as she rushed past me toward her mother.

The rest of us watched, keeping such a respectful distance from Mother and Grandma that several travelers used the space as a pathway, momentarily blocking them from our sight. The two women faced each other and gripped hands, their knuckles white. Being Japanese, that was all they did, but with such trembling intensity, like lovers, that I almost shriveled with embarrassment.

Mother and Grandma stayed indoors during the entire month of our visit, chatting away with hardly a break. They paused only out of politeness to others: my Aunt Miho, who lived a few houses away; Grandpa Ichiro, asking questions about America (Do they eat bread at every meal?); phone calls; visitors. "I'm *bored!*" I said. "Can't I go swimming? Can't I go to Summer Haunted House?"

"Go with your cousins," they suggested. "We'll just stay here." They waved good-bye from the doorway as Aunt Miho, with us four children in tow, headed down the alley to the bus stop under the glaring summer sun. When we reached the corner and looked back for a final wave, the two of them were bending over some potted bonsai trees, already engrossed in conversation. They saw us, quickly straightened, and waved in unison.

I grew familiar with the ebb and flow of their talk. In the mornings—while cooking breakfast, washing up, walking to the open-air market—it was bright and animated, bubbling over with bits of gossip, or additions to previous conversations, which had risen to the surface of their memories during sleep. Afternoons—in the lull between lunch and four o'clock, when the local bathhouse opened—gave rise to more sustained, philosophical topics. Since Grandpa Ichiro took his nap then, it was also a good time for whispered confidences. "Nobody knows this except you," I heard Grandma say many times. They sometimes discussed mysterious financial issues: in the trash can I found scratch paper with hastily scrawled calculations using multiplication and long division.

I hadn't caught such nuances when I was eight; now I watched these comings and goings with avid foreign eyes. But even more fascinating than these allegiances was the change in my mother.

Five years earlier, my mother, my Caucasian father, and I had sold our home in Japan and moved to a small logging town in northern California, surrounded by miles of walnut and plum orchards. "Did you meet up with your husband when he was in the service?" Americans always asked Mother. She hated that question. "Don't these people *think*?" she fumed in private. "Do they even realize what they're insinuating?"

"No...he was never in the service," she always replied, as if in apology. "I have never had the honor of meeting a service man."

"Oh honey," the neighborhood women told me, "your momma's just *precious!*"

Back in America, Mother spoke English: heavily accented and sometimes halting, but always grammatically correct. When she felt light-hearted, she broke into Japanese with me. For the most part, however, she was a severe disciplinarian. She never lounged. She never snacked between meals. She scrubbed, gardened, hand-laundered, even in cold weather when the skin on her fingertips split open in raw cracks. She pulled back her hair, which was glossy even though she used nothing on it but Johnson's Baby Shampoo, into a French twist. Only occasionally at bedtime would I see it undone at shoulder length, making her face look unformed and girlish.

But here in Japan, she gossiped, giggled, teased. Once or twice I caught her watching me with that eager, open look of someone in love.

While Grandma made miso soup for breakfast, Mother stood before the cupboard and nibbled on red bean cakes, beckoning for me to join her. I did, warily.

"Koraa!" Grandma scolded, coming in from the kitchen with the tray.

"But Mama," Mother protested in a loud voice, with a conspiratorial glance at me, "these taste so *good*... Meli-chan and I are so *hungry*..."

I remember thinking that each language carried its own aura, its own mood, and that people fell under its spell.

"I suppose it's only courteous," Mother said, "to visit Miho's house in return. After all, she's always coming over here."

"Yes, you're absolutely right," Grandma said. "But hurry back."

"How come Grandma likes you best?" I asked my mother as the two of us walked toward Aunt Miho's house.

She laughed it off with her new, playful air. "Saa, I have so many special qualities," she said. "I'm irreplaceable."

Aunt Miho was young and pretty; I had often fantasized about having her for a big sister. She and Mother were half-sisters, due to some family complication I grasped only dimly at the time. Aunt Miho's father was Grandpa Ichiro. Mother's father—my own true grandfather—was long dead.

"How's your visit so far?" Aunt Miho asked me at the lunch table. "Are you having lots of fun?" Her intonation was gentle and courteous, like that of a JAL stewardess, with each word hanging in perfect balance.

"Yes, Auntie," I said.

"Hajime said he heard lots of laughing the other night," she said, "when he passed by your place on his way home from work." We all looked at Aunt Miho's husband who glanced up, discomfited, from his plate of skewered miso dumplings.

"Oh, there must have been something funny on TV," Mother said. "The Nishikawa Gang, probably. Do you ever watch it? That is a *hilarious* show."

"Oh it *is*!" I assured Aunt Miho. "Grandma was saying she hasn't laughed like this in years!"

"Oh," said Aunt Miho. "How nice."

On the tatami floor, right under the low table where we all sat, I noticed a leather-bound Bible. By overhearing—or eavesdropping—I knew that Aunt

Miho had turned Christian during our absence. I lifted the book out into the open; Mother frowned and jerked her head no.

I put the book back.

"You can look at that anytime you like," said Aunt Miho in her serene voice. "It's filled with strange and wonderful stories. About loving without limits. Despite anything others might do."

"Even if they're *murderers*?" I asked. Mother shot me a cold glance.

Aunt Miho smiled. "There is no power," she said, "greater than forgiveness." Aunt Miho's husband, a quiet man, got up and went to the bathroom.

"A *hilarious* show…" murmured nine-year-old Sachiko, who was an admirer of Mother's. I glanced over at my three younger cousins— Sachiko, Keiko, and Tomoko—sitting quietly at the far end of the table. With what must have been ease of habit, they had filled their glasses with exactly four ice cubes each and had lined them up, side by side, on the table. They peered, unblinking, as their mother poured the Fanta Orange, the children hunching down at the low table so as to be eye-level with the glasses, thus ensuring that no sibling got a milliliter more than the others.

"Did you see them with those drinking glasses?" Mother said on our way back. We were taking a long detour to Heibuchi Alley so that she could buy some rice wine for dinner. "If you had brothers and sisters, that's what you'd be doing. See how lucky you are, being an only child?"

I did. I would undoubtedly lose out in a competition of favorites. With a flush of shame, I remembered my behavior back home: how I constantly contradicted Mother in an exasperated tone, taking advantage of her ineptness in what, for her, was a foreign country.

But my behavior had changed since our arrival; the language also cast its spell over me. I was fluent in Japanese—it was my first language—but since our move to America, my vocabulary had stayed at a fourth grade level. So in Japan my speech, even my thoughts, reverted from those of a cocky teenager to the more innocent, dependent child I had been five years ago. Here I was no longer capable of arguing with the contemptuous finesse I used back home. Here I was at a loss.

"But don't worry, Meli-chan," my mother said. "I could never have feelings for any other child but you." I was still unused to *chan*, that tender diminutive to a little girl's name for which English has no equivalent. Hearing such words, after all those years in America, made my throat grow tight. I could not have talked back, even if I had the words.

Mother took advantage of my weakened state. She slipped her hand into mine, a big girl like me, right in public. During the course of our stay, she would do this several times—tentatively at first, then with increasing confidence as the month wore on. This would not last once we flew home; the mere act of standing on American soil would destroy that precarious balance.

Now Mother strode along leading the way. Among the local Japanese, she seemed much taller than her five feet three inches. Near the steps of Heibuchi Shrine, we ran into Mr. Inoue, her former high school principal. "I hope you take after your mother," he told me. "She was the first girl from Ueno District to pass Kyoto University entrance exams." I stood with my hand damp and unmoving in my mother's, still bashful from our newfound intimacy. I watched the old man bowing with slow, ceremonious respect. I heard their polite conversation, replete with advanced verb conjugations. My mother's sentences flowed sinuously, with nuances of silver and light, like a strong fish gliding through Kamo River.

The next day, I asked Mother whom she loved best in the world.

"My mother, of course," she replied. We were coming home from the open-air market. She was walking ahead of me; the alley was too narrow for the two of us to walk abreast. Dappled shadows jerked and bobbed on the back of her parasol.

"And my dad?"

"He's number two."

"Who's number three?"

"You! Of course." But I suspected, with a flash of intuition, that I was a very close third, probably even a tie for second. Not that I deserved it. I was an unpleasant teenager, whereas my father was a good, kind man. Nonetheless I belonged to this Japanese world, whose language and blood ties gave my mother such radiant power, in a way my American father never could.

"Who's number four?" I asked, assured of my good status. "Who's number five?" Too late. Mother's thoughts had drifted somewhere else.

"When you come first in someone's heart," she said, "when you feel the magnitude of another person's love for you..." Her gait slowed, along with her speech. "You become a different person. I mean, something physically changes inside of you." Her voice choked up behind the parasol and I hoped she was not going to cry. "I want you to know that feeling," she said. "Because it'll sustain you, all your life. Life...life can get so hard."

So hard.... Was she referring to my behavior back home? Guilty and defensive, I trailed my fingers along a low adobe wall in nonchalant fashion, over its braille of pebbles and straw. A smell of earth, intensified by midsummer heat, wafted toward me.

My relationship with my mother was not a bad one, by normal standards. I understand this now. But back then, the only yardstick either of us had was the bond between Mother and Grandma; it must have been a disappointment to my mother, as it was to me that summer, that we could not replicate it.

"You're Grandma's favorite grandchild," my mother said eventually in a recovered voice.

"Really?" I said, gratified. That question had been next on my agenda.

"Don't flatter yourself," she said, "that it's on your own merits. Not yet. It's because you're my child. You reach her through me. Remember that."

"Okay," I agreed. The *k'sha k'sha* of gravel was loud beneath our sandals. The buzz of late afternoon traffic floated over from Shinbonmachi Boulevard, several blocks down.

"You and I are lucky," Mother said. "Some people never come first." I thought of Aunt Miho, how she had turned back at the corner to wave.

In silence we entered the shade of a large ginkgo tree, which leaned out over the adobe wall into the alley. Its fan-shaped leaves, dangling from thin stems, fluttered and trembled.

Mother stopped walking and lowered her parasol, turning her head this way and that. The *meeeeee* of cicadas was directly overhead now, sharpened from a mass drone into the loud rings of specific creatures; each with a different pitch, a different location among the branches.

"Take a good look around, Meli-chan," she said, attempting to make a sweeping gesture with an arm weighed down by a plastic bag full of daikon radishes and lotus roots. "This alley hasn't changed a bit since I was a girl. It's still got the *feel* this whole city used to have, once."

I looked. My eyes, still accustomed to California sun, registered this new light of a foreign latitude: a hushed gold approaching amber, angling across the alley in dust-moted shafts as if through old stained glass. An aged world. I pictured Mother playing here decades ago, to the drone of cicadas and the occasional ting of a wind chime: countless quiet afternoons, their secrets lost to the next generation.

"Ara maa!" Mother said regretfully. "Somebody's gone and replaced their slatted wooden doors with that all-weather metal kind."

Aunt Miho visited us frequently. Several times, when the grown-ups were reminiscing about old times and everyone sat basking in familial warmth and intimacy, she took the opportunity to slip in something about Love or The Lord. Our laughter trailed away, and we fell silent as she talked: Mother, nodding with restless eyes (When did Miho start using that *voice*? she said in private); Grandma, her gaze averted with a certain sorrowful submission.

Aunt Miho targeted Grandma and Mother. Grandpa Ichiro was spared; he was losing his hearing, usually off in a world of his own. I, too, was excused, since my vocabulary was insufficient for grasping the finer points of Christian theory. "Wait, what does that word mean?" I demanded anyway at crucial moments. "Wait, wait! What does it *mean*?"

In the late afternoons, I overheard Grandma and Mother talking. "Childhood insecurities," Mother whispered.

Grandma sighed. "It's all my fault," she said.

"It is *not* your fault!" Mother said.

It came to a head one week before our departure. My cousin, four-year-old Tomoko, came into the kitchen where Grandma and Mother and I were sitting. "Mama says you don't want to come with us to Heaven," she accused, clasping her tiny arms around Grandma's knees and gazing up at her with moist, reproachful eyes. "Ne, is that true?"

"Tomo-chan, it's very complicated," Grandma said.

"How come you aren't coming to Heaven with us? Don't you want to be with us?"

"Ara maa…" Grandma protested, and stood helplessly stroking Tomoko's head over and over.

Mother's lips took on a compressed look I knew well. I followed as she strode down the hall to the room where Aunt Miho was watching a cooking show on television. Mother slid shut the shoji panel with a *pang* behind her. I listened from the hallway, on the other side of the panel.

"Raise your child any way you want, but don't you dare use her that way against my mother." My mother's voice was barely audible. "Can't you *realize*, how much pain she's had in her life?" she said. "How many times, since we were children, have I *pleaded* with you to protect her in my absence?"

"And speaking bluntly," Mother continued, "what you want from our mother is impossible. *My* father's in Buddhist heaven, waiting for her. And when she dies, I'll be at the temple chanting sutras for *her*. Third-year anniversary, fifth, tenth, fifteenth, thirty-fifth, fiftieth! For the rest of my life. Even if I burn in your Christian hell for it!"

Her wrath was magnificent and primal. At that moment, it didn't even occur to me to feel sorry for Aunt Miho. I was swept up in an unexpected sense of vindication as well as a powerful loyalty to our trio. Over the following week, I was to sit before the vanity mirror and practice pressing my lips together the way Mother had. I would watch my face, with its pointy Caucasian features, become transformed with authority and passion. It would be many years before I felt the poignancy of Mother's belligerent, childlike loyalty, with which she shielded Grandma from the others.

Mother's voice now softened, for Aunt Miho was crying. "Someday," she said, "you'll understand, Miho. You'll understand, the way love works."

Even then, I sensed that my grandfather—not Grandpa Ichiro but my true grandfather—was the key to our family relations. That summer, for the first time, I was shown my grandfather Yasunari's photograph album, concealed in a dresser among layers of folded winter kimonos. "Now remember," Grandma and Mother told me, "this is just among us. The rest of them wouldn't like it if they knew. Grandpa Ichiro either. Especially Grandpa Ichiro!" The album was bound in ugly brownish cloth which, according to Grandma, was once a beautiful indigo; it had matching brown tassels that were still dark blue in their centers. I was discouraged from touching it.

Grandma and Mother turned the pages, with hands smelling of lemony dishwashing soap.

Mother never knew her father; she was only five when Yasunari died in the war. Throughout her childhood she, too, had been shown this album, during stolen moments when the others were away. It was hard to believe this young man in the black-and-white photographs, her own true father, was as much a stranger to her as he was to me. Yasunari was handsome, like a movie star, with finely molded features and eyes like elegant brushstrokes.

"We were happy, very happy," Grandma told me. "Yasunari-san loved children. Every minute he had free, he was carrying your mother. Walking around, always holding her in one arm."

"I think I remember being held by him," Mother said.

"When he finally set your mother down, she'd cry. And keep on crying. Your mother, even back then, she could read people. And sure enough, he'd laugh and pick her back up. She even sat on his lap at dinnertime."

I learned the rest of this story when I was nineteen, after Mother's sudden death from mitral-valve failure. Holding an adult conversation with my grandmother was an adjustment; I was so used to being the nonessential part of a threesome. But in the wake of Mother's death we took on new roles: she as surrogate mother, I as surrogate daughter. In this new capacity we spent hours discovering each other, with all the excitement and raised hopes of a courtship.

Before the war, Grandma told me, Yasunari was a highly paid executive in the import/export business. When he died, he left young Grandma with a sizable inheritance. But her in-laws, determined to keep Yasunari's money in the family, pressured her into marrying his elder brother, Ichiro. Family obligation, they argued. A father for the child. Protection from wartime dangers.

Ichiro was a dandy. Despite the grinding poverty of those war years, he insisted on sporting an ascot and not a tie. A social creature, popular with both men and women, he drank with a fast set and then, flushed with sake, shook hands on tenuous business deals. In a short time he had gone through much of his younger brother's inheritance. In contrast to his outward persona, Ichiro was surly at home; irritable and quick to find blame for the smallest things.

Even today, more than a decade after Mother's death, Grandma revisits this as she and I sit alone, looking through Yasunari's album. She speaks in a whisper, the same whisper she once used with Mother in the late afternoons, even though Grandpa Ichiro is dead now too, and we have the house to ourselves.

Many nights, Grandma tells me, she stood at the kitchen window while everyone slept, gazing at the moon caught among pine branches. Many nights she dreamed the same dream: Yasunari was outside in the night, standing silent in the alley. She could not see him but she knew, as one does in dreams, that he was wearing a white suit like that of a Cuban musician.

"Take me with you! Please! Don't leave me here!" she screamed after him in the dream, and woke to the sound of her own moaning.

Grandma went on to bear two children by Grandpa Ichiro: my Uncle Koku, then my Aunt Miho. In old photographs little Koku and Miho are always out in front, their beaming, gap-toothed faces playing up to the camera; although Grandpa is out of the picture, one senses his presence behind the lens, directing jokes to his favorites. Grandma stands off to the back and Mother does too, her torso turned toward her mother in an oddly protective stance.

In this atmosphere, Mother's social awareness developed early. She massaged her mother's shoulders when no one was looking. She secretly threatened her half-siblings when they misbehaved. She became a model student as well as a model daughter, thus depriving Grandpa Ichiro of any excuse to harass Grandma on her account.

In my mother, Grandma found an outlet for all the ardent romantic love she had felt for Yasunari. This child, she thought, is all I have left: of his genes, of his loyal, solicitous nature. Often Grandma left her chores and hurried over to the neighborhood playground where, using sleight of hand, she would slip a treat into Mother's pocket: a bit of baked potato in winter to keep her warm; in hot weather, a tiny salted rice ball with a pinch of sour plum at its center. This was during the post-war days, in the midst of food rationing.

There just wasn't enough, she tells me now, for the other children.

Aunt Miho dropped by last week during O-bon Week of the Dead, bringing one of those 7,000-yen gift melons that come in their own box. She sat alone at the dining room table, sipping cold wheat tea. All afternoon we had visitors: friends of Mother, dead thirteen years now; friends of Grandpa Ichiro, dead three years. They all trooped past her into the altar room, bowing politely as they passed. Aunt Miho listened from the dining room as they chanted sutras at the family altar and struck the miniature gong. Christians cannot acknowledge Buddhist holidays, much less pay homage to their ancestors.

I put the melon on a dish and took it to the altar room, placing it on the slide-out shelf among a clutter of orchids and boxed pastries. "Mother and Grandpa Ichiro used to love those melons," I told her, coming back into the dining room. "Auntie, you're the only one who remembered."

She smiled, with a warmth that her daughters rarely show me. She is still pretty. She now wears her hair swept back in a French twist, a style similar to my mother's.

This afternoon, Grandma and I discuss Aunt Miho's new hairstyle as we stroll to the open-air market to buy *hiramasa* sushi for supper. Our conversation has the same familiar rhythms I grew up listening to as a child. "She copies a lot of little things from your mother," Grandma says, amused. "She always denies it though. Between you and me, I think she honestly doesn't realize she's doing it."

"Mmm," I say. Unlike my mother, I am uncomfortable discussing Aunt Miho. It's bad enough that I, a mere grandchild, have usurped her rightful place as Grandma's only remaining daughter. "This heat!" I exclaim, adjusting our shared parasol so that it shades her more fully. This solicitousness is a habit I've developed since Mother's death, partly to carry on my mother's role but also, especially in those early days, to provide an outlet for all the tenderness I never gave my mother. It seems to impress the elderly neighbors. "What a comfort your granddaughter must be, in your old age!" they say wistfully. And Grandma replies, "She's just like her mother. Sometimes I actually forget who I'm talking to."

"A! A!" Grandma now exclaims. We have just crossed Shinbonmachi Boulevard and are entering the crowded open-air market. "Good thing I remembered! Remind me, after the fish store, to buy plum leaves for your dinner. To go with the sashimi."

Whenever I accompany Grandma to the open-air market, the fish vendor—a shrewd older woman—sidles up to us with her most expensive items. "Madam!" she greets Grandma today. "After she's back in America you'll be kicking yourself, with all due respect, for not letting her taste these highest quality roe eggs! At their absolute prime, madam, this time of year!" She waits with a complacent smile, as Grandma wavers. "Over in America," she informs my grandmother, as she wraps up our sashimi plus two other unbudgeted purchases, "those people eat their fish cooked in *butter*." She turns to me with an apologetic smile. "You sure have your granny's laugh, though," she says, exempting me from her earlier slur against Westerners. "Startles me every time, miss, coming from that American face."

It's true I bear little resemblance to anyone on my Japanese side. Sometimes I imagine Yasunari rising from the dead, and his shock and bewilderment upon seeing his own wife walking alongside a Caucasian, channeling to her all the love that was originally meant for him. But Grandma is adamant about our physical similarity. The way my thumb joins my hand, for instance, is the same as Yasunari's, and I have the same general "presence" he and my mother did. And she recently confessed that in the early days, whenever I said "moshi moshi" over the telephone, she would have a crazy lurch of hope that Mother's death had all been a big mistake. My voice, she insisted, was identical to my mother's.

We turn homeward onto Temple Alley, walking abreast. Three years ago this alley was gravel; now it is paved. Our summer sandals make flat, slapping sounds against the blacktop, and I miss the gentle *k'sha k'sha* that had reminded me of walking on newly fallen snow.

The houses have changed, too, since my last visit: many have been rebuilt Western-style, with white siding and brass doorknobs. Shiny red motor scooters are parked outside. In the middle of one door hangs a huge wooden cutout of a puppy, holding in its smiling mouth a nameplate spelling out THE MATSUDAS in English letters. A bicycle bell tings behind us: we stand off to one side as a housewife rides past, straight-backed, her wire basket filled with newspaper-wrapped groceries for dinner.

"Where was that little alley that never changed?" I ask Grandma as we resume walking abreast. She gives a short, puzzled laugh as I describe the alley to her.

"I have no idea what you're talking about," she says. "Ginkgo tree? *Cicadas?* What kind of clue is that to go on?"

"There was an old-fashioned adobe wall," I say.

Grandma shakes her head, baffled. "They've torn a lot of those down." She stops short. "Meli-chan," she says, "did we remember to lock the back door when we left?"

Perhaps in the future when Grandma is gone, I will walk with my small daughter—who may have even less Japanese blood than I do—through these same neighborhood alleys. And a certain quality of reproach in the late afternoon sunlight will remind me with a pang, as it does now, of my mother's confident voice saying, "I'm irreplaceable."

"Once, when I was a girl," I will tell my daughter, gripping her hand tightly, "I walked these alleys just like you, with my own mother." Saying these inadequate words, I will sense keenly how much falls away with time; how lives intersect but only briefly.

"Thank goodness I remembered the plum leaves," Grandma says now. She peers over into my shopping basket. "You're always so particular about wrapping them around your *hiramasa* sushi."

"That's not me, Grandma," I say. "That was Mother."

"Oh. Well…" She is silent for a moment. "That would make sense," she says. "Poor thing. It was never available during the post-war years, and she craved it for years after she moved away to—"

"Grandma," I interrupt gently. "It's too late for that now. It doesn't matter."

Grandma quickens her pace, as she sometimes does when she is annoyed. "One doesn't always get the luxury of timing," she says.

The Naked Circus

G. K. Wuori

M ichael bought May for $7,500 plus shipping and handling.

At the Port of Leaving Everything (loosely translated), while May recalled the party her husband had given for her—a One Pot party with a whole barrel of beer—a man approached her with a small device in his hand, a steel machine. Before she could inquire as to his purposes he'd lifted her shirt and brassiere and May felt the bright light of pain shining in her mind. Looking down, she saw a wire piercing her nipple, and a numbered tag attached to the wire—quite industrial, she thought, yet not all that far from jewelry. She had no time to grimace, however, or to squeeze some tears from her eyes because the man quickly sprayed something from a can onto her nipple and the stinging pain went right away.

May appreciated that thoughtfulness, even as the port men led her into a ship container with thirty men and two other women. The port men also conveyed information (shouted, actually, the whole moment quite embarrassing) as to the virginal state of the three women, along with the warning that, if they arrived at site in any state less than that, their diminished value would be distributed over all the men, plus a substantial penalty.

May was a black-haired woman of thirty-seven who'd spent fifty-one days of passage and transfer and sickness and contractors getting to Michael's house, a deal made solely on a computer and, thus, somewhat unique. May's husband knew little of her arrangements, something they'd both agreed upon. Sometimes May's husband said her bravery in this matter of saving the family simply took his breath away.

May had children as well back home, two boys burdened with this or that illness nearly all the time. Her husband, though, had a better hand with the children—softer, a firm yet pleasant father—where May often felt impatient, occasionally confused in responding to her children's needs. They had, thus, never discussed the possibility of her husband undertaking this so-distant salvation.

No heroine, though. She would not allow anyone to look upon her in that way. If she had expansive ways, what somebody once called "an eye for the pearl in the honey jar," she had ambitions, too, that something would come of her having been upon the earth.

"My darling, you do not look at things that way," May said to her husband one time, her frankness not unexpected. "If someone gives me a coin I will double it, perhaps triple it. You will admire its beauty. We are like that, but we are not like each other."

Her husband freely confessed as well—delicately—to a certain neglect of her marital needs during this same conversation. He knew how deep the well of his wife's passions went, and he knew how infrequently his own cried out for release.

"Necessary," he said, as May sadly agreed with him. The poor man, indeed, already worked twenty hours a day and they had yet to live in a place with locking doors.

"Sometimes," he said, "it is good for one person in a marriage to be incredibly dull, the other less so."

That—May had not understood that at all, though she always knew when kindness lay at the root of her husband's words.

These oblique conversations, these indirect apologies May saw as his desperate desire not to be forgotten, since in all likelihood they would never see each other again. The many sacrifices of this quick life all but required permanence in their parting. She told him she would not forget: that the cut of his ears, the shape of his toes, even the hesitant start of his laughter that always turned into a roar—"those things, husband, they burn in me like the lights down on the shopway."

He could see, couldn't he, that how someone lives and how someone loves are often paths that split wide apart? She had monsters screaming at her *living* with such force she thought she would go mad.

"But I *love*," she said, "only you. That is my peace. It does not change."

"Yes, yes, yes," he said. "All I ask is that you keep me in mind, that now and again you pull up a memory of me and let me play in your heart and maybe dance playfully in and out of your eyes. I am not being only a general man here, May, like a poet or a negotiator. I am thinking of those times when ardor taps you on the shoulder like some helter-skelter fiend and you have to rent some American boy to fuck the nervousness and all your many dissatisfactions right out of you. All I would ask of you at such a time is that you not think me dead. I would not expect you to tell your lover my name, though you could perhaps say that I was handsome.

"After all," he said, "we have known each other since we were babies. Our muscles are the same, our bones, perhaps it would be good to tell your lovers your smell is the same as that of your husband. No, no of course you could never say such a thing; only, don't ever forget it, perhaps make it one of those memories you can never tell anyone, but that you never let slip away completely."

Though all the women were beautiful, no one believed any one of them even had a memory of her virginal state. Nevertheless, economics governed this journey, along with this new thing called globalization, and everyone understood that. The women endured no touches beyond a few beatings for laxity or impudence, but that happened to the men, too.

Food and water sat in one corner of the container, and concealed holes for air dotted the metal walls, a relief to everyone (they'd heard stories). A low barrel soon proved inadequate, however, at holding the waste of thirty-three people.

For twenty-two wretched days they bounced and slid their way across the sea before they reached port in South America, a dark warehouse in the coastal town of Chrizone. They were stripped of all their belongings and clothing and put on a rickety old bus that had the words THE NAKED CIRCUS painted colorfully on the side.

"Do you suppose they've sent our clothing out to be cleaned and pressed?" someone said.

Derisive laughter greeted the comment, although no one had any other explanation.

Since they'd all felt each other's physical crudeness during the sea journey, and since no one had escaped the minor or torrential leap of someone's sour vomit at least once, or avoided the unfamiliar eating sounds and sleeping sounds of whomever they'd been next to in the container, their nakedness shocked only those not in their group. May decided that if nakedness made you feel quite vulnerable, it also functioned as a strength—a small element of power, since the clothed never quite knew what to do with the naked.

As they took their places naked on the bus someone said, "Who *am* I?"

"You're me," came the answer with a great whoop of laughter.

Philosophy, May thought, is never more freely dispensed than it is among those who have been willingly imprisoned. May imagined her husband chiding her for always thinking in flowers and ribbons when the world wanted most of its thoughts in nails or stainless steel screws.

They traveled over the mountain places, crossed deserts and farmlands, drove quietly through small villages and cities that thrilled May with their different styles of housing; a love of color she did not share, but unique, special. May loved to find soft things before her eyes, not all of this brightness; neutral things—grays, pastels, the silent colors of winter, especially.

Except for traffic, they never stopped in those places, especially since word of their arrival always preceded them. Young people took to the streets and jumped up and down trying to look into the windows of the bus. Less energetic people stood on stair stoops or looked down from the roofs of houses to see THE NAKED CIRCUS. May thought these demonstrations seemed a little rehearsed, perhaps formulaic, as though the bus brought its weary, if occasionally chilly, crew through on a regular basis.

"Is there really such a thing, this naked circus?" one of the women asked the bus driver.

The driver looked around at them and smiled, an exquisitely rolled Cuban cigar in his mouth. He looked at all of them longer than anyone thought safe given the narrow road they were on. He said something, finally, in what someone said sounded like Portuguese, and which no one understood, then finally turned back to his driving.

Their clothes were returned when they finally reached Belize, although, for no reason that was ever given, their small satchels and bags had disappeared. An almost comical chorus quickly arose on the many ways to say, *Where is my toothbrush?*

"Not uncommon, even when you travel first class," someone joked.

May couldn't remember the last time they'd laughed as a group.

A full moon, too, made magical sparkles over the choppy sea. May hoped some of the others noticed it. She wished her sick children could see this devilish, this black and boiling spectacle. More importantly, she hoped just then that the others wouldn't forget that the world had some things to offer, that it was good to look at, that it could perform (occasionally) as you needed it to. She said as much during a long silence within the group. The silence remained.

Near dawn, they were put in the cooler of a small fishing boat, about a thousand pounds of pollock, tilapia, and grouper nearby in the early stages of rot. Everyone in the group was hungry, but May thought it unwise to eat even the small bits of flesh some of the men and women tore from the slimy fish. Sure enough, a great outburst of vomiting began within a few hours and it had nothing to do with the roll of the sea—fairly calm at that. There was weakness, even tears. May worried that the poisons leaving with the tears could cause blindness, but that didn't happen. Sometimes she wondered how many of these truths she'd learned over the years were actually true.

May's group split up when they got to Biloxi in the Mississippi. Some met entrepreneurs there, others pulled wrinkled papers from within their underwear to see what their next venture required them to do. Of course, none in May's group were friends, none were family, so the severed bond was one of discomfort, occasionally fear. They had shared sweat and stink and pain, and nearly all of them knew the secret names for loved ones that had been cried out during a restless or feverish sleep.

Never, May knew, could they exchange true names, and no one had any address at all yet—New York, for most of them; Chicago for two others, and May finally found out that her purchase by the American man was complete, a lucky thing. She was told nothing about the man at the time.

Those remaining, including May, found themselves on a long truck, their destination a huge chicken farm where they would await their next transport. May loved chickens, but she'd never seen so many in one place at one time. She thought of them as worker chickens, vital in the aggregate, though such details as names, heritage, and place of birth had either disappeared or had never existed. She also knew how easily you could attach that analogy to people, too.

She'd known people who worked so hard they did nothing else and then they died. It seemed as though work had shaped their lives, with an unremarkable death their major accomplishment. May wished she could put it in a more clever way, but the chickens reminded her of her husband. She hoped, once she began sending money home, he'd buy some cigarettes and heavy beer once in a while.

On her third morning of living with the chickens, a milk truck of shiny metal pulled up and two men helped May into a small compartment of the big tank that had been walled off from the milk. May liked the idea of traveling with milk. She thought it slightly romantic, slightly amusing. Milk was soft and life-giving; truly, precious stuff. "As am I," she said quietly to herself as she once again found herself stripped of her clothing, then covered with a heavy grease and pushed through a hole into the compartment.

For a moment, May remembered THE NAKED CIRCUS. She thought of herself as yet one more act. Quite amusing, yes. Quite revealed. Sometimes the traveling shows back home featured women well known for removing their clothing. Only the men were allowed to see that, of course, and they always exited those performances looking slightly gray and very sheepish. May didn't think her husband had ever seen one of those shows, but she hoped he had. Being average, as he so regularly thought of himself, did not mean you couldn't climb the hill once in a while to see what lay beyond.

May's trip lasted nineteen hours before another pair of men looked down on her naked body and then pulled her into the fresh air. They were not careful in what they touched of her, although one of them did give her a bottle of water right away. As she stood next to the truck and stretched her cramped muscles and bones she saw two other men off to the side exchanging papers. One man looked at the number tag on her nipple, then said something to the man holding all the papers.

May thought this place amazing, quite stunning, as she looked around at the hundreds of trucks parked in precise lines, some with engines running, some not. This must be the end of the journey, she thought, yet nothing seemed familiar, no earth signs (rivers, trees, mountains) or things she might think about as being a part of her new home. Overhead, the air rumbled around thick with fumes, the trucks lit by many, many pink lights on poles high overhead.

It was night, though, and May understood the night. At home, she would meet her husband outside late at night when he came home from work. She walked with him so they could talk before he staggered to their bed for his few hours of sleep. Night had made their marriage, even if her husband hadn't made their children. He knew that, of course, though it wasn't something easily talked about.

"My name is Michael," one of the men said to her. Quite gently, she thought, he placed a blanket over her shoulders.

May wrote home:

He keeps me in a boathouse, my husband. I feel safe and warm. It is also dark and so I bruise my knees constantly. There are so many memories, however, in the slow lap of the water and all the smells— of fish, seaweed, gasoline. When the sun shines, the tin boathouse heats up and I feel comfortable. I remember how our own tin houses glow in the sun, and I know that mine must be glowing because at least once a day, often twice, on a sunny day a bird will mistake the glow of my house for freedom and crash into it and die. Sometimes the dead birds float into the boathouse. Do you know that I am writing to you? Can you feel my words on the back of your neck, maybe your knees, as I scratch them out with a fisherman's pencil on an old paper bag?

Michael told her about the snakes in the water. He said don't even think about bathing in there (or trying to escape? May wondered, Is that what he thinks?), in the opening where I usually keep the boat. She could relieve herself there. That was all right. Of course.

"You're not a prisoner," he said, "and this is all temporary."

"This is not your home?" May asked.

"Only a part of my home," Michael said. "The rest is up on the hill. You probably didn't notice it when you first came here."

May didn't know what to make of that, if she had shamed herself already or embarrassed herself, or if she had already displeased him. Perhaps he thought her ugly or simply too fat, since it had been two days now and he had yet to feed her. She finally decided it was much too early to try to figure out what any American man might be saying to her. Still, she was very hungry.

On the morning of her fourth day, Michael came down to the boat-house with clothing and food for May.

"Dear Jesus," he said to her, "I simply forgot."

"Things are on your mind," May said.

"I deserve no forgiveness at all," he said, "but thank you."

He brought her puffy baked rolls with butter, grapes, hard-boiled eggs, water, Coca-Cola, and some cheese that smelled like her husband's back—very odd.

He'd brought the food in a plastic box, but he also had a paper bag and from the bag he took out a pair of sandals and a white dress. May put the sandals on and then the dress—a cut, she thought, not at all familiar to her. She giggled politely.

"Is this something funny?" Michael asked. "Did you think you would stay naked all the time? Do you realize how cold it gets up here?"

May could see that this Michael once again appeared angry with her. She wished she knew how many more failures he would grant her.

"It is a dress," May said, "an American dress. I have never worn such a thing so it makes me nervous. I'm very sorry. It seems to be a very fine dress."

May took the dress off quickly and gave it back to Michael.

Then Michael apologized—again. Finally, he smiled at May and said, "We're working pretty hard to make all of this as awkward as possible."

"Am I the first person you've ever bought?" May asked.

"Yes. Hence, my bumbling along here."

"Hence?"

"Um, therefore. Anyway, the dress is my wife's and I was hoping it would look on you the way it always looks on her.

"A kind of glow," he continued, "as though no darkness could ever contain her. You both look so much alike, whether hands or hips or lips, a certain way the toes grip the ground, a smell, too—"

Then May interrupted Michael and said, "Do you want to touch me? Do you want to see if I feel the way she feels—or felt? Is your wife still with you? Is she alive?"

"Yes, she is," Michael said. "Would you like to meet her?"

"Of course I would like to meet her," May said. "Will this prove difficult for her?"

"If you could talk to her," Michael began, "if you could listen—"

"Michael?"

"Yes?"

"You say 'if,' but I belong to you. I am owned by you. Perhaps you find that troublesome, but I don't. It's why I'm here. If I were firewood you could burn me. I am what you will determine I am."

Later that night, May once again wrote to her husband using the fisherman's pencil and a paper bag.

> As they say in America, my husband, here's the deal: I am to be another woman and live in a house of many sad tidings. The woman I will be is a dying woman. My name will be Carol, which I think means something like singing. You must use that name whenever you think about me. Perhaps you could begin saying that word in front of the children. They will not find it a hard word.

Michael's house had three floors and cedar siding, very woodsy as might be depicted in any number of housing magazines. A small warehouse adjoined the main house, May noticed. The warehouse held four automobiles, all of them different, and all of them very old, like a vehicle her grandfather drove before he disappeared. There were many gables formed by the steep-sloping roof, and on the lower floor a deck faced the lake and the tin boathouse. May noticed that all of the floors had carpets on them, big and small, and that many of the walls were either marble or inlaid with mirrors. She began to think good fortune was about to strike her like a hammer on a mushroom.

Michael apologized for the clutter and all of the mess. He said his wife had neglected her work since taking sick, and for as much as he'd been willing to do it—"she will not allow me to get a girl for the job"—Carol had said no, she would not be given up on that easily.

"It would give me great pleasure, Michael," May began. "I know all about the things that are pleasing to woods, porcelains, ceramics, all of the—"

Michael would not let her finish.

"When it is time," he said.

Together they walked the broad stairway that went upstairs. Wooden and curved and more elegant than anything May had ever seen, the hardwood steps echoed from Michael's shoes but barely squeaked beneath May's bare feet. May knew Michael was taking her to his wife and she wished she were wearing some clothes. She supposed the harlot of any house spent a lot of time undressed (although Michael had not suggested that—yet), but no woman likes to meet another woman naked, as she remembered from the baths back home. You always wanted to tell the world how grandly life had blessed you, but the body spoke with only true words. The body told no cheerful lies.

Michael's wife lay in the biggest bed May had ever seen; a king, Michael said to May, a notion not at all clear to her. He meant the bed, she supposed, since she knew that even this English, this most energetic and abrasive language, never defined its women as kings.

The bed held lake water, Michael said, warmed with a heater.

"It moves Carol's body around quite easily," Michael said, "and I like to think it just as gently moves her spirit."

Carol smiled at May and May thought for a moment she was looking in a mirror. Carol was gaunt where May was full, but the sickness had done that. Otherwise, Carol's eyes, her nose, her lips, even the tiniest of clefts in the chin—she and May shared something, as though a delicate genetic flower had put its pollen into the wind many years ago.

"Please get into the bed, May," Michael said as he pulled back the blankets.

Carol said something, her voice soft, not clearly audible. Still, May said thank you and realized Carol had told her she was beautiful, had said it in words May could not hear. May told herself there are some things a woman—any woman, anywhere—will always hear.

She reached over and took Carol's hand in hers. The hand was very cold. May felt Carol's heartbeat in her hand as well, a strong beat but slow, as though the heart were more than willing to go on but time, that fat house rat, had things to do elsewhere.

Michael would not let May leave the bed after that.

He brushed Carol's hair in the morning and brushed her teeth. He put a clean diaper on her, then rubbed her feet and helped her drink some coffee. A sponge bath came later in the morning along with a few delicate touches of makeup.

Michael always entered the room smiling, often reciting some interesting bit of news he'd heard on the radio. He opened the curtains to the bedroom so that the dawn chop of the lake sprinkled the room with sparkling light. Sometimes he sang, quite spirited songs that May, of course, had never heard before. Carol ate little, but Michael fed her whatever she would take down, talking all the while and reading the newspaper aloud.

After doing Carol's dishes, he came back into the bedroom, announced a hearty "Good morning!" and then repeated everything for May.

Carol and May talked all the time. With May right next to her, Carol needed only the force of whispers to break the silence her body had forced on her, the force of weakness and lassitude, the force of a dying that, until May had arrived, kept telling her, *No, that's not important. No, not that, either.* Carol began to see that everything was important. She asked May about her homeland, though not about her husband and children.

"Politics," she whispered, "what's that all about? I have heard your country is reaching for democracy. Is that a good idea?"

Before May could answer, though, Carol went elsewhere.

"Plays," she said, "theater—you have countrymen who do that better than anyone else in the world. Do you enjoy that sort of thing?"

May had never seen a theater performance.

"My town," May said, "my village is very small."

"It's all right," Carol said. In only a moment, she was asleep.

One morning Carol asked May if she liked martinis.

"What is a martini?" May said. "I have never heard of this martini. Martin, I have heard of. We have something like that name in my country. A martini—is this a small Martin? Now laugh, please. I think I'm terribly wrong."

"It's a drink," Carol whispered, "with a tiny vegetable in it called an olive."

"I know olives!" May said.

"They're very good—the martinis."

Since Michael refused them nothing, they sipped the funny drinks that day from noon until early in the evening, stopping now and then to sleep or doze or simply to stare out the window at the lake.

The drinks made May's toes numb, and they made her think about her husband and her children. She remembered the day he'd walked out of his small shop and saw her standing there with her dress caught in her bicycle chain. He could have ignored her. He could have ripped the dress out of the chain. He could have laughed at her as some children had already done.

Instead, he'd picked up the rear wheel of the bicycle so that the chain and sprocket would no longer move, and then walked to her house—a long walk—even politely turning his back as her mother came out and helped May out of her dress and into a shirt and a pair of jeans. Carefully, then, he removed her dress from the bike. It was dirty near the hem, but untorn.

They were married one week after that.

"Michael?"

"Yes, May."

"It is good for Carol to drink these martinis? They are intoxicating. They are very strong."

Michael said that badness no longer existed for Carol. She could drink.

She could think uncharitable thoughts. She could write nasty letters to political officials. Had she strength enough, she could foment revolutions in small countries, with all of it, each small minute of the most minor of days, written in goodness and wonder.

"There is no longer waste in Carol's life, dear May, no longer anything inconsequential—especially laughter and, above all, your friendship."

"Sometimes, Michael, when I dream at night, I feel like I float in and out of Carol's body. I can see memories and hear people whispering her name. I can also see children inside her that she never had. They look like my children."

"How sweet you are," Michael said. "I noticed the other day and even more tonight that you're starting to sound like Carol. That pleases both of us. I want you to know that."

"We are very much alike," May said. "Do you know, one night her eyes were dry and hurting her, so I cried my tears into her eyes and she said that made them feel soothed and peaceful. I wasn't sure what soothed meant, but it sounded comforting the way she said it."

Michael quickly left the room after May told him that.

As May weakened from her bed rest and began to lose weight, she and Carol decided to play a trick on Michael, a funny deed to pull some of the misery out of his eyes and send it down to his belly as laughter.

Slowly—May had not been out of bed in weeks—she stepped to the floor. Her legs wobbled and felt like they were made of cooked noodles, but she made it across the bedroom to the dresser. Delicately, she took hold of the hand mirror, surprised at how heavy such a common tool now seemed.

Back in bed, May and Carol were shocked by their first look in the shared mirror, shocked at the streets of sadness lining their faces, shocked at the hills and valleys of woe that marked time's impatient progress. Carefully, though, with May walking slowly around the room gathering the containers and bottles and packets of Carol's makeup, they daubed, they painted, they spotted—they made of each other's face a canvas and pulled from the canvas the most generous and the most raucous of clowns: clowns of beauty and delight. "This passing clown," Carol said at one point, "and her replacement."

"If I am worthy," May said.

"You are more than we had hoped, my darling," Carol said.

"Someday I must tell you about the naked circus," May said.

The next morning Michael entered the room and looked down at them. He smiled and said, "Carol—," then realized he could not tell which was Carol and which was May.

"A couple of pranksters," he said.

May opened her eyes and said, "We tricked you because we love you."

"You did a good job. May?"

"It's me. Are you angry?"

"Oh, no," Michael said. "Not at all. You must have had a good time."

"It took so little," May said. "Eventually we decided that Carol was May and May was Carol. We invented new people for ourselves and a new world where confusion no longer existed. We decided that if one of us was dying it wasn't important which one. Such joy in that, Michael! For a time, we felt like we were sleeping out under the trees, where you look up at the sky and the stars and you can see anything you want to see. If there are monsters, so also are there heroes. We decided the best kind of hero was the clown because you owe the clown nothing but your joy."

"I'm very pleased," Michael said. "I used to make Carol laugh all the time, but lately—well, I mourn her. That's a terrible thing since she isn't even gone yet. She hasn't—"

"Michael?"

"Yes, May?"

"Carol died last night."

Michael left for a few minutes then, leaving May alone and weary next to Carol, alone and saddened, although there had been fright, too—fright during those nameless hours as death came to a body so much like her own she feared it might make some mistake. Death could do that, death the only permanent owner of bodies, death who could take possession at will and who was never held accountable.

Michael returned and May thought he would take her down to his room so that she would be out of the way when the emergency people came. He didn't, though. He had some cream he used to clean Carol's face, and then May's. When he finished the cleaning, he picked Carol up and left the room with her, returning once again after what seemed like no time at all.

"It's time," he said to May.

He pulled the blankets down to May's waist and, using a small tool, quite silvery and shiny, he clipped the wire and pulled the numbered tag from May's nipple.

It didn't hurt at all, she noticed, and she smiled at him as he smoothed her hair and gave her a sip of water; as the tears rolled down his cheeks, though there were no sobs.

"Go to sleep now," he said. "I know this has been very hard for you."

"There was joy, Michael. Truly, there was joy."

"I know, Carol," Michael said. "I know."

Attila The There

Gina Frangello

A PRIL

Camden was atoning. Sometimes, during the ten, twelve-hour stretches he spent wandering around Amsterdam without uttering a word to anyone, he felt like a monk on a vow of silence. Dutch sifted through his ears like background noise, easy not to notice at all. He played games with himself: passing his student ID to the ticket seller at the Anne Frank House or negotiating vegetable purchases at the Boerenmarkt, all without verbal exchange. Alone at home, he gratefully turned the TV to Dutch shows. *Over de Rooien*, a program where people had to do stupid things in public and find strangers to participate, was his favorite since you didn't need to understand what anyone said to follow slapstick. His mother had enrolled him in a weekly Dutch course, and to his relief they were allowed to speak only Dutch in class. Most of the students—techies over on jobs from the States and England—formed clinging friendships; Camden watched them transform from a conglomeration of nerdy strangers into giggling cliques. A decade younger than the others, he remained on the outside. They didn't even invite him— a legal child at home—for drinks after class. Camden didn't mind. Part of his atonement for what he'd done to Aimee, his deliberate abstinence from girls altogether, entailed steering away from any pack mentality.

Camden's mother, Ginny, had a fetish for handicapped women. Lisle, the Dutch poet with whom he and Ginny were now living, had been in a wheelchair for eight years due to a riding injury. Before Lisle, Ginny had dated: an epileptic, a deaf woman (or a "beautiful human being who happens to be deaf"), two bipolars—one of whom was suicidal—and another woman in a wheelchair, from spina bifida. Lisle was the first of the girlfriends to be obese. Her spine rested so straight against the back of the chair that her breasts shot out like life-threatening torpedoes, her thighs spread on the seat. She had a breathtaking face.

At one time, in New Zealand, where Lisle had lived for reasons Camden had yet to ascertain, Lisle had been an artist's model to earn money. There were pictures of her nude—chatting with older men and other beautiful women—pasted in a big scrapbook she kept in the floor-to-ceiling bookcase by the fireplace. Camden could not quite believe it was her—maybe a sister or something?—but he avoided the scrapbook anyway, worried he'd do the unspeakable: get a hard-on over Lisle's twenty-year-old, nubile self; that he'd progress to imagining her now, nude and twisting around on the bed with Ginny, even her orgasmic yelps political and abrasive. Since he had first witnessed a female orgasm four months prior, it was difficult to keep from transposing the image onto every female he encountered, but in Lisle's case, he managed with ease, as long as he avoided the scrapbook.

Ginny and Lisle liked parading it around for guests, though. Not because they were proud of how hot Lisle used to be, but as an illustration of her earlier, oppressed self: the duped woman who used her body as a form of economic exchange; the innocent girl who became an "objectified object" of the "male gaze." Lisle orated on this subject frequently to her poetry group, which met at the apartment every other Wednesday. Camden's mother, who was not a poet, scurried around serving coffee and cakes, and though the members of the group all spoke and wrote in English, they lapsed into Dutch when Ginny entered the room. Ginny didn't seem to mind; she liked assisting people. She often quipped that she would make the ideal personal assistant to a movie star. Lisle had published little poetry, but Camden doubted even movie stars could compete with Lisle's ego and sense of entitlement. While the handicapped girlfriends in the past had accepted Ginny's ministering with gratitude, Lisle seemed to punish Ginny for her normalcy, rejecting her efforts to help, driving her toward a more marginalized existence—as though being gay weren't enough. Camden once overheard his mother and Lisle arguing about a club Ginny didn't want to go to, and when he looked the name up under "gay" in his guidebook, he discovered the bar was S&M oriented. For days, he studied Ginny for bruises, but she looked fine, healthy if thinner.

He did not ask his mother what the hell they were doing in Amsterdam when it seemed clear already that things weren't working out. He had long since given up on finding logic in what women bore in the name of what they believed was love.

In order to relocate to Amsterdam, Ginny had pulled Camden out of school in Illinois three months before the end of his junior year. He'd left over the protests of school counselors, teachers, his grandparents, and most of the girls at Oak Park/River Forest high school, who aspired to sleep with him either again or for the first time. Camden and Ginny settled into the trendy Jordaan district during a time of year when the weather in Amsterdam was constant rain. While his friends back home were breaking out springtime shorts that hung low on their hips, Camden and Ginny trolled Amsterdam museums in wet wool coats, fighting nonstop sore throats. Before Camden even unpacked his clothes, three ex-girlfriends' e-mails had arrived at the Jordaan apartment. *It's 65 degrees today*, one wrote. *Hugh threw a party while his parents were in St. Martin, and got arrested having sex with some skeeze in the master bedroom because in the throes of passion, ha ha, they didn't hear the cops burst in*, wrote another. *We're watching the Cubs' opening from Hugh's brother's roof in Wrigleyville*, wrote a third. Each typed at the end, before her name, *I miss you, I miss you, I miss you*. Camden did not write back.

It would be five months before classes started in Holland, and Ginny couldn't work here for three years, until she could apply for legal residency. Meanwhile Lisle paid all the bills, leaving Camden and Ginny stuck in the apartment together like siblings home from school with measles. Though Ginny brimmed with plans for places to go, things to see, she spent her actual days fussing around the apartment, perusing Lisle's Andrea Dworkin library and watching CNN so she could complain about world events later when Lisle got home. Camden, under pressure, developed an unhealthy interest in the Torture Museum. He listened to the audio tour of the Van Gogh museum until he could have written a paper on bipolar Vincent without even getting on the internet. Every day for lunch, he ate apple pie stacked tall on a white plate. He learned not to feel rain.

The closest he came to picking up a girl was at an Irish pub, Mulligan's, with Lisle and his mother looking on. An abysmal folk band played loudly. The girl was with her mother, too, who knew the band's singer. The girl's name was Roos, "the spelling of Rose in Dutch," she explained. Camden quipped, "A rose by any other letters is still as sweet," expecting the reference to be lost on her, but she replied in the flawless English that never stopped unnerving him among the young A'dam set, "Every American guy I've ever met has said some variation of that line, and I haven't gone to bed with any of them yet."

Their mothers watched them talk but didn't speak to each other. Roos' mother, a painter, sat alone and silent, listening to the music and smoking hand-rolled cigarettes. Ginny and Lisle argued about the guitarist, who was Lisle's ex. Roos was pretty if tomboyish, with full, heavy breasts that he and his buddy Hugh would have nudged each other about back home. Camden broke the conversation off abruptly, though he watched Roos for the remainder of the evening. She had a stillness, like her mother. She was as tall as he and wore leather pants with sneakers. Her hair was short and dark, which almost made her appear foreign—he had never seen so many blonds—but her cheeks bore the unmistakable pink glow of a Dutch girl, even without makeup. Although she was dateless too, he felt embarrassed about being at the bar with Ginny and Lisle, although he saw restraint as a victory, indicative of his new life.

Aimee had leaned over, trying to whisper to him, breasts swaying. "After, it'll be the same, you and me? This'll be the only time he's with us, right?" Hugh's torso, stretching to intercept her path of intended intimacy, blocked Camden's access to her ear. Would he have warned her if he could reach her? It'll never be the same between us either way—get up and leave right now. If you don't, this is only the beginning. *Then Hugh's hand, reaching to scoop her tit like an udder, vulgarly kneading; Aimee's eyes, scared but aroused, rolling back. So easy—it was so easy every time....*

Morality was paradoxical in Amsterdam: prostitution legal, soft drugs decriminalized. Locals didn't seem interested in either. Some of his mom's friends back home had spouted that letting women do what they wanted with their bodies—to sell them if they chose—was liberated, even feminist, but Ginny told the Oak Park bipolar on the phone that it wasn't like that, it didn't look like what she imagined. Camden knew what she meant. He'd figured if there weren't so much stigma on sex for girls, everybody would have as much of it as possible. Women would hire hot guys for the night too, sure. Why not? But mostly boys his age and younger went for rent here, and old men did the buying. The commercial hype focused on women: bare breasts sold everything from soap to beer. Boobs were plastered on billboards, starred in the commercials before films. A poster selling ice cream at the Albert Heijn portrayed a female mouth giving a chocolate-covered bar head.

Even if you kept out of the Red Light District, there were mini prostitution clusters all over the city. Innocuously walking down the street, you might encounter a woman in her underwear, sitting in a picture window staring at you. The District itself had a giant German, British, and American frat-party vibe, as if all the brothers were on X. Eastern European and Indonesian women in fluorescent bikinis stood behind elevated glass like animals in the zoo. The hot ones were up front, so gorgeous it was easy to succumb to the gawking, to figure the prostitutes must get off on their power. But the farther you walked among the labyrinthine streets, the more you encountered the fat, broken-down chicks, the hunchbacked, dwarfy, older whores behind their glass windows like circus freak-shows instead of proud lionesses strutting. The tourists of the District—nearly all male after nightfall—had a violent, frenzied undertow about them: you had to watch your wallet. Junkie-skinny drifters would offer to sell you H even if you were walking with your mom. The greedy desperation of it was more creepy than sexy—Camden only had to survey the revved up, shoving guys crowding the streets to wonder which were really the zoo animals. Man's neediness for a hole was embarrassing.

According to Lisle, Holland was light years behind North America when it came to women's "economic independence." Ginny dully recited the statistics into the phone, seemingly only vaguely aware that she remained unemployed. When Camden left the apartment in annoyance, cabs at taxi stands displayed Yab Yum cards on their dashboards, receiving kickbacks for referrals to that infamous brothel where educated, beautiful Dutch girls would fuck your brains out for a price no sixteen-year-old could afford. In Amsterdam, those too lazy to go out to buy drugs could have Thai stick or skunk delivered to their homes. The Netherlands seemed full of contradictions: in busy restaurants, strangers cordially invited Camden to sit at their table—yet since he and his mother had been here, none of their Dutch acquaintances had yet invited them home for a visit.

"Friendship is not casual here," Lisle explained. "It can take years, and then it is formal, like a declaration—*I think of you as a friend.* In the United States it's more like, *Oh I sat next to you on the airplane and told you my secrets and now you are my friend.* Here we may be repressed, but our friendship is true."

It seemed an odd thing to say for a woman who, at a poetry workshop in London, met an American tourist at a lesbian bar and proceeded to utterly disrupt her life in the course of a few months. The ground here was constantly shifting, sticky. Lonely.

MEI

He remembered her name visually: Roos. When he saw her selling tickets at Bananenbar, he would have turned and run had he not been with three English girls and a German guy from the youth hostel, all four engaged in hyped-up double entendres, full of hope for an evening of debauchery and trying to ignore the Disney World atmosphere of the tourist sex clubs. *And now, ladies and gentlemen, Minnie and Mickey will skate on ice naked—they may fall into each other's genitalia while they're at it, but don't worry, they won't enjoy it.* Roos stood in the doorway, sporting the same leather pants from Mulligan's, hair still shorn like a boy's, no lipstick to brighten her white and pink face. The first night he met her, Camden had thought she might be gay, but now he knew Dutch girls often went au natural. She held her hand out, smirking, though he didn't think she'd remember him. He wished the German guy behind him would take some initiative and deal with her instead.

Amsterdam had changed for him on Koninginnedag, April 30—not Queen Beatrix's actual birthday, but her mother's, a good time of the year to party in the streets for about thirty-six hours nonstop. Even preparations depressed Camden: the buzz of incoming travelers and never-closing bars and restaurants, of the city being transformed into a musical flea market of wandering musicians and market stalls. The thought of sticking close to the Isle of Lesbos while his mother waited on Lisle and her friends,

proved too much. He'd stalked off in the hope of finding a quiet corner
in which to refrain from the bacchanal, but instead he saw students everywhere, his own age or a year or two older, descending on A'dam from all
over Europe and the U.K.

They spoke to him as though he were one of them—they did not know
he'd changed. He remembered how to form the words, the banter and bullshit: *What bands do you like?* and *Where have you traveled?* and *Wanna see
my tattoo?* He woke the next morning in a hostel, full-bladdered and naked
next to a girl on a tapestry blanket thrown over a straw mat.

All his vows—all his efforts—and how long had his atonement lasted?
Just over a month. It was the same weakness; he couldn't trust himself.
That evening at Lisle's, he had allowed himself to think consciously of Aimee
for the first time since his arrival—*Stop, Cam, I think I'm gonna pee!*—of
how suddenly her back had arched, torso flowing like a wave that lapped
toward him and receded away, her shoulders limp in his arms after.... He'd
felt godlike and clueless, cocky and nervous as he held her. Remembering,
he bawled into his pillow leaving wet circles of saliva, trying to hide the
sounds from his mother and especially from Lisle.

But he'd gone back to the youth hostel. The crowd kept changing every
few days or weeks, but usually there was some straggler remaining who
could introduce Camden to the next pack of travelers, recent high school
or college grads. They bore guidebooks, though they mostly got too stoned
to do anything but sit at the Bulldog, nearly passed out at their tables.
Until they met him. Camden knew things by now—knew to take fellow
Americans to the "Boom Chicago" comedy routine at the Rembrantplein,
knew girls loved the salad Niçoise at Café Luxembourg, knew that the
shabby Dutch Flower coffeehouse around the corner was small enough
that both employees and regulars greeted him by name, which carried high
cachet for his new friends. ("The Bulldog and The Grasshopper are the
Hard Rock Cafés of hash," he told them. "They're industries that sell over-
priced T-shirts, not real local flavor.") At the Albert Cuypmarkt, he ordered
in Dutch: olives, cheese, and other foods girls found romantic. Weather
permitting, he rode his date on the back of his bike all the way to Vondelpark
for a picnic and free classical concert. Most tourists, even the girls, thought
of A'dam as a walk on the wild side—so he knew how to find Casa Rosso
and navigate his "charges" inside before they could realize they were being

taken to the Hard Rock Café of live sex shows, since anything off the tourist path would freak them out. He could tell which girls were hot enough to get into RoXY, and would take them to the Bazaar Attitude flea market near his house to look for club gear in case ugly-American shorts and Nikes downplayed their lithe legs. He lied about his age: eighteen, a graduate taking a break before "university" to hang out where his mother's lover, "a poet," had an apartment. He never mentioned that Lisle was wheelchair-bound. Once, after an exceptionally lousy blowjob, he admitted (through some kind of free association?) that the poetry Lisle wrote was bad.

Seeing Roos again shamed him, as Pavlovian as if he were face-to-face with Aimee. Stupid—the girl sold tickets to a sex club of all things! Still, she seemed a bitter reminder of his early days in A'dam when he'd believed himself capable of change.

Now she waved her fingers in front of his downcast eyes. "Hey, you aren't going to say hi? I'll tell your mother. They don't let anybody in at Mulligan's who doesn't have good manners!" She grinned wide.

Camden blushed. He felt it all over his head like a rash, a scalp itch. At once, his face seemed all wrong—seemed to invite this tall, unkempt girl to find him obvious, to read between the lines of his life and agenda. *Pretty boy with three girls, showing off, looking to get laid. Trendy American tourist thinking he's decadent for going to see naked girls shoot bananas out of their snatches. GQ poster-boy poseur, little suburban twit.* Anything he did, with this face, would seem calculated, a contrived effort to be charming. If only he'd taken his new friends to Casa Rosso, even though he was so bored with that show he thought he'd kill himself if he watched Batman go soft one more time. At least then he would never have run into Roos.

Suddenly, it dawned on him, how to turn things around. "I didn't figure you for the kind of girl who would work at a place like this."

Roos sighed. "You Americans always say 'this kind of girl' and 'that kind of girl.' It's just like your politics—one party is for the rich white people, another for all the poor people and the immigrants, you say. You all believe it and run out and vote for this person, and you marry this certain type of girl, and I always wonder do you wake up one day and realize that any outsider can tell from watching your TV sitcoms or news shows that you are all exactly the same?"

"What a bitch," a Brit girl muttered. The German guy snickered.

Camden felt hit by strange relief. "Go on in without me, guys," he said. "I have to stay here and defend my country's honor to this totally misguided, but very pretty woman."

"You can't just stand here and block the door," Roos countered. "It's bad for business, for the male customers to see me talking to you."

"Wat doen jij achter werk?" he whispered, unable to let her go but desperate for his chortling cohorts not to hear.

She let her eyes run down him, as though sizing him up for the first time. "How old are you?"

"Sixteen." The four hostelers made noises of shock and irritation. Two swarthy men behind them made as if to push ahead. Camden said, "I'm going to go have a drink somewhere and wait for you. An hour? Two? Four? Where should I go?"

"Don't be so silly," Roos said. "It's too rude to leave your friends." Then, "So, you know, I do the same thing every Sunday. Meet me at the Engelbewaarder tomorrow afternoon, and maybe you'll like it too."

JUNI

After four weeks, Sundays belonged to Roos. A phone call in the morning, then the routine began. He rode his bike to her mother's houseboat, also an art studio; went inside for coffee. Roos would be reading the paper at the old, farmhouse-style kitchen table, which was full of dents, grooves, and smears of paint. Her cup would sit half full, lukewarm, no lipstick around the rim or makeup oil floating on top of the coffee, so Camden would have a sip and wait while her mother poured him his own cup. Next came bread and jam, or sometimes cookies, but Roos and her mother took little interest in them. Sometimes people would drop by, to see Roos' mother's paintings or talk about an upcoming show, and they would come into the kitchen, too, and her mother poured them coffee. Camden would feel like an insider for already being perched on the wooden bench with his own lukewarm mug, his own section of the *Herald Tribune*. Roos' mother spoke little English, so all conversation took place in Dutch—Camden would only pretend to read, straining to understand. Whenever Roos spoke, she addressed him in English, as though they were a unit, conspirators. The thrill was inexplicable; he had to keep his face calm though he wanted to dash up and kiss her hard to show all the guests what was between them. Except that *wasn't* between them—not yet—and besides, he had garnered enough about Dutch reserve to know a display of messy, over-eager passion would only position him as an outsider again. So he sat, sipped, read, waited.

Though Roos (of course) had a bike too, they usually walked to the Engelbewaarder. Across the street, kitty-corner, was a coffeehouse displaying the Jamaican flag, but the only time they had ever entered was for Roos to purchase a bottle of water, which she promptly brought back onto the street. The Engelbewaarder was up a narrow flight of stairs, dark and brown and tentatively seedy in its bohemianism. The crowd was largely middle-aged Dutch and arty expats; there were chessboards. Smoke was thick. He had seen a group of grungy Gen Xers smoking skunk once out in the open, but never dared light up himself. Roos did not smoke, cigarettes or anything else. She drank infrequently, but at Engelbewaarder ordered one whiskey straight up and sipped it while Camden drank Duvels like Lisle so as not to be mistaken for a Bud Light-gulping tourist.

They were there for the jazz—a wild scene that rarely started on time but got going around 3:00 PM or so, as musicians slowly filtered in, dragging their instruments behind them. They set up in front, under the gray glow of the window, and then, for no cover charge to patrons, began an hourslong improvisational jam session featuring a rotating group of some twenty musicians. Sometimes a dozen played at once, sometimes only a few, as they sat out sets and joined in, leaving Camden dazed and aroused in a way music never before had. In the large, open area in back, full of tables, bar life went on as usual with the jazz serving as a backdrop, but up front, where Roos and Camden crammed in at the bar or snagged one of the two tables directly in front of the stage, conversation halted; the music reigned.

Most of the players were men over thirty, scruffy with unwashed clothing in muted shades of black, buttons missing. One saxophonist, a woman scarcely older than Roos, showed up twice to play, her toned biceps flexing as she manipulated her horn. Her hair was long and blond, her face the clean, simple prettiness of Holland; she wore, each time, a black tank top and tight black pants over her tall swaying body. Watching her blow into her sax—face growing pink with effort, hipbones shifting positions as she grooved, her entourage of men accompanying her in a cacophony of sound—

Camden felt stirred in a way he never had at Casa Rosso. She was like an Amazon goddess, and in those moments he felt he would have given anything to feel her body moving against his, to have her wet mouth to himself. But in the next instant, she would jump offstage, and there would be Roos, flushed with pleasure and her tiny whiskey, beaming at him, and the saxophonist would seem like a beautiful sunset they had witnessed together, shimmering and magical, and he would feel glad to see Roos in the dim light of the bar, real and tangible, neither of them mourning that the splendor of what they'd seen was gone.

After Engelbewaarder, even the usual haze of early evening in Amsterdam felt too bright. They walked shielding their eyes, blinking. They needed to "come down," Roos said, so they headed all the way to Centraal Station, to a surreal spa as modern and New Age as Engelbewaarder was a dingy sixties throwback. Roos' best friend from school worked here, at Oibibio, as a massage therapist, and Roos had a standing Sunday appointment just before closing. Inside, the place felt like a strange cross between a giant dance studio and a shopping mall—after his fourth visit, Camden still felt incapable of navigating between the shop, the café, and the spa on his own. Roos, on their first "date" following Engelbewaarder, had taken the liberty of booking Camden a massage too—not that he minded. When she'd gone right along with him to the co-ed dressing room and stripped, his anticipation overrode his embarrassment and he'd chucked off his own clothes, lingering with the smell of Duvel and smoke. But when Roos turned, still naked and holding her towel to her side like a handbag, and pranced into the lobby, sat down and started reading a magazine, Camden freaked. His own towel wrapped around his waist (he'd done it before he could even notice that she hadn't), he surveyed the lobby in a panic: all around him, business types of both genders sat in the buff reading, talking on cell phones, sipping water and tea. A few had towels wrapped around their waists (thank God!), but most appeared oblivious to their nudity, including the fully dressed, hot young receptionists and the walk-in customers off the street inquiring about the availability of appointments without batting an eye at the hoards of dangling penises and perky—or sagging—breasts.

Roos' own breasts, only eighteen years old, nonetheless suffered from gravity, given their size. Her pubic hair was sparse and black; she didn't shave her lean thighs and the hair was likewise thin but dark like a pubescent boy's. Camden's heart rate returned to normal when his massage therapist fetched him, but she ushered him to a private room exposed through a wide, glass door so that all—especially the hot receptionist with her bird's eye view—could watch his ass being kneaded. He thought he might pass out. Just last year, visiting Hugh in the Hamptons, Camden and the crowd they'd run with that summer had formed their own nudist colony down a stretch of mostly deserted beach—they only invited the prettiest, potentially promiscuous girls to join them. Occasionally an adult would hap upon them and stare, disapproving or maybe envious, but the sense of themselves as spectacle had only heightened Camden's enjoyment, his feeling of power. He could tell that some of the kids they'd met, even ones with nice bodies, wanted to join in but just couldn't overcome their shyness; he'd felt disdainful of their conventionality, superior. But now it was the sheer lack of spectacle—of sex—that so unnerved him. He seemed to be the only person in the building conscious of all the nakedness.

And that was Roos. A normal girl living with her mother, dabbling at painting, going to school part-time, abstaining from cigarettes and drugs—but in boutiques, if she saw a shirt she liked, she'd take her top off right there and try it on without going into a changing room. He had seen other Dutch girls do this too and, not knowing them, had assumed they were wild—partying, rave-hopping, X-taking, slutty chicks the Oak Park Camden would have made it his business to know. Instead, Roos lived something like her forty-year-old mother; neither of them dated much, from what Camden could tell. They cooked dinners in, talked about art. After Oibibio, Roos would take him to Shizen, her favorite macrobiotic Japanese restaurant, and Camden, exhausted, would sit beside her sipping green tea, having traversed the entire city by foot on little sustenance beyond beer, wolfing down his raw-fishless maki while Roos expertly maneuvered chopsticks to place tender sashimi slices into her naturally bright red mouth. She never seemed tired; her feet never hurt. Shizen was between their homes, so she would bid him good night upon leaving, kiss him swiftly three times on the cheek—left, right, left—their lips never meeting, and promise to call him tomorrow. She was reliable, did not play games, did not seem to keep track of who had phoned whom last. When she referenced former lovers, which she did rarely but always with good nature, it was impossible to ascertain whether she meant to give him hints or was merely confiding in him as one would a friend. (She had yet to announce *I think of you as a friend*: some small relief.) She seemed to have no idea of how to flirt.

And so, over a series of four Sundays and sporadic other-day-of-the-week "dates" (Were they dates? They went, as they saying went, Dutch), Camden's confusion grew. He did not know how to approach her as a lover and despite thinking of her constantly, was not even quite sure he wanted to. She made him nervous at the same time as making him feel more at ease, more *himself* than he could recall having felt with a girl—with anyone. His handsomeness, a currency in which he was accustomed to dealing, seemed not to register with her, though she was always polite and gracious, interested enough in him on some level to spend extensive time with him. For a woman who got naked at every opportunity, she seemed almost asexual, or at least defined less by her sexuality than seemed normal. Didn't she have desires? Did she fantasize about him? Was she seeing someone else? Like throwing himself upon her in a tackily American display of passion in front of her mother's art-patron guests, the prospect of blatantly hitting on her seemed clearly inappropriate, contrary to the intimacy he hoped was building between them. He feared—like a girl—that if they fucked, it wouldn't mean anything to her. They would, he decided—every Sunday night alone in his bed, listening to the sound of his mother and Lisle's arguments, or worse, his mother's shuddery sobbing alone—simply be friends.

Ginny was in front of the television when Camden entered the apartment after his fourth Sunday with Roos. The silence made it immediately apparent that Lisle was not at home. Since coming to Amsterdam, his mother had taken up cigarettes again after ten years, and now she turned to look at him, her frail, lovely face lit by the TV, her body like a brittle stick aflame at one end. Camden was about to walk past her and go to bed, but she said, accusation somehow always in her voice, "I was waiting for you."

He didn't say anything. That was the one thing about having a mother, about having his particular mother—you did not have to say anything. She would just keep talking at you, and eventually, if you listened hard enough, she would tell you how she wanted you to behave, and if you felt like it, you could fake it, and then you could leave.

"I'm thinking—well, I'm...you got your wish, after all. I guess we're going home."

The words should not have felt like a jolt. But they felt like sliding down the long, spiraling plastic slide of the playground Ginny used to take him to as a kid in Chicago, his body wild with static electricity so when she lunged forward to catch him at the bottom, despite his protests that he did not need her, she always gave him a shock. *Aversion therapy,* he'd quipped to Aimee once, trying to make light of the calls he hadn't returned. *My mother totally smothered me, but she didn't even know how to do it right, to make me dependent like she wanted. It's not you. She accidentally taught me to like my space.* He stood now in front of Lisle's sofa, in her *gezzelig* little living room, his skin bristling with an electric pain. "Who says I want to leave?"

His mother snorted. "Isn't it apparent? You can't stand to be in this house for more than five minutes. Not that—"

"Maybe that's because I'm trying to take advantage of living in another country, so I'm out doing stuff. Maybe I've been trying to make the best of it."

Ginny sighed. "I was going to say, not that I blame you. Lisle and I can't be pleasant to be around. You *have* been making the best of it. You haven't given me any trouble, Cam. You never do. It's not you—I said it all wrong. It's me."

"Well who says you have to be with Lisle for me to stay here? Maybe I'm tired of being dragged around because of who you're sleeping with. Maybe I'll just stay."

There was nothing, then. Only his mother, too demure to point out that at sixteen, he had no money, no legal right to be in Holland, no high school diploma even. He was tied to her, dependent, and this he knew was the one comfort of her life, even though living with him was like living with a ghost. Even though he couldn't wait to leave.

"I didn't realize you'd become happy here," Ginny ventured. "Are you seeing someone? A girl?"

"Of course it's a girl," Camden snapped. "What would it be, a guy?"

"I didn't mean that, honey."

"Whatever." On the tip of his tongue: *Excuse me for liking girls—if I promise never to impose my disgusting male libido on one again, can we stay?* But Ginny would receive the words like a cruel, irrational blow; there was nothing, truly nothing she had ever said to him to give him the idea that his heterosexuality—his sexuality at all—was unacceptable or repugnant to her. Always she had given him freedom, with the obvious exception of these sporadically predictable relocations-for-love. Yet he had never brought a girlfriend home, it occurred to him abruptly. He'd never had a girlfriend he treated well enough to bear his mother's scrutiny. Her fault, or his? How could he explain to her now that after four weeks some Dutch girl had transformed him, made him into something better? His mother of all people, who was transformed and uprooted and reinvented every few months, every few years, but never got anywhere beyond her own skin. Hadn't he learned from the master how foolish it was in the end, when there was only one person you ever could be?

"I'm glad you met someone," Ginny placated, with that stupid thera-pisty voice. "You may find it harder to leave now, but it comforts me, knowing you gained something positive from this experience. It makes me feel less guilty for uprooting you, again."

"Yeah, well, it shouldn't." He stared at her hard. How utterly ironic that a woman so fragile would build a life around wanting people to need her. Maybe the Oak Park bipolar missed her, wanted her back after she'd increased her cachet by running off to live with an Andrea Dworkin-spout-ing radical Dutch poet. Maybe she had gotten wind that an American Sign Language convention was going to be held in Illinois and she couldn't resist. Maybe he should let himself collapse into her arms and cry and give her what she wanted, and then if she had him she wouldn't need everyone else. But he didn't know how to do that, didn't want to, and couldn't remem-ber anymore if he had turned into an asshole to escape her, or if he had just been born that way. What did he have, anyway, to offer Roos? A dick already used up before adulthood, that had squirmed up every hole he could get into, even when it ruined lives? His pretty face? Some "cool" status meant to make up for the fact that his mother was a lesbian with embar-rassing lovers—for the fact that something in him was dead and cold?

But how could he go back?

Under fluorescent basement lights—whose party was it?—keg beer in trans-parent plastic cups: a too-bright yellow. Sudsy Easter egg dye. Hugh's brows *drawn back from his eyes, lips curled, a snarling dog...*all over us, man...couldn't get enough...didn't have to talk her into anything...comes like a fucking eel...tell them, Cam...why not ménage à cinq?...*Words like the buzz of someone else's radio; his own footsteps an echo in his ears, ascending the stairs.* Awww...Mr. Fucking Sensitive...like she's his girlfriend or something...dude...not even fucking midnight...come back....

They sat at Café Luxembourg after class, five of them now who had signed up for another Dutch class after the first eight-week course ended. The second session was already half over, but Camden wouldn't even finish it before he left. They were a motley crew: a techie and his girlfriend (both Brits), an ex-Peace Corps couple, and him. He was almost ten years younger than the others, but they had taken him in, won over by his earnestness to learn the language. He'd been the class star in the end— that was one plus about being a high school student. Rote memorization was still fresh in his mind. The others stumbled over speaking aloud in class, were embarrassed, didn't seem to actually study and then lamented their own stupidity. But being a student was second nature to Camden, even though he'd never been a particularly great one. It was still the only thing he'd ever done.

At Café Luxembourg, they drank cappuccinos and watched beautiful people mill. Camden liked the anonymity he felt with his classmates, his youth and chiseled features shielded by their preppy plainness and coupled normalcy. They sat, an unabashed cluster of foreigners with an open Dutch dictionary, trying with absurd futility to converse in their broken phrases. He saw their thrill over a string of foreign syllables when a moment of understanding clicked. But for Camden, it was more: a sense of difference, a reinvention of meaning. He remembered learning in his very first Dutch class that *hun* meant *there*, and the shock, the recognition of meaning's ambiguity. *Attila the there*, he'd muttered, to the amusement of his classmates. That was how easily language could be recast, violence becoming merely the absurd. One twist of articulation and poof, everything could be different. *A Roos by any other name....* *Verkrachten.* His fingers paused in his dictionary, ran over the definition: *rape.* Some words could not be reconfigured to lose their danger.

Camden's mind hovered half on Roos tonight, but the other half loved these dorky, bookish interludes. He delighted in the progression of his own vocabulary in a way he had never permitted himself to enjoy classes at home. Most of the techies had dropped out when they realized anytime a foreigner attempted to speak Dutch in Amsterdam, the answer came back in fluent English, so practicing was almost impossible—the only students in Dutch II were the diehards. Camden always promised himself he'd speak to Roos' mother in Dutch, but something about the calm silence of those Sunday mornings, about the separation between himself and Roos from her mother's Dutch visitors, precluded introducing his own agenda into the scene. He sat quietly now, not much inclined to show off. He had not told his study group that he was leaving.

"I never get over how ugly Dutch sounds," Peace Corps Girl said. She wore her hair in braids now, to assimilate. Amsterdamers, though they were an oddly earnest lot, had an almost unintentional appreciation of kitsch: that summer all the teenaged and twentysomething girls were parading around in blond braids like stereotypical Dutch girls, with their leather pants, hand-rolled cigarettes, platform heels, and irrationally gorgeous breasts. The Peace Corps couple was short—she only about five feet— and dark, so on her the braids had more of a Frida Kahlo vibe that was still strangely appealing.

"I think it's beautiful," Camden said quietly, and they all looked at him incredulously. He realized he had chosen his words in part to be contrary, and amended: "I mean, I think the total lack of beauty in Dutch is attractive. There's something dignified about not having to be flowery and romantic all the time. You've got to admire the Germanic languages for having the confidence to be guttural, you know?"

"You're a weird kid," the techie Brit said, rumpling his hair. Indignation rose in Camden's throat, then quickly settled. He let his lips smile. Someone else said something. His moment had passed.

Grandparents and small children had set up folding chairs. Camden watched, amazed: most of the spectators watching spectacular floats drift by weren't gay. They were all ages, many with families. In Chicago, whenever Ginny had dragged Camden to the Gay Pride parade as a child, protestors used him against her—corrupting the children, *blah blah blah*. In the United States, kids were like sofas covered in plastic: to be admired but never broken in. Here—where the age of consent was foggy, somewhere between the unofficial twelve and legal sixteen—the treatment of children seemed less precious, more matter of fact, like sex itself, like everything. A float of The Village People sailed smoothly down the Prinsengracht's murky waters, and the small boy on an old man's shoulders next to Camden and Roos cheered. Neither of them, reflected Camden, probably had any idea who the pseudo construction worker and his buff buddies were supposed to be, had ever heard the band's songs even in jest.

Roos was coolly friendly today, had been since he'd told her of his impending departure. He couldn't finger the change exactly—she still called, still made plans to take him around the city on her continual campaign to make a proper Dutch teen of him, useless as it now seemed. She still kissed him energetically and briskly—left, right, left—on meeting and departing, and if anything, her touches in-between had become more frequent, more affectionate. A swat on the arm; a surprisingly small hand resting momentarily on his thigh. But something felt off.

His mother was home today. Lisle had gone off with her friends to party, though from outward appearances this day was more about men than women. The nomadic lesbian scene here, mostly about one-night parties advertised beforehand almost like raves, couldn't compete with the theatrical flair of Amsterdam's enormous and vibrant gay male culture.

These floats and costumes were mind-blowing, the spectacle beyond anything in Chicago. Tonight he and Roos were supposed to hit Melkweg for the end of Gay Pride Week's festivities: comedy shows, art exhibits, you name it. But Roos had friends visiting from France; Camden was frustrated—he wanted to be alone with her, even if he knew the results would only yield more of the same.

Roos leaned over the canal whooping with the rest of the crowd, happy for their space close to the front, the chairs they'd dragged from Lisle's apartment. What was the big deal? He was sick of these parades. Putting it on water, adding professional flair didn't change anything. He was tired of watching from the sidelines here, waiting for his own life to happen. Now it would all be over before he could even tell Roos he loved her. For

God's sake, couldn't she *tell* he loved her? What kind of guy would spend more than a month following her around without so much as a taste of her cheerful pink tongue if it weren't love? Or was she used to this sort of thing? How could it be love if Camden didn't even know?

"My friend tonight," Roos said, rap-a-tap-tapping his knee in staccato, "he is someone I met traveling, you know, when I left school. We sleep together sometimes, when we see each other, but he is bisexual, that's why he came for this weekend. So maybe tonight you want to come with us—if we do that, I don't know if we will—and then it will take some pressure off, you know? Then I think you and I will both feel better when you go."

He stared at her. Had he misheard? Her English was not usually faulty, but the crowd was booming, and sometimes she had lapses. He blinked.

"You want me to have sex with you and your boyfriend?"

"Oh, no," she giggled. "He isn't my boyfriend—I told you," she squinched up her face, "really he likes boys. But only sometimes girls. He's very nice."

A light dawned. "Oh. *Oh*…" and a wave of nausea hit him—all this wasted time—"Roos. Do you think I'm gay? Because of my mom—I mean, I've told you, and you've seen me with girls, when we met and everything—I'm not interested in guys that way. I'm interested in…I like…well, actually, I like *you*."

"I know!" She slapped her forehead—the Dutch were so animated, strangely camp when speaking, despite their reserve. "I'm trying to think why I'm not saying this clearly—no, I understand that you don't like men sexually. I'm—well, I'm just thinking because you and I are so close, you know, and we like each other maybe too much, that when you leave it will be hard for us both, if we have sex. But I know you want to do it—so I'm just thinking, maybe this will make it easier, you know? Not so personal, but to satisfy curiosity. Then we will still be friends, and when you go, it won't be so sad."

"Not so sad." He did not know what to say, felt his words echo, trampled by the crowd. To fuck her with some random bisexual French man seemed about the saddest thing he could think of in the world.

"Yes, exactly!" Beaming at him with her exquisite apple cheeks, their small flaws—a whispery scar from a girlhood fall; a littering of tiny pink veins when she laughed—visible without the shield of makeup and even more endearing than perfection could be. She was trying to make him happy; she had said, *I know you want to.* He shook his head slowly, made himself cross the ocean of his fear to take her hand.

"Roos. I'm in love with you. I don't want to share you with some other guy like a toy. I would rather nothing happen between us at all than it be something degrading like that, that would cheapen the time I've had with you. Do you understand?"

But she didn't. It was visible on her face, the position of her untweezed-but-still-delicate eyebrows. "Why do you say *like a toy*? He is my friend— I am not a toy."

"That's not what I meant." He sighed—language was sticky. "I just want it to be nice—*romantisch*—not some kinky threesome with you blowing some other guy while I'm—while I'm screwing you doggie-style or something. Come on! Look, I've done that—I know what it's like for the girl—"

"Done *what*? What is it you think I'm asking you to do? Why do you think it's something ugly, like you using me with some other man—I told you—he's my friend and he likes boys too. We would all be the same. Maybe he is our toy—yours and mine—and he would like to be! Maybe *you* are the toy! Why does it have to be me? I don't know what you have done, but—"

"No. You don't." Not yelling back—he couldn't yell, not this, what he was about to say. "What do you want me to tell you? That I don't live in some little idyllic world where everybody's always friendly and polite and sex is oh-so-civilized like shaking hands or going for a beer? That I had a girlfriend—that there was a girl I knew, who I used to sleep with, *fuck buddies* we call it at home, and I let one of my friends have sex with her, and next thing you know I was inviting her over so two more guys could fuck her with us too? They raped her, OK? She didn't know it—she never reported it—she's still spreading her legs for them now, doing whatever they say. But my mother would tell you they raped her. My mother would say...I think we raped her, Roos."

She was shaking her head, slow then faster. "You let your friend have sex with her? Like she is your property? Why do you say it that way?"

"For chrissake!" He stood—next to him, the old man glanced disapprovingly, his display of negative emotion more threatening to the grandchild's well being than the gyrating, half-naked men kissing each other on their gay-orgy floats. "I can't say everything perfectly! She wasn't my property—she was just a girl I liked, and I let her down—I was afraid to admit I liked her and didn't want to share her. I was afraid she was too slutty and I'd look bad. Aren't you the one who told me Americans are obsessed with what kind of girl somebody is before they'll date her? Well you're right—I was like that. But now I'm not anymore."

"I think you still are. I think you think if you make love with me with my friend, you will make me into the kind of girl you can't like anymore."

Camden sat down. His hand was still gripping her wrist, too tight, it must be too tight. But she was as tall as he was, older, probably as strong—she made no move to pull away. "That's not true. That's not what I'm talking about. I just don't want to cheapen it. I don't care about your friend—I don't want him there. I just want you." Then, suddenly letting go, he watched the blood flow back into her wrist, rushing red. "But you don't want it to be something special. You want it to be just a game, a fun activity like going to a parade. You're afraid to feel sad when I leave." Tears were clogging in his throat—he wasn't sure if it was her, or what he had revealed—if maybe it was that she'd had almost no response to learning he'd raped a girl, but instead wanted to argue semantics. "I said I *love* you, Roos. Do you even care about me?"

"Of course I do!" Her exasperation had gotten the better of her now; she folded her arms, glared at the staring old man. "But what is the point, tell me? You're leaving! You're some kid! You have to go home! What do you want me to say?"

Aimee on the backseat of Ginny's car, his head resting on her thigh, her other leg vise-like over his neck, but loosely. *Thank you.* His veins instantly hot inside. What had happened between them had been accidental—no skill of his own. She looked like somebody who had seen God—this girl he knew from parties—just some easy freshman Hugh and the rest would never think worth much with her frizzy locks and slight baby fat. Only good enough—always good enough—to screw. *Thank you.* He'd expected her to be awkward, nervous, maybe mad. No girl had ever thanked him before....

Maybe it was true that Ginny had somehow made him feel guilty about being a man, fearful of his desires—that her conviction in male violence,

her urge to nurture the weakest of women, had inspired in him a reactionary craving to fit into a male pack at any cost. It hadn't always been
easy—sometimes with his pretty face, at new schools, and when they heard
about his mother, there were assumptions. But the girls always straightened that out—always flocked to him—and once he'd proven himself with
them, the guys followed. It was always understood: the girls were only a
means; his male peers were the ones whose opinion counted. Until Roos.
Was this how Aimee felt when Hugh suggested a threesome and Camden
sat right there smiling as his best friend talked a fourteen-year-old girl into
setting her high school career under some terrible stone she would never
escape? He and Hugh were popular—she must've felt, if scared, also desired,
honored. But later, when there had been four of them, coked-up and slur-
ringly drunk…she was only a bonding ritual then, like a playing field or a
war. She had tried to make eye contact with him, but he wouldn't look;
even when he entered her, he made sure to flip her over first. He'd been
so sick afterward he couldn't sleep or eat for days, sure the police would
show up at his door any moment. But the next weekend, she'd only shown
up at the usual set of parties, gone upstairs with Hugh. When Hugh beckoned for Camden to join them, he pretended not to see. What girl would
want to be forever labeled as "that freshman who was gang raped?" Even
"slut" was infinitely preferable. When Hugh and the others had teased him
about not wanting to hook up with Aimee again, he'd insinuated that being
naked around three other guys was not really something he wanted to do
on a regular basis, and maybe they should be a little worried if they thought
it was so much fun—that shut them up. To tell them that what they'd
done was *wrong* was unthinkable. He had the feeling that by now, if he
found Aimee when he got home, apologized to her, she would be far beyond
understanding what he was even talking about.

"Does this mean you don't want to go to Melkweg?" Roos asked, and for
a moment his heart soared—maybe she would say never mind, maybe
she would stay with him for as much time as they had left. But when
he hesitated, he saw only that she hoped for a way out of this drama—
that he would stomp off now and make it easy, or come and play along,
admit she was right the way he usually did, chalk it up to his unworldly

American-ness. Her wrist, resting on her knees, had returned to the living, breathing color of the rest of her skin—his flash of violence now invisible. He had the urge to grab her again, to mark her, to keep her from slipping away. His hand stayed still.

"Not everything can work out," he said quietly, as bodies around them filed past, heading home or toward other scenes of merriment, the parade done. "Sometimes you have to take a risk and get hurt for anything to be worth it or real." He realized he knew this, too, from his mother—the hopeful and brave parts of his psyche as sure as the parts of which he was ashamed—while Roos' mother would never run across an ocean for love or disappear into the bones of her own body in the grief of its disillusionment. Right now Roos' mother was probably smoking and serene, lost in the abstract pictures of her head, alone on the houseboat, a model to her daughter of how to live a perfectly self-possessed, independent life free of pain. Did it work? Could you close yourself off that way, even with the best plan? He'd thought he could, but his mother's blood ran through him, impulsive and naive and full of some blind capacity for love he had never known he possessed—and that Roos would not give him the chance to explore and see if it was real.

"I think I'll take a pass," he said, and touched her wrist once more, gently this time. "I'll call you before I leave, though."

She stood to fold her chair, hoisted it without difficulty under one arm. Her blinking eyes at a rare appearance of sun seemed doll-like, confused, slightly dazed as to how meaning had proven so slippery between them. Then she lifted his chair too, when he stood stupidly failing to do so, and headed over the bridge toward Lisle's empty home.

Slave Driver

Wanda Coleman

Trudy recognized them immediately, three silver-haired gents—father, uncle, son, all regular patients—as they entered the central-city doctor's office that evening. They were small men, businessmen, originally from Eastern Europe, proud shrewds radiating the arrogance of acquired American wealth. Clad in casually elegant sweaters, slacks, loafers, they looked frail, obviously feeling changes the clock had wrought. Even the son was well into his sixties.

Trudy's stomach tightened. As the front office receptionist and back office general worker, she would greet them stoically, if not enthusiastically, but could not help but anticipate the moment when their assault would begin.

The son and uncle struggled as they dragged August, the father, through the outer door into the lobby. He was past ninety and, as far as Trudy was concerned, as evil as he was platinum-haired. He had made it a ritual to insult her. He did so freely in front of Mona, the Japanese office manager, knowing that she would keep quiet. No one sane would risk gainful employment defending a nigger, went the implication.

Trudy never challenged Mona's silence. Together, they manned the physicians' front office counter and examination prep area. As a child, Mona had survived internment in one of the stateside camps of World War II. Her family lost everything. Mona still had the disturbing habit, Trudy observed, of never throwing away uneaten food. Her desk drawer was filled with stale packets of cookies and gritty candy bars. She would keep leftover fruit from lunch on the counter until it blackened with rot or whitened with mold.

There was nothing in the way of friendship between them. Not even the neutral pop-culture chitchat that usually bridges that treacherous void between workers of different social stripes. Trudy had tried to no avail.

She made mental notes of instances when a patient cracked a racist joke or made an ugly comment in front of them. Mona's back would stiffen, but she never said a word—of reproach to the patient, or in empathy to Trudy afterward. Trudy weathered every difficulty, except those presented by August and his kinfolk.

Last time, August actually called her a "colored wench." She had gone hot and cold. She had fought to keep from snatching the reprobate through the reception window and blessing him with every pound of her strength. Her eyes had begun to tear in repressed rage. Her hands had trembled as she mentally forced the faces of her children into view, envisioning what it would mean to them if she ended up in jail on charges of assault. She left old August smirking as he stood at the window, went to the back of the building and remained there.

Mona had come in and had seen August sitting quietly on one of the sofas.

"Are you being helped?" she had asked.

He had smiled and shrugged.

She then unlocked the inner office door, saw the reception area was untended and went around back. Trudy was sitting behind the back office counter, typing away at the day's dictation, earphones in her ear.

Mona had rapped loudly on the counter. Trudy looked up. It was hard enough to be unappreciated by her employers, difficult enough to bear Mona's warped indifference, but excruciating to endure repeated abuse from their aging, well-to-do clientele. Trudy had battled to maintain her mask of front-office decorum. It continually galled her that this was something Mona failed to understand.

"Why are you back here, when there's a patient up front?"

Trudy looked at her and said nothing. Mona cocked her head.

"Are you all right?"

"No," Trudy said, "I'm not all right."

"Aren't you going back up front?"

Trudy stared at her without offering an answer.

Mona looked at her blankly and shrugged. "I swear, I don't know what's wrong with you people."

Now, in unspoken protest, whenever Trudy spotted a troublesome patient coming into the office, she abandoned the counter without a word, and went around to the station in back, leaving them to Mona. But on this visit, Mona was out running errands for the doctors, and the lab technician—a recent arrival from Palestine—was analyzing the morning's urine specimens. Trudy had no choice but to cope with the trio.

August's son, a willowy man, looked as if he were going to snap under his father's weight. Trudy was struck by how docile and infirm August had become. The uncle closed the front office door with his foot. Then the two younger men labored to get August onto the waiting room sofa where he lay breathlessly moaning as the uncle approached the reception window and glared defensively at Trudy.

"We don't have an appointment," he said anxiously. "Think the doc'll see him?"

"Sure," her bright smile was phony.

Trudy went to the physicians' chambers, knocked on the door, and informed the doctor on call that he had an emergency patient. She alerted the technician that tests might be needed, then quickly prepared an examination room. That done, she returned to the inner office door, invited the men in. Again they wrestled with August, bouncing him against the waiting room sofa until they managed to pull him to his feet. Unable to budge him any farther, they stood there, staring at her blankly.

"We can't lift him," the son said softly. "And he can't walk."

She heard the exquisite pain in his words. The anguish in his face was mirrored in the silent frown of the uncle. Three old men. This was relentless recognition, a profound admission of diminished manhood—their notions of manhood. She could not help but respect their pain.

"Here, let me help." She said it so sweetly she could hardly stand herself. She imagined herself rising above their level of bigotry. They had treated her very nastily, especially the crusty old August, who went out of his way to demean her. And they knew she knew it was because she was black. She had never complained to any of the doctors. The physicians she worked for were white men themselves, immigrants and the sons of immigrants. Without discussion, it was understood that no matter how liberal in their hiring practices—at root—they basically shared August's contempt for the African American.

Trudy had resisted temptation to return the abuse she was subjected to, ever mindful of how badly she needed to keep her job in order to care for her children. An economic recession was on and, nationwide, decent-paying alternatives were scarce. She liked her job and had no desire to quit, as said to friends, "behind the racist bullshit of busybodies."

What the immigrants didn't know was that Trudy could drive herself far harsher than any so-called boss. It was she who insisted that her ghetto apartment sparkle as if it were a mansion, dusting and polishing everything that could be dusted and polished. It was she—in the role of mother and father—who fed and clothed her children, washed and ironed the laundry, shopped for groceries, washed and waxed the car, paid all the debts. It was she alone who minded the children, drove back and forth from school to babysitter, and scheduled what entertainment was affordable in her efforts to give them a decent life. It was she who spent loveless night after night addressing envelopes by hand, for a mail order outfit, to earn extra money—after the kids were asleep.

She believed she could make time her ally by finding the cheapest clock with the loudest alarm. She set it religiously after midnight before she fell into an exhausted sleep. It woke her at four-thirty every morning, allowing her barely enough time to tend to her person, wake and feed the children, get them to school and then begin her thankless workday anew.

First to arrive every morning, before making the coffee and taking messages from the answering service, she brought in the daily newspaper, one she'd take home each night to glance at before bedtime in concert with the TV news. The headlines invariably left her numb and deepened her sleep. She had few opinions about anything that could not be reduced to an elemental right or wrong. Keeping up with local politics was impossible beyond noting the skin color of the candidate for whom she might vote. Headlines that thundered the unilateral invasion of a country to send strident messages to enemy nations concerned her only to the extent that one of her kinfolk had joined the military.

Otherwise, fear and frustration defined her dreams. They were the dreams of a statistic she knew uncomfortably well: working class poor, single mother.

It was she who spent any available waking moment wondering what she could do to escape poverty, wondering what it would take to free herself and her children from its misery. She counted those neighbors who fell around her, families destroyed, lives taken, knowing it was only a matter of time before she, too—and her children—became victims of some inevitable violence. Too often she had stood among onlookers when a lover or spouse was taken away in handcuffs; or carried oven-fresh casserole dishes to bereaved families following the gang-related funeral of a child or teenager. Nightly, she listened as police helicopters swooped over rooftops, as sirens and shouts echoed up and down the block.

All I have is my high school diploma and my back.

The dread drove her so fiercely that it spilled over into her workplace, manifested as compulsive neatness, resulting in a medical office where every chart, desk, file, and ledger was in perfect order. She did the billing, made appointments, transcribed dictation, assisted the laboratory technician and the office manager, was Janeofall.

The white man hadn't been born, she thought, who could drive her one centesimal harder.

Trudy positioned herself at August's side, pausing briefly to cushion his apparent shock at being touched by a large ebony woman for the first time in his life. Trudy was dark-skinned, a full six-feet in height and weighed a firm, high-busted two hundred pounds. Her thighs were thick, her legs sturdy. Opening her arms, she cradled August as if he were a slightly hefty infant.

He looked at her with grateful amazement.

She was surprised at how light he was as she carried him through the waiting-room door.

The son and uncle followed. They watched helplessly as Trudy lowered August onto the examination table, handed them a paper dressing gown, and instructed them to undress him to his waist. The three men stared at her, gasping, hands and fingers twitching in befuddlement.

"You're a strong one, aren't you," the uncle finally muttered.

Appreciating the complexities of embarrassment and tarnished masculine pride, she tried to offer some simple explanation to defuse the situation, perhaps break their spell of wounded self-esteem.

"My father was a boxer back in the '40s and '50s. When I was little,

I used to work out with him during training sessions."

"Oh," August nodded. The men smiled at one another awkwardly.

Trudy left them in the doctor's care and returned to her front office duties. Almost as soon as she sat down, consternation set in. She realized that they had accepted her explanation about her father because it played into the stereotype of the Negro as superior work animal.

Mona finally came and relieved Trudy, who avoided the geriatric trio the rest of that evening, working at the back desk until August was rolled from the office in a wheelchair.

A month later, during lunch break, the reception window quietly slid back, pushed open from the waiting room side. Old man August stuck his head and hands through the opening. It was his first visit since Trudy had carried him into the examination room. He stared at her without a hello.

Mona was across the street at the hospital cafeteria. As usual, Trudy ate while on duty. She neatly put her lunch aside and smiled at August warmly, recalling how sick he'd been. She wiped her hands thoroughly and rose from the counter to face him at the window.

He had recovered. His eyes sparked with mischief. In his hand was a slip of paper she recognized as the bill she had prepared and sent. It dangled loosely in one ancient, liverspotted paw, just within reach.

"Let me talk to the doctor!" he barked in her face, brusqueness underscored by his thick-tongued accent.

Trudy sighed. August was up to his old wickedness. He was familiar with the office routine and knew the doctors were out on lunch break. Yet he demanded she be put through paces.

"The doctor is at lunch," she repeated stoically, trying to echo her former sweetness, "as you well know."

"I SAID I WANT TO SEE HIM!" August roared.

The invoice fluttered loosely in his hand.

"If there's a question about the bill, perhaps I can help," she said as she reached for it. August snappily withdrew it from the window.

"YOU?" He snorted it like a dirty word. "You help me?" He trumpeted like a bull elephant. "You—you're just the SCULLERY MAID around here!"

Instantly, her eyes glassed over.

She fought herself to keep still. Her mouth opened, her jaw hinged and unhinged but no sound came forth. Her nose began to run, and dripped down onto her smock. She did not dare move a whit, and did not raise a hand to wipe it clean, teetering before her tormentor, frozen with rage.

His eyes laughed in her fury.

The click of the back-office door, followed by the rustle of a skirt and the soft padding of Mona's feet, brought her out of the trance. Mona peeped around her, through the service window, trying to see what she was staring at. Her eyes swept the waiting room.

August was gone.

Oblivious to Trudy's state, Mona glanced down at the counter and saw the unfinished lunch nesting between the phone bank and the appointment book.

"You take that around back and finish up," Mona snapped.

"My name is Trudy," she snapped back. "T-r-u-d-y. And I like to hear it said."

The Wolf Story

Irina Reyn

When I first stepped into Frederick Chopin Airport, I was afraid Lauren wouldn't be there to meet me. The airport was smaller than I imagined it would be, just a long corridor of faded carpet, with one small newspaper stand. I tried to decipher the airport signs, standing there with my wrinkled coat slung over an arm, realizing that I had expected to encounter Cyrillic letters. Around me, families were embracing; I heard the plastic crinkling of flower bouquets, the loud smack of kisses. But then I saw her. Frail and compact, fistfuls of hair behind each ear, she lunged for me in her rickety, coltish way, and I tried to secure a grip across the lattice of her bony shoulders.

"Welcome to Warsaw," she said, surprised, it seemed, that I was here. I followed her to the baggage carousel. There, the passengers of my small connecting flight from Munich were gathered, watching the mechanical mouth spitting out one lumpy bag after another. Lauren darted for mine, grasping its torso around the middle. Two men mobilized to her rescue; the suitcase probably weighed more than she did.

Outside we were greeted with blinding sleet, mounds of gray snow, a ferocious wind. Over e-mail, Lauren had warned me that a Polish winter would extend deep into the spring, but it had seemed impossible to grasp while I was packing; it was that kind of April in New York.

On the bus, I watched the looming buildings, some hidden beneath the skeletal trellis of construction, some still charred from World War II-era bombing, others gleaming and intimidating. The pedestrians below were a dark, scurrying mass. Only a few people seemed to be bothering with umbrellas; the rest were plowing ahead grimly, head first, into the storm.

This was not the most pleasant introduction to Poland, and I wondered at Lauren's resilience through the months of January, February, and March. How could she not feel isolated, cut off from language and friends, navigating one dreary day after the next?

We were all surprised when she left New York, announcing right before New Year's that she had bought a plane ticket to Poland to find its remaining Jews. She would teach English in the evenings, she said, and by day, she would conduct research at the Jewish Historical Institute—interview survivors, speak with the Jews who decided to stay. She saw a larger project emerging, a book maybe; in any case she would figure it out once she got there. We were stunned. None of us were doing much of anything in our early twenties. We were photocopying manuscripts for tyrannical editors or verifying phone numbers in magazine articles. We were flirting with news producers, sneaking into film premieres, balancing ourselves on wobbly stilettos, mourning Princess Diana. We would get our free meals at whichever company was having the party: Naomi would send something around about MTV; I would get us into *Saturday Night Live!* holiday functions; Joanna would sneak us into wine and cheese lectures at NYU.

Our men still had nicknames—"The Guy Who Only Eats Salmon," "Mr. Hoover," "Pepé Le Pew." We went to synagogue on the high holidays, but broke the fast at Union Square Café. We voted for political candidates with our gut and considered length when buying a novel. We responded, but rarely initiated. So when Lauren told us she was off in search of Jews, we knew a major shift had taken place in our lives. Some of us (for it could not have been only me) were made to feel ashamed— in our silver lamé tank tops, our knee-high suede boots, our push-up bras, our vodka cranberries—of our own pursuits.

And then, four months later, she called me from Warsaw. "I'm pregnant," she said.

"You need me." I was already reaching for my Filofax and the number of a travel agent. "I speak Russian." She begged me not to come but I refused to hear it; Lauren was in trouble and there was no one to help her but me.

Her building was a Soviet-style concrete structure that was only three floors tall but spread over an entire block, each entrance indistinguishable from the next. Only one of us could fit comfortably into the elevator with the suitcase, so Lauren got in first, holding open the accordion flaps of the door, while I flattened myself against the wall. The apartment was a sublet from a Polish academic on sabbatical in Berkeley, Lauren explained from the other side of the bag. I assumed this was where she and Mateusz had been together.

We walked into the apartment. The white lace curtains, the rug on the wall, the television, small and square with protruding knobs, the floral-patterned china—all nearly replicated my grandmother's place in Brighton Beach. When I sat on Lauren's cot, covered by a wool blanket tucked inside a duvet cover, I heard the squeaks of the springs as the canvas adapted to my body.

"I'm lucky, I guess," Lauren said. "I rarely feel nauseous."

But that didn't surprise me; Lauren always found a way to separate herself from the crowd.

"Aren't we disengaging ourselves from the soft center of life?" she had said to us suddenly when we sat down to dinner at Balthazar, a reservation acquired after Naomi's boss at MTV put in a phone call to the owner. We ignored Lauren then—the wine list was extensive and our resident French expert, Joanna, wanted to take a stab at it. "Pouilly-Fumé okay with everyone?" she smiled, looking up from the list.

And after dinner, we knew we looked good with our bare legs, our curves and painted mouths; we convinced the bouncer to let us cut the line at Limelight. Some soccer players from Granada bought us a round of whiskey sours, and Ace of Base was pounding over the sound system. Lauren drank more than the rest of us and, barely weighing one hundred pounds, had to be dragged out of the club, her arms warm and heavy around my neck. We piled into a cab at four in the morning, smudged mascara around our eyes, ash-like splotches on our cheeks.

As usual, it was up to me to see Lauren home; I can still see her hunched over the lock, the tautness of her concentration as she stabbed at the keyhole with her key.

The appointment at the medical clinic was not until late afternoon, so we had practically an entire day at our disposal. Sleepy and jet-lagged, I was thinking a late start, a café, maybe a museum if we were feeling ambitious. But Lauren had other plans. She wanted to show me the remains of the Warsaw ghetto.

She got dressed, which meant rifling through two suitcases in the corner of the room. The nightgown she removed was floral, cotton, and boxy. My grandmother used to make my lunch dressed in a nightgown like this— an immigrant nightgown, I would call it—frying chicken cutlets and cubed potatoes on her small stove, rubbing her oily hands on the apron. By the time I finished lunch, my grandmother would be dressed for the synagogue, the nightgown tucked carefully under her pillow. And here it was, the very same one, on Lauren's body, engulfing her.

"The Warsaw ghetto. Great," I said, if only so she would take off that nightgown and fold it away out of my sight.

There was not much left to see; if I wasn't with Lauren, I would have bypassed this fragment of wall and found nothing significant in the strip of railway, where cattle cars were used to ship victims to concentration camps. An innocent bus stop stood where the train station used to be. An unremarkable residential neighborhood took the place of the former ghetto. As we walked, Lauren took notes on a pad. She tried to show me what she had written but must have sensed that I was eager to get indoors.

"A Jewish star!" I pointed to a scrawling on the wall.

"It's a slur," she said, barely looking up. My umbrella had failed to cover her head, and snowflakes formed a thin veil over her hair. "It's how rival soccer teams insult one another, by spray-painting a Star of David."

We went up a few steps to stand at the Monument to the Heroes of the Warsaw Ghetto, but I could barely see its entire form for all the snow flurries. The memorial was a granite square; tucked into the front were sculptures of men standing, kneeling, one slumped over. And when Lauren walked us around the back we found an inlaid panel, a row of families, marching.

"I'm dying for a cup of coffee," I said after we stood by the monument for what felt like hours. I was impatient for Lauren to bring up Mateusz. That's why I was here, after all.

I thought I had finally met a kindred spirit when I first glimpsed Lauren at our college's Chabad House. Neither of us was Orthodox, so we sat awkwardly on the women's-only side, the men a mass of shadows behind the opaque screen. We had heard of the rabbi, a charismatic man known throughout the campus for inspiring spirituality in secular Jews, and so there we were, following the Hebrew with great difficulty, helping one another keep up with the service. I was immediately drawn to Lauren's obvious indifference to fashion—white Keds paired with an unflattering, ankle-length dress, hair gathered messily by an oversized lime green clip.

After the service, we found our way to a local diner where we ate grilled cheese sandwiches until midnight. It was the way she spoke, I remember—quickly, sucking back words—using her hands as well as her mouth. I told Lauren about my grandmother, and she seemed to understand. She was working on a genealogical project, tracing the lives of her own great-grandparents, Polish Jews who emigrated before the first World War. She had all that conviction—even if back then it was still wobbly, fastened to nothing solid.

Once I invited her to join my budding social group, it became clear that Lauren, like me, had difficulty finding boyfriends. Naomi was a redhead whose chutzpah when inebriated paved the way to male introductions. Joanna had the gait of a gazelle, and she spoke French. Lauren was wiry and intense, a vegetarian who loved cheese above any other food. I tried to explain to her that a guy who's meeting you for the first time doesn't always want to hear that his clothes were sewn by underpaid labor workers in China. As far as we knew, Lauren had only a single boyfriend in college, a guy we never met. But then one day, she reemerged, even thinner than before. She gathered us into our dorm's common room, ordered pizza and cheese sticks, paid for the entire order, and apologized—then we knew he was gone. I was relieved but a bit ashamed at being relieved. If Lauren, of all people, had discovered love, how could I justify my own empty bed?

So many Polish words are similar to Russian and yet not the same. At the Casablanca Café, I experienced flashes of understanding, a word here and there. "Saturday," for example, scratched on a chalkboard—*sobota* in Polish, *subota* in Russian. When Lauren first called to say she would be getting an abortion, I knew she was asking to be rescued. Who else would take care of her?

"They will understand me even if they don't want to," I had assured her.

Lauren ordered a *herbata* and a *kawa*. I was impressed with the way she was able to form complete Polish sentences, but she still squinted in mental calculation as the café server told her the price. The teenage girl leaned down to Lauren to enunciate the words.

We found a seat by the window at a round, Parisian-style café table, with a view of miserable pedestrians sliding around in the slush.

"Mateusz." From the way she said his name, I knew he, too, was gone, and the old sensation, like the relaxing of taut rubber bands, returned.

They met at the Jewish Historical Institute, she said, while she was doing research on Polish Jewish history. He was part of that new generation of twentysomethings who were excavating their Jewish pride, who tried to make it to the Nozyk Synagogue at least once a month, who gathered in wine bars to discuss Poland's Jewish future, who vowed to marry only another Jew. They were responding to their parents, Lauren told me—Polish Jews who didn't want to be reminded they were Polish Jews; who were driven by anticommunist politics rather than religious identity; who had little interest in confronting their country's role in the Holocaust. So it became the goal of people like Mateusz to spark a flame, to attack the country's historic anti-Semitic impulses. He invited Lauren to join their group.

"That's very interesting. But how does he feel about all this?"

"He's just like us, Galya. Figuring out who he is." Lauren gulped down the last of the tea and took my hand.

I wriggled out of her grasp. "It doesn't sound like he's figuring anything out. It sounds like he got you pregnant and ran away."

"I guess it looks like that." Her hand remained on the table and she leaned forward, as if to pluck an eyelash from my cheek or brush away a crumb on my chin.

I maintained my patience; with Lauren, it wasn't easy.

"If you didn't drag her in with us in college…" Naomi used to tell me, glancing at her watch as we missed the beginning of yet another movie or entered a party just as its heat was becoming diluted or lost our prized table at Mercer Kitchen. Then Lauren would come running in, a backpack strap sliding off one shoulder, wearing that horrible swamp-green Land's End jacket she insisted shielded her from the crosswind, a thick book in her hand.

"Give her a chance," I would tell the girls again and again.

Was it after she insisted we start attending Friday night services, that Naomi and Jo made their first plans by themselves? They claimed neither Lauren nor I was home to pick up their call, that it was a last-minute invite to a film screening. But I had been home all day with nothing to do, waiting for the phone to ring, for my night to take shape.

The medical clinic was scrupulously clean with cheerful yellow walls, but the consultation room was narrow, with peeling wallpaper. I sat in the chair while Lauren dangled her feet off the table. I realized that I had no idea how to say "abortion" in either Polish or Russian.

"It's gonna be fine," Lauren said, so close to me that I could touch her ankles. The doctor walked in, a middle-aged woman in thick glasses and a low bun. "Slucham," she began, writing on her clipboard.

The three of us, at different levels, were so close to one another that for a moment my mind swept clean the little Russian I retained. How often had my grandmother warned that if I didn't keep speaking every day, I would lose an integral chunk of myself?

"You see," I began in Russian, "my friend is living in Poland and needs to have 'abortion.' We can pay in dollars or…whatever."

"Zloty," Lauren said.

"Zloty. But it should be safe, please. You see she doesn't want baby but might want baby in future. She is doing important research on Jews in your country. She cannot leave before she finish research on Jews. Do you understand?"

When my grammatically dubious Russian sentences finished pouring out of me, there was silence from the doctor. She was old enough to have grown up during the period when Russian was required in Polish school-rooms, but her face hardened, without registering that she understood me.

"You want I speak English?"

"Prosic," Lauren said, and I knew then that I was not needed, and

I felt foolish, wedged into a constricted room with Lauren and an English-speaking doctor.

"If you would please leave us," the doctor told me.

I stepped outside, huddled beneath the awning. The snow and sleet had ended, but the wind remained barbaric, gripping my breath in its fist. I could see chunks of the city below, church spires protruded out of the concrete like needles. Just when I couldn't stand out there another minute, Lauren came out to meet me. The abortion would not be until next week.

"I don't think I'm going to have it," she said.

"Why the hell would you do that?" I asked this question several times, but Lauren didn't answer me.

We started walking, with a purpose that I hoped would lead to a quiet place for us to discuss the matter further, or at least a museum or historical sight unconnected to Jewish stars or the Holocaust. We walked for almost half an hour and then turned into the entrance of yet another clone of her apartment building. Slowly, sounding out the words, I read the weather-beaten sign out front. We were on the steps of a nursing home.

"What are we doing here?" I asked. "Don't you want to talk?"

"I've been interviewing one of the few Holocaust survivors who decided not to vacate Poland after the war." Lauren held the door open for me. "Can you imagine? After everything your own people did, to stay, to live among them?"

We walked into the building. Every muscle in my body rebelled, wanted to go back to New York. I smelled a mixture of rubbing alcohol and perfume; before me was a long hallway lined by waxy linoleum. I paused at the front door. What were my friends doing now? I wondered. On a Friday afternoon, the workday would lack serious purpose, so they would touch base by telephone to firm up plans for the night. A snack at someone's after-work happy hour, then in quick succession: a book party, a jazz concert, drinks in the kind of chrome place that required slipping by a beefy security guard. A loft soiree, maybe, with its anonymous owners and generous bartenders. An exchange of cards, the names printed in assertive blue and brown and black inks, their significance dissolving by the following morning.

"You'll love Agnieszka," Lauren said, pulling me by the wrist. I could already imagine what lay ahead: a woman with blinking blue eyes, the warm touch of her hand. She would speak to me in long-buried Russian, no doubt, as the memories erupted out of her. I've seen those Holocaust documentaries. She would find in me an entry into her younger years, and then what horrors would she translate into speech? I resisted Lauren's tug and stood where I was.

Lauren let go of my arm; perhaps my reluctance was what she expected. "I thought it might be interesting for you," she said, and I watched her slip through one of the doors at the end of the hallway.

Outside, I thought of my grandmother, who often tried to unload her own tales of the war next to her chicken cutlets and potatoes. She would lace her food with stories of the extermination of her family, in their own home, of her subsequent forty-one months inside a Ukrainian ghetto.

"Babushka, let's not," I would say. "Tell the wolf story instead." And she would oblige, launching into my favorite childhood tale of the wolf who came to an elderly couple and sang:

> *There once was a farmer*
> *Who had five sheep*
> *A colt and a calf—*
> *Seven beasts in all!*

The old woman was so charmed by the song that she told the old man to offer the wolf a sheep. The wolf gobbled up the sheep, and returned the following day, singing the same song. He received another sheep, and another three, and eventually, the colt, the calf, and the old woman herself. When he came back again, the old man understood that this time, the wolf had come for him.

Who could blame me for preferring a wolf to a ghetto? I was nine years old and the day was pulsing with warmth and unfilled hours, and downstairs, in the playground, kids were chasing each other. You could hear the choir of their laughter all the way up on the eleventh floor and I longed to run around with them, to feel the unconditional sunshine across my cheeks.

Later, kids my age were taking their first trips into the city, and I informed my grandmother that I no longer had time—just a peck on the cheek and a plate of cutlets and potatoes. I would see my contemporaries on Broadway, buying ripped jeans and crystals, tie-dyed T-shirts and shoes with chunky soles. I would watch them in their groups—their laughter menacing, superior. They could smell an immigrant, those American kids. It was emanating from my braided hair, my cheap sneakers and unfashionable corduroy, my flushed cheeks. I remained shy Galina, the Russian girl with no friends.

Then, the day after taking the SATs, my parents called me out of school. And there were no more potatoes or cutlets or ghettos—there was only silence.

My flight back to New York was still three days away, so we wandered through Jewish cemeteries, past eroded headstones compressed against one another like rotting teeth, lying face-up or teetering dangerously to one side. A few headstones in better shape had rocks piled up on top of them, of different sizes, from grainy pebbles to the kind of stones that required two hands to lift. Always, we were alone. At one cemetery, the elderly caretaker emerged from his cottage and screamed at us to get out, as if we had trespassed on private property, as if he feared what we might find. We were walking in the footsteps of ghosts; the entire city, it felt, was vacant of Jews.

"What are you going to do?" I asked Lauren in many different ways over the next few days.

"I'll do private tutoring; it's more lucrative," Lauren said once, and later, "I hope it's a girl."

We spent the evenings in Old Town cafés, drinking Zubrowka vodka with apple juice, watching streams of people our age pour in and out of clubs and bars, but we had no inclination to join them. We walked by peddlers selling ceramic figurines of religious, black-robed Jews clutching what appeared to be satchels of money. The faces of the figurines were contorted: darting eyes with bushy eyebrows, sloping backs with bent knees, shoulders curved inward. No longer astonished, I bought one, slipping a rabbi into my purse.

As the day of my flight neared, I thought of the job I left behind, as a production assistant for a television news show. My main task was to Xerox the night's script onto colored paper and disperse it to all the departments. Sometimes, a news story would break and the old script would have to be collected, an updated script circulated. On my last day at the office before coming to Poland, I handed the anchor his script. "Jesus," he said, looking fully at me for the first time. "Why can't you number these goddamn things?"

I let Lauren drag me to the Nozyk Synagogue, where we watched the rabbi lead services for no more than eighteen congregants. We were dwarfed by the soaring ceilings, the chandeliers with their flickering candles, the walls, the stained glass windows, the altar all white and round like the curved, sturdy bottom of an egg. We sat in the women's section, feeling the vastness, the emptiness between us and the rabbi, whose voice rose and fell, a black blur wrapped in a shawl. It was as though he were singing directly to me, which was easy to imagine with all those unoccupied seats; prayers my grandmother hummed, their seductive peaks and plunges. Once my grandmother died, my parents stopped going to the synagogue, and I had not realized what this music would recall. The service was over too soon, the final fade-out of song abrupt.

My eyes were closed when I heard Lauren, her jacket on. "It's time," she said.

Afterward, we gathered at a wine bar with Lauren's new Jewish friends. The girls were stylish and pretty—our Polish counterparts—and the guys neatly dressed, gentlemanly, sober. The best-looking one was wearing a leather jacket, an oversized Star of David around his neck. His hair hung long and dry, like unmowed grass. His face was the face of an older man, with a creased, determined jaw. In my plunging, peacock blue blouse, I asked him to order me a piwo at the bar. The prayers had twisted open a valve in me. Taking the beer, I caressed his thumb.

"This is Mateusz," Lauren said, suddenly beside me. I could hear a grind in her voice, her teeth pressed too tightly.

I backed away. I had gotten it into my head that Mateusz had receded into the past, but he was very much here, exuding the bitter scent of lemon peel, long hair sweeping the collar of his jacket.

"Does he know?" I whispered.

"To the Jewish future of Poland!" Mateusz said in near-perfect English. He raised his glass. Some of the other patrons looked up from their candlelit tables, their romantic tête-à-têtes, their glasses of Bulgarian reds, but then they looked away.

"How many of these young Jews are there?" I asked Lauren.

"What does it matter?" she said, with uncharacteristic impatience, as if I had posed the same question twice. "Not nearly enough."

She was watching him, and he, as if drawn to the fierceness of her gaze, gave Lauren a kiss on the lips. "Moja kochana," he said.

He squeezed her hand, a series of slow, reassuring pumps. She was wearing her Land's End special; underneath, a bulky, cable-knit sweater, taupe leggings that lent her the appearance of sagging flesh. She nodded at him, grinning foolishly.

I watched them kiss; this strange Adonis bending down to meet Lauren. I had never seen her giving herself over to an embrace, clutching shoulders inside a leather jacket, reaching up on her toes. I had thought her to be alone, in a foreign country. When she found the Jews, she would return to us, I had believed—to New York, to the only life that mattered.

The night before I was to leave, we went to bed early. I fell asleep on the cot, and Lauren on the couch, but in the middle of the night, I shuddered awake to voices coming from the kitchen. The light from the naked bulb on the ceiling was filtering into the living room, shadows shimmering on the floor.

"The future of Poland," Lauren was whispering, "is a Jewish baby."

"I can't believe this. A baby, it is impossible," a male voice said. "To have a baby right now? You must be joking."

"But it's the right thing to do," I heard, the voice now weaker.

The conscious part of me wanted to eavesdrop, and I contemplated confronting Mateusz—his curls and his dimples, his Star of David—to lecture him about responsibility, but too many glasses of Zybrowka and apple juice were weighing down my eyelids. I went back to sleep.

In the morning, I said good-bye to Lauren, who looked as though sleep had eluded her. Her thin hair was tied in a messy knot, skin creased around her eyes. She stood among the Soviet relics of my youth: the shabby brown furniture, the worn, faded carpet on the wall. On the kitchen table stood two glass mugs full of cold tea and a plate of fanned cheese slices, their outer edges turning a deep, crusty orange after sitting uncovered for several hours.

I hugged Lauren, wanting to know how to confide in her again. In the gray chill of morning, the apartment was homey, with its interplay of brown and orange, its warm shabbiness. I stepped out into the hall.

"Why did you come here?" she asked, in her immigrant nightgown, her hand ready to shut the door behind me.

I muttered something about wanting to help one of my best friends, but suddenly I couldn't recall whether during that phone call from Warsaw I had been summoned, or if I had summoned myself. Had I remembered it incorrectly? Had it been I who dialed Lauren in Poland, struggling to make myself understood in Russian, finally tracking her down through the Jewish Historical Institute? She needs me, I told myself on one of those Sundays when the phone didn't ring, all those people outside—all of New York City, it seemed, enjoying the first bursts of spring—and me, indoors, shades drawn, with no idea of what would hold any meaning. Lauren needs me. I had thought of my grandmother, then, no doubt. Where had I been when she collapsed on her own stairs?

When Nazi soldiers came to her village, my grandmother told me, she hid out in the cabbage patch. She pressed her head flat on the ground, inhaling the smell of earth and potato, not daring to look up. All night, she heard screams. Some of them may have been her mother's or father's or uncle's, and at one point, it did sound like her mother's—low-pitched, staccato— and my grandmother was ready to run back. But instead she stayed still.

"Go," her mother had told her. "And stay in the patch, until there is silence."

Lauren was clearly growing cold in her nightgown; she wrapped her arms around her shoulders, pressed her feet close together. Down the hall, we heard a shuffling of feet, the slow clicking of a cane.

The corridor was badly insulated; the wind easily penetrated my stylish winter coat. I thought of the porcelain rabbi at the bottom of my purse, of the vast, empty synagogue. New York, my only home, now felt like yet another hiding place. Soon, not even Lauren would be able to guide me out of the delicate shelter I'd created for myself. I thought of my grandmother's wolf, singing its song, and knew that it would eventually come for me too.

But when I was ready to answer Lauren's question, when I began to understand why I had come, I realized that her door was closed, and that it had probably been closed for a very long time.

Before Tonde, After Tonde

Petina Gappah

O ur dhedhi slammed the door behind him so hard that my new red coat fell on the floor on top of my brother Shingi's parka. Against the black of Shingi's jacket and the dark of the carpet, my coat looked like bright blood on a dark road. He didn't take the jacket with him when he left, Shingi, and Dhedhi hadn't seen it. He would have thrown it out with all of Shingi's other things if he had, but like Dot on *Eastenders* always says, sometimes you don't see the things that are right in front of you.

Rozzer from next door barked when the front door banged. Through the walls, I heard Mo shouting to him to keep quiet. I peeked out of my room when I heard the door and saw the jackets on the floor. I also saw my mother doing what she always does when my father shouts and bangs doors behind him: she sat on the stairs with her mouth falling down at the corners. Dhedhi's anger remained in the house even after he left. It formed a cloud that settled in the cracks, seeped up past the staircase and Mhamhi's falling face, to the bedrooms and the bathroom.

They were fighting about Shingi again.

"We have to find him," Mhamhi had said. "Things can't go on like this. He is our son, our only son now."

"I have no son," Dhedhi said.

"We must submit to God's will," said Mhamhi. "If we put our faith in God and trust him to find a way, he will bring Shingi—"

"I do not know anyone called Shingirai."

He used Shingi's full name, and he shouted at Mhamhi in Shona, two things he does when he is very angry. My Shona is not that good anymore. I mean, I still speak it and everything, but I don't always remember the right words to say to my grandmother when my mother makes me talk to her on the phone. I remember afterward, but not when I am actually talking to her. I can hardly follow my grandmother when she uses old totems and proverbs. We have only been here two years, since I was nine, but I am not so daft that I could forget a whole language just like that.

When I am not at school where it is English all the time, Mhamhi complains about Dhedhi. And Dhedhi hardly talks, he just shouts orders. It is really hard to keep up a language when all you hear are complaints, commands, and the same stuff over again. It's not like back home where everyone says all sorts of different things in Shona. I should say back in Zim, really, because London is our home now.

Mhamhi sat for about ten minutes before I heard the stairs creak. She came up to my room, her face all puffed.

"Did you hear your father?" she said.

I tried to pretend that she had not spoken and kept my eyes on my PlayStation. I pushed the buttons on the analog controller to see if I could get Trinity to kick two of the Matrix agents at the same time. Shingi could make Neo and Morpheus kick ten agents, and when I remembered this, I missed him so much that I forgot I had sworn never to talk to him again. I managed to kick two of the agents, and it might have been three but I found it hard to concentrate because Mhamhi said again, "Did you hear your father?"

"Uh huh," I said.

"What manner is that of talking to your mother?"

"I mean, yes Mhamhi, I heard him."

"You see the way he talks to me? Like I don't exist? I pray to God that when you get married, your husband will not treat you in this way!"

She went on about how she is the one who works to put the food on the table, and is it her fault that he cannot get a job, and I tried to switch off my mind, but that is hard to do when your mother is sitting in your room, telling you your father is an awful, unfeeling person. She never explains why they shout at each other, and worst of all, why Shingi just up and left without saying good-bye. Then she said we had to pray for Dhedhi and for Shingi, and she made me switch off my PlayStation so that we could pray together.

He is angry all the time now, Dhedhi, and he shouts over every little thing. Like the time I asked him if I could change my name. "No one else is called Patience," I explained. "It's a word, not a name."

"Patience is a perfectly good name," he said. "That was your aunt's name."

"Yes, but no one here is called Patience. I mean, Dhedhi, this is not like Zim, where people are called funny things." There was a boy, Genius, who won the hundred-meter race, and a girl, Memory, in Miss Mashava's class.

"*Zim Zim kuita sei*? What do you know about your country? Is this the way that a girl of your age talks to her father? Why does your mother not teach you some manners?" He really lost it then. He shouted that I was not to question his authority; if Patience was a good enough name for his sister, it should be good enough for me.

I said, "Sorry, Dhedhi."

We watched *Eastenders*. Dawn kissed Ian and they were rubbing their arms all over each other, and I was so afraid that Jane would catch them, but just when it was getting really exciting, Dhedhi told me to do my homework in my room.

"But, Dhedhi, I *have* done it. I want to watch."

"Go to your room this minute."

When Mhamhi said, "Why not just let her…" he told her to get out of the room as well.

"*Kamani*," he said. "Both of you out, get out now."

Mhamhi and I went up the staircase and she pushed me into her room. We sat on the bed. She held me and cried, and all I could think was: Jane had caught Ian and Dawn, and what would Jane say if she learned that Ian had given Dawn a credit card? That Dawn had agreed to pretend to be Ian's wife, even though Jane was his real girlfriend? I sat there wondering what would happen next, trying to listen to the sound of the television, but Mhamhi kept crying. Then I heard loud cheering, which meant football, so I wrote and rewrote the story in my mind and tried to block out Mhamhi's voice saying, "Look, look, see what your father is doing."

He didn't always shout, Dhedhi; he used to laugh. He whistled, too. Whistles that were not any tune in particular but that were just a sound that was always there, like our maid Sisi Annie singing Chimbetu songs in the kitchen, or Mhamhi laughing with Auntie Sue from next door. But that was ages ago, back in Zim, before we came to England, before Tonde died.

I wrote a story last term for school about the thing that I miss most about Zim. I thought for a long time about what I missed. I suppose I could have written about Tonde or our dog Spider, but they are not *things*. I miss things like the sun always being there, or having a garden. I miss Blakistone, my old school, and answering questions in class without worrying if Kylie and her friends are going to make fun of me and laugh at me afterward for knowing the right answers. I miss walking home with my friend Mandy, and going around the greenways and walking without our shoes on. Most of all, though, I miss our swimming pool, and that's what I wrote about.

Miss Norman said I was creative and had a good imagination. She thought it was just a made-up story. Kylie even said there are no pools in Africa; people there live in huts in the jungle like on *Survivor*. She doesn't know anything though. Our house was really nice and everything. It was not a very big swimming pool, like I explained in the story, but I could swim five lengths when I was in grade two, and I was only seven then. Tonde could swim ten lengths and one time he even did twenty but he had to sit and throw up because he swallowed so much water. Mhamhi found him coughing by the side of the pool and yelled at him because he had asthma and was not supposed to do anything that might cause an attack.

He died anyway, and we moved to England.

They talked about it even before Tonde died, moving to England, I mean. But Dhedhi wanted to stay. "We will not run from our problems," he said. "These bastards will not be around forever, and if we leave, that is just what they want. Things cannot get worse."

Things did get worse; everything started to change. Not quickly, like what happens on *Eastenders*, but slowly in little bits. The pool was the first thing that changed. It got all yucky and green because Dhedhi said there wasn't enough money for the chemicals. Sisi Annie had to cook outside all the time because there was never electricity. Mhamhi yelled into the phone all the time at the electricity people. "One hundred and thirty five power cuts in the last four months," she said. "And your bills get higher and higher. This is intolerable. Don't make stupid excuses. Hello? Hello, hello?"

We stopped eating all sorts of nice things because Mhamhi said everything was expensive. We couldn't even go to Sweets From Heaven or to Scoop for ice cream. I didn't mind too much because the ice cream had started to taste all funny. The Scoop people said that was because the power cuts meant that the ice cream wasn't always fresh and it melted a lot and they didn't always have enough milk. The new farmers had killed all the cows and eaten them. In the end it didn't matter because the Scoop people closed the shop and another one opened that sold all these toys that had funny signs on them because they were made in China. Tonde got a remote-controlled car from there for his birthday. It went around the room once and got stuck under the sofa, and it wouldn't move even when Dhedhi changed the batteries.

Other things changed, too—lots of things, like having to carry lots of the new money called bearer cheques just to buy bread. You had to be careful with it because it was almost like newspaper, it tore that easily. And we couldn't have Cartoon Network or Nickelodeon any more on DSTV because Mhamhi said we didn't have foreign currency.

The biggest thing that changed, though, was that Tonde died.

We don't have a maid in England. Sisi Annie stayed behind, so there is no one to look after me when Mhami is at work. Shingi used to look after me, but since he went away, I look after myself. Mhami is breaking the law because the law here says adults are not supposed to leave kids alone.

"We did not come to England to end up in jail," Mhamhi said, "so make sure that you do as I say."

She said that I have to look after myself after school.

"None of us can count on Dhedhi," she said.

He is never here in the afternoon, and when he is, it's like he is not here anyway. He doesn't have a job even though he went to university and had a really good job as a manager with this company that makes beer back in Zim.

It's okay, we have food and clothes and everything because Mhamhi has a job as a pharmacist at one of the Boots on Oxford Street. After Dhedhi failed to find a job, there wasn't enough money for us plus everyone he has to help in Zim, so Mhamhi took another job looking after old people five nights a week. It was really weird at first, not having her around at night. Sometimes she came home after I was in bed. It was even weirder having Dhedhi cook for us, and he laughed when Shingi and I complained about his funny meals.

He went to loads of interviews, Dhedhi, all over London, even once to Birmingham. He tried a job in a factory but lasted only a week. Months went by, then a whole year passed and still he didn't have a job. Mhamhi said he should try registering with her agency because there was always work there, and that was the first time he shouted, really shouted I mean. "I did not come to England to wipe white people's bottoms," he said. Only he was much ruder than that, saying *matuzvi evarungu*, a really bad way of saying white people's shit, and it is such a bad thing to say that you are not supposed even to think it.

Then one day, just like that, he stopped looking for a job and began to spend all his days typing really fast on the internet. When he is not on the internet, he watches boring *Sky Sports*. I hate football more than I hate anything else in the world. One time, Shingi and I looked at the computer to see what he spent his time doing. We tried his and Mhamhi's and Shingi's and my name for the password, but that didn't work. "Try Tonde," I said, and Shingi tried it and it didn't work.

Then he typed TONDERAI and it worked.

We found that Dhedhi was involved in a forum where people from Zim wrote really awful things to each other about politics and stuff like that. The forum said, WELCOME, ZANUIMHATA. That's the name that Dhedhi used on the forum. He had been shouting there at all the politicians in Zim, at people on the forum, calling them morons and idiots.

"We are stuck here, estranged from our homeland, fucking economic refugees because a moron called Mugabe who shits like you or me won't give up power," he wrote. "And *mhata* like Mukoma, Pakuru, and Senior defend him, even as the country dies because your shallow minds are wrapped in liberation bullshit." The people called Mukoma and Senior had shouted back at Dhedhi, saying he was the *mhata*, and Dhedhi shouted back and on and on it went. It felt so weird to read these things written about my father who was pretending to be someone else.

I walk home fast after school, without talking to anyone, like my teacher Miss Norman told us. That's because the streets are full of pedophiles who like to have sex with kids and then kill them. They don't look evil or anything like the Nazis in my Indiana Jones game. They drive around in their white vans looking just like anyone else and that's why we are not allowed to talk to strangers. I found it weird at first to ignore adults all the time because in Zim you are supposed to greet older people and be polite to them even if you don't know them.

So anyway, I walk home on my own without talking to anyone, and I let myself in. Sometimes Mhamhi leaves food for me to heat in the microwave. But one time after Shingi left and Dhedhi had thrown away all his things, I came home and there was nothing to eat in the kitchen and he was drinking beer and being Zanuimhata on the internet. "You should learn to cook," he said without looking up when I said there was no food. "My sisters could all cook at your age."

In the kitchen, I switched on the gas stove to make scrambled eggs. It wouldn't light up, and I remember Mhamhi saying that sometimes she had to switch on all four plates at once just to get one lit. I did that and turned the knobs up really high and then clicked on the gas switch and the flames were ever so big and my braids were on fire and melted and burned my face and neck and I screamed. Dhedhi put out the fire, and the only good thing about being burned was that he put his arms around me just like he used to even for no reason, and he picked me up and helped me put on my coat. And I cried and cried even though it was not that bad, because I wanted him to continue holding my hand and he did, all the way to the hospital.

"Superficial burns," the doctor said. "You know better than to play with fire." I opened my mouth to tell him what really happened but I closed it again.

So I woke up one night to hear Dhedhi, Mhamhi, and Shingi yelling at each other. Shingi banged the door behind him and never came back.

I waited and waited and he never called to explain or to say hi. When Mhamhi was at work, Dhedhi put all of Shingi's things in bin bags and threw them out.

He became really strict, had all sorts of new rules for me. "I do not want you to wear trousers," he said.

"But it's part of my uniform," I said.

"Wear the skirt," he said, and to Mhamhi, "Make sure the hem is below the knees and cut her hair. No child of mine is going to look like a whore."

Mhamhi said, "She is only eleven."

"All the more reason for her to start learning values."

Mhamhi said I should pray for Dhedhi, and said nothing more, not even how cold it would feel with just a skirt and tights. I prayed so hard but Dhedhi didn't change his mind, and everyone laughed at me because I was the only one in a skirt on days it was freezing. I thought it was *so* unfair, because whores are people who have sex with lots of boys and I hate boys almost as much as I hate football.

Even Mhamhi got weird after Shingi left.

She didn't talk about him, except when she pleaded and argued with Dhedhi. She started to go to this new church called the Temple of God's Deliverance. She made me wear frilly dresses and sit while people sang and danced and prayed aloud all at the same time. Something about their faces reminded me of the man with the dirty dreadlocks who stands near the lions at Trafalgar, who says "Lord take me back to Jameeeca, *please* take me back to Jameeeca." Shingi said he was a mad, sad bastard.

Some of the ladies dance up and down the middle passage where there are no chairs, and then they fall to the ground and start shaking. I used to worry because all the ladies wear skirts, and I didn't even want to imagine if their knickers started to show; that would be too awful. But there are ladies called Sister Jocelyn and Sister Mattie who rise up from their seats to straighten the skirts of the fallen women so that nothing shows. They don't need to do that for the men, of course, because they wear trousers, and anyway, it is only women who tumble over and fall with the Holy Spirit.

On *Eastenders*, it is always the littlest things that change the way the big things turn out, like Jane remembering that she didn't switch the lights off in the café, which means she goes back and doesn't see Ian together with Dawn, or Pauline not having enough change for her underground ticket, which means she has to go ask the newsagent and misses the train, and that's how Joe catches up with her and they get married.

That's what happened with Tonde, little things that didn't go right.

His asthma medicine ran out and none of the pharmacies had the stuff to fill up his inhaler. Mhamhi and Dhedhi looked everywhere. Mhamhi asked Auntie Sue to get it when she went to South Africa, but her flight was cancelled because there was no fuel for the plane. She went later, but came back too late. On the day before she returned with Tonde's medicine, he had an attack at school. His teacher, Mrs. Mawere, had called the ambulance, but they said there wasn't one, again because of the fuel. Mrs. Mawere drove him to the hospital herself, and he died in her car before they got there.

Mhamhi carried Tonde's inhaler with her to the funeral and would not let it go. Tonde's coffin was really small. I didn't know that they made coffins the right size for kids. Dhedhi got very drunk at the funeral. Shingi says he saw him crying, but I never did. He kept saying *achamudya Mugabe mwana wangu, achamudya chete*, that the president should eat Tonde.

"This is what happens when life becomes cheap," Uncle Steve whispered to himself, but I didn't know what that meant exactly, because Mhamhi said our life had become expensive.

Seven months after Tonde died, Mhamhi and Dhedhi sold the house and car and everything. Auntie Sue took our dog, Spider, and two weeks after that, we moved to England. It's like everything is divided up in halves—there's the half before Tonde died, and the half after Tonde, only it doesn't feel like a half, more like that's how things always were, like Tonde had never been.

No one wants to talk about Tonde, not even Shingi. He is seventeen and I am eleven, and the gap between us is even bigger without Tonde in between. Only my grandmother talked about him sometimes. She introduced me to people in Zim as *hanzvadzi yeuyu mushakabvu*, which means the sister of the dead one. I wish she would just say his name, Tonde, like they do on *Eastenders* when people die. Den is still Den, and Mark is still Mark. No one pretends they don't have a name anymore. No one calls them just the dead ones.

I close my eyes sometimes, and I try to remember his face. All the pictures of him are in a drawer in Mhamhi's bedroom that she keeps locked. It has all her secret stuff like her contraception pills. Tonde is locked up in that secret drawer.

I am trying hard not to, but I am forgetting his face.

Mhamhi didn't go to work that day Dhedhi banged the door so hard because she felt sick. There was a ring at the door and I opened it, and there was Shingi. I screamed so hard that I felt my ears sing, and I clung to him and wouldn't let him go.

"Whoa," he said. "Where's the fire?"

He lifted me up and I put my face next to his. He smelled like Dhedhi smelled when he had been drinking. Mhamhi came down to see what the noise was, and when she put her arms around him, it was both of us that she hugged. I was so glad to see him that I forgot I was angry that he went without saying good-bye.

"I can make Trinity kick two agents at once," I said. "Let's have a game."

"Sorry, Peshi *shaz*, I can't right now," he said.

"You shouldn't have come," Mhamhi said. "Your father is still so angry."

"I came to tell you that I am moving north."

"Where? Where will you stay?"

We never heard the answer, because at that moment the door opened and Dhedhi walked into the room. He looked at us like he couldn't see. He walked straight over to the computer.

"*Manheru*, Dhedhi," Shingi said.

"I don't greet animals," Dhedhi said.

"Animals, Dhedhi? Animals? But you can do better than that, surely. Pigs and dogs, isn't that the phrase you are looking for? Isn't that what Mugabe calls us, too, pigs and dogs?"

"Leave this house this minute," Dhedhi said. "I will not tolerate a sodomite under my roof."

"*Your* roof? What, have things changed that much since you kicked me out? Because here I was thinking that Mhamhi is the only one who is working. Or is it only your roof because *mune machende*, and she does not have them too, your dick and your balls?"

"Shingi, please." Mhamhi started to cry with her hand over her mouth. My heart was beating so fast I thought that everybody could hear. I was too shocked to say anything, because Shingi was saying all these words that you were not even supposed to think.

"But hang on, I have balls too," Shingi said. "But that does not make me a man, now does it, not to you anyway, right, Dhedhi? So I am not a man, but tell me—are you a man? Are you a man?"

"Patience," Dhedhi said without looking at me, "go to your room this minute."

I knew better than to argue. I fled without even looking at Shingi, but I didn't go to my room. I sat looking down at them from the top of the staircase. They were so busy looking at each other that no one noticed me there. When Dhedhi spoke again his voice was low. "I will not have a sodomite under my roof."

"This is England, Dhedhi. England," Shingi said. "I can suck dick and no one cares. I can take it up the ass and no one cares. I can even marry if I want to." He started to hum that tune that people play in church when a woman is walking down the aisle to get married. He did a twirl around the living room that he did not complete because my father struck out with his fist and hit Shingi hard.

Shingi laughed, so Dhedhi punched him again in the face. It was not one bit like Indiana Jones punching the Nazis or even Dennis hitting Phil Mitchell that time on *Eastenders*, because it was real and it was my father doing it to my brother. It was real and Shingi's face was full of blood. I did not know that Shingi could laugh and cry at the same time.

My father said, "Sodomite, sodomite," every time he hit him. Then he kicked him with his feet.

"Fight like a man if you think you are a man," he said.

He raised Shingi and hit him again, and this time Shingi's head hit against the staircase. Mhamhi cried and shook him. She said, "Shingi, Shingi, Shingi." She said it over and over and still he did not get up. When Dhedhi walked out of the house, he did not slam the door behind him. It closed softly, and my red coat and Shingi's parka remained on their hooks.

The View From The Mountain

Shauna Singh Baldwin

I met Ted Grand soon after he came to Costa Rica and built the Buena Vista. He didn't know of me then, but I knew of him—every day during the construction of the hotel, I sat on my veranda in the morning, nursed my first bottle of Imperial, and squinted to gauge his progress. The Buena Vista's walls capped a peak three miles away, at first gray, soon white. Trust a gringo, I thought, to buy that view, with all the lights of San José twinkling in the valley below. A man was beaten to death by the local bosses and found picked clean by crows right where Ted Grand was building. Trust a gringo not to care that he was building on blood-soaked land. I refused to go see the hotel.

Ted wouldn't remember the day we met. I still do—my annual day of sadness. All my days were days of sadness then, but that day was the worst, the anniversary of the fire. The night before, I went through tequila, guao, Heineken, Pilsen, and whatever else was in my cupboards to prepare myself. But Madelina and Carmen were before me. My little Carmen, only six years old. Screaming, crying. A bout of dengue seemed to be upon me. In the morning, I soaked a towel in ice water, went out to the veranda, sat down in my wicker chair, and put the towel over my eyes.

I heard Jesús's Isuzu stop on the road below, but I didn't budge. He came in without knocking, the folds of his pelican neck wobbling, his shirt flapping about his paunch. He stuck his big nose into a cupboard in my kitchen, removed a steel bowl, returned to the twin aluminium vats sitting in the flatbed of his truck, and ladled out enough milk to last me a week. He talked the whole time, as he always did, and some words got through the buzzing and screaming in my head.

The gringo of Buena Vista, said Jesús Martínez, needed someone to look after his garden. Wanted someone who could care for ten coffee trees.

"Listen to me, señor Wilson Gonzales." His sombrero creaked and I knew he was tipping it back the way he did when he was serious. "The man who gets that job at the hotel can have all the coffee. Can you believe— he doesn't want it."

"What for are you telling me?" I mumbled. "I drink a lot of coffee, but I never took care of coffee trees."

"What for—?" Jesús shook my shoulder. "If my son was old enough, I'd make him go talk to señor Grand, tell him he knows all about coffee. Tell him looking after coffee trees is what his father and grandfather knew in their cradles. But my son is too young, and he doesn't speak English like you. So I tell you, mi amigo."

I lifted a corner of my towel and thanked Jesús for his tender concern and suggested he was wasting his time and gas.

"You're drinking more than milk—an educated man like you." Jesús, like my long-gone mother, would be silent only when he had finished saying what he planned to say. "And señor Grand might need a man who can cook too. He should get a new wife. I hear his old one left him the very day the hotel was completed. Went to Florida with the man who sold señor Grand the chandeliers."

"I always said I'd never go up that hill. A man was killed there." I took the towel off my eyes and wiped it over my face.

"Yes, he was killed. And he died. A man died there and there and there." Jesús pointed at the hill, the valley, and the road dotted with crosses between them. "Everywhere you look, a man has died. Men keep dying, and what does it matter where they died or how? We all die." He spat to emphasize his irrefutable logic.

I groaned.

"Even I, Jesús, will someday die, and I won't be back to save you if you don't save yourself right now."

Having delivered his message, Jesús pulled his sombrero forward again and crunched away to swing into his cab.

What did Jesús know? He was just one of my many creditors, that's why he wished me a long life and prosperity enough to pay his bills. And he didn't charge interest like the others. Eyes closed behind my wet bandage,

I took mental inventory of my creditors. All would agree with Jesús. It took all day, but the thought finally pushed me from my wicker chair so I could drag my alcohol-soaked body up the hill.

As I made my way into the hotel, I ignored what Jesús said. It should matter that someone dies, even a stranger. Death should matter so Madelina's and Carmen's would matter.

I can never tell an American's age, because so many tourists have had plastic surgery, even men. Ted's face seemed older than mine, and his hair was sparse and turning gray, but his spine was more erect. The new hotel was spacious and airy. A "bow-teek" hotel, Ted called it, as he showed me around. Each of its twenty rooms had a balcony with a view of the valley. Each would be uniquely decorated, each would have a name: the Bird Room, the Conquistador Room, the Monsoon Suite.

Ted said Costa Rica attracted his investment with a large middle class, democracy, no military, no oligarchy.

"I do not know what it is like to live in an oligarchy," I said, "but we now have a military. It lives in los Estados—the USA, yes? When the president of Nicaragua said he wanted to drop a bomb on our president, what did our president do? He picked up the phone and called Mr. Reagan. And Mr. Reagan sent troops to Nicaragua."

I was only joking, but Ted didn't laugh.

"Out of friendship, because we are just like los Estados," I added hastily. "A democracy."

"Don't count on that, Wilson," said Ted. "It's all about interests. There's no friendship, only interests."

I thought of my friends, even Jesús. I could not have survived the years since the fire without them. They had no reason to help me. I said—not to Ted, because I didn't wish to offend him, but to myself—that I hoped I never thought like him.

Ted had built himself a white stucco villa beside the hotel. Modern, with a few Spanish arches and flourishes. He took me to see it the next morning. I felt comfortable inside, though it was not quite finished and had little furniture.

"I hired a Costa Rican architect," said Ted, when I mentioned it.

I warmed to him immediately—what gringo would hire a Costa Rican archi-tect? We went out to look at the coffee trees and I assured him I would look after them. He said I could keep the coffee. I protested we would share it. We shook hands when I left.

"Wilson," he said, quoting some great American poet, "I think this is the start of a beautiful friendship."

Jesús was pleased that I'd followed his advice but warned, "Señor Grand is here for la pura vida, but give him a little more of the pure life and maybe he'll go home. He could sell the hotel as soon as it's finished the way he wants it, you know."

In the next few days, I drove Ted to the SuperMaas so he could buy peanut butter; he didn't blink at paying 1150 colons. He bought coffee for 2530, an avocado, an onion, and a tomato for 1500. He didn't ask how I could afford to eat. Perhaps he knew what we all knew: to buy anything at the SuperMaas, anything packaged, you must work for gringos or be in the tourist business.

Driving home, I translated a street sign for him: "Despacio—eslowly." He corrected me: "Slowly."

When we stopped, he bought a USA Today from an expat-run van service, and from then on he read a few stories aloud to me every day. That's how my English got better.

And for once Jesús's fortune-telling was wrong. First, Ted didn't sell the hotel. And second, we opened.

Ted put me in charge of the ground staff, then the inside staff. I hired willing women—not too pretty, but happy at heart—and put attractive, sen-sible Consuela in charge, though she was the youngest. I forgot all about the dead man, just like everyone else, being too busy even to take one drink or lie around like a sloth anymore. I paid Jesús back, with a sub-stantial tip for passing on information, and even more important, I began paying my other creditors back as well.

In October I harvested the coffee cherries from the trees. I brought the sacks of cherries to my own veranda, and Jesús helped me pack them carefully into his Isuzu. I sent him to a factory in Heredia for the best wet processing and roasting. The coffee returned, now dressed in silver bags, each with a generously flourished "Arias" label—Oscar Arias Sánchez had just won the Nobel Peace Prize. Its aroma turned heads in the hotel.

And in April, I hired younger men than Jesús and supervised the planting of more trees down the side of Ted's hill.

One day, just after I set up a huge satellite dish for his TV, he said, "Wilson, let's take a drive." So I took him in his new SUV and we drove through the mountains. I pointed out teak, mahogany, Brazilian cherry, bocote, and purple heart where I could. At Rio Tarcoles we stopped in the middle of the bridge to gaze at the crocodiles. Ted didn't admire the scaly brown shapes nosing the shore—fifteen on one side of the bridge, ten on the other. He said they were animals that ate other animals.

"You like vegetarian animals only, my friend? Horses, cows?"

"Yeah, I was in the service. I had enough of killing," he said.

Does killing or dying in war matter more or less than a death from accident? Again I was thinking of the fire. The fire killed, but I blamed myself. I should have come home earlier, should have had some sixth sense as a husband and a father. We strolled over to the other end of the bridge, where palms rustled like a whisper of Madelina's best dress. I became Ted's tour guide as we entered a store, identifying packets of rellenos, dried bananas, cashews, and coconut cookies. Behind pyramids of watermelons and mangoes, a little girl laughed—I heard my Carmen.

When you have lost the little girl you created with the only woman you have ever loved, when you have failed your family and disappointed yourself, it takes someone like Ted to make you believe it is possible to create again.

And create we did. A hotel with a bar, a restaurant, an organization. In 1993, we opened a tiny grocery store in the hotel and Ted taught me to stock Skippy low-fat peanut butter, Entenmann's doughnuts, and SP-45 with Aloe sunscreen. The Buena Vista offered internet service with a cup of Arias in 1996, before anyone else in Costa Rica had an internet café. And Ted taught me to hang paintings by local artists above the computers and call them primitive art.

He took a buying trip to Florida and returned with more chandeliers. While I stood on a stepladder, installing them in the lobby, he handed up tools and the delicate globes, telling me how he visited his ex-wife and forgave her. I went home and told Jesús the next day how much I admired that, when I can't even forgive myself.

Hurricane Mitch did a little damage in 1998, and I would have just renovated the hotel to look the way it used to, but Ted said destruction is an opportunity for change. He moved things around in the dining areas, redesigned the kitchen, redecorated the bar. Change, he said, sends a signal to customers that we are growing, not standing still.

"It tells people you're with it."

I wasn't easy to convince. Most of our customers came once in their lives and then went somewhere else. But Ted said, "Change is like music, felt but not seen."

Even so, I saw no reason to tear out a perfectly good swimming pool and talked him into simply repaving ours with blue floral ceramic tile. And after my days of hard work installing the tiles, Consuela told me the bright tiles uplifted the whole garden.

Some changes I liked immediately: he decreed the Buena Vista would play no more Kenny G. That music had been playing in every bar, restaurant, and hotel nonstop since 1993. He said people might like to listen to Costa Rican salsa and mambo, and I told him he was becoming one of us after all.

I didn't tell Ted the salsa and mambo reminded me of Madelina—we used to dance. He had never asked me anything about my past or told me anything about his. Whenever I asked, he said the past wasn't important. Yet he called me brother.

"Individuality, that's what we need, Wilson," he said. "Dis-tinction. We don't want to be like the cookie-cutter resorts, bringing in hundreds of people on charters and storing them in high-rise hotels, turning them over like meat on a grill and sending them back tanned on both sides."

Individuality, I learned, was available to those who could afford it. I was shocked and apologetic each time Ted printed out a new season rate card. Ted had to spend a lot of time teaching me not to stutter when I said *only* $175 per night, *only* $185 per night, *only* $200 per night.

Every time something broke down, Ted asked, "Don't you have anyone who can fix that?"

"Nobody," I would say. "Okay, maybe my cousin…" and I'd call. Soon I had every Gonzales working for Ted at Buena Vista. Slowly and "eslowly," relatives I had pushed away in my grief came back into my life.

The clock over my stove moved forward, circled three hundred and sixty degrees three hundred and sixty-five times in a flash, then another and another. Ted and I moved in lockstep into the new century. I couldn't remember what forty and fifty felt like. I only realized Ted was on the other side of sixty when he told me he needed a hearing aid.

I was in the gift shop helping a couple from New York make up their minds—modeling a sombrero one minute and spinning folk tales about hand-carved parrots the next. They had to catch a plane, so I had arranged for my cousin to take them to the airport.

But just as I was packaging the parrots, Ted came in. In a very professional tone, he informed the couple that he had just heard no planes would be flying to New York City that day. He said he just saw New York on CNN and…and…his face caved. Amazement hit me like a thump across my chest: Ted was holding in tears.

I juggled rooms and accommodated the New York couple and a number of others for extra nights while we sorted out rumours from news. The net, the TV, the *Tico Times, La Nación, Al Día, La Republica* and *USA Today* offered an intermingled dose of both. Bit by bit we learned a crime had been committed in New York by nineteen men, and the death count was growing. The New York couple kept saying this was just like Pearl Harbor. I think they really believed some other country had attacked los Estados. The death count passed a thousand, then two thousand, then three thousand, and then I watched President Bush II say he was on a crusade; he too thought the country was under attack.

Now I regretted installing the satellite dish. Suddenly Ted was not with us at the Buena Vista anymore, except for collecting his money every evening. He bought a small TV and made me install it behind the reception desk so if he was there he could watch the sad and angry norteamericanos on CNN and FOX News all day long. If I was on duty, I watched it too, and I felt the same sadness of the families. I too wanted all those deaths to matter. There were donations, there was talk of insurance—norteamericanos seemed much more valuable than my Madelina or Carmen ever were. I watched so many wearing or waving flags, but only for los Estados, though CNN said people of many countries died in the towers.

One day, two days…it became five days since Ted made morning rounds with the housekeeping staff. Then I began doing it for him so he would have time to cheer that man Bush. And he was still cheering a month later when that man Bush dropped bombs on people in Afghanistan. So Ted hadn't had enough of killing after all.

Late one evening, I was watching a CNN special report on bioterrorism after an anthrax scare in Washington when I heard shouting and crying. I rushed around the reception desk into the hall to find Ted standing over a cowering maid as if he meant to rip her apart. No, not a maid—Consuela, my most efficient housekeeping supervisor. Consuela, who had been with us since our grand opening. The heat of Ted's anger hit me though I was standing three feet away.

"Ted!"

He turned to me, and I saw the face of a man I did not know. "Wilson, don't you protect her. The clumsy bitch was about to break one of the globes on the chandelier."

Not a shard of glass on the floor, all the globes intact and in fixed orbit above.

"Which one has she broken?" I said reasonably, hoping to calm him.

Consuela's hands covered her face; she was weeping.

"None yet, but she was going to."

Dark tear-filled eyes met mine in mute appeal.

"Ted, Consuela has been dusting and cleaning this chandelier for years."

"You too, Wilson. You and your whole family…I know all of you…going to cheat me."

Insult churned in my belly. "Yes, you do know us, Ted." I knew I should be respectful but my voice climbed away. I heard myself almost shout, "Ted, we are your friends, not your enemies!"

A gleam came to Ted's eye, a gleam I didn't like at all.

But he did turn away from Consuela.

He strode back to the reception desk, but instead of going behind it, he stood arrested before the TV. Retired generals debated preemptive strikes. "Motherfucking bastards," said Ted. I thought he was swearing at CNN. "Bastards! Nuke the lot. I'll sign up again. Do it myself."

His face—like a cold sun.

I came up behind him. "Do you remember the first time you saw the crocodiles?"

"What crocodiles?"

It was many years ago, but if he chose not to remember the crocodiles, he would not remember what he had said. So what use was discussion? I went back to Consuela.

Her shoulders were fragile under my clasp. She looked up at me, confused. Teardrops on her lashes like dew on petals. I led her to the garden gazebo, and we sat bathed in the sweet scent of flame vines. The evening view from the mountain, the carpet of lights spread below, calmed us both. I wiped her tears and apologized for Ted.

Normally, Ted would have invited me next door to his home for a nightcap after the last guests left the bar. He'd usually have a little Courvoisier in a snifter. I always had a Pepsi, because if I took anything stronger, I might keep drinking, and I knew it. But this night I would not yearn for what had flown.

I stopped at Jesús's shack on my way home to my cabin in the valley and told him what happened. And I admitted I had wanted...yes, I wanted very much to kiss Consuela and make sure no one made her cry ever again.

Jesús reappeared the next morning. "Señor Wilson," he said, "I delivered the milk to Buena Vista and I tell you the gringo has gone mad. He says maybe I have poison in my milk. He said, Milk—*venenoso!* I told him, The cows are tethered in my yard and I milk them morning and night. Where from would there be poison?"

"He has anthrax on his mind," I said. "He's annoyed even with me. Things will calm down."

But they didn't. I was working with two laborers on the hillside below Ted's home, picking crimson coffee cherries, when Ted swaggered over and pointed at the burlap bags hanging at our waists. He told me to load them all onto the hotel truck. Our agreement was over at his whim, with no mention of payment to the laborers—or me. Embarrassed, I turned to the laborers, translated what Ted had said, added an apology on Ted's behalf and paid them myself. Maybe Ted's shares in some big American companies—Enron or Worldcom—had fallen. But then I saw on TV that Ted's president had also decided he was not bound by previous agreements—larger ones, international ones.

Ted was just following a bad example; he would return to normal when his president did.

Jesús said a good friend would leave Ted Grand alone because that's what Ted wanted. "You yourself were like that only a few years ago."

"You didn't leave me alone."

Ted's anger and suffering wouldn't leave me alone. I could not be his brother anymore. I hoped I was still his friend, but I remembered him saying there are no friends, only interests. Did I have any right to call myself more than an employee? Servant, perhaps? I sat on my veranda that evening as the sun faded over the rainforest and the cicadas pulsed sí, sí, sí all around, while my blood pulsed no, no, no.

My Suzuki Samurai was all beaten up and rusting out, and my cabin was little better than Jesús's shack, its only claim to beauty being a shrine I built to the Virgin from half a concrete pipe. Actually it was a shrine to Madelina and Carmen.

I talked to the Virgin now—I told her I had neglected my own life in favor of the gringo's. I made him my center. The hotel was my life because it was important to him. But all Ted cared about now was cheering his country's troops through the liberation of Iraq. Fool, fool! What did I have for myself if he went away? I hadn't even saved very much.

During Holy Week everything was closed in Alajuela and no alcohol was being sold anywhere. I drove Ted to the coast, his air-conditioned van sealed against the humid warmth—slower than usual, as everyone had the same idea. We drove in silence, as if neither of us could think of anything to say. I longed to blow foam from a chilled mug of Heineken. Coffee trees flowered in surrounding farms; I opened my window a crack to get a whiff of their fragrance. Woods of teak and mahogany flowed past.

Madelina and I used to take Carmen to the coast every Easter. One time I drew two concentric circles in the sand. We each caught a hermit crab, placed them in the inner circle and blew. Madelina's crab moved first, and went far from the center—and better still, out of its shell. I think she won.

It didn't matter who won.

Afterward, we warned Carmen about the poisonous manzanillo trees by the beach, and she listened solemnly, then ran into the Pacific, shouting her glee.

This day, the drive did Ted some good—he closed his eyes most of the way. I wondered if running the hotel was becoming too much for him. I resolved to help him more.

Jesús brought his new monkey, Luisa, and she swung from my rafters, her funny white face hanging below her long curly tail as if righting our upside-down world. She reached for peanuts, and I confided to her, though really to Jesús, "It's cancer. It's eating señor Grand from inside."

"In the brain?" said Jesús.

"No, in his spleen."

"If it was in his brain, it might explain his behavior," said Jesús. "But the spleen—that excuses anger and pain, but not injustice."

"I went to see him in the hospital," I said. "He complains of insatiable hunger and unquenchable thirst. They have told him he can go home because they can do no more for him."

"So of course he called you to come bring him back to Buena Vista?"

I nodded. "Ted said he has been through difficult times before. And he has resources I never had."

"You're comparing your loss to his illness," said Jesús. "But each loss, each trouble is itself. Right now he's not here with us. In his head, he's in los Estados, in New York."

I had to agree. Ted was only following what had happened or was happening in los Estados, and he seemed to believe no people ever, anywhere, at any time, had suffered as great a tragedy as norteamericanos. Could I blame him? All he ever read was USA Today. And the many stories he read me to improve my English featured only norteamericanos. No norteamericano, no story. As if the rest of the world was inhabited by non-persons and monkeys. And he never heard my story or had any point of comparison because he never asked.

I should have asked more questions. I should have tried to find that thing in his past that was eating him now.

"Is it good that his head is in the United States?" I wondered out loud.

Jesús nodded. "Sí, sí, it's good. If his body was also there, not only his mind, he'd have to pay a lot more for doctors."

"He has extra expat coverage. Six months free hospital in los Estados."

But Jesús's compassion had fallen low. "Señor Grand has everything he needs. He lives in fear and anger anyway. But, amigo, why do you look so anxious?"

"Should I go with Ted to los Estados? I mean, when he goes for treatment?"

Jesús said, "Señor Wilson, I will say to you what I would say if you were my son: don't go. Mr. Bush's Injustice Department would stop you at the border. And now they take people who want to stay a long time in los Estados and put them in camps and prisons. We wouldn't even know you were gone; we wouldn't know how to find you."

I thought about this. I thought about never seeing Consuela again. Then I thought about the employees of the hotel—some of them my relatives—who all relied on me now. I thought about how many years I might have left and the things I still wanted to experience. I decided I did not wish to disappear.

But Ted once called me brother. What should a brother do?

Eventually, I didn't go because Ted didn't ask for my help. He believed he could do everything by himself: be angry alone, fight cancer alone. And he still needed a caretaker to run his hotel and send money to the hospital up north.

Ted left Costa Rica on a night the monsoon decided it must arrive. Torrents hammered the roof and pounded the broad leaves of trees. Titi monkeys swung downhill before us as I drove his van to the San José airport.

It wasn't exactly good-bye, but I didn't sleep much that night. A clay-colored robin woke me with its drunken *dudududu*. After Jesús delivered my milk, I got in my Suzuki and drove to the coast. The rain lifted early in the morning, and I eventually noticed I was in Manuel Antonio. In the Parque Naçional, I sat facing the beach, my back to the smooth trunk of a Naked Indian tree that had sloughed off its bark.

On the path behind me, a park guide had set up her telescope on a tripod. "Some species have adapted so well they can't survive any place else," she chirped for a group of tourists. White-maned waves reared and tossed on the shore. Turquoise water, shady palms. In the distance a smooth hard island rose from the water, a lighthouse at its peak.

This was what Ted saw: the postcard he had crawled into for a while. Maybe he could only be blown so far from his origin. Maybe he feared that if he crossed into the next circle of the world, he would lose his American shell.

Ted went into remission a few times but never completely recovered. His cancer claimed him one day in a hospice in los Estados. My sorrow at this death of a friend and brother shouldn't have been so vague, so much like the sorrow I once felt for the man beaten to death at the top of the Buena Vista hill. His death should have mattered more than the death of that stranger.

But one-way caring has become difficult for me.

The same year Ted died, Consuela and I agreed to care for each other. She did me the honor of marrying me. Jesús brought his only son to play the guitar, and our friends and relatives danced the salsa with us at our wedding. Soon after, Jesús moved closer to Irazú, the smoldering volcano—his family said he was needed there. More opportunity for his son, he said. More swinging-trees for Luisa. He comes to see me when he needs a favor for someone—that's as it should be.

Now Consuela and I operate the Buena Vista, take salaries and send profits to its new owner, Ted's nephew in Portland, Oregon. The view from the mountain continues to bring joy to its guests: people from los Estados and the rest of us.

Bhakthi In The Water

Shubha Venugopal

Bhakthi sat in the front seat with her hands clasped under a fold in her sari. The seat belt felt too tight across her lap, but she didn't adjust it, or fidget, or lift her heavy braid to cool the back of her neck.

"We're here," Tarun said, stating, as he often did, the obvious.

Bhakthi didn't look at her son.

"Mom? We talked about this. You can do this."

He unbuckled his seat belt, but before he could move over to Bhakthi's side and pull her out—he was fully capable of tugging on her arm the way he did as a child—she released herself and stepped away. She didn't turn her head when he called out, "Have fun!" She didn't, as she wanted to, run after the car, begging him to take her back. She reached for the glass door of the swim shop.

The air in the swim shop felt heavy with the weight of water. Monsoon air, Bhakthi thought, remembering India, how she used to wait for rain. Unlike the scent of freshness she had known when she'd lean over her windowsill as a girl, the American swim shop smelled like wet rubber.

Bhakthi walked past the Bermuda shorts splashed with purple palm trees and the bikinis tied with bows. She passed the wall of masks with protruding plastic noses and windshields for eyes. She avoided the dive section, frightened by twisting breathing tubes and streamlined wetsuits. She glanced at the poster of sharks baring double rows of teeth. They were aligned by size: cookie-cutter to great white. She stood still, memorizing the edges of fins, and didn't hear the insistent voice asking, "Ma'am? Can I help you? Are you lost?" until a young man touched her arm.

Her gold bangles jingled when she jumped.

"Swim lessons," she told him. "My son signed me up."

He beckoned for her to follow—glancing at her sari, her black-and-gold beaded *mangal sutra*, and the bangles she still wore—and led her to the poolroom behind the shop. She trailed behind, eyeing the dolphin tattoo on the back of his neck. She studied the dolphin's arc, its beatific smile.

Bhakthi hesitated at the entrance to the rear room. Dominating the room was a large, rectangular pool. Steel bleachers lined one side, and next to them, a few feet away from the pool's edge, was a small office.

The thick, chlorinated air in the poolroom felt even wetter and warmer than it did in the swim shop. Envisioning damp circles staining her sari blouse, Bhakthi kept her arms pressed to her sides. Tarun had talked to her about wearing antiperspirant to stop the stains; she had bought a tube, displayed it on her dresser, but had never opened it. She preferred instead to dust herself with fragrant frangipani talc. But in this room with its strong chemical odor, she couldn't smell herself.

"This is your instructor, Karen," the young man said, indicating an athletic woman with short, dark hair who had just come out of the office. "Karen teaches swimming and diving, group lessons, and private lessons like yours. I'll let you two get acquainted." He gave the woman a look—the kind of look she'd seen Tarun give others about her when he was amused—and left.

Bhakthi tried not to stare at Karen's wetsuit with its fuchsia stripes bold against the thin-stretched black that enhanced her slim, curved body.

"You must be Bhakthi. Ready to learn to swim?" Karen drew out the *a* in her name far too long. Bhakthi shook her head. "No? Well, you're here, aren't you?" she said. "That's the first step. Soon we'll have you doing the butterfly."

"I'm afraid of water," Bhakthi said, so softly that the woman had to lean in close enough for Bhakthi to see the drops of water dotting her tightly curled strands of hair.

"Then, honey, why are you here?" Karen settled onto the bleachers and stretched her muscled legs. She motioned for Bhakthi to join her, but Bhakthi didn't. "My son is a lawyer. He's going to Mexico—a long business trip." She paused. "Yes?" Karen said.

"His trip won't start for several months. He said if I want to come, I should learn swimming."

Karen nodded. "You wouldn't want to miss out on all that water."

"My son is sick of my being afraid," Bhakthi said. She thought, *I'm sick of him being ashamed.*

Her son disdained all her fears: her hesitation to drive a car by herself, her wariness at venturing on fast roads even when she was a passenger. When he was twenty-one, Tarun had taught her to drive. He made her study manuals after dinner and took her to the parking lot of a nearby supermarket at night to weave between cones he set up.

"I can't believe you've lived thirty-some years in this country and never learned. Wasn't it hard to go out?" he had said, his hands spread on the kitchen table.

"I walked," she said, not looking up from rolling chapatis for dinner. "If desperate, when he was around, I asked your father."

Tarun pushed back from the table, his chair scraping against the floor, when she mentioned his father.

"But what if you had wanted to go out by yourself?" he said, and then, anticipating her *Where would I go?* before she asked, he said, "To the mall. To a salon maybe—even though you'd never go to one, I know. Maybe to have some fun."

Fun. It was a word her son used often growing up, and still used now at twenty-seven. She'd never been sure what he meant by it. *Duty,* she knew. Had lately even managed *relax.* But she hadn't had fun since she was a child creating an imaginary tea set for herself out of rocks from her mother's garden.

She was still afraid to drive. Afraid to leave the house at night, and to live without Tarun in the house. Afraid to speak more than a few words in passing to Americans. And most of all, she was afraid of large bodies of water. She had managed fine, tending her husband's house, raising their child, meeting with relatives on occasion, until her husband left her and her son began to speak up. Now, when he mentioned getting his own apartment and finding one for her, she did everything she could to dissuade him, to keep him always with her.

"Wait until you try it. You might be surprised." Karen stepped closer to the pool to explain depth, length, water temperature, and the plans for the lessons. Iridescent nail polish gleamed like pearls on Karen's long toes.

Bhakthi's own feet, soft and brown, decorated with silver marriage rings, remained hidden by her sari. She didn't move closer.

"Did you get all that or was I going too fast?" Karen asked, and then said, on seeing Bhakthi's expression, "You weren't listening." She brushed aside Bhakthi's *sorry*, saying, "It's your lesson, hon', not mine. I already know this stuff."

Bhakthi touched one of the bleachers; it felt hard and cold.

Karen got down and knelt by the pool's edge. Patterns of light rippled turquoise across her smooth face. "Check it out." She looked up at Bhakthi, who didn't move, and sighed. "Look, sweetie, I'm not going to push you in. You could at least *try* to come closer. Do you want to change into your swimsuit?"

When Bhakthi said she didn't have one, Karen straightened, saying, "You don't have a swimsuit? Never heard that one before. Well, you're not going to swim in *that*." She laughed.

"My mother swam in rivers wearing cotton saris," Bhakthi said, and then, as if to herself, "Wish I were more like her."

"Seriously? In a sari?" Karen looked Bhakthi up and down. "I don't think I could manage that and I've been swimming all my life. She must've been quite a woman."

Bhakthi looked away. "She was."

"Anyway," Karen said. "You still need a suit—our shop sells them." She noticed Bhakthi's empty hands and said, "Let me guess. You didn't bring money, right?"

Bhakthi said again, "I'm sorry." She said, "Except to bathe, I never take off my sari."

"So what you're saying is that you're not going to buy a swimsuit? Lord. I'll have to think about this one."

Karen dipped her fingertips into the water. "Might as well be taking a warm bath." She stared at the waving black lines on the pool's bottom for a moment, and then said, without turning, "Mexico, did you say? I lived there once." She smiled at Bhakthi. "Want to see some pictures?"

Bhakhti let her hands, which had balled into fists, uncurl. She felt a tingling in her fingers. "I'd like that," she said, looking, for the first time, directly at Karen. The woman's eyelashes—thick and dark, lighter at the tips—reminded her of Tarun's.

Karen led Bhakthi into the small office containing a desk cluttered with diving gauges and two plastic chairs. On the wall was a framed picture of Karen holding on to the outer railing of a boat, about to let go and fall into the ocean. Bhakthi examined the picture—the sun outlined Karen's cheekbones and curved shoulders, and her skin shone like polished gold.

Karen motioned for Bhakthi to sit and pulled from a drawer a stack of photographs. Bhakthi bent forward to better see the glowing blues, the brilliant colors of coral. Colors as vivid as India's. In one photograph: Karen reclining against the muscular chest of a man with teeth gleaming white against the dark of his face. Karen quickly flipped it to the back of the pile. "Don't know why I still have that," she said. She held out a photograph that looked like a postcard with the camera lens half in and half out of the water. Bhakthi saw mountains in the distance, rocks in front. Too much water. "Wouldn't you love to be there, right behind the lens?"

"Is that yours?" Bhakthi asked Karen, and pointed to a large black camera with protruding buttons that sat on a shelf behind Karen's desk.

"Yes. You like photography?"

Bhakthi said she never tried.

"That's what we'll do," Karen said, standing abruptly, leaving Bhakthi to blink up at her, uncomprehending, from her plastic chair. "We'll take pictures." She reached for the camera. She said, "You *are* paying me, or at least, I guess, your son is, so we might as well do *something*. Want to learn how to use this?" She handed Bhakthi the camera.

The camera felt heavy in Bhakthi's hand. She closed her fingers around it. "My son takes the pictures now that my husband's gone," she said.

"You can't fight me on this one. It's too easy. Give it a try?"

Bhakthi followed Karen out of the office. Holding the camera, Bhakthi squatted near the pool's edge near where Karen was sitting, feeling less afraid with the camera in her hands. She peered through the scratched window and saw, in the glass, black lines waving through blue. She asked Karen, "Do you do this a lot?"

Karen said, "When I was a kid I used to lisp. You know—speech impediment? I got to be afraid to open my mouth, what with other kids laughing every time I tried. Kept myself closed in my room."

Karen slipped her hands underneath her hips and leaned forward toward the pool. She let her legs hang in the water. "Then one day, I came home from school and saw a camera on my bed. Dad's idea. Mom threw in a photography book."

Karen lifted one foot and watched the water stream off her skin. "At first, I took pictures of objects in my room. Then I took photos from my window. Couldn't contain myself after a bit and started to explore the world through my camera lens. I could handle just about anything, as long as it was framed in that little box."

She glanced at the camera in Bhakthi's hand. "Now, here's my suggestion: hold it with one hand and put your other in the water. It will make a cool picture with those gold bracelets you're wearing."

Bhakthi studied her greenish hand in the camera glass, her fingers distorted and bent. Her bangles caught the light, glinting like the fish scales in Karen's photos.

That night, when Tarun would ask, *Did you get in the water?* Bhakthi could, without lying, give her assent.

Bhakthi hadn't wanted to come to America. She never thought she'd have an American son. She liked living with her parents, cooking for them, going to the vegetable market where she daily greeted familiar vendors. She missed her routine. After waking at dawn, she'd cut vegetables, wash clothes, and hang them on the clothesline outside. She'd have an hour before preparations for lunch. In that hour of freedom from chores, she would go out on the roof of her parents' flat and sit among the drip-drying clothes, listening to the nearby rivers. Sometimes she would knit or read, but most often she'd watch birds cawing and fretting in leaves. She felt safe there, listening to the cacophony of crows, far removed from the world below. She had no desire to go down and join it.

After her father located for her a moderately wealthy banker (the son of one of their neighbors), he told her it was time she cared for a man, not just for her parents. That, he said, was a woman's role. Bhakthi remembered how her mother looked down, eyes wet, saying nothing. Bhakthi couldn't understand how her mother could betray her. How her mother could let her leave. Her father explained that the banker's mother wanted her son to come to India and take back a bride to America to help him keep his home. When Bhakthi asked, "Why must it be me? Why must I go so far?"

directing her question at her mother, her father answered, saying that it was her destiny to go. No one could escape what was fated.

Bhakthi had convinced herself she'd be fine in the new country as long as she stayed inside. Once she got to America, though, her husband demanded she go out. He frequented formal dinners and company events, and wanted her by his side. He tried to teach her the rules—shake hands like an American, don't bow your head and press together your palms. Converse with people, make small talk, don't act like a shy village bride. Don't make me ashamed. Be sociable: befriend my colleagues' wives. How about getting rid of the sari and wearing a dress? He said, more than once, "Why are you so backward, always sulking in corners?"

She asked him why he returned to India to get married if he didn't want someone like her. He said he did it to satisfy his mother. "I tried to do as she asked," he explained. "I followed the Indian way—always obey. She said I had to marry an Indian, so I complied. Though perhaps I made a mistake?"

Soon he gave up trying to change Bhakthi and left her alone, safe within the confines of walls.

Her husband began to fly to conventions each month and didn't invite her to accompany him. Bhakthi would thumb through his suitcase after he returned—when he wasn't home—and sniff at the samples of expensive lotions and soaps he brought back from fancy hotels.

After work, her husband went to the gym or to bars to drink what he called *martinis*. He said, "Maybe you'd have liked drinking them too, if you had ever let yourself." When he was home, he read the newspaper or rearranged files in his bookshelf. She didn't talk to him much; she assumed he couldn't be bothered with domestic concerns as he was a busy man. Bhakthi wondered if her presence reminded him of his success in obtaining not only a house, but along with it, a wife—one he could afford to keep at home. On weekend days, he golfed, and at night, he left to play cards. She rarely saw him, and he rarely spoke to her, except to say, "Can you make more of that sweet potato dish?" or "When you iron my pants, be sure to put the setting on 'wool.' I don't want my expensive clothes burned."

Bhakthi thought things would change when they had their son, but Tarun was—her husband said—a "Mama's boy." He complained she monopolized Tarun, but when she was around he didn't overexert himself. When Bhakthi let the infant sleep in her bed, her husband no longer entered it. He complained of getting disturbed and slept down the hall instead. Bhakthi stitched clothes for her son; she strapped him to her chest and went shopping for him. When he grew older, she walked him to school and stood waiting for him outside the school door as soon as he finished. She sang to him her mother's lullabies and painted for him landscapes of her Indian home. She kept him close and made sure he didn't wander. She taught him Hindu mythology. Her favorite story: when Lord Krishna was a child and his mother, Yashoda, saw in his open mouth the universe—worlds spinning, moons and stars—and realized her son was divine. Yashoda, Bhakthi told Tarun, became her son's devotee.

They never went on family vacations—her husband used his time off to visit his relatives who had immigrated to Europe. She returned to India only twice—after each of her parents had died, to make the funeral arrangements. Her husband bought her tickets and mandated that she return in a week.

When he told her he was leaving her, that he had met someone else— a strawberry blond lawyer from Yale, Bhakthi later found out—the only thing she could think to ask him was, "But now who will manage your things, keep everything clean for you?" He said, "I'll hire a maid." He told her she'd be happier this way—he was leaving her his house and young son, after all. In his new life with a new wife, he'd have little time for Tarun.

After he moved out, Bhakthi placed a bird feeder outside her kitchen window so she could watch ruffling feathers and a flash of beak while sitting for hours alone at the table. It was the only thing she did for herself. Now Tarun, grown into a man who bore resemblance to his handsome father, kept pressing her to do more, to improve, to seek fulfillment.

"Why don't you throw out that old couch and buy yourself another?" Tarun said, banging dust from the red-and-brown furniture positioned at a slant in the family room—as it had from the first day she had moved in, thirty-five years before.

"Mom, it's time you got a new mattress," Tarun said, dragging her mattress with its baby stains off her scratched wood bed.

"I'm going to get you some decent artwork to hang on your walls," Tarun said, taking down the pictures of himself as a child, which she had used to decorate her walls.

When he said such things, she felt as she had on that day, years before, when one of his school friends stopped over unannounced. Tarun was thirteen then. Bhakthi answered the door in a sari marred with cooking stains; Tarun stood on the stairs behind her. He had looked from his friend—a girl in a pressed pink mini and matched tank—to his mother, his face blotchy, and then he had run upstairs. After that, she never appeared where those who knew him might see her—a dusky, dowdy, Indian housewife. He never brought friends back to his home, and Bhakthi didn't question his decision. She didn't question him later when he became determined to challenge and change her, when he said, "Wouldn't it be nice for you to not depend on me for everything—living in your house, driving you about, your only company? Wouldn't you feel better about yourself if you became braver, more independent?" She wanted to ask him, What would she do? What use was she to anyone now he was grown?

"You need to travel and see the world," Tarun said when he first told her about Mexico. Bhakthi had proposed India, but then he told her it was a business trip. "You don't have to go," he had said. "You could stay here alone for a month." When she asked about Mexico—"But what will I do there?"— she had nearly dropped her tea when he responded, "Swim, of course."

Bhakthi's mother had been a strong swimmer. She'd learned by herself; she had been around water since she was a child growing up near a fishing village. She'd carried Bhakthi to the riverbank every morning and had told her daughter to wait quietly while she strode without fear into the rapids. Bhakhi would squat, miserable and cold, her feet making sucking sounds in mud, waiting for her mother to return. Sometimes her mother would let the river take her downstream, and Bhakthi would stand on tiptoe, peering over the tips of reeds, to catch sight of her mother's streaming clothes. She'd always come back before Bhakthi called out, before Bhakthi felt sure she'd lost her.

Once, as her mother carried her to the river just before dawn, Bhakthi reached up to touch her mother's cheek and found it wet. Bhakthi wanted to ask her mother if she'd had a nightmare, if that was the commotion she'd heard the night before. Though a nightmare couldn't explain that strange male voice. The voice couldn't belong to her father, who had gone traveling to visit his family. Bhakthi hadn't heard it before and had left her room to investigate, only to find her mother's door locked. Inside: the muffled sound of a man's voice and then something even stranger—her mother's laughter, light as wind chimes. In her father's presence, Bhakthi's mother rarely laughed, and never like that.

Afraid of what she heard, Bhakthi had returned to her bed and fallen asleep waiting for her mother to come out. The next morning, Bhakthi asked her mother about the nighttime noises. "You are six years old," her mother had said, sounding angry. "What you thought you heard exists in dream-worlds. Now it's time to wake."

That morning, Bhakthi's mother went farther downstream than ever before. Bhakthi strained to catch sight of her. She forced her feet to enter the frothing river as she searched for the red spread of her mother's sari. In the distance, she saw her mother's head disappear under the water in a swirl of white foam. Bhakthi's throat grew hoarse from yelling. She waded in deeper, slipping on rock, sinking in mud, all the while calling out. She lost her balance and water filled her mouth. She sputtered and choked, flapping her arms, her face going under. She opened her eyes to mossy green, a green that would, for years, consume her when she slept. She struggled to breathe until she felt her mother's strong arms lifting her from the river. "What were you thinking, child?" her mother said, her voice breaking. "I told you to stay out. This river is far too dangerous."

Her mother carried Bhakthi home, cradling her like an infant. Wrapped in her mother's arms, Bhakthi listened to the crows and vowed to never again immerse herself in water. That was the last time she saw her mother swim. Her mother never mentioned what happened when her father was gone. Her father didn't comment on his wife's silence, one that, even as a child, Bhakthi noticed. From then on, her mother's feet remained rooted to ground, and Bhakthi kept vigil close beside her.

When Tarun asked her why she was so against learning to swim, Bhakthi didn't tell him what had happened to her mother, how she had watched her mother wane and fade.

The next week, when the young man with the dolphin tattoo greeted her, Bhakthi waved back. She walked without lingering past the masks, fins, and shark posters, and entered the pool area, looking immediately for Karen. She saw her, clad in a simple black swimsuit through which

Bhakthi could see the rippling of her ribs, the flare of her hipbones, the hollow between her breasts.

Karen said, "You going in today?" When Bhakthi said no, Karen tapped her fingers against her leg and said, "We've got to figure out something to get you moving."

Bhakthi asked if she was Karen's worst student. Karen said, looking at Bhakthi's peach cotton sari, "You are certainly the most uniquely dressed!"

Bhakthi rearranged her pleats and worried their folded edges.

Karen said, "I work with small kids. They have the opposite problem as you—they have no fear. Given the chance, they'll leap in and sink."

Bhakthi said, "What do you do to stop them?"

"Hold on a sec," Karen said. "That reminds me…" She rummaged through a tall storage cabinet wedged near the desk in her office and emerged with her hands full. She said, "I had to find a way to slow the kids down. Get them calm enough to wait until they can safely enter."

Karen tossed down what she held onto the tiles near the pool—large sheets of paper and a bag from which spilled out paints and brushes—and went back to get two collapsed wooden easels. She set them up and stood in front of one of them. She balanced a tray of paints in her hand and extended, to Bhakthi, a brush.

Ignoring Bhakthi's confusion, she said, "Ever paint?" When Bhakthi said that she used to, Karen said, "You can try your hand again."

Karen pointed at the blank page propped against the other easel. She placed in front of Bhakthi a palette of watercolors. She said, "I thought I'd try using art to demonstrate proper swimming techniques to the kids— I illustrate swim strokes and breathing methods, and have the kids try to paint what they're going to do. It's fun."

She said, "If you don't want to get into the water, why don't you at least try painting it? Imagine yourself inside. It helps to visualize before you act."

Bhakthi frowned. "But I don't know what to paint!"

"Bhakthi. Work with me here? I'm running out of ideas." She leaned over and placed a bushy brush in Bhakthi's hand. "Remember my Mexico pictures? All those underwater colors? What about drawing something like that—nothing frightening. Why don't you get some paint on that page and see what comes up? Who was it, anyway, that taught you?"

Bhakthi clasped the brush's handle tight with her fingers. She said,

"My mother." Painting was one of the many things her mother could do that she had rarely revealed to anyone.

Bhakthi brushed on a stroke of green—lime, not moss. She had enjoyed drinking lime juice, *nimbu pani*, with sugar on hot days when she was a girl. She applied an arc of yellow: a tropic sun. She swirled on orange: ripe mangoes she had eaten with her mother by the riverbank. A line of blue became a river lit with sun.

Gray spirals became, for her, the music of water, the cool breeze that lifted her mother's hair. Bhakthi painted a girl squatting by the roots of a banyan tree, her hands dripping with fruit. Then: a woman wading in a red sari, her long hair loose and free. Bhakthi could barely remember now how her face grew damp from river winds.

When Bhakthi finally put down her brush, she saw what Karen painted: palm trees, coral, a man hovering in black shadows. Bhakthi didn't ask her who he was, or why he loomed over the brightness of Karen's canvas.

Later, at home, Bhakthi told Tarun she had been playing for a whole hour in watercolor. He seemed pleased, and Bhakthi knew that he didn't hear *color*, that he heard only *water*.

"How did you become a swimming instructor?" Bhakthi asked Karen the next class when they sat by the pool, Bhakthi's sari hitched up, exposing her slender ankles that she dangled over the edge.

"I'd tried odd jobs all my life—dancing lessons, photographer, camp counselor. Even learned sign language. Then I began to travel and wound up waiting tables at a resort in Mexico." She said, "I spent days by the ocean. With a friend's help, I eventually got certified and got a job teaching swimming and diving—what I did most of the time anyway. When I moved back home, I continued."

Bhakthi kicked her feet and sent up a spray that showered over them. Wiping her eyes, she said to Karen, "That man in your Mexico pictures? Was he the one who got you into swimming?"

"Yes. He got me into it—that and other things. I ended up in too deep after a while."

Bhakthi surveyed Karen's legs—strong, the thighs sprinkled with downy hairs. Today Karen wore a red suit that brought lights into her hair. Bhakthi said, "What happened with him, if it is okay that I ask?"

Karen tried a laugh. She said, "You know. Same old story. I thought he was the one. He couldn't be with only one. An old tale, too boring to repeat. I just can't believe I let it happen, you know what I mean?"

Bhakthi put her hand on Karen's and felt the younger woman's surprise at her touch.

"Okay," Bhakthi said, "if I lean forward enough for my face to make contact with the water . . ."

"Are you going to get in?"

"No, but—will you keep me from falling?"

Karen got in the water and faced Bhakthi. "I promise. I'll hold you up."

Bhakthi pressed her belly into the cold tiles at the edge of the pool and lowered her head almost close enough to stick out her tongue and taste the chlorinated water. She kept her eyes open, despite the antiseptic odor. She felt coolness lap her skin.

"Lean in farther." Karen lightly touched Bhakthi's shoulders.

Bhakthi let the tip of her nose touch the water; when she lifted her head, a wave wet her lips and chin. She felt herself slipping forward, and cried out, struggling to sit up. Water dripped from her face, and wet spots stained the front of her sari. Karen reached for the stack of towels on the bleachers and handed one to Bhakthi. She said, after Bhakthi dabbed at herself, "What's your son like?"

Bhakthi twisted the gold ring on her finger. "He wants to change me. Doesn't like who I am, I suppose. I think perhaps he blames me for his father leaving us."

Karen said, "Do you know that? Has he told you?" She said, "Does he want you to change, or only to grow?"

Bhakthi studied Karen: her tanned skin, the fullness of her lower lip, her cheekbones. She'd seen occasional photographs of women in Tarun's drawers when he went to work and she hunted for glimpses into his life. Professionals in starched, tailored clothes, their hair pulled back in chignons. Every so often, a new woman's image would replace the old; they all looked similar to her, but none of their pictures ever remained for long. Until the latest one—the one with blond hair—not strawberry but platinum.

When Bhakthi found a picture of Tarun's new interest in his wallet, she asked her son if he had been seeing anyone. He said, "Perhaps. And what if I have?" She asked about his woman, about what the woman did. He said, avoiding her stare, "I'm seeing a lawyer." Bhakthi said, before she could stop herself, "Like father, like son."

Tarun narrowed his eyes. He looked—for a moment—not like son, but husband.

"If you really believe that," Tarun said, "then why are we having this conversation? I should be gone by now." He grabbed his jacket and left Bhakthi in the kitchen clutching the back of her chair, the sounds of birds loud in the background.

Bhakthi never tried to persuade Tarun to marry an Indian. She longed for a daughter-in-law who would understand her, who would give her a role to play—mother again, grandmother perhaps, if things went well. The image in her mind—sari-clad bride, long-lashed eyes demure and downcast—became replaced with one of herself, a rejected housewife. She wouldn't let Tarun repeat that mistake and break an Indian woman's heart. She thought, *I'll let him choose; I won't impose my will only to lose him.* She thought, *But please, don't let it be that lawyer.* That sophisticate, that blond, who would be sure to take Tarun away from the mother she found unworthy.

Let him marry an American, but not one like his father's new wife, Bhakthi prayed. She wanted her son's choice of bride to be someone who would respect, not dismiss her.

At the pool, Bhakthi planned how she would say to Karen, You should meet my son. Karen, with her tousled curls and easy smile, the form-fitting suit that allowed her to move unhindered. Bhakthi would say, He'd ask you to explore the world with him; he'd make you try new things, do things you haven't before. She thought of the photograph of Karen about to jump from the boat and said aloud, "Or maybe that's what you'd do for him."

"What, hon'? Did you say something?" Karen looked up at squares of fluorescent lights positioned between ceiling tiles. Bhakthi didn't reply. Karen said, "Anyway, after my bad luck, I've decided I'm done with men. I'm much happier, you know, without. I like my independence."

Bhakthi didn't pay attention to what she said, but rather to the way Karen's eyes matched the blue of the water.

When Bhakthi showed up for the next session, as usual in a sari, she found Karen sitting on the bleachers with a wetsuit draped over her lap.

"I know you feel uncomfortable about this," Karen said, "but just check it out. It is a few sizes too big—not too tight-fitting. It won't keep you warm in ocean waters, but in this pool you don't have to worry. And it will cover your whole body—no exposed skin. Not that anyone but me will be looking. Will you try it?"

Bhakthi fingered the hem of her sari palu, and drew it more closely about her. Her husband had never seen her without clothes. Whenever he had rolled onto her, it had always been dark. He had lifted up her sari, not bothering to unwrap it or to undo the many hooks closing tight her blouse. He had tried once, early in their marriage, but Bhakthi had pushed away his hands.

During her marriage ceremony, when female relatives helped her change into her red wedding sari, she had gone into a back room by herself to remove blouse and petticoat. She had not let the women observe her. When she gave birth to Tarun, she had been hidden in the delivery room by a white hospital sheet. No one had seen her without layers of cloth concealing her body except her mother who used to bathe her long ago, pouring over her the cleansing well water.

Bhakthi reached out to feel the wetsuit that hung like an animal hide across Karen's legs. The material was thick and spongy. She said, "In this, I'm not certain I'll know myself."

In the dressing room, Bhakthi stood in front of angled mirrors. "You might like your new self better," Karen had said. Bhakthi thought it might be true. She had never before noticed the shape of her body. What she saw outlined in rubbery black fabric: narrow and rounded shoulders, small breasts, wide hips; slender waist, fullness of thigh. She studied herself from the front and side, and then twisted around to see herself from the back. Without her jewelry, which snagged in the wetsuit when she tried to pull it over, her neck and wrists seemed exposed, belonging to someone much younger than herself. Now that her husband was gone, she should have already removed her jewelry, but she still thought of herself as *wife* and wore the gold trappings that marked her as that.

Bhakthi stroked her hair that she wore braided and pinned up. She loosened the pins and felt the braid fall onto her back. Grabbing the curling ends, she began, slowly, to unwind it, pulling apart the strands. She never let down her hair, except to wash and brush it. Now it waved about her, black with deep brown highlights, with hardly any signs of gray. She imagined it floating like seaweed, caressing her as she swam. She braided it up again.

Karen led Bhakthi to the shallow end of the pool and told her to climb down the ladder and sit on each rung until she was waist-deep. Bhakthi obeyed, perching at last on the final rung. She moved her legs and arms in circles, watching the ripples spread. Then she closed her eyes. Her belly felt warm, like when she was pregnant with Tarun. She imagined him inside her still, dependent on her blood, needing her nourishment and air. Needing her in order to grow, to metamorphose eventually into a man. She could almost feel again his fetal movements as he swayed in her womb's fluids. She imagined herself, then, curled and secure, miniaturized within the womb of her mother. She pictured her mother pregnant, entering a river, striking out against the flow.

Bhakthi opened her eyes and slid in deeper until water covered her chest. She walked toward Karen, who waited in the pool, and felt the water's weight push against her. She stretched out her hand underwater and let her fingers interlock with Karen's. She nearly said to Karen, On my last class with you, I'd like you to meet my son, but decided to keep silent.

The next week, Karen urged Bhakthi to put her face in the water and blow. She said, when Bhakthi started to pull away, "Just take a deep breath and let it all out. Nothing can come in when you are exhaling like that."

Bhakthi obeyed, letting air expand her chest. She closed her eyes and felt her face immersed in soft wavelets. She blew, making a humming noise, and then raised her face to laugh at the bubbles that tickled her nose. She remembered a scene she hadn't thought of for years: Tarun as a toddler, ducking his head in the bathtub, blowing bubbles for her to burst. How he had giggled, clutching her hand, when she gathered up soap and obscured his slick body with froth.

Karen said, "It's good to see you laughing like that."

She handed Bhakthi a kickboard and held one end. She told Bhakthi to lie flat, belly down, and move her legs. "Like this," Karen said, and in one fluid movement, she was horizontal as if on a bed. Bhakthi grasped the board, digging her fingers into the foam, and scissored her legs as Karen pulled her back and forth. She felt her muscles burn and enjoyed their heat, surprised at her energy. She moved as if over a soft surface, like sand—over it, and at the same time, within. The water rushed in through the neck and wrists of her suit, dispersed over her body, and remained inside, cushioning her with a layer of warmth. She felt cradled and protected by the water against her skin. She dropped her face into the water that stung her eyes. Karen's legs shimmered near her. She heard a loud roaring: the sounds a fetus would hear— her mother's rushing blood, the pounding of her mother's heart.

Karen said, "You're doing great. Now isn't this fun? Once you're hooked you'll never want to stay on dry land."

When Bhakthi attempted a backstroke, she felt Karen's hands in the curve above her hips, supporting her, keeping her up. She kept her eyes fixed on the ceiling lines guiding her from above as Karen's fingers laced under her back.

"In a few classes," Karen said, "we'll have you doing a lap."

Months later, as Karen's voice guided her through the basic strokes which she could perform alone now, Bhakthi lost herself in the noise of water. Karen shouted out encouragements from the edge of the pool; Bhakthi finished her laps. She swam uninhibited and uninterrupted, until she saw Tarun, still in dress shirt and tie, striding into the poolroom to pick her up from her final lesson. Bhakthi rubbed at the droplets that burned her eyes and squinted up at her son, who looked to her, from that angle, elongated—a distorted shadow. He watched her from the edge of the pool without speaking until Karen approached him.

Bhakthi clung briefly to the pool's rim as Tarun and Karen greeted each other, Karen's tanned hand clasped in Tarun's brown grasp. Karen sat on the bleachers while Tarun remained standing.

He said, "You must be Karen—the one who performed the miracle of getting my mother into the water."

Karen said, "Tarun, right? No, that was done by your mother."

Bhakthi leaned back to let water weight her hair as she listened to them chatting about her progress, both brimming with pride at what they had helped her accomplish. She imagined herself saying, as if it were the natural thing to say, Wouldn't it be lovely if Karen came with us to Mexico?

She would tell them that she could use some extra lessons. She'd say, Ocean is nothing like pool. Someone who knows it well, who has been there before, could better help me distinguish dolphins from sharks.

Bhakthi saw Tarun rock back and forth on his heels and cross his arms over his chest. His face, she thought, seemed to deepen with color as he noticed Karen's hair, her barely-clad figure, the iridescent polish on her toes.

Bhakthi visualized Karen's eyes opening wide, her hands dropping to her sides, at the idea of going with them to Mexico. Bhakthi would say to her son, I've mentioned before how much Karen has done for me, right? Think of what both of you could get me to do if you combined your persuasive forces!

They would laugh at the thought, and Karen would say, Skydiving, horseback riding.

Tarun and Karen walked a few feet away into Karen's office. Tarun lowered his voice, but Bhakthi leaned her head against the pool's edge to better listen. She heard him say, "You won't believe how scared she's been of everything."

Karen replied, "You didn't know? Your mother is brave as they come."

"I'll take your word for it. You'd know better than I."

Bhakthi waited for Karen to show him her photographs, but then Tarun said, "Did my advance payment cover it? All paid up?" Bhakthi pushed herself up to more clearly see him. His hand was on the wallet in his back pocket—the one with that woman's picture inside.

"You don't owe me anything," Karen said, watching his hand.

"Except for the change in my mother."

"You can thank her for that."

Karen bent to put a file away into a drawer. Tarun reached for his cell phone to check for missed calls. The photographs remained sealed in the envelope on Karen's desk.

Bhakthi let herself sink, then came up suddenly, choking from the chlorine that gave the pool its blue. Her throat stung, and she thought of how, on her trip, she'd be thirsty from salt. Perhaps in Mexico, Karen could fetch for her a glass of lemonade that Tarun would have just made from lemons he picked himself. Bhakthi would drink it and be reminded, as she explored Mexico, of India's moistness, of its bright lights, sweet tastes, and heat.

Tarun shut his cell phone and straightened his tie. He said, before turning to the door, "She will miss you."

"I've enjoyed teaching her. A pleasure I won't soon forget."

"Nor will she, I don't doubt."

Karen said, "Keep an eye on her out in that ocean. She won't know about currents and tides."

"She'll be fine. I'll be there."

Bhakthi licked her dry lips. She propelled herself forward through the water and imagined the pictures she'd take in Mexico with Karen's old camera heavy in her hands: Karen and Tarun wearing snorkeling goggles, water streaming over their faces. Karen and Tarun laughing as dolphins arced over their heads, their skins liquid, alight. Karen and Tarun gifting her with an underwater world, showing her its display of colors. Tarun grateful to her, at last, for introducing him to Karen. Karen, eager and willing to take care of Bhakthi, to draw her out from the walls that had, for so long, held her back.

In Mexico, she'd get Karen to give her advanced lessons and she'd master all the strokes. Maybe she'd even learn to dive! She would finally have fun. Bhakthi imagined herself finally brave, treading deep water, freed in an open sea.

Tarun stepped closer to Bhakthi. He checked his watch, his back to Karen. Karen did not follow him, but stood framed in the office doorway as she stared at the reflection of lights glimmering around Bhakthi in the water.

"Mom?" Tarun was saying, "You done? Let's go?" His words grew muffled as she swam away from him. She kept her head underwater, letting his voice move downstream. She did not struggle to breathe; she did not sputter or choke.

Bhakthi resumed her laps, although her final hour of class had passed. When she glanced at Tarun with water in her eyes, his body became blurry, his features undefined. He looked as though enclosed in a bubble. Bhakthi laughed—a laugh like her mother's, light as wind chimes.

Fresh Off The Boat

Dika Lam

To most people, this isn't a bad place to be: a day's cruise off the coast of Hong Kong, land of my father, land of my first swimming lesson—he threw me into the green sea twenty-five years ago, water wings and all, and when I came up for air, I thought I was spouting emeralds. Now I'm waiting on this island without him, angry because the palm trees look too happy, and because he told the best shark stories, and because he'll never get to see this place again. My mother stayed back home in America, citing paperwork (how much paper it takes to erase a person after death), although the truth is, she never liked my father's side of the family and she doesn't even like water, not trusting anything that can be measured in fathoms, not even love.

Here on the shore, a storm has joined all the other day-trippers, clouds massing in black bean sauce, wind waltzing the boats, and all I can think is, *Damn, I should have learned to speak Chinese*. I wouldn't be left on this pier tonight if I had, everyone boarding ahead of me, my eyes full of rain and the first mate gesturing from my grandmother's yacht, shouting something I just don't understand. (Is he saying go or stay?)

Poh-poh's boat is one of the last traditional specimens: wood the color of old blood, life preservers dangling off the sides like earrings, the roof still stained from where my relatives spread a jellyfish out to die, just for kicks. When the first drops fell, my cousins sprinted ahead in designer dresses (the girls were made in China, but all their clothes are stitched in Italy), ready to sail away from these caves and temples and tourists, but as I watch the crew bear my grandmother aloft like the silver tray of cakes that made the rounds of the beach this afternoon, all I want to do is stay and hike these hills with all the other foreigners, a backpack to ground me, a water bottle in one hand.

My life might have turned out differently if I'd learned to speak Chinese, if I had learned to bark something other than "chocolate" and "give me a Coke" to the servants during those summers abroad; I might not have to sleep at the office, might not have to sip $20 cocktails with clients. I wouldn't be stuck on this pier if I had immersed myself in real words instead of the yacht-club pool during those childhood visits to HK, if my uncles had actually pondered something other than Jockey Club ponies and Mercedes versus Rolls, and later, how I should switch my major to something practical because English is the third degree, my Asian cohorts herding off to medicine or business because they realized that someday they'd have to take care of their parents, my own father shaking his head and saying, "You don't have to worry about us, have some imagination." By then, I'd already applied to law school.

After the funeral, I told everyone back in the States that I was going to Hong Kong to honor my father's birthplace, but really, I traveled because I didn't want to think. I wanted seven million new friends; I wanted to float high above the city on the outdoor commuter escalator that changes flow for rush hour; I wanted tables for twelve, and neon signs trembling in the faces of puddles, and skyscrapers embraced by bamboo scaffolding, which is so much stronger than it looks.

Dad never dressed for the weather. He dressed the way he wanted the weather to be—shorts in late fall, long sleeves in August—but as for me, I can't help but think that if I'd known the humidity would be this mean, I would have spent my summer back in Chicago. At the open-air restaurant where I picked a grouper out of a tank for dinner, my cousins compared the latest cell phones and moved their crabs around their plates under the eyes of lanterns, admiring my purse and asking how much money my boyfriend made as I bit my tongue and tasted the deep and wished for them the fate of jellyfish hung out to dry.

I'm the last to board and I've never felt so alone.

Through portholes, flashes of silk and gin, mahjong tiles crashing on the tables like teeth, and when I look up, the first mate keeps motioning from the lip of the yacht, his hands aflutter, traffic cop and third-base coach in one, the ship lurching like a drunk, the ocean drunk, me drunk on Tsingtao beer that's Chinese but not really, like myself (the Germans founded the brewery), my parents failing to brew any language in me because they left Asia when they were kids, because they were history professors in a small white town, Oxford graduates for goodness' sake, and didn't realize that someday, the linguistic gulf between me and an F.O.B. (Fresh Off the Boat) would make all the difference.

A zipper of lightning shows the gap between slip and gunwale, the tides wet hammers, the deck a seesaw—close, not close, safe, not safe—tired of guessing, I make the call, breaching the tiny divide between good and bad judgment, my gold sandals hoping for polished planks, the first step toward pillows and green tea, simple things I want so desperately once I recognize the look of terror on the first mate's face, his hand grabbing my arm.

I am falling.

I enter the space between dangle and plummet, challenging his grip, below me the rocks and all I can think is, *Damn, I should have learned to speak Chinese*, as if that mantra will help me now, here, where I can feel how much gravity wants me, where I can already taste the salt in my lungs, can practically hear that last merciful crush before it's all over, the first mate looming above me like the moon, if the moon were trying to save my life, burning my skin as he digs into my bones, the tendons in his neck like barcodes, his bare feet rooted to the deck—I think I might be in love with the first mate—why I never noticed him is a mystery, as he was always there, or at least there in pieces: a cleaver blade of hair, dirty fingernails on the anchor, sad eyebrows, and a sympathetic cigarette navigating the twilight the same night Poh-poh fired the chauffeur for having smoke on his breath, chopsticks flashing below-decks two hours after the rest of us had eaten.

The man who holds me by a thread has a tan that comes only from years of working outdoors, and I ponder all the knowledge he possesses—how to navigate by starlight, a family of knots that will never unravel, our children learning to row boats with their feet, the way I've seen old ladies doing it at Causeway Bay—but just then the captain's rope burns my waist in a place I will never ever stand to be touched again as I'm dragged to safety, sobbing and heaving, smelling wet teak and all the mornings that I might have missed, no time to myself as jeweled fingers soothe me with towels, whisking me away so they can fortify my soul with a shot of the world's most expensive cognac, but before they can make me forget, I part my lips, as red as the marks on my arm, the first mate's hands clenching and unclenching, still trying to steal me away from fate as I struggle to say thank you—although I've never known the words.

Asunción

Roy Kesey

It is a beautiful city: flowering jacarandas, old yellow streetcars, Sunday afternoons in the plaza rich with heat and birdsong. It is also an excellent city in which to be mugged. By this I mean that on the whole the muggers here are extremely inefficient.

I have been the intended victim of five attempted muggings thus far during my three years in Asunción. Though my Spanish is perfect and most of my clothes are made locally, it is clear what I am, even from a distance; muggers note my pale skin and the lack of grace in my straight-backed walk, and they know immediately that I was born elsewhere, in a country where salaries are high and jobs are plentiful, where the streets are swept and the air is clean. Do they resent this? Do they rage at my good fortune? I don't believe they do. I believe their only thought is this: here is another foreigner, another soft victim.

Blanco—in Spanish it means both "Caucasian" and "target," among other things. But there is a difference between spotting a target and hitting one. I have never been mugged successfully because I am far stronger than I appear, and because I am not afraid.

They do not like confrontation of any kind, these criminals. When they work in groups it is generally in groups of four, and this is how it will happen: muggers one and two will start an argument in front of you, hoping to distract your attention; mugger three will push you from behind, and mugger four will tug violently at your purse or briefcase. If you do not let go, they will almost always scatter.

There is of course the slight possibility that instead of scattering they will stand their ground and puff out their chests and demand that you give them what they have tried and failed to rip from your hands; in this case, in general, you have only to puff out your chest as well. If you do, they will most likely slink away—slinking is precisely what they do, the slinking of dogs that have been kicked—and you will be left alone, sweaty and victorious.

But of those few who do not run at the first sign of confrontation, there is a small percentage, a very small percentage, who will likewise not slink away once you have puffed out your chest. Instead they will smile. When you meet a mugger such as this, you must swing as hard as you can and you must pray not to miss. If you miss, he will pull a knife from his belt, will stab you in the chest, and will kill you. That is the only rule.

Of course I detest all muggers, but there is a constant roil inside of me, the struggle between acid and base, perhaps, the latter seeking to neutralize, the former to overwhelm: I was taught as a child to hate the sin and love the sinner. I have never been very successful at this, but now at least I know that it is possible. This last scenario, wherein you are accosted by one of the very, very few muggers who smile and do not run, it is how I met the latest great love of my life.

I was on my way home from work, striding through the dense summer dusk, the heat at last relenting. A young woman was twenty or thirty yards ahead of me, walking in the same direction, and the moment I saw her I began to speed up.

It was not that I wanted to speak to her, to compliment her eyes or her smile, to undress her slowly and spread her across my bed—I did not desire any of this. I wanted only to be close to her for a moment. This is something I have felt so many times, man or woman or child, it is all the same, the need to be close. Sometimes it is all that one requires.

This was not, I think, the first time I had seen the young woman. That night she was dressed neither poorly nor well, but cleanly: pressed black trousers, smooth white blouse, low black heels that clicked as she walked. She smelled of jasmine and moved through her own quiet music as I closed in.

Then he came from the side. He was slender and lithe, and he went for her purse but she held to it just long enough for me to reach them. I shoved him in the back, and he sprawled; she gaped at me, her mouth ever so slightly open, her purse on the ground at her feet.

I retrieved the purse and set it in her hands. Now she was not watching me. She was watching the mugger who stared up at us from where he lay.

"Just go," I said to her. "Go now, go quickly, fly."

She nodded, turned away, turned back. The mugger was getting to his feet. I stepped toward him and he raised both hands. The woman turned away again and started walking, faster and faster, and at last she disappeared around the far corner.

If the mugger had taken off just then, he could have caught her in the space of two or three blocks. Of course I would have followed, would have arrived soon enough. But he did not pursue her, not at all. Instead he squared his shoulders and puffed out his chest.

"Your wallet," he said.

I puffed out my chest as well, and he smiled. It was a beautiful smile. I knew that it was time, time to swing as hard as I could, praying not to miss. As long as I didn't miss, one punch would have been sufficient, I think. But I didn't swing. I couldn't. His smile was so beautiful.

There was movement, one hand flitting to his belt, still the smile, still I could not swing; the smile, my hands at my sides, but something failed, something caught, he pulled and tugged and his smile waned and finally I was free of him. I set my feet and drew back my fist, something flashed at his belt and I swung, the blow starting in the strength of my legs, surging up through my back and chest, through my shoulder and arm and into my fist, his hand was rising and again the flash as I hit him and he flurried and collapsed facedown across the curb.

I waited for him to rise, but he did not. His body trembled in that low light. There was a farther movement then, and I looked up, saw the young woman standing at the corner. I motioned, and my motion was unclear even to me—it meant for her to stay or to go, I have no idea.

When she disappeared again I stepped to the mugger and flipped him over, thinking to kick him in the face, to show him that mugging is wrong, that it makes an already hard world still harder. As he slumped onto his back I saw his hand held tightly to his stomach. I saw the blood that bubbled up through his fingers. I saw that what had flashed at his belt was a knife now buried to the hilt in his abdomen.

I bent over him, the knife, his thin chest heaving, his kind and delicate face. One of his eyes was swollen nearly shut, and there were scrapes across his forehead, a gash at one temple. He would not be getting up for some time.

I could have walked away and been done with it, but leaving him there was not possible, not in any real way. He looked up at me and smiled again, that smile. His one open eye was a wonder: long black lashes, a warmth of brown. And at that moment I began to believe he could be taught, began to hope he could be saved.

Rafael is his name. I nursed him here in my apartment. We were fortunate that the knife had not pierced his diaphragm, that his internal bleeding was not unmanageable. I set him on my bed, the knife still in place: from films I had learned that if I pulled it out too soon he would bleed too much too fast, would be lost to me.

I fed him only liquids—my own dinner blended until smooth—and I brought him cups of warm herbal tea whenever he complained of thirst. I bathed his scrapes and daubed antiseptic cream on the gash at his temple. I even consulted a pharmacist and bought everything he recommended, the gauze and tape, the antibiotics and painkillers.

I noticed that the ringing of the telephone often disturbed Rafael's rest, so I had it disconnected. And on the morning of the third day, as he lay sleeping, I called a locksmith, who came and put locks on the windows, the interior doors, the kitchen drawers. I try to think only the best of the people I meet, but there is no sense in taking unnecessary risks.

I sat with Rafael each afternoon as heat thickened the air and the city went still. I tried to amuse him with stories of finance and scandal in Brussels and Baghdad, Bombay and Buenos Aires. Always he turned his face away.

Then for nearly a week a fever came and went, came and went; hallucinations took him and he sobbed in Guaraní. When he woke from his frothing fear I asked what he'd seen. He claimed not to remember. Slowly I cured him, and at last he began to reveal himself to me, but his stories came in fragments: the name of a cousin he hadn't seen in years, the title of a book his mother had once read aloud, and then he'd fall silent again.

Through all of this, the fever and shards of past, I eased the knife out as gently as possible, half an inch per day. Soon the knife threatened to fall of its own accord, and I was unsure what would result if it fell, if the bleeding might resume or additional damage might be done. I braced the knife with damp towels and forbade Rafael to move.

Finally I was able to slip the tip of the blade from his smooth, brown, hairless skin, and we had a small celebration: champagne, strawberries, candles. Our first kiss. He struggled against it, but not, I think, with much conviction.

A few days later he tried to escape. My downstairs neighbors called me at work to say that it sounded as though some kind of animal were trapped and dying in my apartment, and I came home to find claw-marks on the inside of the bedroom door, a broken window, blood smeared along the ledge to where he sat. But the ledge is far too high, the fall would be too much for anyone who wished to live; as well, the streets below are noisy enough that no distant shout would be heeded. I repaired the window, painted the door, and punched him once, as hard as I could. Then I kissed him—his forehead and cheeks and eyelids, his soft and bloody mouth.

It is difficult to know how much is enough. For a week I kept him bound and gagged in my bedroom. The neighbors complained once or twice of thudding sounds coming through their ceiling, but I calmed them with stories of construction. There is no point in worrying those around you.

The last few days of that week there were no more complaints, and from the depth and gentleness of his gaze each time I entered the bedroom, I came to believe that he now understood. I removed the gag, unbound his feet and hands, massaged his wrists and ankles. I told him of my apartment's many comforts, and promised he would learn them all.

The following day a rasping cough took hold in his chest. I went back to the pharmacist for decongestants and more antibiotics, but the cough grew hollow and deep—bronchitis or pneumonia, I never learned for sure.

It was almost a month before he was healthy again, and in that time I grew ever more certain I could trust him and his love for me. Sponge bath and hot compress, Mentholatum and lemon tea, and bit by bit he told me all I wished to know. His home in Bahía Negra on the bank of the Lateriquique, and the brothers and sisters he'd left there. The fortune he'd come looking for and now knew he'd never find. The garbage he pawed through for food, the bridges under which he slept, the alleys where he lay in wait.

He told me so much, and I could only trust him. When the sickness finally burned itself out, I gave him keys to all the doors of the apartment. He had earned them, I thought. That evening I came home to find him waiting on the living room sofa. He presented me with gifts: a gold watch and a beautiful leather briefcase. They were stolen, of course, and I beat him unconscious. There is no point in making a hard world still harder.

We had no further problems for the next several days, and on Sunday afternoon I took him to the plaza. It was still very hot although autumn had begun. We watched the old men sipping their cold tea, the ornate cages at their feet filled with canaries and finches. Rafael begged me to buy him a songbird, and I let him choose. The old man set an unreasonable price, but was not difficult to persuade, and Rafael and I walked slowly home, carrying the cage between us.

Though the canary was a female, Rafael insisted on naming her Teodoro; he cared for her with great tenderness, and she sang splendidly. When I returned from work four days ago, I found him leaning over her cage, whistling something pleasantly serene, a folksong of some kind, perhaps in the hope that she would learn it.

I came to stand beside him, asked if the words to the song were in Spanish or Guaraní, and Rafael turned, kissed my mouth, held me. He drew back and something flashed at his belt, and this time I was not quick enough. Love slowed me, I believe. The knife hit me where his knife had hit him on the day we met, or very nearly so. He must have spent hours sharpening the blade, or it would not have slipped in with such grace, such warmth.

I have been lying on the couch since then, drawing the knife out half an inch per day. By the end of next week I will be able to remove it entirely. And how long after that must I wait for full recovery? A month or so, perhaps less.

The pain is only a nuisance; far more troubling is the manner in which Rafael left me. As I slid down the wall he kissed me again, the softest kiss. He drew my wrist to his face and kissed my hand. He stepped over me and walked to the door. Do you see? Instead of setting Teodoro free, he left her caged, and in so doing surely meant to send me a message. But what does the message mean? There is precisely one way to find out.

Rafael should not be too hard to find. As soon as I am well I will begin my search for him, in the alleys and under the bridges. If he has left Asunción I shall track him to Esteros or Villarica, to Horqueta or back to Bahía Negra. He may even have left the country: Bolivia, Brazil, Argentina. It will make little difference.

I will find him lying in a hammock beside a slow jungle stream, wild parrots eating guava from his hand; or in a shack above the tree line in the mountains, rain thrashing at the roof; or in a small dirty house on the outskirts of some major city, cinderblock walls, a poster of the Virgin curling up at the corners. I will find him and take him in my arms. I will trace his lips with my fingertips. I will teach him the indefatigable strength of love, the rippling force of forgiveness.

Keys To The Kingdom

Diane Lefer

J ody worried about the car, but not half so much as she worried about
Frank. They had argued about whether to drive: he didn't want to take
the subway; she didn't want to park on the South Bronx streets.

"If they really wanted people to show up, they wouldn't schedule it at
night in a neighborhood like that," he said.

They were hip enough so that it was okay to worry about crime and
even criticize people of color—to each other, in private at least. Still, Jody
felt she had to correct him: "Maybe they don't think of it as a *neighborhood like that*. They live there."

They drove. It was, after all, a company car and the company had already
replaced a door lock, two broken windshields, a radio, and a tape deck
without complaint.

The block surprised them: a row of bungalows each on a small lot,
each complete with driveway and picket fence. So aspiring and petit bour-
geois, right down to the clean new aluminum siding, that even the subway—
rattling by on its elevated track—angled away, to avoid casting its shadow.

Frank put an arm around her; he was a companion she could travel
with anywhere. She liked that about him—that he was very adaptable and
quick to make friends—but when the door opened, she thought, Please,
let him behave.

They were, as she'd expected, the only white people there. "I worked
in South Africa for four years," he reminded her. "This isn't new to me."

She'd been attracted to him first by his politics. By his interesting
past that afforded interesting conversation in the present and suggested
courage, good nature, and depth. It was also nice that his vision had not
stood in the way of his getting and holding a quite good job. But lately

he embarrassed her at times with, for example, his air of bonhomie with parking garage attendants and waiters. Maybe his casual friendliness had been subversive in South Africa; looking at him in 1989 New York—tall, cleanly shaved, in his expensive suits—she suspected his behavior was read as condescension, noblesse oblige. Or worse. There was something almost fatherly in his displays of democratic intimacy, likely to provoke not only class antagonism but Oedipal rage. That's what came, she thought, of his having once been a priest.

She had heard about the meeting through a union delegate at the hospital: a discussion, dinner, and fundraiser for the women left behind in the so-called homelands while their husbands worked in the cities or lived in bachelor barracks at the mines. It's about *women*, she told Frank, but she knew she was being unfair. It was also about South Africa, and though it was twenty years since he'd been expelled from the country, it still had much more to do with his life than with hers.

Her friend from the hospital wasn't there, which made it a little awkward, but Jody chatted with the hostess, admiring the house, her poodle, her beaded bracelets, her Mali mud-wrap shawl. Frank had no trouble finding the kitchen (for a beer), the dining room (for the potluck supper—oxtail stew, rice, various breads), and a seat in the corner of the living room. Everyone seemed to be American-born or, judging from accents, Caribbean, and all were well dressed except for the man called "Buddy"—this name pronounced in exaggerated fashion as if to demonstrate that everyone knew it was false. Buddy wore jeans, a black, green, and gold T-shirt, dark glasses, and a beret. Because he hadn't spoken, he could not yet be ruled out as African. He chewed on a toothpick and took responsibility for feeding cassettes into the VCR: interviews with guerrilla fighters, complaints about the scarcity of weapons, a picture of the "collaborationist" Chief Buthelezi with ominous rifle crosshairs superimposed over his face. To Jody's surprise, this revolutionary propaganda came complete with closing credits—several minutes worth—the same as any entertainment film.

"What you t'ink?" asked Buddy. His unidentifiable accent sounded as fabricated as his name.

"I thought this meeting was going to be about the plight of women," Jody said. "And the overseas education plan." She was uncomfortable; she didn't think it was up to Americans to sit safe at home and finance death. But

Buddy—all of them—would think her terribly naive if she said so. "Violence against the white regime is one thing," she said. "It may be—it's probably—necessary. But I can't see any good coming of African people killing each other." No one answered. "You've got your work, I've got mine," she said to Buddy. "You're a revolutionary. But I'm a nurse, and I see the consequences."

Everyone looked at her. Not in a hostile way, but Jody didn't like feeling so conspicuous. She felt exposed, embarrassed at using her job for easy rhetoric, and she soon found herself backing off, then vigorously agreeing to everything that was said. She couldn't stop her head from nodding, even when people talked about necklacing collaborators with flaming tires; even when someone made not-so-veiled threats, calling Archbishop Tutu a traitor to the cause.

Then the plates were cleared away and everyone gathered around the table while Buddy showed them glossy spec sheets for automatic weapons and explained how each worked and how much it cost. Jody wanted to be closer to Frank; she felt herself edging in his direction but wouldn't allow herself too near: the white guests sticking together—that just wouldn't play. Anyway, Frank would be no help. She saw him give Buddy two large-denomination bills. She also noticed that his attempts to speak Tswana fell flat.

We shouldn't be here, she thought, and Buddy asked who wanted to sponsor the next dinner. Oh God, she thought, terrorist Tupperware, and the doorbell rang and she heard greetings and then a voice—"Francis! Francis!"—even those two syllables unmistakably African in their precision.

Frank stood, bemused and transfixed as a more ordinary man might be on suddenly hearing a love song from his teenage years.

Everyone turned to face the new arrival: a short, very dark man with a thick neck and surprisingly massive shoulders below his clerical collar; he dressed in black with all the old-fashioned somberness you rarely saw anymore in a priest. His head seemed slightly bowed—from too much prayer, Jody hoped, not forced submission. He raised his head and spread open his arms as he approached Frank. "This man," he said. "This man, Francis, was such an inspiration to me!" Then the black priest and the white ex-priest stood in the center of the living room and embraced.

Father Sylvester was not actually a South African. He told Jody where he was born, but she couldn't quite catch it—in part because of his accent, and in part because he used its colonial name, a name that had ceased to exist about the same time that Jody was born. He'd attended a mission school run by German priests. ("Do you speak German, too?" she asked. "Ah, no. Our classes were conducted in English and we learned some Latin. They told us German was much too difficult. It was plain they thought our attempts at the tongue would be painful to their ears.") After his ordination, the Vatican reassigned mission territories and his order was no longer authorized in his country. The order that took its place did not recognize his ordination. Father Sylvester had to leave his home, soon to become a free black republic, and go to South Africa to carry out the duties of a priest. In due course, he got in trouble. The order sent him off to Germany, from there to the United States. Now he lived in the South Bronx. He worked part-time at parishes without regular clergy; he visited methadone clinics, city hospitals, and jails.

An ally, Jody thought. She wanted him to set these people straight and imagined him gesturing toward his throat, saying, *This collar is not compatible with a necklace.* But Father Sylvester declined to analyze the South African struggle. "I am not a South African," he said, but then pleased Jody, saying—pointedly, she thought—"As it is not my country, it is not up to me to say how freedom must be achieved."

They left together soon after: Jody, Frank, and the priest. The car was unscathed.

"I'm sorry you had to give them money," Jody said as Frank unlocked the back door to let her in.

"I can afford it."

"That's not what I meant." Of course, she hadn't known what to do either, but it bothered her that Frank sounded entirely unperturbed. "That's a very casual attitude to take when someone may end up dead thanks to a gun you paid for." She waited for Father Sylvester to, she hoped, back her up.

"I've been to these things before," said Frank. "My cousin does them for the IRA."

This got Father Sylvester's attention. "The Irish?" he asked. "And your cousin is Irish-American?"

"They do it the same way," said Frank. "Except the IRA always has music. And a bigger crowd, but fewer women. At least the way Brian does it. I don't know why they didn't have African music tonight."

When they reached Jody's street, she invited the men up for a drink. She assumed they wanted to be alone so they could stay up all night reminiscing, but she wanted to share at least a little in the reunion. And she didn't want to say good night to Frank yet, not feeling the way she did. If he left now, she might decide not to see him again.

She admired the life Frank had led, but it frightened her sometimes—it hardly seemed possible—that she couldn't even imagine what it was he actually believed. He had told her about growing up in a little place in Iowa, the only Catholic family in town, going to parochial school and then on to the seminary. His story was detailed, quite logical, and normal. It had nothing to do with fervor. When he explained his return to the secular world, he never mentioned anything like a crisis of conscience. She wouldn't have known how to live with a religious person—she had no patience with any of that. But Frank got away with too much, she thought. She couldn't quite figure a Catholic with no concept of hell, but that was Frank, all right. All he seemed to know of God was His bounty. As a priest, he got room and board and a total retirement plan; now, as a public relations VP, he lived on expense account. From church to corporation, he still drove a company car.

But once upstairs, Frank was good—she had to admit it—fooling with the CD player, staying out of the way, and letting Jody and Father Sylvester get acquainted.

She showed the priest her African wood carvings. "Frank gave me these," she said. "I've never been to Africa myself though I'm hoping, one of these days. I travel quite a bit as a nurse." She'd gone with medical missions to Nicaragua and El Salvador. And she'd had a call for Armenian earthquake relief, but it had been too hard to make last-minute travel plans. "I prefer ongoing disasters," she said. "That includes New York"—her callous humor an attempt to let Father Sylvester know she was no out-of-touch idealist; she didn't take herself, or her virtuous do-gooding, too seriously. Maybe that was the trick to Frank, she thought: he didn't look serious simply because he didn't let it show.

"What do you think of America?" she asked.

"I find your country exceptional," Father Sylvester pronounced. "You see, I was accustomed to greeting people with 'How do you do?' I came to America and, here, everyone has the right to ask, 'How are you?'"

It seemed to Jody that when he—when Africans—spoke English, they kept the sounds at a distance, forced them through pushed-out lips, as though afraid if they let the language in any deeper, the words would catch and make them gag. Father Sylvester used English skillfully, like a tool, an extension of himself rather than an integral part. His lips, she thought, were like clever hands. "Do you see it?" he demanded. "'How *are* you?' Of course, I understand this is just a polite formula, but how extraordinary, to find the essential ontological question repeated and replied to several times in the course of an ordinary day."

"You know what I've thought?" said Jody. "The reason the Afrikaaners hate you so much is that English is the language of humiliation and oppression. And you speak it so much better than they do."

"English is an interesting language," Father Sylvester agreed. "In many of the European tongues, as you probably know, there are two words for *you*: one is formal and one more intimate. English is different. In English, there is a single word: *you*. Except sometimes it means a person. And sometimes—though the grammar books do not point this out—it apparently refers to your national origin or race."

"Ouch. You got me," she said quickly, though she was not quite sure she'd said anything wrong. "But you're changing the subject. I'm sure you have more to say about America than that." When Father Sylvester didn't answer, she teased him. "You're smiling," she said, "either to charm me or to let me know you're not going to tell me what you really think." She realized suddenly she was flirting with the man. It was bad enough he'd found her with Frank; he would think she made a practice of going after priests. The realization disturbed her, but even after she thought it, she found herself touching Father Sylvester's arm as she handed him another drink. She felt for him, far from home, imprisoned by vows, moved about the world at the whim of the Vatican—jerked around, she thought, by faith.

She wanted to ask, *Do you feel betrayed?* She had no idea what he was thinking. Father Sylvester seemed to wear a perpetual look of amusement, like indulgence, or a mask. Maybe it came from his spirituality, though since getting to know Frank, she'd stopped thinking of spirituality as a quality to be expected in a priest.

"You must be quite surprised," she said, "to find your old inspiration, Francis, living quite comfortably now, thank you, running around with a woman. An *atheist*." She stressed the word. "A Jewish atheist at that."

"Insignificant," said the priest, "compared to other things. Ah, Francis, Francis. Talk about expectation and surprise! I will never forget when you appeared at my door. You were the first American I ever knew. I had never before seen a white man share a black man's meal, or sleep in a black man's hut."

"Wasn't that a wonderful time!" agreed Frank. "We cooked over an open fire," he told Jody. "You wouldn't believe the constellations you see in the African sky. We stayed up talking all night."

"From that day," said Father Sylvester, "my dream was to come to America." He laughed; not the bitter snort of a laugh an American might make. "Do you know, shortly after I arrived, I was asked to deliver a sermon for the birthday of Martin Luther King, Jr. That was the first I knew of the American civil rights movement. Or the need for it." He laughed with happiness, or its perfect counterfeit, as if his understanding now went so deep, it would be foolishness to keep a grudge. "Shame on you, Francis," he said, wagging a finger. His laughter rang out gleeful, like a child's. "So much you did not tell me."

Frank and Jody meant to see Father Sylvester again, but they were both very busy and somehow months went by, and then a year. By then, they had moved in together. They were finding it a hard adjustment. Frank had lived communally but never intimately; Jody knew she wasn't easy to get along with, and she liked living alone, but she'd begun to suspect her preference was profoundly antisocial: how would black and white ever learn to share South Africa if she wasn't even willing to compromise on a few daily life issues with a man she thought she loved? They were trying to work things out, and this seemed to take a lot of energy so that neither felt much like making an effort to see friends.

Jody finally phoned the priest the Saturday morning when she and Frank woke to the news that the South African government was letting Nelson Mandela go free.

"We have to get together," she said over the phone. "We have to celebrate."

"Yes, yes, of course." She heard Father Sylvester's precise tones. "You want to dance in the streets. Just like they do in the townships." She couldn't tell if he intended irony. She began to feel defensive, but perhaps for nothing. "I have no engagement for this afternoon," he said.

"Of course we don't want to keep you out too late. Tomorrow's going to be a big day." Mandela was to be released about 3:00 PM Cape Town time; that meant 8:00 AM Sunday in New York. The black churches would surely be jubilant, and she was hoping Father Sylvester would invite them to morning mass.

"I'm going to show you a side of America you haven't seen yet," Frank said. "Give me directions to your place, and we'll pick you up. How about in an hour and a half?"

"I thought you knew how to get there," said Jody after he hung up.

"I just wanted to make sure," said Frank, and then he admitted he'd never actually driven Father Sylvester home the night of their reunion. "He had someone to see."

"At one in the morning?"

They had driven crosstown, and Father Sylvester had asked to be let off on a block of luxury high-rises and singles bars. Frank seemed embarrassed when he told her, but Jody was pleased. "I'm glad he doesn't take celibacy seriously," she said. Father Sylvester hadn't been permitted to speak German, and Frank had withheld the truth. If you get a partial education, she thought, you have a right to only partial observance of vows.

"It might have been politics," Frank said. "I didn't want to ask." And then he presented his plan, astounding her, as he did so often, with his impracticality. "We're going to take him cross-country skiing."

"Look," she said. "Look out the window. It's pouring rain."

"It's February. Upstate the rain will be snow."

"I'm sure he doesn't know how to ski," Jody said.

Frank thought cross-country would be easy for a beginner, but at last suggested a compromise: "Snowshoes. You don't need any experience for that. And he'll enjoy it. Like walking on water."

Of course, they only had two pairs. On the way to the Bronx, they double-parked in front of the sporting goods store and Jody sat in the car while Frank ran in with his credit cards.

They found Father Sylvester in front of his rooming house wearing a black raincoat, oversized galoshes, and holding a black umbrella. A tree-lined block, Jody noted, but she wasn't sure the trees helped any—

sycamores, now bare of leaves, their shriveled dark balls of fruit still hanging like extinguished Christmas lights. Shreds of cloth, rags, and plastic bags flapped, caught in the branches, fluttering like tinsel.

"Welcome to the township!" he said.

Jody moved to the back seat with the gear and Frank's purchases so that Father Sylvester could sit up front. From the back, she couldn't join in the conversation without leaning forward and straining her voice, and so she sat watching the street. When they'd driven to the Bronx for that meeting, it had been nighttime, too dark to see much, but now the rain let up to a drizzle and Jody looked out the window at people huddled beneath elevated subway tracks waiting for the bus, a confusion of highways and overpasses breaking up neighborhoods, confounding those who tried to walk. Old graffiti on the walls made her think of fading tattoos—blurry, dirty, with no hint of the artistry or the vivid colors that must have been there at the moment of creation. They drove past rubble-filled lots and down avenues where flying pennants announced the stores and hand-lettered signs offered bargains. Then back into the burned-out blocks where clusters of umbrellas identified the unorthodox places of business: a tailoring and dry cleaning service with orders taken out of a van, its broken windows mended with cardboard and plastic; a couple of men selling steaks out of the back of a station wagon; Sam's Coffee 'N Donuts Café housed in an empty lot, in an abandoned school bus without wheels. She wished these signs of vitality could please her—proof of a recovering community—but instead she couldn't shake off her impatience: she was almost sorry to see it, the fighting spirit that prolongs a hard death.

Music suddenly poured out of the tape deck: an *a cappella* chorus in gorgeous African harmonies—oh, Frank had come prepared. The voices thrummed, so many shadings, so much richness. It was truly symphonic. She leaned back and let it wash over her, then leaned forward, trying to hear what the men were saying. She caught many of the same words she'd heard before: the open fire, the constellations. They'd been a couple of Boy Scouts, she thought. They'd been so young. Frank's memories seemed so shallow compared to the music with its levels and levels of sound.

"When's the last time you ate real mealies?" he asked, still in his nostalgic reverie.

They ended up on the Bruckner Expressway instead of the Major Deegan. "No problem," shouted Jody from the back. "Just take it up to the Cross Bronx. Less dreaming, Frank, and keep your eye on the road."

They listened to the rain and the music, words like *freedom* and names like Mandela, Biko. Jody wondered if Father Sylvester would go back.

"Hell," said Frank. He'd taken an exit, but it had led them onto residential streets, not the ramp he'd expected to the Cross Bronx.

"So I'll see a neighborhood I haven't seen before," said Father Sylvester. "This environment seems quite nice." They passed brick houses with bright new cars in driveways and, in the front yards, what looked like modern sculpture and must have been fruit trees wrapped in protective plastic for winter. Few people were out in the rain, but every face they saw was white.

"Look," said Jody. "Catholic American kitsch." In front of a corner house a plaster Virgin Mary spread her protection over a little Dutch boy and little Dutch girl standing in a ceramic wooden shoe.

"And this is also the Bronx? New York City?" asked Father Sylvester.

"I think so. Unless we've crossed over into Westchester. I don't really know."

Frank turned onto what looked like a major route which, instead of leading to the highway, took them into a shopping mall parking lot. He was usually good about stopping to ask directions when lost, but this time Jody hoped he would not. It might be a mistake to draw attention to themselves here. This could be one of those neighborhoods where these days it wasn't safe to be black.

"Aren't you warm, Father Sylvester?" she asked. "Take off your coat." With his clerical collar showing, he ought to be okay.

At last they were moving along parallel to a highway—which highway they did not know—three encouraging lanes of traffic speeding by in each direction on the other side of a chain-link, razor wire-topped fence. The access road turned out not to be. The paved surface stopped at a dead end.

"There're three requirements for being a highway engineer in this country," Frank told Father Sylvester. "Be blind, be stupid, and you're disqualified if you've ever driven a car."

"Another facet of American life," said Jody, "that never got mentioned around the campfire."

"Don't worry," Father Sylvester reassured them. "I'm in good company and I'm finding this a very entertaining day."

They pulled onto a narrow and winding side street, Jody occasionally catching glimpses of houses—bigger now, set farther apart and back from the road behind suburban-style lawns—Frank driving slowly, vision impeded by blind curves and fog. "Well, I don't know about you two," he said suddenly, "but I'm hungry." He parked and turned on the emergency flashers. "Father, you're about to see the campfire of the nineties."

Frank had succumbed to the promise of his credit cards and bought much more than a pair of snowshoes. He'd prepared for an expedition, with a lightweight campstove, bottled water, dehydrated foods. He set up by the curb. The car was their shelter, the open front door served as a windbreak. The propane canister fit easily onto the stove; the flame burned hot, without sputtering. The African chorus sang; the water boiled, and then the coffee was welcome, the lentil curry couscous surprisingly good. They all felt peaceful and adventurous, lulled and stirred by the harmonies, the sudden short bursts of rain. Jody reached over the seat to hold hands with Frank; she didn't think Father Sylvester would mind.

When the yapping and barking started, Frank jerked his hand away. A woman, hooded against the weather, stood looking at them, her mouth open in amazement, pulling hard to restrain her dogs on the leash.

"We got lost looking for the Cross Bronx," Jody called from the back seat. It was probably a good idea to let this person know they would gladly get out of the neighborhood and be gone. "If you could direct us?"

"Oh, dear," the woman said while the little dogs danced on their hind legs. "My husband does the driving." She stooped a little, craned her neck to see into the car. "Oh! What a lucky coincidence. I mean for me to see a black person today." She stuck out her hand at Father Sylvester. "Let me take this opportunity to say congratulations. About your Mr. Mandela."

When she was gone, they laughed and then sat relaxed and happy, all critical faculties suspended. Even Jody felt it now. They are few enough— and worth celebrating—those moments of connection and hope. Those times are real, she thought, though they don't last long. Why ruin them asking, *What will happen next? How many more people will die?* For now, she let herself trust the good feeling. She let it light her: the glow of Frank and Father Sylvester in Africa; Nelson Mandela coming home, released from prison after more than twenty-seven years.

The car seemed to glide. It didn't much matter where they were going. The sun broke through the leaden sky and the rain stopped, leaving the air newly washed. Frank was humming now and Jody and Father Sylvester singing softly along with the tape.

"Who was Howard Gillen?" the priest asked.

"I don't know," said Jody.

"We are traveling toward his house," said Father Sylvester. "We've now passed at least three road markers for the Howard Gillen Historic Home."

And then there they were, staring stupidly at a Gothic Revival mansion.

"Whoever Howard Gillen was," said Jody, "he had money."

"Serendipity," said Father Sylvester. "We must go in."

Frank pulled up and parked by the gate.

The house looked odd, but they didn't understand why at first. Frank and Father Sylvester hit their heads on entering; the door was unnaturally low. Jody complained, "There ought to be a sign."

"I'm your site interpreter." A scowling female no more than four feet tall greeted them. She was dressed for the Roaring Twenties in silk and spangles, sequins, dark-seamed stockings, feathers at her throat. She played with her necklace, a double loop of jet beads. "Five dollars a head."

Frank had ten dollars on him; he paid for the priest and himself. Jody bought her own ticket. The woman slipped their money into a beaded bag.

Howard Gillen, 1880–1925, had inherited part of the Gillen oil fortune in 1902, she told them. A dwarf—she pronounced the word with aggressive and loving emphasis, stretching it to three syllables, her teeth bared on the final *f*—he had designed a home to conform to his own size. She turned and waddled to the parlor, her bowlegs showing through the fringe of her hem.

They followed down the hall, tentative and awkward. Slowing their steps so that she could stay in the lead, they stopped to look at Gillen memorabilia on the walls: studio portraits of a hunchbacked man with thick black eyebrows; in other photographs he wore a tux, pleasantly crowded by long-legged women; in another, a nervously grinning Theodore Roosevelt stooped to shake Howard Gillen's hand.

The parlor reminded Jody of the main reading room at the public library: no books, but the same arches and claw-foot columns, dark wood and marble carved with little curlicues and rosettes. In spite of the high ceiling, the door was framed low. Frank hit his head again; they heard their guide stifle a laugh.

"Notice the placement of the light switch," she said. "Notice the height of the table." Her voice sounded like a computer simulation. She gestured toward a low parlor sofa. "Sit there." Father Sylvester wrenched his back and, not noticing the coffee table, banged his knees. "This house was designed not just for Mr. Gillen's convenience but for another reason as well: to make everyone else—the so-called normal people—very, very uncomfortable."

Though their guide had been prepared, in costume, it seemed the Howard Gillen Home did not attract many guests. There were cobwebs in the expected, unavoidable places—the corners of the ceiling, the chandeliers—but in addition the rooms seemed all but unused: the furniture, windowsills, and windows—even the stained glass—dull, almost fuzzy, with dust.

In each room, they saw the scaled-down furnishings: the miniature piano, the dining room table with kindergarten-sized chairs. "Mr. Gillen often had his financial advisers to dinner," said their guide. The idea obviously pleased her. "This room was designed not just for Mr. Gillen's convenience but for another reason as well. Why? To make everyone else—the so-called normal people—very, very uncomfortable."

By the third repetition of this theme, Jody was aware of her rising anger. Demented flapper, she thought, I don't need this. Then she felt ashamed, which angered her more, but that was the point, after all; the experience she hadn't expected but had paid for. She stumbled on the sweep of marble stairs: she had stopped paying attention and both the risers and the banister were too low.

In the master bedroom, cherubs and women with bared rosy breasts disported themselves across the low ceiling. The guests, close by the enormous bed, were poked at by its canopy. "And why is that?" This time, the guide did not answer her own question but waited patiently for the visitors to chant the response, her eyes glittering and flat as sequins. Father Sylvester's eyes glittered, too. He wore his usual smile.

"How interesting," chirped Jody, unwilling to let the woman see how well Howard Gillen had succeeded in his aim. From the window, she looked out over a river, some cars and buildings shrunk down in size on the other shore.

"Is that the East River or the Hudson?" Frank asked.

Where were they, anyway? Their guide didn't answer, though she continued the tour—at this point just overkill—through several more rooms.

At last it was over. Free and out on the street, Father Sylvester chuckled. "Well, are you very, very uncomfortable now?" He patted Jody's back apologetically when she started to cry. Then he put his hands on her shoulders. "One gets used to it," he said.

"Maybe one shouldn't," she answered.

"One grows quite accustomed," said the priest, while Frank went ahead, humming, to unlock the car. *The company car*, thought Jody. He'd been humming in the house, too, down on hands and knees examining the carpet, stooping to study the marquetry work on the dressing table. Everything charmed and enchanted him. She'd watched as he studied each damn piece of furniture, delighted, as though he'd stumbled into a giant dollhouse, perfect in every detail, made just for him.

Father Sylvester's grip tightened on her arm. "I think you are going to hurt my friend," he said. As usual, she couldn't read his tone. Was he worried or pleased?

"Are you two coming?" Frank called. "I know a great place for dinner."

If we can find our way out of here, thought Jody, but she kept her mouth shut. She wanted Father Sylvester to be the one to say it. He still held her arm and pulled her along, and she was sure Frank didn't see her resist. He was beaming at them, waiting at the car door. How could he, in this world, be so happy? Father Sylvester said nothing and Frank kept on smiling. It certainly seemed he loved them both.

The Wizard Of Khao-I-Dang

Sharon May

Tom treats me like a servant in the day, but he invites me to drink with the Australian Embassy staff in the evening. He's new on the Thai border and my least favorite of the immigration officers, arrogant and short-tempered. But I accept his offer because I consider this, too, part of my job; not only to work as a Cambodian interpreter but also to try to educate the staff, as I've been here longer than any of them. Besides, I know he'll buy the beer, and without the alcohol, I cannot sleep.

Tonight all three of them are there—Tom, Richard, Sandra—sitting at a table outside the Bamboo Garden, which caters mostly to foreigners, under a hand-lettered BAMBU GARDIN sign. I am the only Cambodian man—the only Cambodian here. The other two translators—Thais who speak Khmer with an accent, and who have their own families to return to in the evening—are absent. Only I have nowhere better to go.

My favorite of the three Australian officers, Sandra, looks about forty years old, pale and fleshy. She wears a red felt hat with a floppy brim, as if she must shield herself from the soft glow of the streetlights. Dark freckles dot her body, like bugs in a sack of rice, speckling her face, her neck, her arms. Of the three embassy officers, she is the kindest, and the most emotional, especially when she's drunk.

Tonight, after her fourth beer, she leans her face close to mine and says, "These poor people. How can you stand it?"

Her tears embarrass me.

I don't want pity. What I want is for them to understand. Of course this is a foolish desire. I know what the Buddha teaches: desire is the cause of suffering. And so I have tried to eradicate desire from my heart. I have tried to weaken its pull on my mind. But still it remains. A wanting.

A deep lake of yearning, wide as the Tonle Sap that expands more than ten times its size during the monsoon, only to shrink again in the dry season.

Even after we have lost everything, we still want something. The people stuck in Khao-I-Dang camp, who have escaped Cambodia to Thailand, want to get out to America or Australia or England—or any country that will possibly accept them. They want this not for themselves, but for their children. I, who already made it out to Australia and came back to the camps to help my people, want to go home to Cambodia. And the immigration officers, what do they want?

The next morning, Tom doesn't look at me or the Cambodian applicant, who has been bussed here from Khao-I-Dang for this interview along with the other hundred refugees waiting outside the building for their turn. I suspect Tom is tired or hungover, already worn down by the weariness of bureaucrats. He stares at the file lying on the table and absently twirls a Fanta Orange bottle clockwise between his thumb and forefinger. Drops of water cover the glass like beads of sweat, except near the lip, which he wipes with a handkerchief now before taking a sip. He drinks a dozen bottles of Fanta Orange a day, because—as he confided to me when he first arrived a month ago, nervous and sweating—he is afraid of the water, afraid of the ice, and isn't taking any bloody chances. So every morning, I fill an ice chest in the Aranyaprathet market to keep the bottles cold.

"When were you born?" Tom finally asks the applicant, who stares intently at the floor while I translate the question into Khmer. He wears the cheap, off-white plastic sandals distributed in the camp last week. One of the side straps has broken.

"I'm a Rat," the man answers, glancing up at me, not Tom.

Of course I don't translate this directly. The man, Seng Veasna according to the application, nervously holds his hands sandwiched between his knees. Seng Veasna means "good destiny." He looks about fifty, the father of the small family sitting in a half circle before the officer's wooden desk. I calculate quickly, counting back the previous Years of the Rat until I reach the one that best suits his age.

"1936," I say to Tom. He checks the answer against the birth date on the application, submitted by Seng Veasna's relatives in Australia. The numbers must match, as well as the names, or the officer will think the man is lying and reject the application. Each question is a problem with a single correct answer, only a family's future—not an exam grade—is at stake.

It is my job to solve these problems. To calculate. To resolve inconsistencies.

I did not wish to become a translator or to perform these tricks. I had wanted to become a mathematician and had almost finished my baccalaureate when the Khmer Rouge took over. I'd planned to teach high school, but it was not my fate. Instead, I now work in this schoolhouse made of timber and tin, at the site of an abandoned refugee camp. This building alone still stands, used for immigration interviews. Inside, three tables for three teams are set in a wide triangle, far enough apart that we can see but not hear each other.

The arrangement reminds me of the triangle I have traveled from Cambodia to Thailand to Australia—and now back again, to Thailand, retracing my journey. After the fall of the Khmer Rouge, I left Cambodia, crossing the minefields to a camp like this one on the Thai border. Australia accepted me. In Melbourne, I washed dishes in a refugee hostel and took English classes. Language has always come easily to me, like numbers. I'd studied French and some English before the war. Like a fool, I had even kept an English dictionary with me after the Khmer Rouge evacuated us from the city. For this stupidity I almost lost my life; when a soldier discovered the book, I survived by claiming I used the pages for toilet paper— very soft, I told him, ripping out a few pages to demonstrate.

After the Khmer Rouge, I learned some Vietnamese from the occupying soldiers. In the refugee camp, I learned a little Thai. Still, when I first arrived in Australia, English sounded like snake language, with so many S's, hissing and dangerous. But then the words began to clarify, not individually but in patterns, like the sequence of an equation. A door opened, and I no longer felt trapped. I still felt like a stranger though; useless, alone. I had no wife, no children to keep me there. After three years, I got my Australian passport and returned to Thailand.

First I worked in a transit camp in Bangkok, where the refugees who have been accepted must pass medical tests before they can be sent abroad. The foreign aid workers didn't trust me, because I was Cambodian. And I didn't want to be in Bangkok. After six months, I heard the Australian

Embassy needed translators on the border. That's where I wanted to be, where I could be useful. I jumped at the chance. One step closer to Cambodia, to home.

I had to come back. I think it is my fate to work in a schoolhouse after all.

"Why did you leave Cambodia?" Tom asks the applicant now.

Of all the questions, I dread this one the most. When I translate it into Khmer, Seng Veasna laughs, lifting his hands and opening them in the air in a wide gesture of surrender. For the first time during the interview, he looks relaxed, as if all the tension has drained from his body.

"Doesn't he know what happened in our country?" he asks me. His tone is intimate, personal. For the moment, he has forgotten his fear. He seems to have forgotten even the presence of the embassy officer, although I have not.

"You must tell him," I say in Khmer. I understand the purpose of this question is to distinguish between economic and political refugees, but I also know that this man cannot answer, any more than the last applicant, who just looked at me in disbelief. He cannot answer any more than I can. Still, I urge him, "Just tell the truth."

The man shakes his head no. He cannot speak. He can only laugh. I want to tell him I know this is a nonsense question, a question they do not need to ask.

Why did you leave Cambodia?

I've told the embassy staff many times that if they ask this question, they can never get the right answer. I've explained to the other two officers—although not yet to this new one, Tom—that nearly two million people died. One-quarter of the people in Cambodia died in less than four years. Then the Vietnamese invaded. There was no food, no medicine, no jobs. Everyone has lost family. Myself, I lost my mother and father, two brothers, one sister, six aunts and uncles, seventeen cousins. The numbers I can say; the rest I cannot.

Even now, the fighting continues in Cambodia and on the border. Sometimes in this schoolhouse the muffled boom of heavy artillery interrupts the interviews.

"Why is he laughing?" Tom asks.

"He does not understand the question."

"Ask him again. How can he not know why he bloody left the country?"

I see Tom's bottle of Fanta is almost empty. I take another from the ice chest, pop off the cap, wipe the lip with a clean handkerchief, and set it on his desk before turning back to Seng Veasna to explain in Khmer. "I know, you don't want to remember. But you must tell him what you've gone through." When the man still does not speak, I add, "Uncle, if you don't answer, he will reject your application."

At that, Seng Veasna glances quickly at Tom then back to the floor and begins to talk, without raising his eyes. I repeat his story in English, the story I have heard so many times in infinite variations, the same story that is my own. And when Seng Veasna is finally through and the interview finished, to my relief the officer Tom stamps the application accepted. One done. Ten families still wait outside. The morning is not yet half over.

Here's what I don't say to the immigration officers:

Try to imagine. The camp is like prison, nothing to do but wait and go crazy. Forget your iced bottles of Fanta and beer. Forget your salary that lets you live like a king while you make the decisions of a god.

Imagine. It is like magic. You wake up one morning and everything is gone. The people you love, your parents, your friends. Your home. Like in the film I saw twice in Australia, *The Wizard of Oz*. I watched it first with my second brother's son, who was six, who had been born on the border but raised in Melbourne and cannot even speak Khmer properly. The flying monkeys scared him so much I had to turn off the video. But those monkeys reminded me of home, of when I worked in the forest surrounding Lake Tonle Sap. They reminded me of the monkey god Hanuman and his army who helped Rama rescue Sita. So later, after my nephew went to sleep, I watched the rest of the movie. The next week I rented the video and watched it again alone. I didn't like the singing and dancing, so I fast-forwarded through those parts. But the girl's wanting to go home—that I understood. And I understood, too, the wizard who has no power, who cannot even help himself, although he also secretly wishes to return home.

I want to tell the immigration officers: Imagine, you are in that movie. Then maybe you will understand. You are the girl. Only there is no home to return to. And instead of Oz, you have woken up in a refugee camp.

Each day you have nothing to do but worry and, if you are lucky enough to have a ration card, to wait like a beggar for handouts of rice and canned, half-rancid fish. At night after the foreign aid workers leave, the soldiers who are supposed to protect you steal what few possessions you still have, and they rape your wives and your daughters. You want only to get out. To find a new home.

Every day you hope for an announcement on the loudspeaker that an embassy is conducting interviews. You hope for America but any country will do: France, England, Australia. You check the list on the wall, search for your name, squeezing your body in between the others. The people clustered around the wall have a certain rank smell, almost sweet. You wish you could wash this stink from your body and purify yourself of this place, of this longing. On one side of you stands a husband who has waited for years, checking this same wall; on the other, a mother who's been rejected twice and so has little hope, yet still she comes to look. Behind you a father squats in the sun; he can't read, so his son checks for him while he waits. If you're lucky enough to be listed, you must be prepared to go to the interview the following day.

Imagine. The bus picks you up early in the morning, exiting the gate past the Thai guards with their machine guns, taking you out of the camp for the first time in the years since you arrived. As the bus rattles over the rutted road, your mind clenches in fear. The child in front of you presses her face to the window, enraptured. She points at the rice fields, the water buffalo, the cows, which she has never seen before because she was born in the camp. "What's that?" she asks, curious. "And that?" Her father names these things for her. You know he is thinking of the interview ahead, as you are, and how much depends on it, how her future depends on it; perhaps he is thinking, too, of how the shirt he has cleaned and pressed is already stained with sweat.

All the questions are difficult. Especially the ones that seem the simplest to the immigration officers: What is your name? Where were you born? How old are you?

Take, for example, this morning, when officer Richard asks a young man, "What is your brother's name?"

"Older brother Phal," the boy answers. He is skinny, frightened.

"What is his *full* name?" Richard, over six feet tall, has wide shoulders and a large belly like a Chinese Buddha. Although he smiles often, his height and massive torso scare the applicants, especially when he leans toward them as he does now, both elbows planted on the table, intently studying the boy. The young man stares at the floor. He looks like a real Khmer—wide cheekbones, full lips, chocolate skin. "Don't be scared," Richard says. "Take it easy. We're not going to do anything to you. Just try to answer correctly, honestly."

Still the boy hesitates. I worry Richard may take this as a sign the child is lying about his relationship to the sponsor, although I've tried to explain to him that Cambodians don't call their relatives by their given names; it's not polite. You call them brother or sister, aunt or uncle, or you use nicknames, so you may not know the full given name. Then there are the names you may have used under the Khmer Rouge, to hide your background to save your family's lives, or your own. I have explained this all before, but it does no good.

In the end, Richard says, "I'm sorry," and stamps the front page rejected.

I can do nothing. Although siblings have lower priority, I believe the familial relationship is not the problem. Rather, the boy is dark-skinned and speaks no English. Richard, like the others, prefers the light-skinned Cambodians, who have more Chinese blood, softer features, who can speak at least some English. If they are young and pretty and female, even better.

Just as important is the officer's mood, yet another variable I must consider. Tom is more likely to accept an applicant when he has been to a brothel the night before. Sandra is more likely to approve after she has received a letter from her children in Sydney, less likely if they happen to mention her ex-husband in Brisbane. Richard, usually in good spirits, is most dangerous when he has a hangover or digestive problems. Today he seems to have neither trouble. He has not been running to the toilet or popping paracetamol pills for a headache, so I don't know why the day doesn't seem to get easier.

The next couple is neither young nor pretty. The wife's lips and teeth are stained red from chewing betel nut.

"When was your seventh son born?" Richard asks.

The husband and wife look at each other, confused.

"Was it eight or nine years ago?" the man asks his wife.

"Nine," she says. "No, eight."

"You sure? Wasn't it nine?"

"No, tell him eight." The wife gives her husband a scolding look, then smiles weakly at the officer, showing her stained teeth. By now Richard is laughing and shaking his head.

"Eight," I translate.

"Do they know his birth *date*?"

The husband looks again at his wife. "Dry season," she says. "I remember it had stopped raining already."

"Around December or January," I translate. Then I add, "It's not that they're lying; it's that these things aren't important. Birth dates are not registered until a child enters school, if then."

"How can you not know when your own child was born?" Richard asks me. His generous belly shakes as he laughs. He does not really want an answer, so I say nothing.

"What's wrong?" the wife asks me.

"Never mind," I say. "Don't worry."

I am forever in between.

To the people in the camp, I explain again and again, "Look, you must remember your full names and birth dates. In Cambodia it's not important, but in the West, it's very important. If you don't know, make them up. One person in the family must write all the answers down, and everyone must remember. You must practice."

They look at me funny at first, not quite believing me, like Richard watches me now, still chuckling. Because he is amused, I calculate he will accept the couple. I decide to say nothing and just smile back.

That night at the Bamboo Garden, Richard calls the owner to our table. "Your food is spot on, very *aroy*," Richard says, emphasizing and mispronouncing the Thai word for delicious, using the wrong tone. "But mate, that sign is spelled wrong."

The owner, a slight man in his sixties, nods his head, "Yes. Thank you. Yes."

"I mean, you gotta fix that spelling." Richard points to the sign above him. "Darith, can you explain to him?"

Shit, I think, even here I have to translate. In polite language, I tell the owner in Thai that the big foreigner loves the food very much.

The owner smiles. Richard nods, happy to be understood. I think that's the end of it. But then Richard pulls out a long strip of toilet paper—which is used in place of napkins—from the pink plastic container in the center of the table. In large block letters, using the pen he keeps in his shirt pocket, he writes: BAMBOO GARDEN. He underlines the double O and the E, then points again at the misspelled sign.

The owner's face darkens, without me having to explain. "Thank you. Yes, I fix," he says, as he takes the piece of toilet paper from Richard's outstretched hand.

The young woman sitting in front of the desk this morning is both pretty and light-skinned. Her hair, recently washed, is combed neatly into a shiny ponytail that falls below her narrow waist. As she passed me to take her seat, I could smell the faint sweet scent of her shampoo. She wears a carefully ironed white blouse and a trace of pink lipstick, which she must have borrowed from a friend or relative to make herself up for this occasion. Officer Tom, to whom I have been assigned today, watches the girl with interest, charmed. Her sponsor is only a cousin, so normally she would have little chance of being accepted.

"What do you do in the camp?" he asks. "Do you work?"

The young lady speaks softly. Out of politeness, she doesn't meet his eyes. "Yes, I work, but..." Her voice trails off and then she turns to me, blushing. "I don't want to say, it's a very low job."

"What is it?"

"I work in the CARE bakery, making bread."

Tom eyes me suspiciously. "Why are you talking to her?"

I could answer him straight, but I'm annoyed with him today. I did not sleep well last night. I am getting sick of this job, this place. For all I do, it seems I have done nothing. "She was talking to me," I snap back. "That's why I talked to her."

"What did she say?"

"She says she doesn't want to tell you, because she feels embarrassed." As if on cue, she turns her head away. Her ponytail ripples down her back.

"What exactly does she *do* in the camp?" Tom says this in an insinu-ating way, as if he suspects she's a prostitute. I don't like the way he looks at her. Maybe he is undressing her in his mind right now. For her part, the girl waits quietly in the chair, knees drawn together, looking at her hands lying still on her knees. Her fingernails are clean, cut short. This, too, she remembered to do for the interview.

"She has a wonderful job," I say to Tom. "You know the bread from the CARE bakery in Khao-I-Dang, the French bread you eat every morning? She is the baker."

"That's very good. Why didn't you say so in the first place?" He relaxes back in his chair and takes a drink from the Fanta bottle. I don't know how he can drink this stuff, or how I can watch him drink it all day. I submerge the thought and clear my head to concentrate on the task at hand. He con-tinues, "Ask her what is she going to do if she gets accepted to Australia."

"What are you going to do in Australia—tell him you're going to open a bakery," I say, all in one sentence.

Raising her head to face him now, she answers in a sweet, composed voice, "I want to open a bakery shop in Australia."

I translate, "She wants to work in a bakery in Australia, and when she can save enough money, to open her own bread shop."

"Good, good," he says, and stamps the application accepted.

That night at dinner with Sandra and Richard, Tom asks me out of the blue, "Why did you come back here?"

The restaurant sign is gone, creating an empty space over our heads. I shrug my shoulders and look away, hoping he'll get distracted, perhaps with the attractive waitress waiting to refill our glasses. I glance at her and she comes forward to pour more beer for everyone.

"You came back, didn't you?" Tom persists after the waitress has stepped back into the shadows. "Your mother's Australian, isn't she? And your father is Cambodian?"

I've heard this rumor, too, mostly from foreigners. I think it is their way of explaining why I can speak English.

"No, I am all Cambodian," I say. "But I have Australian citizenship."

"So you went through the Khmer Rouge and all that?" asks Richard.

"Yes. All that."

Sandra, who knows this, watches me. Her jaw tenses under the shadow of her hat.

"I don't get it," Tom says. "Why would you come back? Seems to me everyone else is trying to get out of here." He laughs, lifting his glass. "Myself included. Cheers, mate."

I lift my glass. "Cheers," I say. I should leave it at that.

Sandra is still watching me with concern, her eyebrows drawn together. "How about that storm this afternoon?" she asks to change the subject. "I couldn't hear a thing."

Maybe it is the beer. I don't know. I look straight at Tom. "You don't know how much the people feel," I say. He doesn't respond.

"I couldn't hear a thing," Sandra repeats, more forcefully this time. "I can't believe how loud rain is on a tin roof."

"Yeah," says Richard. "I even had to stop the interview."

"The way you treat people, you don't know anything," I say, still looking directly at Tom. He shifts in his chair and dips a spring roll into sweet red sauce. With his other hand he ticks the Formica tabletop. His eyes study the waitress. As if he hasn't even heard me. I often feel this way around the immigration officers, invisible. Sometimes they talk about the Cambodians, calling them lazy or stupid, as if I am not there, or as if they have forgotten that I am Khmer. I continue, "If you ask me, these people never want to come to your country. If you open the gate, they will go back to Cambodia. They won't even say good-bye." I want to stop, but I can't. "And don't ask them why they leave the country. You think they want to leave their home? They laugh when you ask them that. You should know. The real situation is that they want to survive."

Sandra has stopped talking. Richard looks into his half-empty beer glass, then takes a sip. Tom loudly crunches on another spring roll. I don't know why they are the way they are. It's not that none of them cares. There is Sandra, and others like her. And they are sent from country to country, without time to learn the difference between Cambodia and Vietnam. It's not easy for them. I tell myself that they are just worn down, but the new arrivals have the same assumed superiority, the unquestioned belief that they know everything: what is wrong, what is right—that they are somehow more *human*. I signal to the waitress for another round.

The next night, instead of beer, Tom orders me a Fanta Orange soda, grinning as he slides the bottle across the table toward me. The restaurant sign is still gone.

"No, thanks," I say.

"Go ahead, mate."

"No, thank you," I say again.

"Why not?" asks Tom.

"Oh, leave him alone," says Sandra.

I stare at the orange bottle.

"It won't kill you," says Tom.

"No, not me." I try to make light of it. "I gave that stuff up a long time ago, in 1976."

Tom laughs. So does Richard in his booming voice. For all of their attention to dates from the applicants, for all their insistence that the numbers must match exactly, they ignore what those dates mean. But I am telling the truth. It was 1976, the second year under the Khmer Rouge regime. It was the rainy season, cold and miserable. I lived in a single men's labor camp on a hill in the rice fields. One night I heard the guards calling, "We got the enemy! We got the enemy!" *What enemy?* I thought. We were in the middle of nowhere. The real purpose of the guards was to keep the workers from trying to escape or steal food at night. When I opened my eyes, I couldn't see the man sleeping next to me. Clouds blocked even the stars. Then I saw the feeble flames from lit pieces of rubber tire, burned for lamplight, and got up to see what had happened.

Near the compound's kitchen, three Khmer Rouge leaders gathered around a skinny man kneeling in the mud, his elbows tied tightly behind his back. His shoulders were pulled back like a chicken's wings, tensing the tendons in his neck. He had dark skin and long hair that fell below his bound wrists. I'd heard rumors of resistance fighters, "long hairs" who lived in the forest around Lake Tonle Sap, but I had never seen one and did not believe until then that they really existed. I had thought them the product of our collective imagining, our wishing someone had the courage to fight back.

Comrade Sok kicked the man in his side, and he fell over into the mud. Sok was a big man, twice the size of the prisoner. When Sok kicked him again, the man's head hit a water buffalo yoke lying at the edge of the kitchen. One of the other leaders pulled his head up. The prisoner's eyes were closed. Comrade Sok said, "Why do you resist? Who do you struggle for?"

The man seemed only half-conscious. He opened his eyes briefly, then closed them again and spoke very clearly, slowly enunciating each word: "I struggle for all of you, brothers, not for myself."

"You struggle for me? We have already liberated the country." Sok kicked him again. "We have no need of your help."

The man said once more, "I struggle for you."

Then they threw him like a sack of rice into an oxcart. Everyone was watching. We couldn't help him. We couldn't do anything.

The next day, while I was cleaning the abscesses on my feet using water boiled with sour leaves, the oxcart returned—without the man, loaded instead with bottles of soft drinks and cigarette cartons. Comrade Sok explained this was our reward for capturing the enemy: one bottle for three people, one pack of cigarettes for ten people. The next time we captured the enemy, we would receive an even greater reward.

The cigarette packets were Fortunes, with a lion insignia. The soda bottles were Miranda Orange. I teased the two younger boys with whom I shared the soft drink, dividing the bottle into thirds, the top being the largest, the bottom the smallest. "What part do you want?" I asked. Of course they chose the top two portions. "OK, I'll take the bottom," I said. "You don't mind if I drink my portion first…"

"No, that's not right," they protested together. I was only making fun. I poured the drink into three tin bowls we usually used to eat the rice ration, giving the boys most of it. They were excited about the soda, which they hadn't tasted in a long time, if ever. But all the while I was trying to make them laugh, I felt sad. A man was killed for this.

The drink was flat, not even enough liquid to fill my mouth.

The application lying on the table today in front of Sandra is a difficult case. This morning, when I dropped the files on each of the three officer's tables, I made sure this one came to her. The sponsor in Australia, a daughter, had gotten citizenship by claiming a woman was her mother. Now that the daughter was in Australia, she was claiming the woman was not actually her mother, but rather her aunt, and that the woman sitting before us now is her real mother.

The mother hands me the letter from her daughter, which I translate. In it, the daughter explains that this woman is her real mother and confesses she lied before. She did not know her mother was alive then. She was alone in the camp, with no one to take care of her. That's why she decided to lie.

Sandra asks me, "Do you think they are real mother and daughter?"

"Yes," I say, and hand her the letter, which she adds to the file lying open before her, with the previous and current applications, and small black-and-white photos. "You can even see the daughter looks like her."

"Well, they cannot do that," Sandra says. "She lied. The law is the law."

"I can tell you, this is a story many people face, not just these two. They do not intend to lie, but because of the circumstances they must do it, believe me. Think of your own daughter, if you were separated." And then I add, "Of course it's up to you, not me."

"She lied," Sandra says. "It's finished. I have to reject them."

"I can't tell them straight like that," I say. "Would you let me explain nicely to them the reason they are getting rejected?"

"All right, go ahead."

So I take a chance, a calculated risk. There is nothing to lose now. I know Sandra loves her own children, and also that she has a good heart. I say to the mother in a soft, even voice, "Look, your daughter lied to the embassy even though she knew what she was doing was wrong. A country like Australia is not like Cambodia. The law is the law. When you say someone is your mother, it's got to be your mother. Now she cannot change her story. So from now on, I don't think you will be able to meet your daughter anymore for the rest of your life."

Tears begin to well in the mother's eyes. I feel bad for what I am doing, but I know there is no other way. I keep my voice firm, steady, and continue, "So now, after all you've been through in Cambodia, after how hard you struggled to keep your family together, to survive, now you are separated forever."

The mother begins to wail, a long piercing sound that fills the entire room, so that the teams at the other two tables turn around to look at us. "Oh, my daughter, I will never see you again!" she cries. I translate what she says for Sandra. "After all we survived in the Pol Pot time—when you were starving, I risked my life to steal food for you. When you got sick, I looked after you. When you could not walk, I carried you in my arms. And now you lie. You lie and you are separated from me. I cannot see you for the rest of my life. *Ouey…*"

I translate it all, word for word. The father is crying now, too, but silently. He sits in a wooden chair, with his back straight. Their young son watches his mother's face and sobs as well, echoing her wails.

"Please, tell them to go now," Sandra says. She looks away and wipes her eyes with the back of her hand.

In Khmer, I dismiss the family, "Go, go. Don't cry anymore. Even if you die, nobody cares. You will never see your child anymore."

As the mother walks away, the applicants at the other tables watch her leave. The building is silent except for her voice. She cries all the way out of the building, gripping her husband's arm. Her son whimpers too, clinging to her legs through the sarong, almost tripping her.

I start to laugh. "Well, Sandra, that's it," I say. "Send them back to the Killing Fields. Don't worry. There's more coming."

Sandra looks at me, stunned. She opens her mouth and closes it again, without saying anything, like a fish gulping sea water. The freckled skin around her eyes is red and puffy. I can see the beating of her blood in the translucent skin of her left temple, a small pulsing disk, like the flutter of a bird's heart. She looks away, down to the table, and starts idly shifting through the papers. She isn't really looking at them.

"I'll get the next family," I say.

She nods, her face still turned away from me. I grab the list and go call the next family from the dozens of others waiting outside the building. Some stand in the sun. Others squat in the shade of three small coconut trees, fanning away flies.

"Keo Narith," I say. No one steps forward. The crowd looks agitated, nervous. The mother is still crying, "My daughter, I can never see you again!" A group has gathered around her, asking, "What happened? What happened?"

"Keo Narith!" I call again.

Still, no one answers. I remember the name because it rhymes with my own, and I saw the family members board the bus when they were called in the morning. They must be hiding somewhere now in the crowd or behind the coconut trees or around the corner of the building. I hear a man to the left of me say, "The embassy is not happy today. They reject easily." It's true, when too many people are rejected, the next applicants don't dare answer. They'd rather wait for months or years until they get back on the list again.

After we drive back to Aranyaprathet, the embassy staff meet again for dinner at the Bamboo Garden. The owner has fixed the sign: two small, oblong Os are now squeezed into the space that held the *U*, and the *I* has been changed to an *E*, only the shades of paint don't quite match. Tom and Richard are talking the usual bullshit. Richard expands on his most recent stomach problems. Tom no longer talks about leaving. He has a Thai girlfriend now, a prostitute who he claims is a waitress at the bar who has never slept with a man before him. "She's been saving herself," he says.

Sandra looks at him, disgusted, and interjects, "Yeah, right. You really believe that?"

As the men continue talking, Sandra turns to me and whispers, "Darith, I changed it. I changed the file, when I got back. I'm letting them go now. I believe you."

I say quietly, "You made the right decision."

"I know," she says, her eyes shining, urgent. "I understand."

I think there is more than any of us can understand. I feel something I cannot express: an opening, an exit. It is like the feeling I had when I first crossed the border after the end of the Khmer Rouge regime: gratitude, mixed with weariness, hunger. The day I arrived I could still taste the foul pond water I had drunk in darkness the night before, so thirsty, not seeing until morning the corpse of a woman—not long dead—who lay in the pond, next to where I slept. I didn't know then what would come, how many years I would work to return to this border I had fled. I wonder, does Sandra—whom I can see still watching me, out of the corner of my eye as I look down at my beer glass on the table—really understand? How many families will remain stuck in the camp if I can no longer do this job? I weigh all of this: duty, desire, two halves of an equation, as I turn the glass in my hand.

All the while in my heart I am thinking, hoping, I can quit now. I can leave this place. It is time to go home.

Ishwari's Children

Shabnam Nadiya

We lived in Dhaka, but my dadajan lived at Noapara, our ancestral village. He was a large man, his girth befitting a man of his worth and station in life. His eyes crinkled when he smiled and sometimes when he wanted to but didn't. His beard was mostly white with slivers of black proclaiming the youth that still flowed in his veins. He always wore a freshly laundered and starched white skullcap. These were never purchased; my grandmother knitted them for him.

We would visit Dadajan twice or thrice a year. He, however, visited us frequently. He would arrive with a man in tow carrying coconuts, earthen pots full of live fish, and, twice a year, gargantuan sacks filled with rice from his fields. He himself would come bearing stories. Invariably the stories were about Ishwari—the river was swallowing up land like a starving mad-woman. "She's a hungry one," Dadajan would tell me. "She's eating me right out of house and home." The rampaging waves of Ishwari were engulf-ing huge chunks of land—a lot of which belonged to my grandfather. She was washing away houses and fields; villages disappeared in a matter of days. But Ishwari also gave it back, he told me. "She chews and chews, and spits it right out. No saying where that land'll turn up, though it's better and more wholesome than before." Still, it was these regurgitations that Dadajan had so much trouble with. There were frequent arbitrations required and even visits to the law courts over whom the newly arisen *chars* belonged to. The fertile lush lands that emerged from Ishwari's womb were desired by many—whether they were rightful claimants or not. Dadajan would come to consult my father frequently on these matters: as the only son, all of it would most certainly be his one day. I would sit by Dadajan's lap, submerged in sleepy comfort as they discussed the status of this piece of land or that, hearing about the violence and the persistence of *charuas*, *char-bandhas*, as these char-people strove to settle the newly surfaced land-masses, learning of squatter's rights and other legalese of land disputes.

Whenever we were visiting, I would always accompany Dadajan on his business errands. However, I remember being taken to see a char only once. It was winter then and Ishwari was at her driest. Dadajan was going to see some people on a newly arisen char. We went part of the way on the small *kosha* that Dadajan kept for his personal use. As the slim shape of the kosha slid along the dark riverbed, I longed for the clearer waters of the rainy season. We had two of Dadajan's *kamlas* with us. Abdul Chacha and Alam Chacha were the most trusted of all the men who worked for him. They were brothers and there were other members of their family who worked for ours—had done so for generations. Abdul Chacha, the elder, had worked for my dadajan ever since he had been capable of bludgeoning sun-hardened clods of earth to ready the fields for planting. He accompanied my grandfather everywhere, a black umbrella and a cloth bag containing necessities for both men hung from his shoulder. Alam Chacha's responsibility at that time was to lug me (and another black umbrella) around whenever Dadajan took me on his business errands to show me off—the only son of his only son.

Alam Chacha had rowed the single-oar kosha as far as the river had allowed. "We'll have to walk now, Babu," Dadajan told me in his rumbly voice. He led the way, striding with his silver-topped walking cane in hand. Abdul Chacha followed holding the umbrella over his head. I was put astride Alam Chacha's shoulders. He had to hold the umbrella up higher than usual to accommodate my head. It must have been quite uncomfortable for him, perhaps even painful—for carrying a six-year-old boy is no joke—but he never complained or even appeared put out. Or perhaps he did and I simply remained unaware of it, secure in the unfeeling obliviousness of the young.

The banks on both sides were splotched here and there with dried *kaash* and grass, like the fine sun-bleached thinning hair of the very old. The verdant riverbanks of Ishwari in full spate had disappeared. As we walked on, the sparse vegetation dwindled as the recognizable riverbanks melded into white sand. The pale winter sun had found the one place where it could live its former glory and showed no mercy. The sand and the sun dazzled and benumbed my little-boy eyes: the stark whiteness was everywhere, everything around me seemed to glow. It seemed a landscape of an unimagined world, as if I had entered dream-time. Even the sounds of the world appeared to have changed. Gone was the steady thrum of Ishwari; the calm bustle of the household and of the village as they went about their day was a distant dream. Instead, all I could hear was the constant rhythmic swishing as the sand shifted beneath our feet and the discordant cry of a hawk as it circled far above us. This was Ishwari with her water gone, sucked away by winter. The river lay like a tired old lizard sunning its underbelly. I have no idea how either my grandfather or his men knew where we were, or where we were going, for it seemed an endless journey to me as we trudged on and on within that unchanging lucent glare. Safely ensconced on Alam Chacha's shoulders, it seemed as if it was I who was becoming weary with each step.

And then suddenly harsh green erupted in front of my eyes. There were trees and houses. As we neared I saw that although they looked fairly new, the houses were built similar to our cowsheds. Simple structures of woven mats and bamboo slats held together with twine, they were easy to dismantle and put up again. Yet even our cowsheds were roofed with tin, while these were thatched. There were children playing in front of the shacks. Most of them were dressed in rags of indeterminate color while a few were naked except for talismans and *tabijes* tied to their waists with the traditional black string. They stopped as they caught sight of us and stared. Abdul Chacha called out, "Hey, where's Kamrun Munshi, do you know?" None of the children moved. "Didn't my words reach your ears?" he bellowed. "Call Kamrun Munshi and tell him that Chowdhury Shaheb of Noapara is here." They scattered before him like a flock of sparrows.

We moved into the shade of the few banana trees that bordered the settlement and waited. Alam Chacha lowered me to the ground. A few minutes later a woman appeared, her head and part of her face covered with the *anchal* of her ragged sari. I could see more women gathered a bit away, craning their necks trying to get a glimpse of us and keep their heads covered at the same time. The woman stood in front of Dadajan and touched her hand to her forehead in greeting, "*Salaam Aleikum.*" My grandfather inclined his head graciously in response.

"Well?" It was as if Abdul Chacha's curtness, not a sudden breeze, ruffled the sand at her feet. She said something in an inaudible voice.

"Speak up, woman," ordered Abdul Chacha. "Where is Kamrun Munshi?" She raised her face slightly and repeated, "He's not here." She paused and added, "He's gone to the market. This time of day, the men..."

"So who are you then?" It surprised me that Abdul Chacha seemed to be speaking to her as he was; why was he so angry at this woman? "I'm his wife," came the low reply.

"Wife! Oh, you're his woman. You *charuas*—"

"Abdul," the calm voice of Dadajan interjected. "There is no need to be like that." Abdul Chacha immediately bowed his head and took his place behind Dadajan. "So you are Kamrun's wife? Well, I am Akram Chowdhury from Noapara. We have come a long way. And I have my grandson with me. Do you think we could sit in the shade somewhere and have a drink of water? It is unfortunate that your husband is away. I had business with him." The covered head bowed and turned away murmuring an indistinct invitation. We followed her to her yard. The other women trailed behind us, their chatter a gentle susurration like the swirl of river waters.

When we reached her yard, Kamrun Munshi's wife set out a wooden *jolchouki* for Dadajan to sit on. She said something to some of the other women who slipped away immediately. They stood there, the rest of them, just behind Kamrun Munshi's wife, as we inspected the ramshackle shed of her home, the neat yard with its corner covered with pats of dried cow dung, chewed-up pith of sugarcane, and a heap of unidentifiable rags to be used for fuel or perhaps to be sold. A washing line was drawn taut from the house to a banana tree, on which hung a red and green striped sari as tattered as the one she was wearing. A few scraggly looking chickens were clucking about aimlessly.

"You seem to have settled in quite nicely," Dadajan said with a proprietary air as he sat on the jolchouki. He pointed his cane to the chickens, "Do they lay well? Do you have a cock for breeding?" There was a coarseness in Dadajan's voice and the way he spoke, as unfamiliar to me as the shimmering terrain we had just traversed. As he spoke, the women who had left returned—one of them carried a small wooden *piri* and the others came with eatables. She placed the piri near Dadajan's feet and motioned for me to sit on it. Two tin mugs were placed near his feet for us as well as a few *batashas* and coconut *narus* in a battered tin bowl. To offer just water to a visitor was unthinkable, even to these people.

Kamrun Munshi's wife came and stood near me. She motioned to me with her hand and said in her soft voice, "Eat, Babu." Her anchal had fallen away and I could see her face clearly for the first time. She had the kind of spurious prettiness of the countrywoman, that faded with age and work. I chose a creamy brown batasha and sucked on it, the crumbly sweetness melting in my mouth. Dadajan picked up a mug and took a sip. "This is very good. Go on, Babu, try it." I drank from the other mug. Sugar water. Dadajan smacked his lips and asked, "Where is Kamrun Munshi? Leaving his young wife all alone in this place. Where are the other men?" The children appeared suddenly—their ghost-faces peeked out from behind the women, peered out from the corner of the house. They watched us as silently as their mothers.

"The menfolk are not home this time of day. It is so in the villages too."

"Why has Munshi gone to the marketplace?"

"We had some eggs, and some vegetables. Also some fish from Ishwari. He will sell them and bring rice."

"Eggs, vegetables. I see you've begun planting," Dadajan said as he looked at the patches of darker earth to the west. "Watermelon, tomatoes, cauliflower. That is good, it will hold the soil down. So you have quite settled in. How many of you are there?"

The woman stood in front of us with her eyes lowered and dug at the earth with her toe. "In our house?" she asked. "No no," Dadajan waved his cane impatiently. "All of you, here. How many?"

"Oh, a few households," she replied vaguely. Dadajan looked at Alam Chacha and inclined his head slightly. Alam Chacha slipped quietly away through the yard into the settlement. There was a sly chittering of insects all around us. Dadajan smiled, "Listen, *beti*, you people have just come here. I know it will be very difficult; mainlanders often have no understanding of the hardships of the *charua* life. But I am a man who lives under Allah's eye. I have to see to it that all within my power live lives that are useful and fair, and that justice is done to them." Kamrun Munshi's wife looked at the ground as she said softly but distinctly, "We work. It is very hard, but we work as Allah allows us."

Dadajan nodded, "Yes, yes, that is as it should be. But there are many kinds of people in this world of Allah's. There will be men who will say that this land is not ready to be settled yet, that you must not live here yet. The chars that arise, there are many disputes as to who owns them." He stroked his beard. "Me, I am a simple man. I leave it to the laws of Allah and the laws of the land to tell me what is mine and what I should have. But others, you see, they are not always so scrupulous. That is what I wanted to talk to Kamrun Munshi about." There was a silence as Dadajan paused. Kamrun Munshi's wife looked away to the half-hidden children. They were losing their unaccustomed diffidence and were edging closer to us. "There are those who think nothing of burning up a few houses, uprooting fruit-bearing trees, bullying and intimidating innocent people." Dadajan resumed, "They tell themselves that the things that they destroy, belong, after all, only to *charuas*. I do not say that this is right, merely that they think like this. Yet it is a sin to see hardworking people like you get hurt this way." Dadajan paused again. He picked up a naru from the bowl in front of him and nibbled on the flat brown-colored disc. "You must tell whoever comes that you live here for me," he said abruptly. "Then they will no longer bother you." Kamrun Munshi's wife raised her face suddenly and looked directly at Dadajan for the first time. "But no one has bothered us."

"They might. They will." Dadajan popped the whole naru in his mouth and munched noisily. "Make no mistake—they will come." He took a sip of water and picked up a batasha. As he was about to take a bite, the woman said, "We have lived on chars before. Our men know what to do." Dadajan smiled. "Of course they do. But what I say will make your life easier. Tell Kamrun Munshi to come and talk to me. Then he can talk to the others." There was another pause as instead of putting it into his mouth, Dadajan crumbled the half-moon of the batasha in his hand and let the pieces drop away to the ground. "The fish you talk about, the fish that he has gone to sell, Ishwari's fish is not just for everyone. Most of the river and the fish *ghers* in this region; I own the leases." Dadajan shook his forefinger at her playfully. "Where is he catching them from?" The woman pursed her lips as if words that had already escaped her mouth had been too much. "I will be going to see the administrative officer. As a local man I feel it is my responsibility to watch over these new lands. I must tell him that he is not to worry, that I have let good people, good *charuas* settle here. I must tell him how many houses and people and animals are here; it is important that he know these things." He pointed his cane at the chickens as they ambled mindlessly nearer. "You have chicks too, I see. You breed them to sell?" The woman hesitated for a moment, then nodded.

Just as Dadajan asked, "How many do you get a month?" Alam Chacha walked back with a rooster held tightly under one arm. He came and stood behind me. "Boro Amma will want to cook *morag-polao* with this for the Young Master," he said. My grandmother always cooked this dish for my father when we came visiting. Usually she had two or three roosters all plumped up awaiting our arrival. Perhaps she had forgotten this time.

Dadajan smiled indulgently and stroked his beard. "My son, my only son, has brought his family to visit his old parents. He grew up here, and so my men they all feel like brothers to him. They are always careful to look after him properly when he is here." He spread out his hands, palms upward. "They love him like a brother and like to give him all they can." He turned to Alam Chacha. "Why don't you tie its legs up? You'll find it easier to carry." The woman had been looking steadily and unblinkingly at the rooster while Dadajan spoke. Suddenly she spoke in a very clear voice. "Of course. Your only son, of course, he must have this. There is no need to pay us for it. You must take it as a gift, from us poor *charuas*." She became silent again as if this speech had wearied her, and she had said all that needed to be said for the measure of that day.

"We must leave now. Tell Kamrun Munshi to come and see me," said Dadajan and strode toward the path by the banana grove, swishing his cane in the air with a casual disregard. The delicate silver filigree on the handle winked in the sun with a knowing air. Suddenly it slipped from his hand and whacked the face of a little boy who was standing close to the path watching us leave. "Ahha. Poor thing, is he hurt too much?" The half-naked child gave a soft whimper and tottered toward the women who stood silent. None of them moved to gather him in, none of them even looked at him. "Is he one of yours?" Dadajan asked Kamrun Mumshi's wife. "Abdul, give a ten taka note for the child. Poor thing. Hey, *baccha*, buy some chocolates, okay? Come, Babu," he called me. "We must go." The woman did not answer nor did she move to take the money from Abdul Chacha. Dadajan walked away. Abdul Chacha waited a few moments then tossed the note to the ground and followed him. Alam Chacha had already picked me up and sat me on his shoulders for the return journey.

We were well on our way before I asked why none of the women had picked up the child; wasn't his mother there? "*Charuas* are like that," Dadajan told me. "They move around so much. The very soil that they settle on, that itself is temporary, no saying whether it will remain the same or even be there in a month's time. So they become different than us. They hold this life Allah has so graciously given us lightly, as of no consequence. And so they do not have proper family feeling, not even for children."

The rooster squawked once, then subsided to a guttural cackling as it hung head downward from Abdul Chacha's left shoulder. "They are like that. Still I try to do what is within my power for them. In the eyes of Allah, we are all one, all equal," I remember Dadajan saying as the boat slid smoothly into the water. If the journey there had seemed long and arduous, the return trek seemed as endless as the weary waters of Ishwari.

It seems to me that it was merely the shimmer of sun and sand that burned that visit so permanently into my mind. The char that I had seen is as dead as Dadajan now, and it is only my act of remembrance that gives life to that *charua* woman. The clarity of those images dulls other child-hood memories that I so desperately long to relive. I remember listening to the steady splash of the oar for a while. And I remember Dadajan stroking his beard with a quiet satisfaction.

White Night Fire

Yelizaveta P. Renfro

On Keith's last night in St. Petersburg he and Svetlana walked the streets in a stupor of unspoken ardor and regret. The city was aglow with the hazy, blanched light of summer, and the Russians were out strolling arm in arm, celebrating the brief month of perpetual Arctic light.

"Tell me again—what is it like here in the wintertime?" Keith said, tightening his arm around Svetlana's waist. They were walking down Nevsky Prospekt toward the Neva River.

"It is very cold and very dark and not very much people are outside at night, not like this," Svetlana gestured at the people strolling around them. "There is ice and snow. Not such a nice time for American to visit."

"I wish I could see it."

"Well, you come visit then, and I take you on special tour, show you my city in winter," Svetlana said and looked up at him, then blushed and looked away.

"I'll have to come back then," Keith said lightly.

"You will?" Svetlana looked up again.

"I—I don't know. I will try," Keith stuttered.

"Ah," she said, then looked away.

"You'll probably be glad to see us go," Keith said. "You'll think, Finally those horrible Americans are gone and I can get some peace."

"About the others—yes."

"And me?"

"About you—no." Svetlana turned her head away and looked at a stone lion on a high pedestal that guarded the small bridge they were crossing. Keith too looked up at the lion, noting the beast's frozen roar, wondering vaguely how long it had stood there, keeping watch over the small tributary.

She turned back to him. Her eyes were lowered, and her bottom lip trembled slightly, as though she were about to speak.

"Svetlana," he said, reaching one arm around and stroking her back, but she would not grace him with her gaze.

"Do you want a beer?" he asked finally, spotting a beer café down the block.

"If you want," she replied, still not looking up.

"Here." He pulled a wad of wrinkled rubles from his pocket. "Get us two of anything you want."

Svetlana took the money from his hand and pulled off a single bill. "You are crazy," she said, meeting his eye. "Do you know how much money is here?"

"Spend it all. I won't need it after tomorrow anyway."

"Here," she insisted, putting it back in his hand.

He stood to the side of the pedestrian traffic and watched her walk off to the café. The first two nights he had made an attempt to be a gentleman and order the beers himself, but Svetlana had quickly taken over the job after having to rescue him from three muddled transactions; he knew only the word for beer—*pivo*—and as soon as the conversation got into the intricacies of price and change, he was lost.

In several minutes she returned with two bottles.

"Thank you," Keith said, taking an enormous swig of the beer.

"We walk more now?" she asked.

"Yes," Keith said, slipping his hand around her waist—the preferred strolling position for Russian couples. The beer churned in his stomach, and he felt exuberant and reckless. What a wonderful country this was— a place where you could stroll down the street drinking a beer, your arm around a gorgeous girl.

For his first forty-eight hours in the city Keith had found the white nights disconcerting. He went to bed at his usual ten, but he couldn't sleep because daylight poured through the gap in the thin curtains; he thrashed in the narrow bed until finally falling into a fitful dream state at six o'clock. Two hours later the alarm clock bored into his frenetic sleep.

The first night Keith went out with Svetlana he discovered the secret:

you simply don't sleep. At least the Russians didn't seem to—they were out strolling, drinking, kissing, smoking, shouting at all hours of the indistinguishable days and nights.

"I can't believe this place," Keith said.

Svetlana waved his incredulity away with a broad sweep of her hand. Her gestures seemed to be exaggerated in order to make up for her occasional difficulties expressing herself in English. "It lasts only a few weeks," she said. "And some sleep during the day."

"What about work?"

Svetlana shrugged. "You see—it is mostly young people," she said. "The old—they are used to it, they sleep. My parents—they have enough when they are young, now they sleep."

So Keith and Svetlana began to walk up and down Nevsky Prospekt every night, stopping for a beer now and then, and at first Keith wondered what the point of all this walking around was, but then the whole thing became a wonderful mélange of sights and sounds: people strummed guitars, sang Beatles songs in accented English, necked along the rails on the waterfront, strolled back and forth over the bridges, waiting for the magical moment that came each night at a quarter to two when the bridges all up and down the river would open at the same time, slowly lifting up their stately arms, to let the ships pass through—and you had to make sure to end up on your side of the river when the bridges went up or else you would be stranded for a couple of hours on the wrong side. But no one really seemed worried about it, for things always worked out here.

After a few beers, Keith would incredulously tell himself: I'm in Russia. I'm in fucking Russia! It wasn't quite as exotic as being in the Soviet Union, perhaps, and the truth was St. Petersburg was probably the most European and civilized corner of Russia, but still, for a boy from Southern California it felt like the hinterlands, and Keith thought often of that crazy czar, Peter, who decided to build his new capital in this eerie swampland. That was a man with vision.

Some of his late night rambles caused Keith to be a little inattentive at his endless real estate and city planning meetings during the day. He had to keep reminding himself that it was an honor to be included on the panel of esteemed realty and municipal experts who had been invited here to meet with local city officials so that Russians could learn how better to handle the tricky business of private ownership. Keith himself was a real estate lawyer and, at thirty-one, the youngest of the American guests. Back home, Keith drafted contracts for multi-million dollar beachfront properties, followed a low-fat diet, did his treadmill for forty-five minutes every morning, slept eight and a half hours a night, lifted weights at the gym on the weekends with his friend Ted, and dated professional career women who were not especially beautiful but were educated and could hold up their end of a conversation. He knew firsthand that divorce could be a nasty business. He had seen it with his own parents, and Ted was a divorce lawyer. Keith had had a couple of long-term relationships, and he had a vague plan that involved being married by thirty-five, but so far he hadn't felt strongly enough about any one woman.

But after just four days in St. Petersburg, he fell in love with the city, with Svetlana. Only he couldn't be in love with her, because she was poor and Russian and probably only wanted a ticket out of here.

The first time Keith saw Svetlana she introduced herself to the Americans as their cultural guide.

"I will take you on tour of my city, St. Petersburg, the most beautiful city in the world," she had said with the haughty pride of someone who has never been anywhere else.

She had a Roman nose, blue-black hair, and eyes of a blue so pale as to be nearly white, and the combination was striking, even frightening. She was the type of woman who became beautiful only after you got used to looking at her. She was not at all like the other Russian beauties, who were fair and tall and lean. Svetlana was beautiful in another way altogether: she was small, bordering on plump, with curves everywhere—rounded calves, dimpled elbows, swelling hips—except her face, which was a series of geometric planes. A sharp chin, the straight plane of her nose meeting her squared forehead, the perfect triangles of her canines—a series of lines that came together in her exquisite face.

Svetlana showed them the immense Winter Palace, so grand and unreal that it looked like a fairy tale, plopped down in the middle of Russia. She showed them the famous statue of Czar Peter on a horse known as the Bronze Horseman. "Maybe you know this poem—'The Bronze Horseman'—written by Pushkin?" she asked. Her question was met by several puzzled expressions. "Pushkin was our great national poet," she said brusquely. Barely pausing for breath, she continued: "OK, now we go to see churches.

"This church is built on exact place where Czar Alexander II was murdered by bomb in 1881," she explained. Keith looked up at the bloated, multi-colored heads of the domes, and it was like an attraction at Disneyland. The garish, exaggerated exterior seemed comically contrary to the rigid antiquity of the faith: the bearded, morose church fathers and devout old women in kerchiefs; the tarnished icons and standing dimness broken only by the tiny glow of candles; the occasional slant of direct light through an open door—it was like real life housed inside a cartoon.

"Why don't Russian churches have anywhere to sit?" someone in the group asked Svetlana.

"This is part of Orthodox faith, of long tradition," Svetlana replied. "There is saying that for Russians faith is in the legs."

Whenever one of the Americans asked a question, Svetlana's answer was always gruff, bordering on angry. Her tone seemed to say, *How dare you be so ignorant about my country?* That was why Keith rarely asked her questions that would expose his ignorance of art and architecture. He knew all the laws that governed the ownership of buildings; he didn't need to be acquainted with every brick as well. Svetlana was just the opposite—charmingly naive about law, but grimly serious about the beauty and history of the building itself.

"We are opposites," Keith had said to her one night.

"That is good, no?" Svetlana had quickly retorted, and Keith was surprised. She was twenty-four years old and Russian; she could not possibly know what he meant.

After their first afternoon of sightseeing was completed, Keith lingered until all the others drifted back to their rooms, then approached Svetlana.

"I was wondering," he said, "if it would be possible to see a Russian nightclub."

"Nightclub," she said. "Yes, we can go, but I think best time to go is at night."

"Fine with me, let's go at night. Are you available?"

"Yes, I can do. Your friends will come too?"

"No."

"They do not want to see Russian nightclub?"

"No."

That night she took him to a nightclub located underground in an old fallout shelter. It was a smoke-filled room with no windows, full of pulsing lights and Western techno music, writhing bodies. They sat at a cramped table in the corner and sipped beers.

"Maybe you want to dance?" Svetlana had shouted at him over the music.

"No, I just wanted to see, that's all."

"I do not much like nightclubs," Svetlana called back.

"Well, let's go then."

After leaving the club, instead of heading straight back to Keith's hotel, they walked the streets around it in a sinuous fashion, neither of them eager for the evening to end.

"So," she said, "now you have your wish. You see Russian nightclub."

"Do you know what else I want to see? The real St. Petersburg."

"Real?" Svetlana wrinkled her forehead.

"I want to see where people live," Keith explained. "Not monuments or museums, but houses, your neighborhood."

"It is not so interesting," Svetlana said, surprised.

"It is interesting to me."

"OK," she finally assented. "Your friends—probably they do not want to go?"

"No," Keith replied. "They do not."

Keith settled into a routine. In the mornings he attended meetings with city planners and local real estate specialists and discussed how to privatize government-owned apartments, how to do all of the paperwork and create the necessary legal paper trail. Then in the afternoons Svetlana took the group out for a couple of hours to see the sights, and finally in the evenings, after a bland dinner in the hotel, he and Svetlana met alone.

It was three days before Svetlana finally took him to her neighborhood. Each night he asked her to go, and each night she said, "Not today. Maybe tomorrow." And then one evening they were in a part of town Keith hadn't seen before. Apartment buildings rose all around them, crumbling at the corners, paint peeling. Faded laundry dried on balconies. Occasionally they passed an overflowing dumpster or a pile of refuse, smelling of rot.

"I thought you said St. Petersburg was the most beautiful city in the world," Keith said.

"It is."

"What about all of this?" Keith pointed at a heap of rusted metal in a yard.

"Poverty does not make it less beautiful," she said, with the characteristic proud tilt to her head, and Keith, suddenly giddy, rested his hand on the small of her back.

Emboldened, he pressed his face to the top of her head and said, "You are beautiful."

Svetlana pulled away from him and looked like she was about to speak, then simply shook her head.

"You are. You are perfect." Keith reached over and pushed a lock of hair behind Svetlana's ear.

"I know you Americans like thin women," she finally said. "I have seen your magazines. *Cosmopolitan, Vogue.*"

"Those are just magazines."

"Ah. And they say nothing about you?"

Keith felt a flash of anger. I am not like the others, he wanted to declare.

"They say something about the people who publish and read those magazines, perhaps," he replied. "But I belong to neither of those categories."

"OK," she said. "I am sorry."

They fell into step again. This time when Keith put his hand on her waist she reciprocated, tentatively hooking her thumb into a belt loop on his khakis.

Svetlana led Keith through a labyrinth of narrow streets, and finally they entered a tall, gray building, indistinguishable from the others. The light was dim in the musty entranceway, and as Keith's eyes adjusted, he saw a row of mailboxes on the wall, some of them hanging askance, others battered and dented.

"We must take stairs," she said. "Lift is broken. Do not worry—it is only to fourth story."

Keith followed Svetlana up the stairs. The walls were filthy and covered in graffiti, much of it in English. FUCK OFF AMERICA, he read as he walked, SERGEI IS KOOL.

"I don't understand how the Winter Palace and all of those churches are kept in such great condition, and the rest of the city is like this," he said.

"City officials—they want tourists to come to St. Petersburg, so they spend money on places tourists see. And it is the best way, I think. It is not so important where you live, but what would happen to our country if we did not take care of historical places?"

They stopped in front of a door, and Svetlana produced a key.

"You will meet my mother," she said, opening the door.

In the hallway shoes and boots of various sizes were jumbled on the floor, and an ancient refrigerator hummed and clacked in the corner. A clothesline was stretched across the hall with a series of men's white undershirts hanging from it, obstructing Keith's view of the rest of the apartment.

"Take off your shoes," Svetlana commanded as she slipped out of her sandals. Keith bent awkwardly and pulled off his sneakers.

"OK," she said, "come with me."

Keith ducked under a shirt and followed her past a closed door into a crowded living room. Sitting at a table covered in piles of minuscule beads of all colors was a woman who looked very much like Svetlana, except that she was more portly than plump and her black hair was streaked with strands of silver.

"Mama, this is Keith," Svetlana said in English.

"Hello," Keith said.

The woman nodded her head at Keith without smiling. Then she looked at Svetlana and spoke Russian. Svetlana answered briefly, then the woman spoke again.

"My mother is angry because I did not tell her you are coming," Svetlana explained. "She want to clean first. But do not worry. I explain to her that you want to see how real Russians live."

"What did she say?"

"She said she think maybe you crazy." Svetlana laughed. "OK, so this room is main room and bedroom of my parents."

"What do your parents do?"

"My mother—she is bead artist," Svetlana said, pointing at the table. "My father—he is physicist at university."

"This is your mother's work?" Keith indicated a collection of beaded jewelry on the table. He picked up a pair of dangling earrings—purple and yellow beads in an intricate fleur-de-lis pattern. "Tell her they're beautiful," he said. Svetlana quickly translated Keith's compliment, but her mother continued to sit quietly, regarding him impassively.

"And where is your room?" Keith finally asked, returning the earrings to the table.

"I sleep in corridor," Svetlana gestured from the direction they had come. "On cot."

"You do what?"

"I have sister, Lena. When we were small we have room together," Svetlana led him out into the hall and knocked on the closed door.

"Then my sister—she married Finn and moved to Finland, so we keep foreign exchange student in my room. Each year we get new student. Now the student—she is from Germany, but she is not here, I guess."

"She gets your room, and you sleep in the hall?"

"Oh yes, it is quite good arrangement, because we make much money from students. And we must give them private room—this is part of agreement with university. Come—I will show you kitchen."

Keith scanned the narrow kitchen briefly. He understood why the refrigerator was in the hall—there was no room for it here. Two people could not stand in the room at the same time without touching.

"OK, well, we go now," Svetlana said, her manner brusque. She spoke briefly with her mother, then led Keith back outside.

"Well, what do you think?"

"I think," Keith began, "I think it must be very hard to live that way."

"You become used to it. When my parents were young before they have children, they live in communal flat with three families, and everyone share one kitchen and one bathroom."

"That's rough," he said, immediately feeling like an idiot for saying it. He slipped his hand around Svetlana's waist and drew her nearer to him.

They walked on silently; Keith looked sideways at Svetlana, at her pressed pale green blouse and brown skirt, her white sandals, her hair

neatly gathered into a beaded butterfly barrette that repeated the colors—
pale green, brown, white—and he wondered how she could emerge into the
world so poised and polished each day, after spending a night under a line
of laundry beside a clattering refrigerator. It seemed like no life at all; there
was no place in the world she could call her very own. Keith wondered whether
all of those other women who walked and walked and walked up and down
Nevsky Prospekt—the ones who could have stepped right out of the pages
of a fashion magazine—also came from a non-place such as this. Where did
they find the resources to put forth such a beautiful and brave—yes, that
was the word—front each day? Was it their only chance for a way out?

Two days later, as they were parting for the night, Keith asked Svetlana
if she would go up to his hotel room. She told him she would not.

"Why not?" he asked.

"I do not want you to think I will go to bed with every American because
he is American."

"We're not talking about just any American. We're talking about *me*."

"No," she said.

And because he wanted her to know that he respected her, he did not
ask her again, but he wanted to, and each night after they parted he went
up to his room and fell into an angry, disturbed sleep for the few hours
he had before meetings. Was she leading him on? Did she sleep with
Russians? Were they not off limits? No iron curtain to get in the way there.
Maybe she slept with Russians but couldn't marry a Russian—there was
clearly no future in it. Her sister had married a foreigner, and maybe she
was waiting for the same opportunity.

Keith leaned back in the plastic chair and grinned at Svetlana. They were
sitting at a small rickety table in the looming shadow of the Kazan Cathedral,
but in the anemic light Keith could make out little more than the dark out-
lines of colossal Roman columns. He was now mildly drunk and feeling content.

"How come you never ask me about America, Svetlana?" he asked her.

Svetlana paused, a pensive look on her face, before answering. "If somebody asked me what it is like to live in Russia, I do not know what I would
say. It is difficult question, because I live here always, and so it is everything I know. So it is like everything and nothing." Svetlana frowned, prob-

ably trying to think of how to express herself more clearly. "And also," she continued, "every time there is American here, there are Russians all around him, asking questions. 'Tell me about America,' they say. 'Tell me everything.' And it is not so good, because then American has not so good time, he does not learn anything about Russia because he is always answering the questions about America, and maybe too he thinks that his country is better than Russia, the best in the world, because everybody want to know so much."

"And you don't think America is better than Russia?" Keith asked her, only half in jest.

"I am Russian. I think every person should think his country is best."

"You don't ever want to leave Russia?" he pressed.

"Well, perhaps..." She was clearly confused. "The time here is very hard, you see, and many people go to find better life somewhere else."

"Like your sister."

"Yes, but you must not think she is bad person. She love her husband."

"You were afraid if you asked about America I would begin to believe that you want to go there too much. And then you would make an unflattering impression of yourself." Keith was instantly sorry he had said this. He could see the hurt and anger in her eyes.

"I am curious about America, yes. I would go to America, yes. But not without good reason."

"I am sorry," said Keith.

Svetlana looked down at her hands and didn't reply. Keith reached across the table to the new beer she had brought him several minutes before. He took a long drink.

"Oh, it is almost time to go," she said suddenly, looking at her watch. "The bridges will open in ten minutes."

"We can't miss that, not on my last night," Keith said with forced animation, and then he raised the beer to his lips and guzzled it until the bottle was empty.

As they began to walk, his head spun a little, and he leaned more heavily on Svetlana. At the waterfront there were people lined up all along the railing—talking, laughing, waiting. Svetlana led Keith down the sidewalk until they came to an open section of railing. Keith leaned his back against the railing, and Svetlana stood in front of him. He closed his hands around her waist and kissed her once on the lips. Then he pulled back a little to look at her face, which was pale and eager. He tried to gauge her thoughts, but his head kept spinning.

"Penny for your thoughts," she said, and Keith almost laughed. Every once in a while she used phrases that sounded uncanny coming from the lips of someone who did not speak the language fluently. We are taught idioms, she had explained to Keith once, so that we can have real conversations with native speakers. When Keith didn't reply right away, Svetlana looked miffed, and then quickly asked, "What are you thinking about?"

"I am thinking that you are beautiful, and I will be sad to leave tomorrow."

Svetlana waited for more, and it was Keith's moment. He looked down into her pale eyes, empty of color in the watery light, but he could not tell what she was thinking; she was mysterious and remote to him. What was it that some world leader had once said—that Russia was a mystery wrapped in an enigma inside of something else? That was still true; it would always be true.

"And that is all?" she finally prompted.

"I am thinking that St. Petersburg is the most beautiful city in the world," he said.

"Ah," she said, sadly, "so now you believe me."

"I am thinking that it is sad that I am an American and you are Russian, and there will always be so much distance between us."

"Always?" she asked.

"I don't know," he said. "I don't know."

"I too will be sad when you leave," she said, and her eyes glistened. She looked down at the water, then out across the river.

"We missed it," she said.

"What?"

"The bridges—they are up."

Keith turned to look and saw that the arms of the bridges were open, the ships already passing through. The people gathered around had begun to disperse.

"I am sorry," she said.

Without speaking, they began to walk again, slowly, and the regret between them was almost palpable. I can still do it, Keith told himself, I have the rest of the night. But the bridges were open, the rush was gone, the white nights were waning. Now it was after two, and there were fewer people out. Only infrequently did they pass a ghost of a person, thin and insubstantial.

"I have gift for you," Svetlana finally broke the silence. She reached into her pocket and produced a miniature book, its cover a tiny mosaic of beads depicting an onion-domed church.

"Svetlana, it's beautiful," Keith said, taking the book. "Did your mother make this cover?"

"Yes. It is address book, see? Only, it is Cyrillic alphabet."

Keith flipped the cover open and glanced over the tabs: **А, Б, В, Г, Е, Ж, З, И, К**…"Well, some of them look familiar," he commented.

"I guess you must learn Russian," Svetlana said lightly. "I write my name and address. I show you." She flipped the pages to one that contained an entry in her neat script.

"So you will remember me," she said.

"I'll remember you."

"And because I will never see you again." Svetlana bit hard on her lip and began to walk again.

Keith slipped the book into his pocket and walked beside her, not touching her, not speaking. He wanted to contradict her last statement, and yet he could not bring himself to do it. He would not lie to her, and as he did not know what the truth was, he said nothing.

"I'm sorry I have no gift for you," he finally said, to say something, and he felt cheap and ashamed. He was the one who should have given some memento to her, for all of the hours she spent taking him around her city, but he had not thought of it until now.

"Oh, it is nothing," Svetlana said, briskly waving the thought away with her hand. "I did not expect gift."

They fell back into silence and continued to walk. They were headed, via a circuitous route, to Keith's hotel, and they both knew it. He tried to think of a place he could suggest they go instead, in order to prolong the night, but there seemed to be no place for them in all of St. Petersburg.

"Look," Svetlana said suddenly, pointing.

Keith looked up and saw a thick surge of black smoke against the pale sky.

"A fire," he said.

"Yes."

"Let's go see."

"If you want."

They headed toward the smoke. The fire was farther away than it first appeared, and Keith was weary of walking before they arrived at the right street. There was so much smoke that it was difficult to see anything clearly—just the square looming shapes of buildings and the smaller, darker figures of people moving through the gloom. As they neared the fire, a woman walked past them, staring at the sidewalk and shaking her head in emphatic denial of something, her hands blackened. The building on fire was an older six-story apartment building; Keith saw smoke wafting from several top floor windows, but he saw no flames. The air was so dark here that it was as though night had finally come.

On the sidewalk in front of the building, a group of people, many clad in pajamas and robes, drifted about in tight circles through the gloom; uniformed officers and firefighters moved more quickly in broader circles, keeping the others reined into a semi-circular area.

"Stay here. I will ask what happened," Svetlana said. As she moved away from Keith she seemed to lose all color and dimension. If she didn't return to him, he would never find her among these monochrome, two-dimensional shapes, and he would be lost in the city without her. Surprisingly, this thought did not awaken any anxiety or regret in him. In a few minutes Svetlana returned from the gloom, frowning.

"Three people are dead," she said.

"Dead? What happened?"

"There was man on sixth story—he was smoking in bed and go to sleep," she explained. "He died from fire, and then the fire—it goes to next flat where two old people live."

"And they died too?"

"Yes," Svetlana furrowed her brow. "Well, the fire was not completely in their flat, but maybe they smell smoke, maybe they get scared, maybe they think there is no way out of fire."

"What happened to them?"

"They jump from balcony."

"They jumped?"

"Yes, from six stories up. But everybody else—they get out safely."

Keith stood, staring at Svetlana. Her face was a mask, impassive.

"Come on, let's go away from here," Svetlana said, pulling on his arm. "This is not so nice for your last night."

They had walked two blocks when Keith stopped and bent over, suddenly nauseated.

"What is the matter?" Svetlana asked anxiously.

"I am sick."

"Sick with what?"

"I don't know. The beer, the smoke," Keith said, and then he retched.

"Keith, it is OK, it is OK," she murmured soothingly, stroking his back.

Keith stood upright when the queasiness eased, trying not to think about the fire, the old couple.

"Keith, they thought it was better to die that way than to burn, you see?" said Svetlana. "They died together."

He stared into her pastel eyes. Abruptly he felt dead sober.

"I am tired," he said. "I have to be up early. I want to go back to the hotel." Tomorrow he would board a plane and this world would become a dream.

"Of course," she said, and they began to walk again.

What Will Happen To The Sharma Family

Samrat Upadhyay

The Sharma family's trip to Bombay didn't go well. The Royal Nepal Airlines plane started acting funny after half an hour—a strange sound choked the left wing, and the plane began to hiccup—so they had to land in Patna, where the passengers were forced to stay in a hotel for the night.

The mishap would have been tolerable had not twenty-one-year-old Nilesh sauntered out of the hotel after dinner to "check out the territory." Within two minutes he was mugged in an alley, where two hoodlums pocketed his wristwatch, his gold necklace, and the twenty thousand rupees Indian currency stashed in the inside pocket of the coat he had on that warm evening. "I told you to get traveler's checks," Mrs. Sharma shrieked when Nilesh came back, his face bruised and the arm of his coat ripped off. Mr. Sharma slapped him, for that's what he often did to his children in situations where he felt helpless. Their eighteen-year-old daughter, Nilima, fat and smart, said, "Maybe this is a sign we should turn back." She had strongly resisted the trip, saying she needed to study for her A-level exams, whereas everyone knew she didn't want to be away from her Jitendra, who was so stunningly handsome, with a sleek body and a puff of hair on his forehead, that Mr. and Mrs. Sharma often wondered what he saw in their fat daughter. Mrs. Sharma was convinced Jitendra wanted to marry Nilima for her parents' money, which didn't make sense as the Sharma family wasn't super rich. Mr. Sharma thought Jitendra wasn't right in the head, and that the puff of hair hid an anomaly in his brain.

Fortunately, the cash wrenched away from Nilesh wasn't the only money they'd brought for the trip. Mrs. Sharma had another twenty thousand, which they hurriedly converted to traveler's checks at the airport before boarding their plane to Bombay the next morning. Throughout the ride,

Mrs. Sharma berated Nilesh, who had recently dropped out of college and spent all his time in cinema halls, dreaming of becoming an actor. "Who will marry you like this, huh? So irresponsible. You'll lose your wife during the wedding procession." She mimicked him, "Oh, I lost my wife. I don't know how it happened. One moment she was in my pocket, then these hoodlums came and snatched her away." Mrs. Sharma laughed loud at her own impersonation, and a stewardess signaled to her to keep it down. Nilima was engrossed in a Stephen King novel, ignoring her mother's rantings and her brother's sullen face and timid objections. Mr. Sharma was reading the brochure on emergency steps to be taken should the plane plunge toward the earth. Yesterday's jolts and screams had frightened him. He didn't want to die yet; at least not before making love to Kanti, his neighbor's maid who smiled at him coquettishly and didn't mind his sexual jokes.

At the airport in Bombay, no one came to pick them up. They waited. Mr. Sharma called Ahuja's home, but no answer. Nilima saw this as another indication that they should hop on the next flight back to Kathmandu. Nilesh got into a staring match with two big, unshaven Indian boys who appeared ready to come over and do something to him had Mrs. Sharma not scowled at them. After two hours of waiting the Sharmas decided to take a taxi to Andheri, where Ahuja lived. Mrs. Sharma said that they should take the train, but Nilima outright laughed at the idea. "I'd rather spend the night here at the airport than take the crowded, smelly train." So they took a taxi. Mr. Sharma wondered what it'd be like to visit Bombay with Kanti. They could run away together and live in one of the numerous shacks scattered throughout the city. She would wear skimpy clothes, her midriff showing, and he'd make love to her all day long and into the night. Mrs. Sharma worried about how she was going to get her fat, smart daughter and her stupid son married. A couple of offers had come for Nilima, but the boys had balked once they saw her, and Mrs. Sharma never heard anything further about the proposals. As for Nilesh, he'd acquired a reputation as a no-good loafer, so no proposal had even winked his way. In her mind Mrs. Sharma saw Nilima married to Jitendra, which gave her a shudder, and she saw unmarriageable Nilesh roaming the streets, getting into drugs and fights, ending up in jail.

As the taxi crawled along the congested Bombay roads, Nilesh replayed last night's mugging in his mind, over and over, but this time as soon as the muggers approached, Nilesh's left foot shot up like lightning, instantly cracking open one man's jaw; Nilesh whirled and slammed, without looking, the back of his right fist into the second hoodlum's nose, shattering it so a fountain of blood sprang forth and drenched a crowd of onlookers, who had miraculously appeared to see this brave young man in action and who now applauded as the two muggers crumpled to the ground. With squinting eyes and small lips, like Bruce Lee, Nilesh asked, "Anyone else?" Nilesh fast-forwarded and rewound this scene over and over, perfecting his kick, making the muggers beg for mercy, and replacing the "Anyone else?" with a howl.

Nilima turned another page of the novel: the family dog, it turned out, had supernatural powers. But was Rusty going to use it to ward off the evil forces? Or was he going to join the dark side and destroy the family?

Ahuja lived in a nice neighborhood in Andheri, on a quiet, tree-lined street. But no one was home—there was a giant padlock on the door. "They must have gone to the airport," Mrs. Sharma said. "Let's wait."

It was only after they'd waited for nearly two hours that a neighbor came over and told them that the Ahujas had gone on a vacation to the mountainous Nainital for two weeks.

"But that can't be," Mr. Sharma said. "He knew we were coming. I talked to him on the phone a week ago, and I sent him a telegram from Patna about our flight's delay."

"You're not the first ones," the neighbor said. "The Ahujas do this to their relatives all the time."

The Sharmas dragged themselves into a taxi for a ride to a nearby hotel in Juhu Beach, which they knew would be heart-chillingly expensive, but they were too tired and hot to go hunting for a cheap hotel.

They stayed in Bombay for only three days, not only because money was running out but also because Ahuja's betrayal had soured everything. Nilima showed very little interest in the sightseeing they did, except for the Hanging Gardens, which she thought were "fabulous." Nilesh became obsessed with the transvestites who roamed the city in groups. He stared at them, commenting upon their "manly" features. One time he laughed loudly as they passed by, and the *hinjadas* circled the Sharma family and made threatening gestures. Only after Mr. Sharma handed them a hundred rupees did they leave, singing and clapping. Immediately Mrs. Sharma took off her sandal and smacked Nilesh on his head.

On the flight back to Kathmandu, they hardly spoke to one another. The trip had turned Mrs. Sharma even more apprehensive about her children's marriage prospects—they were either stubborn or stupid. Mr. Sharma could hardly breathe in anticipation of touching Kanti's midriff, which he knew he had to do the next time they were together alone. Nilima was devouring another book she'd bought at the Bombay airport, a romantic thriller by Danielle Steele. Nilesh woke up from a short nap, scared. He had dreamed about making love to a transvestite and now had a terrific hard-on. He put the airline magazine on his lap so his mother, sitting next to him, wouldn't notice.

"That's the last trip we'll take as a family," Mrs. Sharma declared as they entered their house. Mr. Sharma immediately went for a walk, hoping that he'd catch a glimpse of Kanti, hanging laundry or dusting a blanket, on her balcony, and that he'd quietly approach her. Nilesh went into his room to practice his drums. This was another of his dreams—to become a rock star. He'd tried guitar, but he couldn't change chords fast enough and his fingers bled. With drums, all he needed to do was bang away, and there was a semblance of a beat. In his mind, women screamed and men danced as he played. The King of Drums, he was called.

Nilima didn't come home that night. She'd gone to see Jitendra soon after they reached home, and the two of them decided they missed each other so much that it was time to consummate their bond. "Let's stay in a hotel tonight," Nilima had said. "It'll throw a real scare into my parents. Maybe then they'll stop bad-mouthing you and get us married."

"But they'll be so worried," Jitendra said. He was a sweet boy—he really loved Nilima and, by extension, her parents. But Nilima was too persuasive for him, and they ended up in a hotel in Thamel.

Mr. Sharma did spot Kanti, not on her balcony but outside a shop in the neighborhood. She was talking with a man. Their body language told Mr. Sharma that this was more than a casual conversation. The man was young, about twenty-five, the same age as Kanti. With pangs of disappointment and anger, Mr. Sharma approached them.

"How was Bombay?" Kanti asked when she saw him. Laughter was etched around her lips, and her eyes.

"Don't you have work at home?" Mr. Sharma asked sternly. "Why are you chatting here?"

"I just came to buy something," she said.

"Go home, go home," Mr. Sharma said. "Who is he? It's not good to be standing here, chatting. It doesn't look good."

The young man appeared indignant. "I'll see you again," he told Kanti and walked away.

Kanti and Mr. Sharma began walking. He used his soothing, intimate voice, the one he'd never used on his wife, to mollify Kanti's anger. "You shouldn't do these types of things in public. It'll only bring criticism from everyone, and might even get you fired. I'm a good man, so I won't tell your employer. But someone else might not be so nice. I am nice because I like you so much. You're a nice girl. And I'm a nice man. That's what we have in common, and when people have things in common they can do many things together. I can teach you many things you didn't even know existed. Who is that man? What can he give you that I can't, huh? Tell me, what do you want? Just utter the word, and it's yours."

Kanti, who was no fool, said, "What gift did you bring me from Bombay? I want a gold necklace."

They were nearing Kanti's house. Mr. Sharma had to think fast. "Is that what you want? You are my queen, so you'll get what you want. But you also have to do what I ask." His hand touched her midriff.

"We'll see," she said. "Let me see the necklace first," and she slipped into her house.

Nilesh knew what his father was up to. His room was on the third floor of their house and commanded a view of the surrounding alleys. He saw his father talking to the maid. Remembering his father's slap in Patna, Nilesh wanted to go down and usher his mother outside so she could witness her husband's desire. But Nilesh also remembered how she had berated him throughout the trip, and he thought—let her be ignorant of this, fun to watch her face when she finds out. Wouldn't it be spectacular, Nilesh thought, if the maid became pregnant by his father and demanded a share of their property? He envisioned a little stepbrother looking exactly like his father—the same prominent Brahmin nose, the long earlobes. Nilesh laughed and went back to his drumming.

By dinner, Mrs. Sharma had begun cursing Nilima. "At her age she should be helping me cook dinner so that when she gets married she won't be an idiot in the kitchen. We've got to put a stop to this, do you hear me?"

she addressed her husband, who was wondering if Kanti would be able to tell the difference between a gold-coated necklace and a real one. He concluded she would, and ate another mouthful of rice.

"I don't trust that Jitendra. What are you going to do about it?" Mrs. Sharma asked her husband, then turned to her son. "And you, loafer supreme, how can anyone call you an older brother when you don't take care of your sister?"

"What can I do?" Nilesh said.

"Leave him alone," Mr. Sharma said. "And leave us alone, at least for tonight. I don't care what our daughter does. Just be quiet."

Mrs. Sharma was going to retort, but she thought the better of it, and they all ate their meal in silence.

At ten o'clock that night, Mrs. Sharma called Jitendra's house, something she'd never done before. When she identified herself, the man at the other end said, "Oh." No, Jitendra wasn't home, neither was Nilima. Jitendra had called and said he was going to a late-night party. Had he gone with Nilima? The man didn't know. Mrs. Sharma didn't ask him who he was—probably the boy's father.

She went to her bedroom and woke her husband, and the two of them made phone calls to Nilima's friends. Then Mrs. Sharma woke Nilesh violently from his sleep and sent him out to search for his sister in the neighborhood. They talked of going to the police station, decided against it; they talked of skinning Nilima alive were she to appear at the door shamefaced the next morning. Mrs. Sharma called Jitendra's house again and argued with the sleepy-voiced father, telling him to keep his son away from her daughter. By one o'clock they were exhausted. Mr. and Mrs. Sharma sat on the couch, Nilesh on the floor leaning against the wall. He really wanted to go upstairs to sleep but was afraid of his mother's tongue-lashing.

Nilima received a slap from her mother when she entered the house the next morning.

"I want to marry him," she told her mother, nursing her cheek. "I don't care what you say—I won't marry anyone else but Jitendra."

Helplessly Mrs. Sharma looked at her husband.

"You're still too young to be married," Mr. Sharma said. "Why don't you finish your A-level exams, then we can talk about it. But you can't spend nights with him in hotels. People will spit at you, and tomorrow if he finds another girl, who'll marry you?"

"If you won't marry us," Nilima said, "we'll have a court wedding. We've already decided."

Mrs. Sharma stepped forward to dole out another slap, but her husband stopped her. "Wait, daughter, what's the hurry? Finish your exams first, then marry him. That's all we're saying."

Nilima considered. "Okay, but get us engaged now. And we'll marry after my exams."

Mrs. Sharma left the room in a huff. Nilesh folded his arms and watched the back and forth between his father and his sister. He knew he was expected to be angry at his sister, probably even shove her around a bit, threaten to beat up Jitendra, but all he felt was admiration. She had a sense of defiance he himself lacked. She'd really shown them that they couldn't push her around.

Later, he went to her room. She was sitting in bed, doodling.

"What did you do last night?" he asked.

"What business is it of yours?"

"Good, very good. My little sister is really grown-up now."

"I'm glad you noticed," she said.

"Did you...really...? You don't have to answer."

"You're a strange brother. But yes, I did."

"Just to spite them?" he asked.

"I don't know. Now go and do your stupid things."

Mrs. Sharma called Jitendra's father, Changu, and arranged for a meeting. That evening Mr. and Mrs. Sharma went to Jitendra's house, a nice-looking building in New Baneswor with a large yard and two cars. Mrs. Sharma told Changu what her daughter had said. "Frankly, we don't think she should be married right now," Mrs. Sharma said. Before, she would have added, "especially to your son," but the family's obvious prosperity had softened her stance toward Jitendra. Instead, she said, "But what to do? Their eyes are fixed on each other."

"These young people," Changu said. "Once their minds are made up, even Lord Indra's dad Chandra can't shake them."

There was silence while they contemplated the mysterious ways of the young. Changu was smoking from a hookah. He took a long drag, then said,

"Well, you're a good family, and we also don't have a bad name in town. If they want to get engaged, let them do it. If we don't agree to this and they decide to elope, our noses will be cut." His index finger mock-serrated the tip of his nose as illustration.

On the way home, Mrs. Sharma said, "Well, at least they're not poor. That was a nice house, and he seemed like a nice man."

Mr. Sharma nodded absent-mindedly. During the hustle-bustle of the engagement, he should be able to siphon off a few thousand rupees for the gold necklace. Perfect, oh, perfect, he thought. That damn Kanti. She had been avoiding coming to the balcony, as if challenging him about his gift. He had to get that gold necklace for her if he wanted to make any progress.

The engagement date was fixed for three weeks later, with a promise from both Jitendra and Nilima that they would spend nights in their respective beds and that Nilima would study for her exams at least a few hours a day. Jitendra had to study for nothing. He'd failed his School Leaving Certificate exams twice, and everyone expected him to fail the third time, too. That her future son-in-law, like her son, was academically inept bothered Mrs. Sharma. "What is he going to become without even an SLC? A peon? How is he going to feed Nilima?"

"She's going to feed him," Nilesh said. Lately, taking courage from his sister's actions, he'd become bolder in talking to his mother.

"Look who is talking," Mrs. Sharma said. "Loafer, good-for-nothing. And what are you going to become? Who is going to marry you?"

"If someone like you could find a husband," Nilesh said, "why wouldn't I find a wife?"

Mr. Sharma laughed, and Mrs. Sharma tried to smack her son but he made a scary face and said, "Don't you dare." And Mrs. Sharma didn't dare— she was losing control over her family, and she didn't even know about Kanti yet.

The incredibly handsome but SLC-failed boy got engaged to the fat, smart girl. Nilima was already pregnant, a fact she hid from everybody, even Jitendra. What she herself didn't know was that the baby would be stillborn, and that it would break her heart, starting her on bouts of depression that would last a lifetime, and that Jitendra, the ever-devoted husband, would stick by her side until she died. They would not have another child.

"I'm dry, I'm dry," Nilima would cry late into the night, and Jitendra would soothe her with his soft voice emerging from those delicate lips. But for now Nilima was pregnant and happy, and she knew she would do well in her A-level exams because she was smart and knew everything.

Mr. Sharma made love to Kanti two neighborhoods away in a small room that belonged to a carpenter who'd done odd jobs in his house. For his "hospitality," the carpenter received five hundred rupees, with a strict warning not to divulge Mr. Sharma's secret to anyone. Kanti had already received her necklace, a ten-thousand-rupee affair he'd found in a shop in New Road. Mr. Sharma hadn't felt so alive in years, certainly not all those times he'd slept with his wife. Kanti was adept at pleasing a man— her tongue did wonderful things to Mr. Sharma's aging body. Loud noises— laughter, coughs, groans, and moans—emerged from his throat that afternoon, and he knew he would do it again and again and again with Kanti, and feel younger and younger. Little did Mr. Sharma know that he'd gotten Kanti pregnant right on that first day (the condom had broken during penetration), and that she'd give birth to a baby boy who looked exactly like his father, as the other son had so faithfully intuited. That afternoon Mr. Sharma also didn't know that Mrs. Sharma would eventually divorce him, something he couldn't ever have imagined his wife doing to him. She'd put all their property in her name, then file for divorce, forcing him to live poorly with Kanti and their new son, shunned by friends, relatives, and even the carpenter on whose bed he'd manufactured his look-alike progeny. Mr. Sharma would deal with this ostracism with laughter on his lips and happiness in his heart. Every moment spent with Kanti would turn out to be heavenly bliss, even though Kanti's midriff would sag after their son's birth. Mr. Sharma would walk the streets with swagger. He would be proud of this incredible turn his life had taken.

Mrs. Sharma worried about Nilima. The A-level exams were only two weeks away, but Nilima had taken her engagement with Jitendra as a license to spend all day at his house. Mrs. Sharma cursed Changu for being so lenient, but she didn't say anything for fear of spoiling the new in-law relationship. In a way, she was relieved about Nilima's impending wedding. Jitendra was foolish and immature, but he doted on Nilima. Despite herself, Mrs. Sharma had grown to like Jitendra, who was always polite and sweet. Not like Nilesh, whose sullen face only aroused her anger.

And Nilesh? What was going to happen to him? Defying everyone's expectations, and surprising even himself, Nilesh would become one of the leading movie actors in the country. He'd haunt the dreams of young girls and boys, who would cover their bedroom walls with his posters and pray to him more than they prayed to Lord Ganesh. He'd ride a fancy BMW, and he would star in movies that would not only become blockbusters but also win him accolades from even the most bitter of critics. He would end up owning his own production company that would make one hit after another. No one could have predicted this, but this is how the world works. One moment you are stuck, and then the moment expands, as if God were forcing it open with his pretty bare hands, and you find yourself in another dimension, and you are still you but the world around you has suddenly changed colors.

Mrs. Sharma's colors would change, too, but right now, wrapped in worries about her children, while her husband explored Kanti's body in the carpenter's bedroom, she didn't know that after her divorce, she would discover, in the temple of Swayambhunath, a swami whose soft words would make sense of the suffering inflicted upon her by her husband. She would see, in a millisecond of remarkable clarity (God's hand at work), that she had invited the suffering upon herself, that all suffering was self-induced, and—this is where her spiritual revolution would begin—that all of life was suffering. This insight would lead her to a place deep inside her where she would no longer feel her physical self. Her body would turn into air, and she would fly over the city, glimpsing in the lives of her one-time family, *their* suffering: "I want to die," bedridden Nilima would say to her husband; Nilesh would laugh at a film clip in the air-conditioned auditorium in his luxury house, his arm around another man's shoulder; Mr. Sharma would accompany his look-alike son to his first day in school.

Le Mal D'Afrique

Francesca Marciano

In a way everything here is always secondhand.

You will inherit a car from someone who has decided to leave the country, which you will then sell to one of your friends. You will move into a new house where you have already been when someone else lived there and had great parties at which you got incredibly drunk, and someone you know will move in when you decide to move out. You will make love to someone who has slept with all your friends. There will never be anything brand-new in your life.

It's a big flea market; sometimes we come to sell and sometimes to buy. When you first came here you felt fresh and new, everybody around you was vibrant, full of attention; you couldn't imagine ever getting used to this place. It felt so foreign and inscrutable. You so much wanted to be part of it, to conquer it, survive it, put your flag up, and you longed for that feeling of estrangement to vanish. You wished you could press a button and feel like you had been here all your life, knew all the roads, the shops, the mechanics, the tricks, the names of each animal and indigenous tree. You hated the idea of being foreign, wanted to blend in like a chameleon, join the group and be accepted for good. Didn't want to be investigated. Your past had no meaning; you only cared about the future.

Obviously, you were mad to think you could get away with it without paying a price.

It's seven o'clock in the morning, and I smoke my first cigarette with sickening pleasure at the arrivals hall of Jomo Kenyatta Airport in Nairobi.

She is on the early-morning British Airways flight.

Her name is Claire; I have never seen her. I was told that she is blond, long-legged, and sexy. She will be looking for me. She has probably been told to watch out for a dark-haired chain-smoker with the look of a psychopath, or at least this is the only honest description that would fit me today.

I hate Claire. She is my enemy, even though we have never met. Yet I am here to greet her and welcome her as part of our family, the baboon group whose behavior I have finally managed to make my own. I guess this is my punishment.

She has never lived here before, but she is coming to stay for good. She will eventually learn all the rules and turn into another specimen, like all of us. That is what everyone has to learn in order to survive here. She is coming to live with the man I am in love with, a man I haven't been able to hold on to. Another possession which slipped out of my hands to be snatched up by the next buyer.

The tourists start pouring through the gate, pushing squeaking carts loaded with Samsonite suitcases. They all wear funny clothes, as if each one of them had put on some kind of costume to match the ideal self they have chosen to be on this African holiday. The Adventurer, the White Hunter, the Romantic Colonialist, the Surfer. They are all taking a break from themselves.

She comes toward me looking slightly lost. I notice her long thin legs, her blond hair pulled tightly into a braid. Her skin is pale, still made up with London fog. She is wearing a flowery dress and a thick blue woolen sweater that makes her look slightly childlike. I wave my hand and she lights up. It's true: she is beautiful. She has destroyed my life.

It's like musical chairs, this secondhand game. When the music stops, one of us gets stuck with their bum up in the air. This time it must have been my turn.

I steer her cart out of the airport toward my old Landcruiser.

"Did you have a good flight?" I try a motherly tone.

"Oh god, yes. I slept like a log. I feel great." She smells the air. "Thank you so much for coming to pick me up at this hour. I told Hunter that I could have easily gotten a taxi—"

"Don't even say that. There's nothing worse than arriving in a place for the first time and having to start haggling for a cab. I believe in picking up people at airports. It's just one of those rules."

"Well, thanks." She smiles a friendly smile. "Wow, you drive this car?"

"Sure." I hop in and open the passenger door while I hand a ten-shilling note to the porter. "Watch out, it's full of junk. Just throw everything on the back seat."

Claire looks slightly intimidated by the mess in the car. Tusker beer empties on the floor, muddy boots, a panga on the dashboard, mosquito nets, dirty socks, rusty spanners.

"I just came back from safari," I say matter-of-factly as I pull out on the main road.

"Oh."

She looks out the window at the gray sky hanging low over the acacias. Her first impression of Africa.

"What a nice smell. So fragrant."

She sits quietly for a few seconds, letting it all sink in, her weariness mixing with her expectations. Her new life is about to begin. I feel a pang in my stomach. I didn't think it would be this hard. As usual, I overestimated my strength.

"Have you heard from Hunter? He's still in Uganda, right?" I ask, knowing perfectly well where he is; I have memorized the hotel phone number.

"Yeah. He thinks he'll be back next week, unless there are problems at the border with the Sudanese troops. In which case he will have to go in."

She sounds so casual, the way she has picked up that hack slang, as if the outbreak of a war were the equivalent of a nightclub opening. Just something else to report, another two thousand words in print.

"Let's hope not." I add more of the motherly tone. "I'm sure you don't want to be left here alone for too long."

"I'll be all right. It's all so new, I'm sure I won't be bored." She turns to me and I feel her eyes scanning me. "I knew when he asked me to come here that he wouldn't be around a lot of the time," she adds nonchalantly.

She's tough, I can tell already; hard inside, under the fair skin and that blondness. She'll get what she wants.

"You live with *Adam*, right?"—to put me back in my place.

"Yes. He's still at the camp up north with the clients. I've just come back from there. You'll meet him when he comes down on Saturday."

"I've heard so much about him from Hunter. He sounds wonderful."

"He is wonderful."

We take the Langata road toward Karen. She looks out the window taking everything in: the tall grass shining under the morning sunlight that has pierced the clouds, the old diesel truck loaded with African workers which spits a cloud of black smoke in our face, the huge potholes. She will learn how to drive a big car, find her way around town; she will learn the names of the trees and the animals.

"I'll drop you at home, show you how to turn on the hot water and things like that, and then leave you to rest. If you need anything just call me, I live right around the corner from you."

"Thank you, Esme, you are being so kind."

She will fall asleep in the bed I know so well which is now hers.

I am glad to hate her. Now I will go home and probably cry.

This is a country of space, and yet we all live in a tiny microcosm to protect ourselves from it. We venture out there, and like to feel that we could easily get lost and never be found again. But we always come back to the reassuring warmth of our white man's neighborhood in modern Africa. It's right outside Nairobi, at the foot of the Ngong hills where Karen Blixen's farm was. It's called Langata, which in Masai means "the place where the cattle drink."

There's no escape; here you know what everybody is doing. You either see their car driving around, or hidden under the trees in their lover's back yard, parked outside the bank, the grocery shop, filling up at the gas station. A lot of honking and waving goes on on the road. You bump into each other at the supermarket while you are shopping, the post office while paying your bills, at the hospital while waiting to be treated for malaria by the same sexy Italian doctor, at the airport where you are going to pick up a friend, at the car repair shop.

Even when you are out on safari, thousands of miles away from everybody, if you see a canvas green Landcruiser coming the other way, you look, assuming you'll know the driver, and most times you do. It's a comforting obsession. So much space around you and yet only that one small herd of baboons roaming around it.

This is our giant playground, the only place left on the planet where you can still play like children pretending to be adults.

Even though we pretend we have left them behind, we have very strict rules here. We sniff new entries suspiciously, evaluating the consequences that their arrival may bring into the group. Fear of possible unbalance, excitement about potential mating, according to the gender. Always a silent stir. In turn each one of us becomes the outcast and new alliances are struck. Everyone lies. There's always a secret deal that has been struck prior to the one you are secretly striking now. Women will team up together against a new female specimen if she's a threat to the family, but won't hesitate to declare war against each other if boundaries are crossed. It's all about territory and conquest, an endless competition to cover ground and gain control.

You always considered yourself better than the others, in a sense less corrupted by the African behavior. You thought of yourself as a perfectly civilized, well-read, compassionate human being, always conscious of social rules. The discovery that you too have become such an animal infuriates you. At first you are humiliated by your own ruthlessness, then you become almost fascinated by it. The raw honesty of that basic crudeness makes you feel stronger in a way. You realize that there is no room, no time for moral indignation.

That this is simply about survival.

Nicole and I are having lunch in a joint off River Road, where you can get Gujarati vegetarian meals. You have to eat off your aluminum plate with your fingers. There is a lot of bright-colored plastic panelling, fans, flies, and a decor straight out of some demented David Lynch set. *Wazungus*, white people, never dream of coming here and that is exactly why we do, because we like the idea of two white girls having a lunch date on the wrong side of town.

"You look sick," Nicole says, gulping down chapati and dal. Her skin is a shade too pale for someone living in Africa, and covered in a thin film of sweat. She's angular, beautiful in an offbeat way.

"I am sick."

"You have to get over it. I can't stand to see you like this."

She has just had a manicure at the Norfolk Hotel beauty salon and her nails are painted a deep blood red. She's wearing the same color lipstick—which is rapidly fading onto the paper napkin and the chapati—a skimpy skirt, and a gauze shirt. Looks like she has just walked out of an interview for an acting job at the Polo Lounge in Hollywood and driven all the way to the equator in a convertible sports car.

"You didn't have to go pick her up at the airport. I mean, someone else could have."

"I guess I wanted to test myself. And in a way it was symbolic."

"Did Hunter ask you to do it?"

"Yes." I nod quickly. But it's a lie.

"I can't believe it. He's such a—"

"No. Actually it was my idea."

"You *are* sick."

"True. But it's all part of our private little war."

Nicole sighs and takes another mouthful of vegetable curry, her wavy hair hanging over the food.

"What does she do? I mean, what is she planning to do here?"

"I haven't a clue. Articles for *House and Garden*? Maybe she will start a workshop with Kikuyu women and have them weave baskets for Pier 1. She looks like she could be the crafty type..."

"Oh *please*." Nicole laughs and lights a cigarette, waving her lacquered nails in the air. "She must be better than that."

I take a deep breath, fighting the wave of anxiety which is about to choke me. I am actually drugged by the raw pain. It is almost a pleasure to feel it inside me, like a mean wind on a sail that any minute could wreck me. If I survive it, it will eventually push me to the other shore. If there is another shore.

I feel as if I have lost everything. It isn't just Hunter. I have also lost Adam, myself, and most of all I have shattered the silly dream I had about my life here: I have lost Africa.

"When I saw her this morning"—I have to say this, to get it out of my system—"the way she was looking at things, so full of excitement...you know, everything must have seemed so new and different...it reminded me of myself when I first came down here. Of the strength I had then. I felt like Napoleon on a new campaign, I wanted to move my armies here, you know what I mean?"

She nods; she's heard this a million times but has decided to be patient because I guess she loves me. She knew beforehand that this lunch would require an extra dose of tolerance.

"She'll fight her battle, and learn the pleasure of annexing new territories. And I don't mean just sexually. She will start to feel incredibly free. Whereas I am already a prisoner here. Like you and all the others. We fought, we thought we had won something, but in the end we are all stuck here like prisoners of war. And we still can't figure out who the enemy was."

"Oh please, don't be so apocalyptic. You are just in a seriously bad mood. I think you need a break. Maybe you should go back to Europe for a while."

"Nicole, why is it that after so many years we don't have any African friends? Can you give me an answer? I mean, if you think about it—"

"What does that have to do with—"

"It does. We're like ghosts here; we can't contribute to anything, we don't really serve any purpose. We don't *believe* in this country. We are here only because of its beauty. It's horrifying. Don't you think?"

Nicole picks up my dark glasses from the table and tries them on, looking nowhere in particular.

"Look, there's no use talking about this again. I hate it when everybody gets pessimistic and irrational and starts ranting about living here."

She stares at me from behind the dark lenses, then takes them off and wipes them with a paper napkin.

"Haven't you noticed the pattern? We're like this bunch of manic-depressives. One moment we think we live in paradise, next thing this place has turned into a giant trap we're desperate to get out of."

"Yes," I say, "it's like a roller coaster."

"I think what we all do is project our anxieties onto the whole fucking continent. This has always been Hunter's major feature and you've just spent too much time listening to him. He loves to ruin it for everyone else because he hates the idea of being alone in his unhappiness. He will ruin it for Claire as well, just wait, you'll see."

This thought makes me feel slightly better. I am not in a position to rejoice at anybody's future happiness at the moment, I feel far too ungenerous. I am acting just like Hunter: working to create as much misery around me so that I don't feel completely left out.

Nicole smiles.

"Come to the loo. Then I'll take you to Biashara Street. You need a bit of shopping therapy."

Nicole is cutting a line of coke on her compact mirror inside the pink Gujarati washroom. I envy the way she always seems to be completely unaffected by her surroundings and carries on living in the third world as if she's simply browsing through an ethnic sale at Harrods.

She snorts quickly, holding back her curls.

"Wow! It's such bad stuff, but what the hell…"

She watches me while I inhale my portion of rat poison, then puts on a naughty smile.

"We'll turn Claire on to this really bad coke and transform her into an addict; that's how we're going to get rid of her. We'll persecute her till she gets a bleeding nose."

I finally laugh. The rush makes me feel warmer. I'd like to hug Nicole now, but she is suddenly looking serious.

"You know, Esme, I never told you, but I feel like I should tell you now…"

"What?"

"I did sleep with Hunter as well. Long before you came out here."

"Oh."

Her cheeks are lightly flushed. I drop my eyes from her face.

"I had a feeling you had," I say. The revelation hasn't shocked or hurt me.

"Why?"

"Just because…oh I don't know. Because of a certain intimacy you two always had."

"Do you mind me telling you only now?"

"No. It doesn't make any difference. Really."

We pause and smile at each other. I feel my heart hammering wildly, and the sudden urge for a cigarette. But I know it must be the cocaine, not her revelation. Strangely, if anything it makes me feel closer to her. She lights two cigarettes and hands me mine. We stand, our backs against the pink tiles, inhaling smoke and scouring powder.

"I am not unaware of what you said before, you know. We are all trapped in some kind of crazy white-people's game here," she says in a soft voice. "I just don't want to get completely engulfed in that kind of dissatisfaction because I don't have any alternatives."

"What do you mean?"

"I wouldn't be able to go back to Europe and function at this point. That's what made me so unhappy about sleeping with Hunter, now that I think of it. I felt he was constantly drawing energy out of me. His bitterness was poisoning me; that's what made me get away from him."

"Hmmm…I guess I am the one who has been poisoned now."

We stand in silence, smoking our cigarettes.

"I'll tell you exactly what it is that hurts, Nicole: the absolute certainty that I don't, and probably you don't either, have the determination, no, wait—the *faith*—to redeem someone like Hunter. We both would rather be poisoned than try to detox him. I never believed I had the power to make him happy. Isn't that stupid?"

"Why, what makes you think this girl will?"

"She has that strength. She will simply drive him out of whatever hole he's trapped in and bring him to the surface. She will love him, it's as simple as that."

"You love him too."

"But she's fearless. Young. And she will have his children."

"Yes. She's a breeder…"

"Right. We are not."

"No. We'd rather snort coke in the loo."

We pause, meditate for a few seconds. Then we do another line and go shopping.

I have to go one step back and try to put things in order. To fabricate some excuses for myself:

You have tried to leave before.

You have woken up in your bed in the middle of the winter, rain furiously pounding on the *mabati* roof, and felt like everything including your brain was turning to mold. You hate the idea of being so far away, forgotten by your friends at home, oblivious to the political changes in the world. You are starved for magazines, sophisticated conversation, films, and good clothes. The person lying next to you is a man who was born here, for whom all that is simply nonexistent. Before falling asleep he has told you how much he loves the sound of the rain pounding on the tin roof at night, how it reminds him of his childhood. You hear him breathing peacefully, wrapped up in the blanket while you are going mad. In the morning you walk out in the garden, holding your hot mug of coffee close to your chin, your last good pair of boots deep in the thick mud. You feel as if your entire soul is going under. Everything around you has the bitter taste of decay: the mangoes rotting in the basket, the corrupted policeman at the road-block who wants a bribe to let you pass, the headlines in the paper about new tribal massacres in the desert and piles of bodies liquefying in the heat. Suddenly the hardness of Africa reveals itself to you. Senseless and without redemption.

When you look in the mirror your face looks drained, armored, no trace of lightness left. You look older. That's when you think there may still be time to save yourself.

You want to leave. And you believe you will never come back.

Nobody is happy to let you escape, since everyone shares the symptoms of your disease. Someone will take you malcontentedly to the airport, in full Kenyan style, still wearing shorts and sandals, opening one Tusker beer after another, hitting the cap on the door handle and throwing the dripping empties on the back seat. They will sway and swear, overtaking *matatu* buses on the way; they will be rude with the porters who are too slow to take your luggage.

You don't care.

You are already on the other side of the ocean, shielded by what's left of your good European clothes, the list of phone calls you have to make tomorrow.

You are out of here.

You check in with a smile, handing your ticket to the pretty stewardess in flawless uniform, the efficiency of Europe already welcoming you behind the airline counter.

You think you will come back, sure, but just as a tourist, to see your friends and your ex-lovers. To see all the places you loved. The Chyulu hills, Lake Turkana, the beach of Lamu, the Ewaso Nyiro River.

You don't know yet that you won't be able to get away.

So many people have tried to define the feeling the French call *mal d'afrique* which in fact is a disease. The English never had a definition for it; I guess because they never liked to admit that they were being threatened in any way by this continent. Obviously because they preferred the idea of ruling it rather than being ruled by it.

Only now I realize how that feeling is a form of corruption. It's like a crack in the wood which slowly creeps its way in. It gradually gets deeper and deeper until it has finally split you from the rest. You wake up one day to discover that you are floating on your own; you have become an independent island detached from its motherland, from its moral home base. Everything has already happened while you were asleep and now it's too late to attempt anything: you are out here, there's no way back. This is a one-way trip.

Against your will you are forced to experience the euphoric horror of floating in emptiness, your moorings cut for good. It is an emotion which has slowly corroded all your ties, but it is also a constant vertigo you will never get used to.

This is why one day you have to come back. Because now you no longer belong anywhere. Not to any address, house, or telephone number in any city. Because once you have been out here, hanging loose in the Big Nothing, you will never be able to fill your lungs with enough air.

Africa has taken you in and has broken you away from what you were before.

This is why you will keep wanting to get away but will always have to return.

Then, of course, there is the sky.

There is no sky as big as this one anywhere else in the world. It hangs over you, like some kind of gigantic umbrella, and takes your breath away. You are flattened between the immensity of the air above you and the solid ground. It's all around you, 360 degrees: sky and earth, one the aerial reflection of the other. The horizon here is no longer a line, but an endless circle which makes your head spin. I've tried to figure out the trick that lies behind this mystery, because I don't see any reason why there should be more sky in one place than in another. Yet I haven't been able to discover what is the optical illusion that makes the African sky so different than any other sky you have seen in your life. It could be the particular angle of the planet at the equator, or maybe the way clouds float, not above your head but straight in front of your nose, sitting on the lower border of the umbrella, just on top of the horizon. Those drifting clouds which constantly redesign the map: in one glance you can see a rainstorm building up north, the sun shining in the east, and gray sky in the west which is bound to turn blue any minute. It's like sitting in front of a giant TV screen looking at a cosmic weather report.

You are traveling north, toward the NFD, the legendary North Frontier District, and suddenly it's as if you were looking at the landscape through the wrong side of binoculars. The ultimate wide-angle lens, which compresses the infinite within your field of vision. Your eyes have never cast a glance so far. Flat land that runs all the way to the distant purple profile of the Matthews Range and then, just when you thought you had reached an end to the space, right when you imagined that the landscape would close itself around you again, that you would feel less exposed, another curtain lifts up to reveal more vastness, and your eyes still can't catch the end of it.

More land stretching obediently under your tires, offering itself to be crossed. Your tracks become the endless flag of your conquest. You fill your lungs with the dry smell of hot rocks and dust, and you feel like you are breathing the universe.

You see yourself as you are driving into this grandiose absolute geometry: you are just a tiny dot, a minuscule particle advancing very slowly. You have now drowned in space, you are forced to redefine all proportions. You think of a word that hasn't occurred to you in years. It sprouts from somewhere inside you.

You feel *humble*. Because Africa is the beginning.

There is no shelter here: no shade, no walls, no roofs to hide under. Man has never cared to leave his mark on the land. Just tiny huts made of straw, like birds' nests that the wind will easily blow away.

Here you are, under that burning sun, exposed. You realize that all you can rely on now is your body. Nothing you have learned in school, from television, from your clever friends, from the books you have read, will help you here.

Only now do you become aware that your legs are not strong enough to run, your nostrils can't smell, your eyesight is too weak. You realize you have lost all your original powers. When the wind blows the acrid smell of the buffalo in your nose, a smell you had never smelled before, you recognize it instantly. You know that its smell has always been here. Yours on the other hand is the result of many different things, from sunblock to toothpaste.

You can't hide. *Le mal d'afrique* is vertigo, is corrosion, and at the same time is nostalgia. It's a longing to go back to your childhood, to the same innocence and the same horror, when everything was still possible and every day could have been the day you died.

Currency

Carolyn Alessio

The agency had told them they might not meet their son until their second night in the country, so Molly and Tom were surprised to look up from the luggage carousel and see a sign raised from the crowd bearing their last names followed by the word SUN. Molly immediately guessed that the writers, non-native English speakers, had intended to write SON, but Tom later would admit he thought the greeters from the adoption agency meant to convey warmth, the rays of happiness their new child would surely bring.

A procession of taped-up cardboard boxes chugged its way out on the luggage carousel behind them. "Let's come back," Tom said, but Molly wanted to wait for their suitcase, which she had filled with soft toys, blankets, and even a copy of *Good Night, Moon* in Spanish. The agency had recommended bringing some "attachment objects" and Molly had come prepared.

In customs, the couple began to unzip the luggage, but the agent just waved them on, smiling as if at a private joke. Molly and Tom moved through the airport, whose main floor looked casual and spacious compared to the tightly packed crowd that loomed above. People waiting to meet flights at La Aurora airport were not allowed to come inside, so they stood instead on an outdoor balcony that looked down on the newly arrived passengers like soccer players emerging onto a field.

By the time Molly and Tom left the airport, the crowd from the balcony had emptied out onto the street. Vendors closed in on the newly arrived, hawking purses, trinkets of skeletons playing the marimba, and corn on the cob slathered with mayonnaise. The smell mixed with bus fumes as Molly and Tom pushed through the crowd, scanning for the sign. It was hard to move forward through the congestion, but finally Molly and Tom saw the sign near the curb where the faded buses and taxis stood waiting. They walked toward the group, and the child they had first seen thirteen months before in a cloudy video clip.

"They've cut his hair," Tom said when they reached him. "They're feeding him more." But as Molly surveyed the child with short, shiny hair, she silently assessed the contrast differently: it's not him. She almost said it aloud, but Tom was already kneeling down next to the boy, holding out his large, pale hand.

Two women from the agency flanked the child. The younger woman, who held the sign, smiled at Molly and Tom. The older woman showed them a badge and papers before greeting them in strained English. She even tried to say their names, pronouncing Molly as "Molé," like the rich gravy Tom always ordered in Mexican restaurants. Molly set down the bags, forgetting the warnings about theft in the guidebooks.

In the battered van that took them to the hotel, the child sat between Tom and Molly and fingered a stuffed soccer ball. The younger woman from the agency squeezed onto the seat with them, and the older one crouched in the space next to the driver where a passenger's seat had been removed, perhaps to make room for luggage. As they rode, Molly watched the child's small hands as he kneaded the soccer ball. She looked at his knuckles that were darker than the rest of the fingers and felt like she was observing the child from an aerial view. On the other side of the seat, Tom was talking to the boy in Spanish, pointing out the windows at the thin trees, the brown, barren parkways that looked to Molly like they did not belong in a country whose name meant "Land of Eternal Spring."

The older woman from the agency called directions to the driver, clucking her tongue at other vehicles that darted in their way. Molly listened to the unfamiliar words and wondered if all adoptive parents first felt a kind of disbelief. She was embarrassed by her initial thought that the child was the wrong one; perhaps she was just scared by the sudden reality of parenthood or had heard too many stories of adoption fraud. Molly and Tom had gone through the same agency as a friend of a friend, and now the child that couple had adopted was a teenager, an ace tennis player in her suburban Chicago home.

"Hugo," Tom called, pronouncing the boy's name the Spanish way, "ooh-go." The little boy looked up, startled, as though his new father had been too forward with him. Molly looked at the child's puzzled face. After their referral from the agency, Molly and Tom had debated for months over the child's name. Calling him Hugo could bring him teasing in the U.S.—a friend had quipped, "Yugo? Like the crappy car?"—but finally they decided it would be too traumatic to change the name. Now, though, as Molly watched the boy turn away when Tom tried to summon him, Molly wondered if the child would ever warm to their voices, their nasal Chicago vowels that surfaced even in Tom's competent Spanish.

The van passed a square with an ornate cathedral on one end, and turned down a narrow, darker side street. "Aquí estamos," the driver called, pulling up in front of a squat gray building.

The little boy roamed around the hotel room, pulling himself up on the bed, the chair, even the faded red walls. Molly sat with Tom on the bed and stared. They watched their new son play with the locks on the suitcases, the fringe on the bedspread. Occasionally Tom reached down to try and tickle him or scoop him up, but then he was off again. Molly marveled at the child's energy, the way he could entertain himself. She thought of many of the children she knew in the States, how they needed adults or a Disney video to occupy them, and Molly wondered if Hugo's easy satisfaction was a by-product of poverty or a more imaginative culture.

The women from the agency stood by the window, talking quietly. When they arrived at the hotel, they had produced more paperwork that Molly tried to review, but most of it was in Spanish. She had put it on the bureau for Tom to read that night.

For the next two days the women remained with them, sleeping at night on bed-rolls they pulled from a duffel bag. Molly and Tom had known about the arrangement ahead of time, but in practice it seemed surreal, like a sitcom set in a Soviet housing project. Only the child seemed untroubled by the arrangement, humming as he moved between chair legs and knees. Once Molly thought she saw his jaw quiver, and she rushed to him, thinking he was crying, but when she reached him, he was still.

The agency had recommended taking their first few meals as a family in the hotel room and keeping the fare simple. Going out to a restaurant would only add more strangers, noise, and possibly new food, the agency had advised, when really they needed to "nest." Molly was uneasy about the term "nest"—she did not quite picture herself bending over her new son with pre-masticated food in her beak—but she understood the concept. The two women from the agency accompanied Tom to the market the first day, and he returned with tortillas and small plastic bags filled with rice, beans, and chopped vegetables. "Everything was in baggies," Tom reported. "Even Coke. They give you a straw."

Molly began to assemble dinner and Tom went to look for ice made from purified water. The women from the agency were still out, and Molly was glad to have the opportunity to take charge without observers. Even Tom, though he probably did not intend to, was making Molly feel like a Girl Scout trying to earn her babysitting badge. She surveyed the room for a table-like surface and came up with two options: the bed and floor. She spread out a towel on the bed and began to empty the bags of food into a few Tupperware containers she had brought along. As she scraped the vegetables from the bags, they looked pureed, like baby food. Back when Molly and Tom had thought they would be able to adopt a newborn, she had read articles in parenting guides on topics like making your own baby food. Gerber was full of sugars, one article alleged. Instead, it said that new parents should buy a food processor and load up on obscure vegetables like parsnips, rutabaga, kale, and yams. When Molly and Tom found out that they probably would not receive an infant (availability was low and Molly and Tom were past the preferable age limit), one of the first things Molly felt was relief that she would not have to shove odd-colored tubers into a shrill machine.

Hugo must have smelled the food because he rose on his knees to peer at the bed. Molly made a beckoning motion. She unwrapped the tortillas and the warm, safe odor filled the room. Molly folded one in half and placed it on top of Hugo's bowl. "*Comer*," she said, embarrassed that she had to use the clunky infinitive, but it was the best she could do. The little boy had put down the truck he was playing with, but did not come over. Molly did not want to rush him. She sat down on the edge of the bed, but noticed that she had spilled squash on her pants. It was the only clean, comfortable pair she had left. Hugo still was on the floor, so Molly went to the bathroom to splash cold water on her pants. She left the door open so as to hear the little boy, but he was quiet.

When Molly returned to the room moments later, both Hugo and the bowl on the bed were gone. "Hugo," Molly said, her throat tightening as though it were jammed with mashed potatoes. "Honey?"

The door opened and Tom came inside, an empty ice bucket under his arm. "He's gone," Molly said, trying to control her voice. She rushed past her husband and into the hallway, where she looked down the dim, empty corridor. She was heading toward the staircase when she heard Tom call her name.

Back in the room, Tom was crouched down on the other side of the bed. When Molly came over, he pointed: in the crevice between the nightstand and the bed, Hugo was hunched over his bowl, shoving the lukewarm food into his mouth.

"Hay mas," Tom said. He tried to help the boy out of the narrow space, but Hugo shook his head and continued to eat. A few moments later, Tom tried again, reaching gently for the child's shoulder and telling him they could sit together on the bed, but Hugo remained crouched over his bowl. Finally Tom got up and went over to stand by Molly. "It's like Dickens," he said in a low voice. "I thought they fed them at the orphanage."

"Wait," Molly said. She went to the bed and made up two more bowls. The first she gave to Tom and the other she took to the floor, where she sat down next to the crevice between the bed and nightstand and ate dinner alongside her son.

At night they all took turns showering in the tiny bathroom, even the women from the agency. The women seemed pleased at the prospect of getting to shower in the cramped, dingy stall, and this embarrassed Molly, who had brought along plastic shower thongs. She wore them only the first night, but felt prissy when the women and even the child stared. Their own shoes were flimsy and not so far from beach thongs. The next day, Molly hid her thongs under the bed and stepped barefoot into the shower stall, risking fungi and bites from the insects that clustered around the drain.

The first afternoon a man from the agency joined them, and went over paperwork with Tom. On a sheet entitled MEDICAL, the man showed Tom some basic information that the agency had already sent him and Molly: dates of recent inoculations, a note that said the mother was not known to drink alcohol or sniff glue. In turn, Tom produced copies of papers that certified himself and Molly as being free of TB, and even a form that said they had never been convicted of any felonies.

The women from the agency went out while Tom and the man reviewed the information. Molly sat on the bed with Hugo, attempting to read him *Buenas Noches, Luna*. She had practiced reading the book at home with Isela, the young woman they had hired to be her son's future nanny. Molly was embarrassed to hear herself attempting to pronounce the Spanish words, so she concentrated on the pictures: the clocks and lights, the bowl and brush. Next to her on the bed, the little boy stared at each page as though it were a puzzling but important document. As Molly read, her chin brushed against the child's glossy hair. It shone so much that it made her wonder if the agency had used a special conditioner on Hugo to prepare him for the meeting.

Molly and Tom awakened the next morning to find swollen patches on their stomachs and arms. Both were redheads, or "orange and pink people" as one of their friends called them, so the inflammation looked especially intense. Molly and Tom stood in front of the mirror, examining their blotchy arms when the child glanced at them and muttered something in Spanish. It was the first time he had truly spoken.

"What, Hugo?" Tom asked. "Qué?"

"He said 'bugs,'" the younger woman said.

"What kind?" Tom asked in Spanish.

The older woman from the agency said something matter-of-fact, prompting Tom to look down at his arms then at the unmade bed.

"What?" Molly said. She was skeptical that a toddler could diagnose a health problem.

"Fleas," Tom said, looking at Molly's freckled face in the narrow mirror. "She says they hide in the beds and we probably have an allergy to the bites."

That night, their last before flying home, Molly left the room to go and buy flea powder. She and Tom had discussed changing hotels, but Tom said the other nearby hotels had even lower cleanliness ratings and besides, he was not eager to offend the agency. Molly was heading down the dim hallway when the young woman from the agency emerged from the room and followed her. "Messus," she said to Molly, and pointed down the hall. Molly shook her head: "No español. Sposo," she said, motioning back to the room where Tom waited, but the young woman shook her head. She continued down the hallway, leading Molly, and knocked on one or two doors until she found one that was open. The young woman motioned for Molly to come inside and Molly followed, but when the woman went to close the door, Molly stuck her gym shoe between it and the hallway.

The room, a storage closet, reeked of mildew and overripe mango. Old wooden mop handles without sponges leaned against the walls like bald, skeletal dolls. Molly squinted. The lone lightbulb that hung in the middle of the room emitted only faint rays, so when the young woman began to talk, her words emerged from the shadows. "Mira," she said, Look. It was one of the few words that Molly recognized, so she nodded. "Cambió," the woman continued, "cambió el bebe."

Molly hesitated, running the words through her head. *Bebe* or Baby was easy, but the first and longer word took Molly a moment. Her Spanish vocabulary was limited, but the woman repeated the word, and after a moment Molly remembered something from one of the guidebooks: *cambio* meant loose change. A currency exchange was called *Casa de Cambio*— Molly and Tom had gone to one in the States to get the money order the agency required. Molly looked at the young woman and suddenly understood. "Momento," Molly said, reaching into the money belt she wore hidden beneath the waistband of her khakis. She and Tom already had paid over $20,000 to the adoption agency, but Molly made no assumptions about how much (or little, probably) the employees here were paid. Besides, Molly had seen this young woman share a piece of sweet bread with Hugo and tenderly wipe the crumbs from his mouth. Molly handed the woman four 50-quetzal notes—about $40 in American currency.

The young woman did not respond right away, but looked at the bills in the trickle of light. Finally she shook her head and said, "Cambió." She smiled weakly.

Molly glanced at her watch. The only store nearby that spoke English was open another twenty minutes, and Molly desperately needed the powder. Her stomach felt itchy as she reached back into her money belt. She presented another bill to the young woman, who shook her head and tried to hand it back to her. Molly murmured, "No, está bien," and left.

On the street outside the hotel, the ancient green buses were completing their rounds for the night. Molly waited to cross at a corner and wondered why the woman from the agency had not approached Tom, since he spoke Spanish. Molly looked up at a billboard of a giant rooster sitting between a keg of beer and a bottle of purified water. Perhaps the young woman was timid around men, Molly thought. Perhaps she believed that mothers had softer hearts.

The store was closed by the time Molly arrived, irking her both because it was five minutes too early and because she could see workers inside, chatting as they watered plants and emptied tills. The only place open nearby was a small restaurant called a *pupuseria*. Molly looked at the red lettering and wondered if the word had any relation to papoose. Probably not— she was proving herself to be bad at cognates. As Molly stood outside the door of the restaurant, she breathed in the warm, doughy smell and realized she had not eaten since a breakfast of bread and black tea.

On the door hung a light-blue and white flag that looked like a pastel version of the Guatemalan flag. Molly went inside, not entirely surprised that she was going to an El Salvadoran restaurant in the heart of Guatemala City.

Piled in a basket on the counter were three puffy-looking tortillas with bits of white cheese and dark bean paste seeping out of them. Molly stared, feeling hungry for the first time since she had reached this somber city.

"Goud mourn-eng," said a man behind the counter, attempting English. Molly wanted to smile—it was nearly 9:00 PM. "Hello," she said in English. She sniffed the air and smiled. The man nodded solemnly.

The guidebooks had counseled travelers never to pull out money before establishing a price, but Molly was in a hurry, so she spread a few bills on the counter. She pointed to the full, golden tortillas. *Pupusas?* Baby tortillas?

The man looked down, picked up one bill and held up five fingers. Molly nodded—the tortillas looked reasonably filling and five of them would be a decent amount for her, Tom, and Hugo. The man turned and called in the order to the kitchen. When he turned back, he pointed at Molly and said in English, "Where from?"

"U.S.," Molly said. "Los Estados."

But the man made an impatient gesture with his hands. "Where?" he asked again, in English.

"Chicago," Molly said.

He paused a moment then nodded vigorously. He wiped his hand on his apron and made the shape of a gun with his thumb and forefinger.

Molly stared at the man's flour-flecked hand. He was smiling. "Oh, Capone," Molly said, remembering the gesture from trips to Europe, where everyone seemed to know two things about her hometown: mobsters from the 1920s, and Michael Jordan. She hesitated, astonished that Latin Americans would know such a thing, too—didn't they have enough of their own violence to contend with?

As Molly waited for her order, she looked out into the darkening night and thought of the group back at the hotel. The little boy was warming a bit to Tom, joining him more in play. The process had been much slower with Molly; so far Hugo had only met her eye once, when she did a few jumping jacks to loosen up. Even then Molly was not sure if the boy was smiling slyly at something on the TV behind her.

Molly looked out the window of the pupuseria. She wondered if the reason she had not been able to bear children was because she was missing a mother gene, like one of those wire monkeys in the famous experiment about nurture. Maybe her physiology had tried to warn her. Until now, Molly—and a few doctors—had concluded that the probable reason for her infertility was Molly's teenage eating disorder. She had suffered from the malady years before meeting Tom, but later, when Molly learned that it might deprive them of a child, she felt like she had exposed Tom to secondhand smoke and he had developed lung cancer.

"Ray-dee," the man said. Ready. As he handed Molly the bag of fragrant, warm tortillas, suddenly Molly realized that she did not have nearly enough for the whole group back at the hotel. She wanted to include the women from the agency; they always claimed to eat on their walks, but more than once Molly had thought she heard their stomachs rumble. In the warm pupuseria, Molly's face burned: she was a new mother and could barely be counted on to address the basic needs of others. She handed the man another bill and said, "Más, por favor?"

The man nodded and called back a string of directions to the kitchen in Spanish. His words were too quick for Molly to pick up anything more than *la gringa*, the white lady. Someone called back a question from the kitchen, though, and the man at the counter repeated the order once more, slowly.

This time Molly caught a bit more—*quatro*, the number four, then another word that was even more familiar, *cambió*. The man said it just like the young woman had at the hotel, emphasizing the final syllable.

Molly held out yet another bill, and the man looked confused. Molly pointed to it and said, "Cambio?"

The man studied her face, frowning. Finally he said in English, "You change order."

Molly pointed at the bill. "*Cahm-bee-OHH*," she said again, feeling like a caricature of a tourist.

The man shook his head and smiled, then corrected her through pantomime. First he held up a dollar bill and said, "Cambio," with emphasis on the first syllable—*CAHM-bee-oh*. Then he took away the money and placed two tortillas on the countertop. He handed one to Molly and took the other. Then he reached for Molly's and switched his golden puff of dough with hers. "Cambió," the man said, emphasis on the last syllable—*Cam-bee-OHH*; a switch. He did the whole exchange one more time.

On the way back to the hotel, Molly stuffed the bag into the front pouch of her Windbreaker. The lump of hot dough pressed into her abdomen as she walked slowly along the street. The women from the agency were supposed to leave that evening to give them a night alone before they flew home, but Molly wanted to talk to Tom before they took off. Perhaps there really had been a mix-up at the agency, and Molly and Tom simply had been presented with the wrong baby. When she returned to the hotel, she could call the other officials at the agency, both here and back home. It might take a few more days in the country, but maybe they could straighten it all out.

As Molly cut through the Central Plaza, she passed the Spanish-style cathedral and remembered a story she had heard about an Italian couple at the agency in the States. They had traveled all the way to the Midwest to adopt through this agency, but the child referred to them for adoption had died while still in Guatemala, before his adoptive parents ever met him. "Sadly, these things can happen," the case worker had told the group of adults. "They're living in a country with all the attendant problems of poverty and war." Molly glanced at the wide steps of the cathedral. She still remembered the case worker's words, mostly because of the word *attendant*; it had made her think of a bridesmaid, of a pastel dress with ruffles.

Back at the hotel, the women from the agency were rolling up their beds, shoving them into the duffel. The younger woman did not look up when Molly entered the room. Still wearing her coat, Molly looked around for Tom. She could hear the child's voice, but could see neither him nor Tom. Finally, Molly walked to the other side of the room and Tom popped his head out from behind the bed. He was on his hands and knees and grinning. The little boy was crawling, too, but when he saw Molly, he stood up and began to make his way slowly over to her. Twice he nearly stumbled, and when Molly looked down, she saw that he was wearing her large, floppy shower thongs. "Clown," Tom called, laughing, but the child did not stop. Molly looked at his small almond-colored feet against the bright plastic soles. How had he found them, or remembered they were hers? The child stumbled again as he reached Molly, and she crouched down to catch him.

That night the boy slept between them, oblivious to the fleas that again kept Molly and Tom awake most of the night. At one point Tom tried to lie down in the bathroom on a blanket, but mosquitoes quickly emerged from the shower drain. They were a species that not even Tom, a science teacher, could identify. Molly lay in the bed, scratching her arms and neck and debating, plotting possible ways to work out her suspicions. Several times before the women from the agency left the hotel, Molly had tried to get the attention of the young woman, but each time, she looked toward the older woman or busied herself in a small task. Molly had even taken out Hugo's immigrant visa. The photo was poor quality, and the child was looking down, but when Molly squinted and held it up to the light in the hallway, she decided that this child had a less defined forehead than the boy in the room behind her. Standing in the hall with the cement walls, Molly tried to picture herself with the passport the next morning at the airport, trying to whisk it past the customs official without seeming nervous.

Later, in bed, Molly thought about other things she had concealed in her life. As a child, she had stolen a Persian coin from a neighbor girl's dresser and tossed it into the family's front bushes. Molly had never found out if it was a rare coin or just change picked up on one of her friend's many trips back to her parents' homeland. Her friend never mentioned it, but for months afterward, Molly had felt strange as she boarded buses and deposited coins in the fare box. During Lent, she put extra dimes into the cardboard rice bowl that her parents kept on the kitchen table.

Just after 3:00 AM, Molly reached over the child for Tom's shoulder, but ended up touching his head, his stubbly red crew cut. He had gotten the buzz on a bet with some of his students at school, and it had left a few uneven spots on his scalp. "Tom," Molly said softly. "Tommy."

Her husband finally turned his head, his hair bristling against the stiff pillow. "Honey," Molly said. "He's not Hugo, I don't think."

Tom blinked.

"I'm sorry," Molly said. When Tom was a little more alert, she went around to his side of the bed and repeated her message: "He might not be Hugo." She said the child's name slowly, dragging out the syllables.

Tom raised his head from the pillow and ran his hand along the side of his face, as though a student had just asked him a confusing question. "What?" he said finally.

Molly stared. She looked so closely at her husband's face that she swore she saw a flea move on his neck and head down toward his T-shirt.

"We'll call him something else," Tom whispered. "Sleep."

At first Molly felt a bewildering but welcome calm, a relief that someone else had assumed her knowledge. A moment later, though, after Tom had fallen back asleep, she realized that her husband thought Hugo simply did not like his name. Molly stood blinking in the dim, damp hotel room.

Molly returned to her side of the bed. The child lay sleeping between them, with his chin resting on the knuckles of one hand, as though he were posing for a high school graduation photo. Molly thought of the first child, the one she and Tom had seen in the video, whose name and photo were on the immigrant visa. She stared at the ceiling. In most of the books Molly and Tom had read about adoption, the parents described their initial meetings as magical, a match even more wondrous and random than the birth of a biological child. Perhaps a switch was just another chance at serendipity.

She did not sleep the rest of the night. Toward dawn, Molly heard a clattering outside the hotel. She walked to the window and pulled back the flimsy shade. On the square across the street, vendors were unloading vegetables and fruit from their trucks and lugging them toward the market stalls. Molly watched them empty one crate after another then load them back, empty, onto the pickup beds.

In the morning, both Tom and Molly had more red hives on their stomachs, but the little boy's skin remained untouched. Molly and Tom dabbed lotion on their stomachs and began to pack. Tom knelt on the floor in front of the suitcase with the child, showing him the different places for clean and dirty clothes with a calm and patient voice, as though he were explaining a biology lab to his sophomores. The child muttered a few words after Tom's, but it was hard to tell if they were in Spanish or English.

When they finished packing, the little boy took a plastic truck and moved out to the hallway. Tom was heading out after him when Molly said, "The tariff."

"Yeah," he said. "Six quetzals?"

Molly nodded.

Tom turned, distracted. The halls had been generally silent so far— so quiet that Molly had speculated about how the hotel made money— but Tom looked anxious, as though he had just left a classroom of freshmen alone in the lab while he went to the bathroom. "Can you get it?" he said.

Molly stared at the side of her husband's head, at the tiny bald spot in his crew cut that he had not even known existed until he had his head shaved. The spot was about the size of a dime, but the white of Tom's scalp shone through the thin layer of red hair that was beginning to gray. Molly understood his impatience to get home, and felt responsible for his irritation in a way that made her feel less than feminist. Tom had told her many times he was glad they were adopting, that he hoped it would bring him even closer to his students who were Latino, but Molly still felt like it was her fault that her husband would never get to examine an ultrasound in a dark room and think he glimpsed his own jawline or nose. "Go," Molly told Tom now, and said that she would finish up inside the room.

At the airport, the officials in customs showed more interest than they had when Molly and Tom arrived. "Documentos?" asked a woman wearing a gabardine shirt. Tom pointed back to Molly and she began to dig around in her bags. Molly was a big fan of hiding valuables and papers in disparate places, such as the tiny, innermost pocket on jeans or the heel of a sock.

"Honey?" Tom asked. Molly could tell by his voice that he was irritated, but also a bit embarrassed; it reminded her of when they once visited Europe and a clerk said it was unladylike for Molly to order both her own and her husband's train tickets.

While Molly searched, the little boy ran his truck along the carry-on bag, curving along the edges and adhering to the sides. He made no motor or "vroom" noises like other little boys Molly had observed in the past, but by the way he pushed, it looked like he was hearing some sort of sound in his head.

"Maybe we should go back in line," Tom said, but Molly held up her finger. She reached into her money pouch but it held nothing but the quetzals for the tariff, something she could easily locate. The woman in customs took off her glasses and squinted. Molly's face burned and she wondered if she had subconsciously misplaced the passports and visa on purpose for more time to consider the act she was now, knowingly, about to commit.

"Honey," Tom said, more gently, and Molly remembered the pouch of her Windbreaker. She reached down to her stomach and unzipped the pocket. First her hands brushed against the empty bag from the pupusas of the night before. Molly's fingers felt numb. She still had time to say there had been a problem, even to pretend she had not known there was a problem. At her feet the child ran his small truck toward the edge of the suitcase, and Molly heard the click of its wheels and tiny axels as it hurtled toward the ground.

"Señora, if you could step to the side," the woman from customs said, but just beneath the bag from the pupusas lay the smaller pouch containing the passports and visa. Molly yanked them from her Windbreaker. Tom let out a sigh and reached down for the boy's hand. As the woman from customs put her glasses back on, Molly spread out the documents in front of her.

In This Way We Are Wise

Nathan Englander

Three blasts. Like birds. They come through the window, wild and lost. They are trapped under the high-domed ceiling of the café, darting round between us, striking walls and glass, knocking the dishes from the shelves. And we know, until they stop their terrible motion, until they cease swooping and darting and banging into the walls, until they alight, come to rest, exhausted, spent, there is nothing at all to do.

Plates in halves and triangles on the floor. A group of ceramic mugs, fat and split, like overripe fruit. The chandelier, a pendulum, still swings.

The owner, the waitress, the other few customers, sit. I am up at the windows. I am watching the people pour around the corner, watching them run toward us, mouths unhinged, pulling at hair, scratching at faces. They collapse and puff up, hop about undirected.

Like wild birds frightened.

Like people possessed, tearing at their forms trying to set something free.

Jerusalemites do not spook like horses. They do not fly like moths into the fire.

They have come to abide their climate. Terror as second winter, as part of their weather. Something that comes and then is gone.

Watching plumes of smoke, the low clouds of smoke that follow the people down the street, I suddenly need to be near the fire, to be where the ash still settles and café umbrellas burn.

I make for the door and the waitress stops me. The owner puts a hand on my shoulder.

"Calm down, Natan."

"Sit down, Natan."

"Have a coffee, Natan." The waitress is already on her way to the machine.

I feel an urgency the others dismiss. I can run with a child to a braking ambulance. Can help the barefooted find their shoes. The time, 3:16, my girlfriend late to meet me. I should be turning over bodies searching for her face.

In a chair drinking coffee holding the owner's hand. "There is nothing to do outside. No one to rescue. Who is already there is who's helping, Natan. If you are not in the eye when it happens, it's already too late to put yourself in."

I trade a picture of my girlfriend dead for one of her badly wounded.

Inbar with her face burned off, hands blown off, a leg severed near through. I will play the part of supportive one. I will bunch up and hold the sheet by her arm, smile and tell her how lucky she is to be alive and in a position where, having discussed it in a happy bed, in a lovers' bed, we had both sworn we'd rather die.

The phones are back. The streets secured. Soldiers everywhere, taking up posts and positions. Fingers curled by triggers.

An Arab worker comes out of the kitchen with a broom.

I'm the first to reach the phone, but I can't remember numbers. One woman slams a portable against the table, as if this will release the satellite from the army's grip.

I dial nonsense and hang up, unable to recollect even the code to my machine.

"Natan will be okay," I promise before leaving. "Natan is a grown man. He can find his way home."

On the street I am all animal. I am all sense, all smell and taste and touch. I can read every stranger's intentions from scent, from the flex of a muscle, the length of the passing of our eyes.

I'm on the corner and can turn up the block, take a few strides into the closest of kill zones. I can tour the stretch of wounded weeping and dead unmoving, walk past the blackened and burned, still smoldering ghosts.

The Hasidim will soon come to collect scattered bits, partial Christs. Parts of victims nailed up, screwed in, driven to stone and metal.

Hand pierced with rusted nail and hung on the base of a tree.

It is with true force, with the bit of higher thought I can muster, that I spare myself a lifetime of dreams.

I follow a street around and then back on the trail to Inbar's apartment.

She is there. We kiss and hug. She holds me in the doorway while I pass through the whole of evolution. The millions of years of animal knowing, of understanding without thought, subside.

We exchange stories of almosts, of near deaths, theories on fate and algorithm, probability and God. Inbar late, on a bus, distant thunder and then traffic. She got off with a few others and walked the rest of the way home.

She makes tea and we sit and watch our world on television.

There is the corner. There is a man reporting in front of my café. And then the long shot of the stretch I avoided. The street I walk on a dozen times a day. There is my cash machine, its awning shattered, its frame streaked with blood. There is the bazaar where I buy pens and pencils. The camera lingers over spilled notebooks, school supplies scattered, the implied contrast of death and a new school year. They will seek out distraught classmates, packs of crying girls, clutching girls, crawling-all-over-each-other-suckling-at-grief girls. They will get the boyfriends to talk, the parents to talk; they will have for us the complete drama, the house-to-house echo of all three blasts, before the week is through.

We watch our life on every channel. We turn to CNN for a top-of-the-hour translation of our world. Maybe English will make it more real.

It does not help. There is my café. There is my cash machine. There is the tree I wait by when there is waiting to be done.

"Would you recognize your own bedroom," I say, "if you saw it on TV?"

Inbar makes phone calls, receives phone calls, while I sit and watch the news. A constant cycle of the same story, little bits added each time. The phone calls remind me of America. The news, of America. Like snow days. Hovering around the radio in the morning. A chain list of calls. "Good morning, Mrs. Gold. It's Nathan speaking. Please tell Beth that school is closed because the buses can't come." The absurdity of the change. Years and miles. A different sort of weather. "Yes, hello Udi. It's Inbar. Another attack. Natan and I are fine."

Inbar tells me Israeli things, shares maxims on fate and luck.

"We cannot live in fear," she says. "Of course you're terrified; it's terror after all." She has nonsensical statistics as well. "Five times more likely to be run over. Ten times more likely to die in a car. But you still cross the street don't you?"

She rubs my neck. Slips a hand under my shirt and rubs my back.

"Maybe I shouldn't," I say. A kiss on my ear. A switch of the channel. "Maybe it's time the street crossing stopped."

A biblical Israel, crowded with warriors and prophets, fallen kings and common men conscripted to do God's will. An American boy's Israel. A child raised up on causality and symbol.

Holocaust as wrath of God.

Israel the phoenix rising up from the ashes.

The reporters trot out the odd survivors, the death defiers and nine-lived. A girl with a small scratch on her cheek who stood two feet from the bomber, everyone around her dead. An old man with shrapnel buried in the hardcover book he was reading, who survived the exact same way when the street blew up fifty years before. A clipping. He searches his wallet for a clipping he always takes with him.

They make themselves known after every tragedy. Serial survivors. People who find themselves on exploding buses but never seem to die.

"Augurs," I say. "Harbingers of doom. They are demons. Dybbuks. We should march to their houses. Drag them to the squares and burn them in front of cheering crowds."

"You are stupid with nerves," Inbar says. "They are the unluckiest lucky people in the world. These are hopeful stories from hopeless times. Without them the grief of this nation would tip it into the sea."

I'm swollen with heroism. The sad fact of it. Curled up on the bathroom floor woozy with the makings for a bold rescue, overdosed on my own life-or-death acumen. My body exorcises its charger of burning buildings, its icy-waters diver. The unused hero driven out while I wait patiently inside.

The chandelier, like a pendulum; the day, like a pendulum, swings.

Inbar will turn the corner in her apartment and find her American boyfriend pinned to the floor, immobile, sweating a malarial sweat.

She will discover him suffering the bystander's disease. She'll want to wrap him in a blanket, put him in a cab, and take him to the hospital where all the uninjured victims, the unhurt, uninvolved victims, trickle in for the empty beds, to be placed on the cots in the halls.

I do not want the hospital. Do not want treatment for having sat down after, for having sipped coffee after, and having held on to the owner's hand.

A call home. Inbar dials the moment she thinks I can pull off a passable calm. My mother's secretary answers. Rita, who never says more than hello and "I'll get your mother." My phone call's precious because of the distance. As if I'm calling from the moon.

Today she is talking. Today Rita has something to share.

"Your mother is in her office crying. She don't say nothing to you, but that woman is miserable with you out in a war. Think about where you live, child. Think about your mom."

There is an element of struggle. Sex that night a matter of life and death. There is much scrambling for leverage and footing. Displays of body language that I've never known. We cling and dig in, as if striving for permanence, laboring for a union that won't come undone.

We laugh after. We cackle and roll around, reviewing technique and execution. Hysterical. Absurd. Perfect in its desperation. We make jokes at the expense of ourselves.

"No sex like near-death sex."

We light up a cigarette, naked, twisted up in the sheets. Again we would not recognize ourselves on TV.

Inbar has gone to work and invited Lynn over to make sure that I stay out of bed, that I go into town for coffee and sit at my café. Same time, same table, same cup, if I can manage it.

Nothing can be allowed to interrupt routine.

"Part of life here," Lynn says.

This is why Inbar invited her. She respects Lynn as an American with Israeli sensibilities. The hard-news photographer, moving in after every tragedy to shoot up what's left.

The peeper's peep, we call her. The voyeur's eye. Our Lynn, feeding the grumbling image-hungry bellies of America's commuter trains and breakfast nooks.

"A ghost," Lynn says. She is gloomy, but with a sportsman's muted excitement.

"Peak invisibility. People moving right through me. I think I even went weightless at some point, pulled off impossible angles. Floated above the pack. My stuff is all over the wire this morning." She pops the top on a used film canister, tips its contents into her palm. "You've got to come out with me one day just for the experience. You can stand in the middle of a goddamn riot, people going down left and right. Arab kids tossing rocks, Molotov cocktails, Israelis firing back tear gas and rubber bullets. Chaos. And you move, you just slide right through it all like a fucking ghost, snatching up souls, freezing time. A boy in the air, his body arched, his face to the sky. He's lobbing back a gas canister, the smoke caught in a long snaking trail. Poetry. Yesterday, though. Yesterday was bad."

"I'm not made for this," I tell her. "I grew up in the suburbs. I own a hot-air popcorn popper. A selection of Mylec Air-Flo street hockey sticks."

"Two of these," she says, and drops two orange capsules in my tea. "Drink up." And I do. "Two before I shoot and two right after I dump the film. An image comes back to haunt me, I take another. The trapdoor in my system. If it gets to be too much, I'll just stay asleep. So to show my utter thankfulness upon waking, I make a pass of the Old City the next day. I stop in every quarter, pray at every place of worship I find. That's my secret, a flittingness. I favor no gods. Establish again and again my lack of allegiance.

"That's what keeps me invisible. That's how I get to walk through the heart of a conflict, to watch everything, to see and see and see, then pack up my images and walk away. In return, nothing. A ghost. Sensed but not seen. That's the whole trick.

"Staying alive," she says, "means never blinking and never taking sides."

"I didn't look, didn't want the dreams. I went the long way around so as not to see."

"Unimportant. Not how you see, but the distance that counts. The simple fact of exposure to death. Same principle as radiation or chemotherapy. Exposure to all that death is what keeps you alive."

"I feel old from this," I say.

"Good," she says. "World-weary is good, just what you should be trying for. Go play the expatriate at your café. Go be the witty, war-watching raconteur. Cock an eyebrow and have them spike your coffee. Ignore the weather and put on a big, heavy sweater. Pinch the waitress on her behind."

I was raised on tradition. Pictures of a hallowed Jerusalem nestled away like Eden. A Jerusalem so precious God spared it when He flooded the world.

I can guide you to the valley where David slew Goliath. Recite by heart the love songs written by Solomon, his son. There have been thirteen sieges and twenty downfalls. And I can lead you through the alleys of the Old City, tell you a story about each one.

This is my knowing. Dusty-book knowing. I thought I'd learned everything about Jerusalem, only to discover my information was very very old.

I move through town, down the street of empty windows and blackened walls. The cobblestones are polished. Even the branches and rooftops have been picked clean. Every spot where a corpse lay is marked by candles. Fifty here, a hundred there. Temporary markers before monuments to come.

I make my way into the café. I nod at the owner, look at all the people out to display for the cameras, for each other, an ability to pass an afternoon at ease.

I sit at my table and order coffee. The waitress goes off to her machine. Cradling my chin, I wrestle images: unhinged mouths and clouds of smoke. Blasts like wild birds.

Today is a day to find religion. To decide that one god is more right than another, to uncover in this sad reality a covenant—some promise of coming good. There are signs if one looks. If one is willing to turn again to his old knowing, to salt over shoulders, prayers before journeys, wrists bound with holy red thread.

Witchery and superstition.

Comforts.

A boom that pushes air, that bears down and sweeps the room. My hair goes loose at the roots.

The others talk and eat. One lone woman stares off, page of a magazine held midturn.

"Fighter," the waitress says, watching, smiling, leaning up against the bar. She's world-weary. Wise. The air force, obviously. The sound barrier broken.

I want to smile back at her. In fact, I want to be her. I concentrate, taking deep breaths, studying her style. Noting: How to lean against a bar all full of knowing. Must master loud noises, sudden moves.

I reach for my coffee and rattle the cup, burn my fingers, pull my hand away.

The terrible shake trapped in my hands. Yesterday's sounds caught up in my head. I tap an ear, like a swimmer. A minor frequency problem, I'm sure. I've picked up on the congenital ringing in Jerusalem's ears.

The waitress deals with me in a waitress's way. She serves me a big round-headed muffin, poppy seeds trapped in the glaze. The on-the-house offer, a bartering of sorts. Here's a little kindness; now don't lose your mind.

Anchors. Symbols. The owner appears next to me, rubbing my arm. "Round foods are good for mourning," I say. "They symbolize eternity and the unbreakable cycles of life." I point with my free hand. "Cracks in the windows are good too. Each one means another demon has gone."

He smiles, as if to say, That's the spirit, and adds one of his own.

"A chip in your mug," he says. "In my family it means good things to come. And from the looks of my kitchen, this place will soon be overflowing with luck."

The waitress pushes the muffin toward me, as if I'd forgotten it was served.

But it's not a day for accepting kindness. Inbar has warned me, Stick with routine. Lynn has warned me, Don't blink your eyes.

And even this place has its own history of warnings. One set accompanying its every destruction and another tied to each rise. The balance that keeps the land from tipping. The traps that cost paradise and freedom, that turn second sons to firstborn. A litany of unburning bushes and smote rocks.

A legion of covenants sealed by food and by fire. Sacrifice after sacrifice. I free myself from the owner's hand and run through the biblical models.

Never take a bite out of curiosity.

Never trade your good name out of hunger.

And even if a public bombing strikes you in a private way, hide that from everyone lest you be called out to lead them.

Contributors' Notes

Carolyn Alessio's work appears in the *Pushcart Prize* anthology, *TriQuarterly, Brain, Child*, and elsewhere. She teaches at Cristo Rey Jesuit High School and is the editor of a bilingual anthology of Guatemalan children's writing, *Las Voces de Esperanza/The Voices of Hope* (Southern Illinois University Press, 2003).

Luis Alfaro is known for his work in poetry, fiction, theater, performance, and journalism. A Chicano born and raised in downtown Los Angeles, he is the recipient of a MacArthur Foundation Fellowship and a resident artist at the Mark Taper Forum, where he is co-director of the Latino Theatre Initiative. He was a visiting artist to the Kennedy Center in Washington, D.C., and an AETNA Fellow at the Hartford Stage Company in Connecticut. He has toured his work throughout the United States, Great Britain, and Mexico. Current projects include the film *Sense & Sensibilidad*. Alfaro is an appointee of Mayor Antonio Villaraigosa as a commissioner for the City of Los Angeles.

Shauna Singh Baldwin's first novel, *What the Body Remembers*, the story of two women in a polygamous marriage in occupied India, received the Commonwealth Prize for Best Book (Canada-Caribbean). *English Lessons and Other Stories* received the Friends of American Writers prize. Her second novel, *The Tiger Claw*—inspired by the life of Noor Inayat Khan, a Sufi Muslim secret agent who searched for her beloved through Occupied France—was a finalist for Canada's Giller Prize. Baldwin's awards include the 1995 Writer's Union of Canada Award for Short Prose and the 1997 Canadian Literary Award. *We Are Not in Pakistan* (Goose Lane Editions, Fall 2007) is her second collection of short stories. She is currently working on a novel.

Wanda Coleman's work is featured in *Writing Los Angeles, Poet's Market 2003*, and *Quercus Review VI*. She has been a Guggenheim fellow, Emmy-winning scriptwriter, columnist for the *Los Angeles Times* ("Native in a Strange Land"), and the recipient of a California Arts Council grant in fiction. Coleman's stories have appeared in *Obsidian III, Other Voices*, and *Zyzzyva*. Her books include

A War of Eyes and Other Stories; the 1999 Lenore Marshall Poetry Prize winner, *Bathwater Wine*; the novel *Mambo Hips & Make Believe*; and the 2001 National Book Awards finalist *Mercurochrome: New Poems*. More of her stories appear in her double-genre collections, *Heavy Daughter Blues* and *African Sleeping Sickness*, and are forthcoming in *Jazz and Twelve O'Clock Tales* (Black Sparrow/David Godine, Publisher, Inc., 2007).

Tony D'Souza was born and raised in Chicago. He earned masters degrees in writing from Hollins University and the University of Notre Dame, and served three years in the Peace Corps in West Africa, where he was a rural AIDS educator. He has contributed to the *New Yorker*, *Playboy*, *Salon*, *Esquire*, *Outside*, the *O. Henry Prize Stories*, *Best American Fantasy*, *McSweeney's*, *Tin House*, and others, and has appeared on *Dateline*, *The Today Show*, the BBC, and NPR. He received a 2006 NEA Fellowship, a 2007 NEA Japan Friendship Fellowship, and a 2008 Lannan Foundation Residency. D'Souza's first novel, *Whiteman*, received the Sue Kaufman Prize from the American Academy of Arts and Letters. His second novel, *The Konkians*, is forthcoming in 2008.

Nathan Englander's short fiction has appeared in the *Atlantic Monthly*, the *New Yorker*, and numerous anthologies including the *Best American Short Stories*, the *O. Henry Prize Stories*, and the *Pushcart Prize*. Englander's story collection, *For the Relief of Unbearable Urges*, became an international bestseller and earned him a PEN/Faulkner Malamud Award as well as the Sue Kaufman Prize for First Fiction from the American Academy of Arts and Letters. Englander was selected as one of "20 Writers for the 21st Century" by the *New Yorker*. He was awarded the Bard Fiction Prize, a Guggenheim Fellowship, and, in 2004, was a fellow at the Cullman Center for Scholars and Writers at the New York Public Library. *The Ministry of Special Cases* (Knopf, 2007) is his first novel. He lives in New York City.

Gina Frangello's first novel, *My Sister's Continent* (Chiasmus, 2006), was named one of the ten best books of 2006 by *Las Vegas City Life* and was selected as a "Read This!" finalist by the Litblog Co-Op for Spring 2006. Her short fiction has been published in many literary magazines, recently including *Clackamas Literary Review*, *StoryQuarterly*, *Blithe House Quarterly*, *Swink*, *Prairie Schooner*, and the anthology *Homewrecker: An Adultery Reader* (Soft Skull, 2005). Her freelance journalism and book reviews have appeared in the *Chicago Tribune* and the *Chicago Reader*. For ten years, she edited *Other Voices* literary magazine, and in 2004 co-founded OV Books, as well as guest-edited the fiction anthology *Falling Backwards: Stories of Fathers and Daughters* for Hourglass Books. Her second novel, *London Calling*, will be published by Impetus Press in Fall 2008.

Petina Gappah is a Zimbabwean writer and lawyer. She holds a bachelor's law degree from the University of Zimbabwe, an LLM from Cambridge University, and a PhD in international law from Graz University, Austria. She lives in Geneva with her son Kush, and works for the ACWL, an organization that advises developing countries on WTO legal issues. Her work has been recognized by the South Africa Centre of International PEN in a contest judged by J. M. Coetzee. Her short fiction has appeared in literary journals and anthologies in Kenya, Nigeria, South Africa, Switzerland, the United Kingdom, the United States, and Zimbabwe. Gappah is completing her first novel, set in Rhodesia and Zimbabwe between 1939 and 1980.

Etgar Keret is the author of three story collections, one novella, three graphic novels, and a children's book. His fiction has been translated into sixteen languages and has been the basis for more than forty short films. His own debut film, *Meduzot*, with writing/directing partner Shira Geffen, won an International Critic's Best Director Award and the Camera d'Or Award at the 2007 Cannes Film Festival. He lives in Tel Aviv.

Roy Kesey was born in northern California and currently lives in Beijing with his wife and children. He's the author of *Nothing in the World* (Bullfight Media, 2006) and *All Over* (Dzanc Books, 2007). His fiction has appeared in more than fifty magazines and anthologies, including *McSweeney's*, *Ninth Letter*, the *Georgia Review*, the *Iowa Review*, *American Short Fiction*, the *Robert Olen Butler Prize Stories*, and *New Sudden Fiction 2007*. His story "Wait," first published in the *Kenyon Review*, appears in *Best American Short Stories 2007*. His dispatches and essays appear regularly at *McSweeney's*, *The Nervous Breakdown*, and *That's Beijing*.

Laila Lalami was born and raised in Morocco. She earned her BA in English from Université Mohammed V in Rabat, her MA from University College, London, and her PhD in linguistics from the University of Southern California. Her work has appeared in the *Boston Globe*, the *Los Angeles Times*, *The Nation*, the *New York Times*, the *Washington Post*, and elsewhere. She is the recipient of an Oregon Literary Arts grant and a Fulbright Fellowship. Her debut book of fiction, *Hope and Other Dangerous Pursuits*, was published in the fall of 2005 and has since been translated into French, Spanish, Dutch, Italian, and Portuguese. She was shortlisted for the Caine Prize for African Writing in 2006.

Dika Lam was born in Canada and lives in Brooklyn. Her work has appeared in *Story, One Story, Cincinnati Review, Failbetter.com*, and elsewhere, and has been anthologized in *Scribner's Best of the Fiction Workshops 1999, New Affinities*, and *This Is Not Chick Lit*. A winner of the 2005 Bronx Writers' Center Chapter One contest, she is also the recipient of a New York Times Fellowship from New York University and a Tennessee Williams Scholarship from the Sewanee Writers Conference.

Diane Lefer is an author, playwright, and activist whose most recent book, *California Transit* (Sarabande Books, 2007), received the Mary McCarthy Prize in Short Fiction. Her works for the stage include *Nightwind*, a collaboration with exiled theater artist Hector Aristizábal about his arrest and torture by the U.S.-supported military in Colombia, that has appeared in theaters, campuses, conferences, and houses of worship throughout the United States and Canada. Lefer teaches in the MFA in Writing program at Vermont College. She received the 2006–2007 City of Los Angeles Literary Arts Fellowship in support of *Phantom Heart*, a novel-in-progress set around a Southern California nuclear waste site.

Rashad Majid is a journalist, editor, and founder of the Azerbaijani newspaper 525. He served as deputy editor-in-chief to the newspapers *Adelet* and *Azerbaijan*, and held positions in the Azerbaijan Translation Center. He is an active member of the World Association of Newspapers, the World Editors' Forum, the Azerbaijani Writer's Union, the Congress of Azerbaijani Journalists, and the Baku Press Club. Majid is the recipient of an Honored Cultural Figure title awarded in 2005 by presidential decree. He lives in Baku with his wife and three children.

Saadat Hasan Manto (1912–1955) was a leading Urdu short-story writer of the twentieth century. He was born in Samrala, in the Ludhiana district of Punjab. He worked for All India Radio and was a successful screenwriter in Bombay before moving to Pakistan at Partition. During his controversial two-decade career, Manto published twenty-two collections of stories, seven collections of radio plays, three collections of essays, and a novel.

Francesca Marciano is a documentary filmmaker and author of the novels *Cassa Rossa* and *Rules of the Wild*. She lives in Rome and Kenya.

Sharon May was born in California of mixed American and Iranian ancestry. She has lived and worked in Southeast Asia, where she researched the Khmer Rouge for the Columbia University Center for the Study of Human Rights. Her stories and interviews have appeared in *Best New American Voices*, the *Chicago*

Tribune, Other Voices, Mānoa, StoryQuarterly, Tin House, Concert of Voices: An Anthology of World Writing in English, Beyond Words: Asian Writers on Their Work, and elsewhere. She has received the Robie Macauley Award, the Julia Peterkin Award, and a Wallace Stegner Fellowship at Stanford University. She is co-editor of *In the Shadow of Angkor: Contemporary Writing from Cambodia* (University of Hawaii Press, 2004).

Ana Menendez was born in Los Angeles, the daughter of Cuban exiles. She is the author of two books of fiction, which have been translated into several languages: *In Cuba I Was a German Shepherd,* which was a 2001 New York Times Notable Book of the Year and whose title story won a Pushcart Prize; and *Loving Che,* a national bestseller. She was a journalist for several years, first at the *Miami Herald,* where she covered Little Havana until 1995, and later at the *Orange County Register* in California. She has lived in Turkey and South Asia, where she reported out of Afghanistan and Kashmir. Since 1997, she has taught at various universities including, most recently, as a visiting writer at the University of Texas at Austin. She holds a bachelor's degree from Florida International University and a master's from New York University.

Shabnam Nadiya lives and writes in Dhaka, Bangladesh. Her work has appeared in the *Texts Bones Journal, The Beat* (the-beat.co.uk), and *Cerebration* (www.cer-ebration.org). She has worked as a translator for a number of literary anthologies and magazines, including *Different Perspectives: Women Writing in Bangladesh* (Eds. Niaz Zaman and Firdous Azim, University Press Ltd, Dhaka), *The Escape and Other Stories* (Ed. Niaz Zaman, University Press Ltd, Dhaka), *In 1971 and After* (Ed. Niaz Zaman, University Press Ltd, Dhaka), and *Kali O Kalam.*

Viet Thanh Nguyen is an associate professor of English and American Studies and Ethnicity at the University of Southern California. He is the author of *Race and Resistance: Literature and Politics in Asian America* (Oxford University Press, 2002). His articles have appeared in numerous journals and books, including *American Literary History, Western American Literature, positions: east asia cultures critique,* the *New Centennial Review, Postmodern Culture,* and *Asian American Studies After Critical Mass.* He was a Fiction Fellow at the Fine Arts Work Center in Provincetown, Massachusetts, and his short fiction has been published in *Mānoa, Orchid: A Literary Review, Best New American Voices 2007, Gulf Coast,* and *Narrative Magazine.*

Josip Novakovich moved from Croatia to the United States at age twenty. He is the author of the novel *April Fool's Day;* three story collections, *Infidelities: Stories* *of War and Lust, Yolk,* and *Salvation and Other Disasters*; and two collections of essays, *Plum Brandy: Croatian Journeys* and *Apricots from Chernobyl.* His work has been published in translation in a dozen countries, including Russia, Switzerland, Turkey, and Italy. He teaches in the MFA program at Penn State University.

Yelizaveta P. Renfro was born in the Soviet Union to a Russian mother and American father, and grew up in Southern California. Her fiction and nonfiction have appeared in *Glimmer Train Stories,* the *North American Review, Alaska Quarterly Review, So To Speak,* and other publications. Her translations appear in *Amerika: Essays by Contemporary Russian Writers on the U.S.* Her awards include the Mary Roberts Rinehart Award in nonfiction, first place in the 2004 So To Speak Fiction Contest, second place in the 2006 Prairie Schooner/Mari Sandoz Prize in fiction contest, and the 2007 Vreeland Award. She holds an MFA from George Mason University and is currently working on her PhD in creative writing at the University of Nebraska–Lincoln.

Irina Reyn's first novel, *What Happened to Anna K.,* is forthcoming from Touchstone/Simon & Schuster. She is the editor of the nonfiction anthology *Living on the Edge of the World: New Jersey Writers Take on the Garden State.* Her work has appeared in publications including *One Story, Post Road, Tin House,* and *The Forward.* She is Visiting Assistant Professor of English at the University of Pittsburgh.

Ehren Schimmel holds a BA from the University of Southern California and an MFA from Emerson College. He was a Peace Corps volunteer in Romania from 2001–2003 and a David L. Boren fellow with the Institute of International Education. He is the editor of the anthology *Unveiled: Stories and Essays from Postcommunist Romania.* His work has appeared in several literary journals, most often on the subjects of cultural collision and American identity. The working title of his story collection-in-progress is *My Search for Osama bin Laden (and other stories by an American).*

Goli Taraghi launched her writing career with a collection of short stories, *I Am Che Guevara Too.* Her first novel, *Winter Sleep,* has been translated into English and French. Her most recent books are *Scattered Memories, In Another Place,* and *Two Worlds.* Two recent story collections, *The House of Shemiran* and *The Three Maids,* have been published by Actes Sud in France. Taraghi lives in Tehran and Paris.

Samrat Upadhyay is the first Nepali-born fiction writer writing in English to be published in the West. He is the author of two story collections, *The Royal*

Ghosts and *Arresting God in Kathmandu*, and the novel *The Guru of Love*. Upadhyay co-edited the anthology *Secret Places: New Writing From Nepal* (University of Hawaii Press). He teaches in the MFA program at Indiana University.

Shubha Venugopal holds an MFA in fiction from Bennington College and a PhD in English from the University of Michigan. She is a professor at California State University, Northridge. Her fiction has appeared in *Post Road*, *Gambara*, *Storyglossia*, *Word Riot*, *VerbSap*, *Elimae*, *Flashquake*, *Literary Mama*, *Antithesis Common*, *The Scruffy Dog Review*, *The Angler*, *Eclectica*, *Mslexia*, *Kalliope*, *Boston Literary Magazine*, and *Women Writers: A Zine*. She has work forthcoming in an anthology of South Asian poets, *Writing the Lines of Our Hands*. She lives in Los Angeles with her husband and two children.

Amanda Eyre Ward was born in New York City and graduated from Williams College and the University of Montana. She is the author of three novels, *Sleep Toward Heaven*, *How to Be Lost*, and *Forgive Me* (Random House, 2007). Her books have been published in more than fifteen countries. Her short fiction has appeared in *Tin House*, and in the MacAdam/Cage anthologies *Politically Inspired* and *Stumbling and Raging: More Politically Inspired Fiction*. She lives in Austin, Texas.

Mary Yukari Waters' fiction has been anthologized in the *Best American Short Stories*, the *O. Henry Prize Stories*, the *Pushcart Book of Short Stories: the Best Short Stories from a Quarter-Century of the Pushcart Prize*, and the *Zoetrope Anthology*. Her debut collection, *The Laws of Evening*, was a Booksense 76 selection, a pick for Barnes & Noble's Discover program, and a Kiriyama Prize Notable Book. *The Laws of Evening* was also chosen by *Newsday* and the *San Francisco Chronicle* as one of the Best Books of 2003. She is the recipient of an NEA grant and her stories have aired on NPR and the BBC.

G. K. Wuori is the author of more than seventy stories published in the U.S., Japan, India, Germany, Spain, Algeria, Ireland, and Brazil. A Pushcart Prize winner and recipient of an Illinois Arts Council Fellowship, his work has appeared in such journals as the *Gettysburg Review*, the *Missouri Review*, *Other Voices*, the *Barcelona Review*, *StoryQuarterly*, the *Massachusetts Review*, *Shenandoah*, and *TriQuarterly*. His story collection, *Nude In Tub*, was a New Voices Award Nominee by the Quality Paperback Book Club, and his novel, *An American Outrage*, was *Foreword Magazine*'s Book of the Year in fiction. He currently lives in Sycamore, Illinois, where he writes a monthly column called *Cold Iron* at www.gkwuori.com.

TRANSLATORS

Karim Emami (1930-2005) was an acclaimed Iranian translator, editor, lexicographer, and critic. Known for his translations of contemporary Persian poetry into English, he became an authority on Persian languages and often worked on dictionaries. His translations from English to Persian include F. Scott Fitzgerald's *The Great Gatsby* and John Osborne's play, *Look Back in Anger*. As a critic, he contributed to a wide range of fields, including film and photography. He lived in Tehran.

Sara Khalili is a writer and filmmaker. Her recent films have appeared in the Tehran International Short Film Festival and the Tehran International Animation Festival. She contributed translations to *Strange Times My Dear: The PEN Anthology of Iranian Literature*. She received a 2007 PEN Translation Fund Award for her English translation of *Seasons of Purgatory*, short stories by Shahriar Mandanipour.

Richard McGill Murphy is a senior editor at *Fortune Small Business* magazine, covering technology and politics. He grew up in the Middle East and was educated at Harvard College and Oxford University, where he earned a doctorate in social anthropology. He started his journalism career in Afghanistan during the late 1980s, reporting for the *London Times* and the *Christian Science Monitor*. His freelance work has appeared in the *New York Times Magazine*, the *New Republic*, the *Wall Street Journal*, and many other publications.

Samed Safarov was born in Azerbaijan in 1987. He is a student at the Academy of Fine Chemical Technology in Moscow, Russia. Safarov writes short stories and nonfiction as well as translations. He has been published in Azerbaijan, the United States, and Russia.

Miriam Shlesinger is an award-winning writer and scholar. She serves as Style Editor to *Target: The International Journal of Translation Studies*, and Reviews Editor to *Interpret: The International Journal of Research and Practice in Interpreting*. She has translated more than thirty stories and plays from Hebrew into English. She teaches at Bar-Ilan University in Israel.

ASSOCIATE EDITORS

Keala Francis is a freelance writer in Honolulu, Hawaii. She is a graduate assistant at the University of Hawaii–Mānoa, where she is pursuing an MA in English/Creative Writing.

Francesca R. Gagliano is a graduate from DePaul University where she earned a BA in English Literature and Creative Writing. She has been a member of the *Other Voices* magazine editorial staff and a contributing editor for OV Books. Her current work appears in the magazines *Threshold* and *No Touching*.

Tracy Miller Geary's fiction has appeared in twenty-five literary journals, including *Harvard Review*, *Puerto del Sol*, *Other Voices*, and *Hawaii Review*, as well as the recent anthology *Fenway Fiction*. She is the 2007 recipient of the Ivan Gold Fellowship from The Writers' Room in Boston. A graduate from Harvard University's Extension School with a Masters in Liberal Arts in Creative Writing, she lives outside Boston with her husband and two daughters.

Anne Flaherty Heekin was born in Boston and attended Georgetown University. She pursued a career in finance with Credit Suisse First Boston. Currently she is a workshop trainer in a variety of literacy-advance and job-readiness programs for young adults. She lives in Chicago with her two sons.

Laura Taylor Lambros lives in Los Angeles. Her collection of stories, *Plastic Has a Memory*, was performed as part of the New Short Fiction Series in 2001. Her writing has appeared in *AfterNoon*, *The Green Tricycle*, *NOHO LA*, *Barrelhouse*, *Margin*, and *Zahir*. Lambros was a 2000 finalist for the James Kirkwood Award for Fiction.

Allison C. Parker is an independent editor for academic and literary publishers, as well as for individual authors, and has been with OV Books since its first release. Her own writing has appeared recently in the literary periodicals *The Sun* and *Deus Loci*, the journal of the Lawrence Durrell Society. She lives a bicultural French/American existence in New York City with her husband, son, and piles of manuscripts. She is working on her first novel.

Barbara Shoup is the author of five novels and co-author of two books about the creative process. Her short fiction, poetry, essays, and interviews have appeared in *Mississippi Valley Review*, *Crazy Quilt*, *The Journal of the Jane Austen Society of North America*, *Rhino*, the *New York Times*, *The Writer*, and other magazines. The recipient of the 2006 PEN/Phyllis Naylor Working Writer Fellowship, she is currently the program director for the Writers' Center of Indiana, an associate faculty member at Indiana University–Purdue University at Indianapolis, and a contributing editor to OV Books. A new novel, *Everything You Want*, is forthcoming from FLUX in 2008.

Credits

"Foreword" by Aimee Liu. Copyright © 2007 Aimee Liu. Published by permission of the author.

"Introduction: Finding the Words," by Stacy Bierlein. Copyright © 2007 Stacy Bierlein. Published by permission of the author.

"Spleen," by Josip Novakovich. From *Infidelities: Stories of War and Lust* by Josip Novakovich, copyright © 2005 Josip Novakovich. Reprinted by permission of Harper Collins Publishers.

"Motherhood and Terrorism," by Amanda Eyre Ward. Published in *Stumbling and Raging: More Politically Inspired Ficiton*, McAdam Cage, 2005. Copyright © 2005 Amanda Eyre Ward. Reprinted by permission of the author.

"Shoes," by Etgar Keret, in the English translation by Miriam Shlesinger. From *Missing Kissinger: Stories* by Etgar Keret, Chatto & Windus 2007. Copyright © 2007 Etgar Keret. English Translation Copyright © 2007 Etgar Keret. Reprinted by arrangement with The Institute for the Translation of Hebrew Literature.

"In Cuba I Was a German Shepherd," by Ana Menendez. From *In Cuba I Was a German Shepherd* by Ana Menendez, copyright © 2001 Grove Press, Inc. Reprinted by permission of Grove/Atlantic, Inc.

"Africa Unchained," by Tony D'Souza. From *Whiteman* by Tony D'Souza, copyright © 2006 Tony D'Souza. Reprinted by permission of Harcourt, Inc.

"Toba Tek Singh," by Saadat Hasan Manto, translated from Urdu by Richard M. Murphy. Copyright © 2003 Richard McGill Murphy. Published in *Words Without Borders*, September 2003. Reprinted by permission of *Words Without Borders* [www.wordswithoutborders.org], an online magazine for international literature hosted by Bard College and supported by the National Endowment for the Arts.

"The Professor's Office," by Viet Thanh Nguyen. Published in *Gulf Coast Magazine*, Fall 2007. Copyright © 2007 Viet Thanh Nguyen. Reprinted by permission of the author.

Acknowledgements

An anthology benefits from the hard work and creative energies of many people. The editor of this project would like to recognize those who saw it to fruition:

A dream team of associate editors—Keala Francis, Tracy Miller Geary, Francesca R. Gigliano, Anne Flaherty Heekin, Laura Taylor Lambros, Allison C. Parker, and Barbara Shoup—spent long weeks reading and discussing stories with a precision that held me in awe.

I am grateful to Marina Lewis, who championed this theme, and to Gina Frangello, who trusted my vision for it. Aimee Liu, amid a rigorous work schedule and book tour, agreed to contribute a foreword the very moment I asked her.

OV Books' dedicated staff of advisors and volunteers embraced this book, especially Steve Almond, Tod Goldberg, Lois Hauselman, Kathy Kosmeja, and Iliana Regan.

We are pleased to have worked with Joan Catapano, Lisa Bayer, Michael Roux, and Joseph Peeples at the University of Illinois Press.

Finally, I hope to thank the hundreds of writers who allowed us to consider their stories. They showed us again and again the wide and affirming voice of human expression. Collectively they granted us the privilege of reading a larger world.

Stacy Bierlein is a founding editor of OV Books and served as contributing editor to the award-winning literary magazine *Other Voices*. Her current fiction, essays, and book reviews appear in various publications, including *Standards: An International Journal of Multicultural Studies*. She has participated in a variety of cultural affairs programs and literary seminars in the United States and Europe and has researched stories in Bhutan, Indonesia, Nepal, Russia, and Tibet. She lives in Southern California.

Aimee Liu is the author of the bestselling novels *Flash House, Cloud Mountain,* and *Face*. Her fiction has been translated into more than eight languages. She has written two memoirs, *Gaining* and *Solitaire,* and co-authored seven non-fiction books. Her work has appeared in numerous anthologies, most recently the essay collections *For Keeps* and *Why I'm Still Married*. Liu is a past president of PEN Center USA and teaches in Goddard College's MFA Program in Creative Writing.